The ELVIS and MARILYN AFFAIR

A
Tom Doherty
Associates Book
New York

The ELVIS and MARILYN AFFAIR

A Neil Gulliver and Stevie Marriner Novel

Robert S. Levinson

This is a work of fiction. All the characters and events portrayed in this novel are either fictitious or are used fictitiously.

THE ELVIS AND MARILYN AFFAIR

This book is printed on acid-free paper.

Book design by Amanda Dewey

A Forge Book
Published by Tom Doherty Associates, LLC.
175 Fifth Avenue
New York, NY 10010

Forge® is a registered trademark of
Tom Doherty Associates, LLC.

Library of Congress Cataloging-in-Publication Data

Levinson, Robert S.
The Elvis and Marilyn Affair / Robert S. Levinson.—1st ed.
p. c.
"A Tom Doherty Associates book."
ISBN 0-312-86968-1 (alk. paper)
I. Title.
PS3562.E9218E45 1999
813'.54—dc21 99-22197
CIP

First Edition: September 1999

Printed in the United States of America

0 9 8 7 6 5 4 3 2 1

For Sandra

Always and Forever

LVY

The ELVIS and MARILYN AFFAIR

SLUG LINE: SWEETHEARTS

By Neil Gulliver

When the phone rang and the stranger's voice said my ex had become the prime suspect in a murder one, I had no way of knowing I was about to stumble into possibly the best-kept secret in all of show business history:

Elvis and Marilyn had a torrid love affair in the fifties, and their sexually charged love letters still existed.

Somewhere.

Whoa!

Come again?

Presley and Monroe?

Imagine:

If there was any truth to the secret, the story was worth a million dollars. The love letters, if they could be found, more.

Ask Jackie O's heirs about that.

But right now the secret wasn't even a rumor, and before it became a whole lot more, other ancient secrets involving lesser icons from the Golden Age of movies would begin to unfold almost as often as bodies began dropping left and right.

"How did you get my home number?" I grouched at the caller, not happy about being interrupted at this crucial moment in my life.

I was sitting in my apartment, in my underwear. I had been struggling for three hours to come up with a clever lead for my next column for the *Daily*, tormenting myself with one false start after another, the way I've been doing ever since I got promoted (if *promoted* is the right word) off the crime beat six years ago.

Yeah, that Neil Gulliver.

That's me.

The one whose face adorns the sides of a million or so buses, his thirty-eight years looking a good ten years younger thanks to a boyish grin, a youthful twinkle in his inquisitive hazel eyes, and a great art department retoucher, who also took away the small scar half-hidden above his right eyebrow—result of an insane moment years ago that put two bodies in the ground—to prettify a set of features that more call good-looking than good grief!—when judged by current standards—and sit well on an angular face not as firm as it used to be and a broad forehead that grows taller as my widow's peak continues its retreat to the rear.

That one.

The Neil Gulliver who writes about people at their best and their worst and most of the time tries to lay in enough humor to get his readers chuckling over their breakfast cereal without dribbling too much milk out the sides of their mouths and down their chins.

I seem to have what Noel Coward called "a talent to amuse," and isn't it better to go for a laugh, something to give people a smile to start their day, than wallow in the kind of blood and gore that comes with the crime beat?

I'll level.

There's a lot about those crime beat years I miss.

Not the killings or man's redundant inhumanity to man.

I never needed a crime beat for that.

Growing up, I heard plenty on that subject from relatives who had marched off to wars in the foolish belief patriotism carried a sharper edge than protest, including my dear dad, who learned first-hand about the phantom pains that attack missing limbs and pounded into me the concept that honorable intentions can begin with saints and end with fools, as easily as the other way around.

I was feeling the old rush now as the stranger said, "Maybe you didn't hear? I tell you your ex-wife is a murder suspect and all you can give me is some smart lip over how I got your home phone number?"

"It's unlisted," I said. "The phone company isn't supposed to give out my number."

"People are not supposed to commit murders, either, but it may be the message never got through to your ex-wife. Anyway, I told her I would call you and she give me the number. Consider yourself called."

"Wait! Don't hang up!"

The silence had a smirk all its own before the unfamiliar voice responded, "Now you're interested all of a sudden?"

In fact, I was interested the moment he spoke Stevie's name, but you're not supposed to show anyone you're carrying a torch.

Especially not strangers.

It's a guy thing.

It allows you to smile on the outside while your heart keeps hemorrhaging on the inside. Mine has been at it for seven years, since Stevie slipped me the legal papers that said we could still be husband and wife, but not with each other.

I was slow to understand that some form of love survives a failed marriage, slower than Stevie, but I got there, learning there is no divorce from true friendship.

I still adored the kid I once loved with unabashed passion.

Always would.

And, I loved the grown woman she had become.

If you knew Stevie the way I knew Stevie, you'd understand why, but first you'd have to get past her image as "The Sex Queen of the Soaps."

Yeah, that Stevie.

Stephanie Marriner.

That's her.

And, please, don't be fooled by what you think you know from what you read too often in the supermarket rags or see on *E.T.* and *Hard Copy*.

You ever get close enough, look deeply into Stevie's eyes so you can examine her soul. And discover the person who exists inside the image. Even if, like me, you have to fight through the act she's putting on most of the time.

"Gulliver? You there?"

"Yeah."

"I said, so now you're interested, huh?"

After another moment, I responded, "You sound like a cop. Are you a cop?"

"No. I'm a schmuck for making this call."

"Definitely a cop," I said.

Lt. Ned DeSantis could have been Scrooge the way he misered his facts, so after he was off the line I swung around to the computer and accessed the *Daily*'s Metro section news bank and scrolled through the first disjointed and sketchy chunks of background.

The victim was one John "Black Jack" Sheridan, a Broadway playwright who had moved to Hollywood and become a widely acclaimed director, but the last thirty years had turned him into a trivia question.

I'm a major movie fan, but I had to be reminded Sheridan was still alive last month. Stevie told me he was the author and director of an Equity-waiver theater production she had agreed to star in, *Marilyn Remembers*, a one-woman show that recreated the great loves in the life of Marilyn Monroe.

She was all excitement over the phone, bubbling with that little girl disingenuousness she turns on and off like a kitchen faucet. The idea was to open the play in L.A., eventually move it to London and—on waves of critical acclaim for her performance—Broadway! (Whenever Stevie said the word, the exclamation point was attached.)

"Blackie Sheridan wrote it especially for me," Stevie said brightly. "He watches my show religiously, and he says I am the best thing he has seen on a screen since Monroe. 'Incendiary sex appeal' is what he said we have in common, me and Monroe, and only Jean Harlow and Rita Hayworth before us."

"Not Madonna?"

Stevie let the question hang for a moment before answering in a dismissive tone.

"Madonna has a mole."

"So do you."

"Not where it shows, honey, although I admit showing it to you plenty of times."

"Earning my eternal gratitude."

"Not how I earned it, baby," she said, falling into her tough act.

I had no snappy rebuttal, only the wistful memory of the sixteen-year-old girl-woman who had swept me off my common sense at a rock concert and soon agreed to share her life with a newspaperman eight years her senior.

Maybe I should have seen it was the kind of marriage that works best for better people than Stevie and I proved to be and was destined to fail.

Maybe I did and merely denied the fact for seven years, by which time Stevie was the reigning "Sex Queen of the Soaps" on *Bedrooms and Board Rooms* and I had learned more about myself than I needed to know.

Was it the father in me that drew me to her in the first place and keeps the protective spirit alive, or was it her need to have a father?

Stevie had grown up an orphan, in the broadest sense of the word. She never really knew her father, who disappeared without a word when she was five, and not a trace since, although from time to time Stevie hired private detectives to go searching. Her mother was hardly more than an overgrown kid herself, who loved her daughter dearly, even when she was off loving somebody else, leaving Stevie to survive for herself.

And Stevie was and is a survivor.

And blessed with a streak of generosity that—given her own bleak upbringing—understandably plays out through charities and causes that help children with histories more desperate and needs even greater than Stevie ever suffered.

Not that you'll ever hear about it.

The money and time she contributes are always cloaked in anonymity. Stevie demands that in order to protect the profane public image she has so carefully groomed and because, as she puts it, "Who I really am is my business. Period."

When Stevie has to be out front, like at a Pediatric AIDS benefit or Jerry Lewis's annual MD fund-raiser, she'll go into a dumb act, maybe let a four-letter word slip out accidentally on purpose, or show more cleavage than the camera lens can handle, to lead the public into thinking she's there only as a publicity stunt.

I keep thinking I'm going to blow her cover one of these days. When I'm angry enough at her to care. Meanwhile, we both love her and she would hate for me to ever stop, and she rarely makes a decision without soliciting my opinion. Sometimes, she even pays attention.

It's not as simple as that, of course, this life after a divorce that was never my idea, where I may have signed off on custody of my soul, but I'm still working on it. Give me another hundred years to get it right, please.

Talking with Stevie about Marilyn and the play, I recognized that the only opinion that mattered was her own.

She declared, "It's about time people in this business took me seriously, Neil. I'm a damned fine actress. The play can be just what I need to show the town I am more than just another—"

"Pretty face," I said, helping her with one of her favorite subjects.

"Exactly! Oh, Neil, honey. *Marilyn Remembers* can do it for me.

My ticket to the big screen and the juicy roles Pfeiffer and Stone and Basinger and, oh, suddenly, Gwyneth Paltrow get, and—oh, you know?''

''I hope you're right, babe. Where's the money to finance this thing coming from? Black Jack Sheridan save his money, or is he planning to dip into your piggy bank?''

Stevie snorted away the suggestion. ''Blackie has the backing he needs from an English producer who is due out here any day. Jeremy Brighton? I talked to him and he sounds legitimate, but I want you to meet him. Blackie, too. Tell me what you think.''

''Of course,'' I agreed, anxious to please.

The meetings were still on hold, although the play had been in rehearsal for two weeks. Stevie did not want me around until she was comfortable with her performance. She phoned daily with a progress report and by yesterday had substituted short-tempered, liquid outbursts for her initial exuberance.

She made no effort to disguise the problems she was having with Sheridan, whom she'd taken to calling Monster Man.

''I'm thinking about walking, honey. I'm going to have words with Monster Man tonight, and either he gets my message loud and clear or they can start looking for a replacement.''

''Don't do anything rash, okay?''

''Have you ever known me to do anything rash?''

''Yes.''

She hung up.

I counted the seconds before she called back.

Stevie always called back.

''Honey,'' she sighed, making the word two elaborate notes on the musical scale. ''Nobody, not even a Blackie Sheridan, is going to come between me and my Broadway debut, so don't be the least bit surprised when I fly you in to the Big Apple for the opening night.''

Forty minutes later, I was negotiating a freeway exit north of Calabasas that put my old Jag on a direct course west to the Motion Picture Retirement Estates. It should have taken twenty minutes longer to get there, but I had ignored the sixty-five mph speed limit.

I was anxious to reach Stevie.

For Stevie's sake.

Stevie has a history of disintegrating under pressure and turning bad situations into Bedlam.

Being accused of first-degree murder is a bad situation even for her.

I followed the posted signs off the main road and past the arched entrance of the Motion Picture Retirement Estates. It was almost noon. The sun was hiding behind slashes of painted cloud in a sky the leukemia-blue color of used laundry detergent.

I had declined numerous invitations to visit the MPRE that started arriving after the *Daily* promoted me to the column. I didn't want to risk confirming my vision of the place as a way station between the glitter and the graveyard for stars who had fared less well in life than on the silver screen.

The MPRE wasn't just a haven for nameless faces. Big names resided here, too. Even Norma Shearer, the queen of the MGM lot who married Irving Thalberg, won an Oscar for *The Divorcee*, and, at the time of her death, was staying several miles down the road in a Motion Picture Country Home cottage full of memories and not much else.

So, I made my excuses and steered clear, fearing permanent damage to the giant screen images I grew up with and still savored through the cable movie channels and the videocassette rentals. I dreaded rounding a corner into someone whose fame was humbled by reality and the passage of time, some withering beauty or a hero hobbling on a cane or confined to a wheelchair.

A Channel 2 news team was packing and stowing gear as I pulled into a space near the front entrance of the mission-style main building. Other news wagons were already on the way out, their coverage done. The parked vehicles included two LAPD squad cars and an unmarked with a red gum ball on its roof.

A frail, nervous woman in her middle forties, small deep-set eyes behind Coke bottle lenses in tortoiseshell frames too large for her emaciated face, sat behind the reception counter. High cheeks and a hawk nose. Small eyes that contributed nothing under her taut

Louise Brooks haircut, a white-streaked, bottled orange instead of black. Wearing a schoolteacher's ink-black dress with a high Peter Pan collar that hung loose from her broad shoulders and hinted at pendulous breasts proportionately out of synch with the rest of her.

A name plaque identified her as "Miss Toby Latch."

I gave her my name, and she put an open palm between us and stopped pulling anxiously on her hanky while she tapped out three numbers on the phone and mumbled into the cupped mouthpiece, her eyes angling to keep me in view.

Behind her in the open clerical area were three tightly placed rows of old-style teachers' desks, nine desks in total, unoccupied. A bank of mismatched file cabinets under built-in shelves jammed with supplies filled the back wall. To her left were three mahogany doors and a massive oil of a proud, hawk-nosed man in a hand-carved, gilded frame that dominated the room. I recognized him—David Wark Griffith, the silent-movie director who is credited with almost single-handedly inventing the vocabulary of film.

The click of a lock.

The door to my immediate right opened.

The heavyset man framed in the archway wore an expensively cut crimson blazer at war with the gold button holding it closed over his ample bay window and a pair of checkerboard slacks that emphasized his long, spindly legs.

"Spoon, Mr. Gulliver. Michael Spoon," he said, in an Irish tenor that fit him better than his clothing. His neck was as wide as his moon-pie face, making it impossible to button his shirt and raise the knot on his subtle silk tie. "Folks call me Mickey. I run this place. Executive director." He moved forward with a dancer's grace, his hand extended, unleashing the kind of smile actors save for auditions.

Spoon's smile was handsome enough to offset undistinguished features showing the effects of too much booze. His alert green eyes tended to disappear inside the upper folds of his doughy cheeks, crackling red and accentuated with slivers of blue vein on loan from the mother lode decorating his puff pastry nose. He was in his early to midthirties, gasping for air like any breath might be his last.

Spoon pumped my hand in a tight salesman's grip, wet with perspiration. That made me aware of the beads of sweat visible across the upper ridge of his small, elegant mouth and raining gently down his high forehead from a jungle of lackluster, sandpaper blond hair. "Ms. Marriner will sure be glad to see you," he said, wheezing and sighing at the same time. His breath smelled of stale mints. "You're all she has been talking about since she woke up and found Mr. Sheridan dead."

Stevie *woke up* to find Sheridan dead?

"Please run that by me again, Mr. Spoon."

The smile slid off Spoon's face. "She was in Mr. Sheridan's cottage when she—" He pressed three fingers against his lips, raised his eyes to the cottage cheese ceiling, coughed his throat clear. "There I go, talking out of turn again. The detective said to just wait for you and bring you on over."

"On over where?"

"Mr. Sheridan's cottage. They weren't finished when he sent me. You should of seen the madhouse. Not this many TV cameras and news people since the time Hal Roach came to visit. You know who that was? Hal Roach?"

"Of course," I said, dismissing the subject with a gesture before he could act on his eagerness to tell me. My imagination pictured Stevie rolling over in bed, throwing out an arm to cop a closed-eye feel, checking to learn why her "incendiary sex appeal" had failed to get a rise from Sheridan and—

The sedative wasn't invented that could get her down from the wall she had to be climbing.

I was close to it myself. "Take me there, okay?"

Spoon nodded.

The receptionist looked up from her hanky pull. "Your cart should be recharged by now. Save you five minutes' walking time."

"Thank you, Toby," Spoon said, acknowledging her with a cheeky grin. A rush of minted breath filled the space between us. "We operate our own little fleet of golf carts, Mr. Gulliver. The Estates grew large and complex in recent years, and they became a way for us to better serve our guests and—"

"You Gulliver?"

A voice behind us interrupted Spoon's commercial. No doubt the man who had pushed open the entry door was the plainclothes cop who probably belonged to the unmarked outside. Most give it away by the cheap cut of their wrinkled suits, the gravy stains on their ties, and a high gloss on their rubber-cushioned shoes. This one advertised it, wearing his gold badge on the outside of his jacket pocket.

"Lieutenant DeSantis. We were just heading your way."

" 'S okay." He crossed his arms on his chest and his hard brown eyes covered me with disinfectant. "The crime lab boys finished up faster'n we expected, so—"

I recognized his voice from the phone call.

"Where's my wife?"

"Your ex-wife," DeSantis corrected me. "What took you so long, Gulliver? Stop to change your unlisted phone number?" He made a production of the word *unlisted.*

"Miss Marriner. Where is she?"

"Where you'd expect to find a television star," DeSantis said sarcastically, tossing a thumb over his shoulder. "Outside there, signing autographs."

He stepped aside as I charged for the door.

Stevie was beyond the veranda, leaning against one of the twin pillars that rose from a used-brick wall three feet high to support the clay-tiled roof, smiling and chatting amiably while putting her name to scraps of paper.

There were six or eight people around her. Most looked old enough to be residents. I thought I recognized one of them from a character part in the original fifties movie version of *The Naked City.* They were either sympathizing with her for the ordeal she had been put through or telling her how wonderful she was on *Bedrooms and Board Rooms.*

Stevie had on a Bugs Bunny T-shirt that flattered her extravagant chest; tight-fitting, stone-washed jeans; soft leather boots that quit at her calves; and a pair of oversized, gray-tinted Carrera racing frames pushed back onto her blond head, the hair pulled off her face into a ponytail that stopped somewhere below her shoulder blades.

Just enough makeup for real life. And all the cameras and media teams that would have raced to the far valley, anywhere, on a murder one call starring a hot celebrity. Eyeliner highlighted the shimmering green and yellow of her eyes; blusher hid freckles that never entirely disappear. A light dab of color revealed the natural pucker of her perfect lips.

Two uniformed officers stood at parade rest a respectful distance away, exchanging tight-mouthed grins, clearly awed at being this close to a genuine star. Most people are, but then, most people have never been married to one.

I thought, Maybe if I'd never started treating her less like a wife than some prized possession, we might still—

I pushed out a breath and called out her name.

She looked up and turned to verify it was me, smiled, and sent me a kiss. "Finished in a minute, honey. I don't want to disappoint these dear fans of mine."

She meant it, but at the same time she wanted to be rescued.

Stevie and I had lived together long enough for me to read that on a glance.

I angled my body sideways and gently sliced a path to her, ignoring grumbles from a few who thought I was trying to fudge a place in line.

Stevie threw her arms around me. Found my lips. Whispered into my ear, "Get me out of here, please, honey. Please."

Her body trembled inside her clothing.

She was more frightened than I had ever known her to be.

2

"At the risk of repeating myself, Miss Marriner has been nothing if not extremely uncooperative," Det. Lt. Ned DeSantis said. The words exploded from his mouth like a string of Chinese firecrackers, making it easier and easier for me to like him less and less.

"At the risk of reminding you, Lieutenant, it's not every day Ms. Marriner finds herself suspected of murder. Maybe she'd have more to say if you allowed her the luxury of an attorney."

"Offer made. Offer refused. Miss Marriner had her heart set on you, Gulliver, and here you are."

"And here I am."

"Her knight in shining armor."

"Her knight in shining armor."

We were sparring over coffee in the conference area of the combination library–meeting room Mickey Spoon had emerged from twenty minutes ago. The room was the size of a master bedroom, with fake adobe walls painted a flat shade of canary yellow, an open beam ceiling of natural redwood, and behind the ceiling-high velvet draperies, French windows that opened onto the veranda.

Outside, the temperature had shot past a hundred.

As well as each other, DeSantis and I were competing with an air-conditioning system droning at full blast. We had never met, but I knew his name. He ran the West Valley Station's detective bureau and had a reputation as an honest, tenacious hot dog with a preference for high-profile collars, who was well on his way to a chief's desk downtown.

I put DeSantis in his early forties. He was a few inches shorter than me, maybe five nine or ten, and his arms hung like he worked out regularly. He had an olive complexion, rich black hair beginning to streak white, a prominent nose with flaring nostrils, dark, riveting eyes, and intensely angled features upset by acne scars that cast eccentric shadows in the deep hollows below his cheekbones. With a little more grooming, he could pass for handsome in an offbeat way.

DeSantis's Adam's apple danced whenever he raised his voice on more than ten consecutive words, as it did now, challenging Stevie to share more information.

"If you still won't take my word for it, how about you ask your ex-husband?" he suggested ominously. He exhaled with audible frustration, reached over for his coffee, and rolled the ceramic mug between his palms. "Mr. Gulliver has been round this corner enough times to confirm how the police desire to work with you. In your own best interests, presuming you got nothing to hide."

Stevie and I were sitting shoulder tight on a small wooden sofa that could have been handcrafted by the Mission Indians a hundred years ago. I had one arm around her and occasionally I squeezed her upper arm, as a reminder to hold her temper. She played one hand nervously on my thigh, unconsciously rubbing it the way a child finds comfort in a pacifier.

DeSantis leaned forward in his straight-backed chair, his head nodding, his gaze shifting momentarily to me, then back to Stevie over a large, handmade sofa table on which historical movie magazines were fanned, stars like Thomas Meighan, Gloria Swanson, and Dustin Farnum on the covers.

He couldn't mask his frustration. He resented my presence and showed it, even before I started playing Ping-Pong with his smart-ass attitude. I supposed he had an adoring wife to go with a house full of worshipful kids. I sensed the basic honesty under his shit-heel veneer.

"If Ms. Marriner has something to hide, suppose you tell me what you think it might be, DeSantis, or cut out your little game of Ken Starr–style intimidation."

"He's been coming on to me like I'm some murderer ever since he got here," Stevie said explosively. "Who does he think I am?" She pondered her own question for a half second. "Susan Lucci?"

Stevie's anger was real. I knew by the way she had started shaking again. I placed a hand against her mouth and locked onto DeSantis with an expression that appeals for understanding.

The cop made a show of appearing baffled. "Susan Lucci? I don't think she's been mentioned before this." He put down the mug, picked up his pen and spiral pad from the table and began to flip the pages, searching.

I sensed it was a put-on but couldn't be sure. "Susan Lucci is also on a soap," I said.

"But I won the Emmy," Stevie said, sounding off just to be heard, trying to mask the fear radiating against my arm. "Twice."

I said, "DeSantis, let me level with you—"

"I wish someone would."

"You want to quit the tough cop act and give me a chance?"

"Or what? You'll write something nasty about me?"

"Worse." I said. "I won't write *anything* about you."

Stevie squealed and patted my leg appreciatively.

DeSantis fought his smile. He pressed down hard on his back molars and his jaws flared, but after another moment he drew a vertical line in the air between us.

"Okay, Gulliver. Level with me."

Stevie's expression turned apprehensive. I sent her a sign that everything would be all right, lifted up from the sofa, and motioned for DeSantis to follow me to the other side of the room, outside her hearing.

Stevie muttered something indiscernible, reached for her coffee and a movie magazine, and rearranged herself on the sofa with her legs tucked underneath her.

I parked by a baby grand, below a portrait of Cecil B. DeMille. The cop made himself comfortable on the piano bench. Patted himself down searching for his cigarettes. "Mind if I smoke?" he asked, once it was too late for me to object. He dropped the pack and a disposable plastic lighter inside his jacket pocket, pushed a thin trail of smoke out of his mouth, waited for me to say something.

"Look, DeSantis, I'm not here to add problems to your life," I said quietly. "Take my word for it, or this conversation will lead nowhere." He thought about it. Nodded. "I'm here strictly because my ex screamed for me."

"Screaming straight into here," he said, pointing to an ear. "I may have to go on disability."

I gave him a conciliatory smile. "I'm not working the story. I'm here for Stephanie Marriner. The tougher you make it on her, the tougher you make it for me and for yourself."

He looked around for somewhere to flick an ash and settled on the tiled floor. "She's the one making it so tough," he said, wearily. "Not a word out of her, not one. Like she don't know the language without a script."

"I can get her to open up," I said, "but there are things I have to know first. You follow?"

"Like I got lessons from Arthur Murray himself."

DeSantis studied his cigarette. He smelled from tobacco and a noxious body odor that seemed to be permanently embedded in his clothing. I had not been aware of it sitting next to Stevie, who was bathed in her favorite scent, Obsession. I tried not to show it and measured my breath. I reevaluated his home situation. A bachelor or divorced. No wife or kids could survive that smell.

I said, "Mickey Spoon told me Stevie woke up in Sheridan's cottage this morning and found him dead."

DeSantis frowned. "I told that peckerwood to keep his yap shut."

"Were they in bed together, Stevie and Sheridan?"

"How *ex* a husband you say you are?"

"Not an answer."

"It's the same question all them reporters asked first," DeSantis continued, as if he hadn't seen my jealousy flare. "You'd of thought they'd want to know the state of the corpus or how we come to figure it a homicide. Journalism has gone down the old one-holer since you worked the beat, Gulliver."

"Not the reason you asked, huh?" He stowed the cigarette in a corner of his mouth, locked onto me with a one-eyed squint. He had seen the jealousy. I shook my head.

"I'll give it to you easy," he said. "I expect the crime lab boys will have more to say later, but so far the only one who can answer the bedroom question is your ex. Emergency said Sheridan was alone in bed when they arrived. His head cracked like a ripe coconut. Brains spilled onto the pillow, owing to contact with a heavy, blunt instrument.

"Ms. Marriner was climbing walls, dressed like you see her now. Already refusing to talk. Screaming after you. Worrying over how she would look for the TV when they got here. Can you believe this shit?" He made a bitter face. "Here's the prime suspect in a murder one, the corpus in the next room, and all she cares about is her eyeliner being on straight."

"I can believe it," I said. I let my eyes wander across the room. Stevie sensed me checking. She looked up from her magazine, her flicker of a smile unable to disguise the anxiety registering on her face.

"Actresses." DeSantis cracked the word and exhaled dragon smoke. "They're all alike," he said and at once seemed to regret having shared the thought, burying it under a cough. I pretended not to have heard and wondered to myself if an actress had once given DeSantis a taste of what I went through. If so, we had more in common than the ugly manners of mankind.

DeSantis doused the cigarette on the sole of his shoe and, when he couldn't locate an ashtray among the celebrity photos in silver frames on the closed lid of the baby grand, deposited the butt in a jacket pocket. The photos were age-stained and carried faded inscriptions and seemed to inspire his next question.

"You ever hear of Claire Cavanaugh?" Either he didn't see my nod or didn't care. "One of them old actresses who live here."

I didn't know she was at the MPRE, but DeSantis didn't have to explain Claire Cavanaugh. My mind already had retrieved one of the truly great faces in movie history, for three decades after they learned to talk. Her immortality had been enshrined after she took a stiff bristle brush to Shirley Temple's backside in *Steamboat Sally* and gave the little dimpled darling her first screen spanking.

"She used to be famous, Claire Cavanaugh," DeSantis said, uncomfortable with the news. "Spoon says she come charging into the administration building out of sorts. The receptionist—" He checked his pad for a name. "Toby Latch. Claire Cavanaugh gets Latch to the point where she understands the babbling. Latch almost drops a load charging after Spoon. Spoon calls Emergency, then he jumps into his go-cart and heads for Sheridan's cottage. Ms. Marriner is waiting outside the front door, not making much sense herself as she drags him into the bedroom.

"Spoon has taken enough Red Cross classes to know the right moves, he tells me. It's apparent to him from the git-go Sheridan has already left for that Great Movie Studio in the Sky."

I asked, "What brought Claire Cavanaugh to the cottage?"

"Her place is next door, so it could of been the racket your ex was making. Way she told it to Spoon, she goes inside and sees Sheridan and knows to call for help, but the phone line has been yanked out, so Cavanaugh rushes off to find someone.

"First she tries the neighbor on the other side, guy name of Polyzoides—" He checked his notes again. "Mimithos Polyzoides. You ever hear of him?" I had, but DeSantis didn't wait to find out. "The guy says he was sleeping off a Seconal and between the pill and a pair of bad ears didn't rouse until after the boys in blue damn near banged his door off the hinges."

"You said it *could* have been the noise Stevie was making that got Claire Cavanaugh to Sheridan's cottage. What did Claire Cavanaugh say?"

DeSantis shrugged and turned his palms to the ceiling. "The old lady turned up missing before we could ask her."

"Missing?"

"You got on your own hard-of-hearing impediment, like this Mimithos Polyzoides? Seems she stayed behind in the reception office when Spoon ran off to Sheridan's cottage. By the time Spoon got back here, Cavanaugh was gone. Nobody has seen her since." DeSantis lit a fresh smoke. "Spoon says it happens all the time around here. Cavanaugh will turn up sooner or later, hopefully with answers for questions and maybe even some unpleasant consequences for your ex."

I put Claire Cavanaugh out of my mind temporarily. "I hear presence, but what else do you have that ties Stephanie Marriner to Sheridan's death?"

DeSantis suppressed a smile. "I'd love to tell you we have her prints on the murder weapon, only we haven't identified the weapon yet. All in due time. The lab jocks filled enough baggies and sprinkled enough powder to get us the whole nine yards."

"To me, sounds like you're not ready to hold Stevie."

He shook his head. "You think I would of let her go and play superstar with the press stupes, answering questions with Barbie Doll tears, if I had enough for the DA's office? She didn't give them a damn word, either, by the way. Just a lot of posture and a lot of boob-heaving and all them Barbie Doll tears."

"But she is a suspect."

"*Primo* . . ." DeSantis sucked up a long pause and said, "Time now for you to show good faith."

He had played fair and I owed him.

I called, "Stevie."

She was on her feet, using the coffee table as the base for a series of deep knee bends.

She stopped and faced us.

I motioned her to join us and her look turned hard.

She waited with her legs apart, hands on hips, head tilted aggressively.

"Doll, I don't see where it would hurt to answer some of Lieutenant DeSantis's questions," I said.

"It would hurt right here," Stevie said, making a grab for her crotch like she was Roseanne on a baseball diamond.

"Actresses." DeSantis spit the word like he was aiming for a memory.

Shortly, the executive director, Mickey Spoon, had a member of his staff cart Stevie and me to Stevie's autumn green Cherokee in the visitors' parking arena about twenty yards from Sheridan's cottage, easy to spot among the dozen or so on a gentle slope of verdant plants that circled like wagon trains around a common parklike backyard and interconnected through a series of winding redbrick walkways. The walkways were lined on both sides by alternating shade trees and lamps shaped like the highway bells that identify the route taken by Padre Junipero Serra when he founded the missions up the California coast from San Diego in the late 1700s. All the stucco cottages adhered to the mission motif, like smaller versions of the administration building.

Sheridan's cottage was the one with yellow crime scene tape barring the arched door and one of DeSantis's uniform cops sitting lazy guard, his chair tilted against the wall and a magazine in his face.

The cop looked up when he heard the golf wagon. He adjusted his sunglasses and stalked us while I guided Stevie into the Jeep and went around and climbed behind the wheel. Stevie insisted she was fine enough to drive but seemed relieved when I snatched the keys away from her.

The top was off and the freeway breeze felt refreshing en route to Sunset-Gower Studios, where Stevie had a five o'clock blocking call on *Bedrooms and Board Rooms*.

I tried talking her into canceling.

"They've heard the news by now and understand what you're going through," I said. "You should take it easy, get some—"

"Neil, do I tell you how to write your column?"

No sense arguing. I made small talk when I wasn't humming along to the Elton John greatest hits CD in her player and trying to hide my concern. She answered my smiles whenever she wasn't staring blankly at traffic or adjusting a wide-brimmed, patchwork floppy that dropped almost to her Carreras. She had found it in the backseat, along with a knee-length, drawstring sweatshirt in rainbow colors that she'd wriggled into just before I pulled onto the 101.

Nearing the studio, she removed the sunglasses and stared intensely at me. "Okay, I'm tired of waiting. What did that cop tell you?"

"DeSantis? It can wait."

"Did he tell you what a bitch I was?"

"Old news travels fast."

Stevie made a little noise to let me know she welcomed my teasing like a hard massage.

"I was acting, honey. The screaming was just an act. I was scared, I cannot tell you how much, and I was not about to tell it to that damn cop. It was all DeSantis could do to not put me in handcuffs and leg chains from the time he got there, like he already had me tried and convicted of murdering Blackie Sheridan and all that was left was to drag me to the gas chamber. I needed you so you can tell me what to do."

"Isn't that what you have Christopher for?"

Christopher was her current fling, a golden haired retriever who pumped iron and gas and her when he wasn't delivering pizzas, waiting for the world to anoint him the next Nicolas Cage. He had started sniffing around Stevie after she cut down Phillip, one of her co-stars on *Bedrooms and Board Rooms*.

"Are you jealous?"

"Always."

"I like that, Neil."

"That's why I said it."

Stevie socked my shoulder, meant to be a playful punch, but it stung, and I winced. She grabbed my arm with hers, hugged it tight, and mothered the spot with her heavenly lips. Elton John finished "Crocodile Rock" and hammered into "Bennie and the Jets."

She drew back and confessed, "I'm through with the SOB."

"Uh-huh. I'm surprised you didn't wise up to Christopher faster than this."

"I won't lie to you. He left me. The SOB left me for another woman. Do you know what that's like, honey?"

"Not exactly, but I suppose it would have been worse if he left you for another man?"

Stevie hauled back to punch me again, but changed her mind. "For a Beverly Hills Pop-Tart in breakaway clothes, barely out of high school. Daddy makes movies in the Philippines. Guts and gore stuff, where lepers run around with their skin falling off. He's there now with his bitch goddess. They're co-starring, if you can believe that! Co-starring!"

Hearing Stevie had gotten a taste of what she put me through gave me a spasm of delight. I wasn't proud of my reaction, but I was honest enough to admit it. To myself, anyway.

It would take a better, wiser man to feel differently, not someone carrying a burned-out torch and waiting for an old flame to come back. I needed Stevie and she needed me, sometimes the same way, but never at the same time, not since Stevie decided being a star to my planet wasn't enough.

I repeated what DeSantis had told me.

Stevie worked it through in her mind and I felt her tension rising again. Several times she nodded agreement. More often, her head wagged left and right.

"Your turn, again," I said when I finished, trying to drag her mind back inside the Jeep. Elton was singing "Candle in the Wind." I turned off the CD over her objection, pressed the FM digital switch until it reached my favorite jazz station.

Some Bill Evans.

Remedial.

Nice.

After a while, she said, "The last people in the world I wanted to talk to was the press. But I did. Like it was a cold reading, only I didn't say anything. Also to put some distance between me and that damn cop till you arrived."

"Tell me something I don't know, sweetheart."

Stevie said, "Not again."

"What's that supposed to mean?"

" 'Not again.' That's what the old woman said to me in the cottage. 'Not again.' "

"Claire Cavanaugh?"

"That who she was, the old woman?" There was a new distance in her voice. "The one from the movie with Humphrey Bogart, where Bogart tells his gun moll to shut her trap if she knows what's good for her, and then he picks up a hot fudge sundae and dumps it onto her head?"

"*Blood on My Hands*."

"That one."

"Claire Cavanaugh," I said, and in my best Bogart, " 'A fat lip like yours doesn't deserve this, kitten. Here, a little dessert for you.' "

I reached over and brought my hand down on Stevie's cap. She laughed to please me before digging back into private reflection. A few moments later, her voice like dry rot, she said, "I killed him, Neil. I killed Blackie Sheridan."

"What are you saying?"

"She saw me. The old woman saw me do it, Neil."

My foot smashed down on the gas pedal.

I got my eyes back on the freeway in time to see an accident in progress.

My own.

I was almost on top of a gas tanker that had edged into my lane, right in front of me.

I slammed the brake pedal hard enough to send it through the floor.

The Jeep shimmied.

The rear end fishtailed and almost creamed a tan Mercedes.

I regained control twelve inches short of the tanker.

"Too close," I squeaked, once gravity had pulled my stomach back where it belonged.

"Too close what, honey?" she said, confused, unaware she had almost become Cream of Soap Star. Stevie, who had just confessed to killing Black Jack Sheridan.

Last night, the night of his murder, Stevie has no trouble finding Sheridan's cottage.

She had visited him once before, weeks ago, a social call before she agreed to undertake *Marilyn Remembers*, to make sure their egos and attitudes meshed. He was full of high-spirited charm and graciousness, truly delicious anecdotes about the old Hollywood, witty and raucous tales filled with famous names and naughty moments, and she can't recall the last time she enjoyed herself this much.

She pulls up and parks next to Sheridan's vintage black Riviera.

His living room is dark. A dim light steals through the curtained bedroom window. She presses the door button. Chimes sound a four-note melody. No answer. She tries twice more; opens the screen door over the protest of rusty hinges. She knocks, graduating from loud to louder. Is the Monster Man ignoring her?

She calls for him by name. Nothing.

She turns to go.

The porch light clicks on.

The door swings open.

Sheridan is dressed out of the Arabian nights in a flowing silk caftan and a fez, the tassel bouncing gently against an ear. Aladdin shoes with pointy toes.

He is displeased and orders Stevie to leave, orchestrating the direction with his cock-shaped cane, its handle shaped like a pair of swollen balls. He starts to close the door. Stevie bars the way with a boot, argues her mission in an avalanche of words.

She declares she is determined to stay there all night, if necessary, until they reach an understanding. Put the past behind them. Failing that, shake hands and part on a friendly note.

Reluctantly, Sheridan allows Stevie inside.

He turns on a floor lamp that instantly bathes the room in the ambiguous glow of his film noir thrillers. After all, isn't Sheridan the man who taught Marlene Dietrich the lighting tricks she didn't learn from her first mentor, von Sternberg? The trick here is to find comfort from shadows.

She follows Sheridan's directions to the massive leather couch and sinks into a corner. He goes to the kitchen to fix drinks. Sheridan will have sherry. She has opted for a light vodka over ice with a lemon twist. Stevie needs the lift to decompress, chill out. One drink won't cause problems driving home.

Sheridan is taking his sweet time.

Anxiously, Stevie wanders the room as she had done the last visit, touching the souvenirs and mementos of his life in what he has made over into a museum to himself. Posters of Sheridan's films dominate the walls. Framed citations, honors. Photographs with stars, most of them acting thrilled to be in his presence. Inscribed photos from world leaders she only knows from history books. Truman and Eisenhower. John F. Kennedy, hiding reality behind a Camelot smile.

She is taken with his great conceit: the Oscar he won for directing *Rendezvous for Two* sits on the plush, brown carpeted floor, propping open one of two glass-paneled doors between the living room and a dining alcove off the kitchen. She does now what she had only thought about doing on the last visit.

She scoops up the golden statuette, clasps it to her breast. The Oscar is heavier than she imagined, maybe fifteen or twenty pounds. She is delivering a whispered acceptance speech, thanking her dear mother for years of encouragement, when Sheridan emerges from the kitchen holding their drinks.

Sheridan is naked, except for his intentions and his Aladdin shoes. He continues past her into the living room, clears a place for the glasses on the coffee table, all the while informing her what she can do to surmount their differences, restore harmony to the production. He settles on the couch and pats a spot for her to join him. Stevie recognizes he's propositioning her.

A mat of hair disguises Sheridan's sunken chest. His hairy, distended paunch crowns his meager thighs. He uses his slender, almost feminine hands to pull apart his knobby knees and display a penis that will need more than direction to act out the role he has in mind for it.

As if reading her mind, Sheridan begins puttering with it. She watches, fascinated. In a few moments, he has what he is proudly calling an erection. His Dickie. He toasts her with his brandy, dips his penis into the snifter. Urges her to undress, get comfortable. Come, have a taste. Give Dickie a kiss he'll remember.

It's all too incredible to fathom, this silly little man in his mid-seventies trying to seduce her, dangling his part and her part in *Marilyn Remembers* as mediums of trade.

Stevie begins to laugh. She cannot control her laughter. She tries, head reared back, hitting the air with her palms, as if that can help.

Sheridan goes limp with rage. He springs off the couch and lurches toward her. He has a bad leg and he drags it behind like an anchor, condemning her with every gasp for breath. He stops a foot or two away, as if not certain what to do next. Eyes molten fury. Blue temple veins straining against the elastic skin of his bald head.

Maybe Stevie should be more frightened than she is, but she is taller by three or four inches and, she supposes, stronger, too, by virtue of her age and the daily training regimen that keeps her in peak physical condition.

Sheridan realizes she is holding his Oscar. He grabs for it.

Perversely, she clings to the statuette.

They grapple for possession as Stevie's thoughts race madly, wildly, trying to make sense of the situation.

A woman's voice calls out, "Not again."

It startles both of them. They freeze.

At once, the combination of surprise and concern crossing his face reveals that Sheridan recognizes the voice. It gives him a few seconds' advantage.

He tugs the Oscar free.

Turns to confront the woman observing them from a position between the alcove and the front door—

Claire Cavanaugh.

"Not again," Claire Cavanaugh repeats, staring straight at her, then at Sheridan, who begins yelling at Claire, waving his arms like a volleyball player at a nudist camp.

Stevie cannot make out his words. She sees the old woman is scared and has started to back away as Sheridan advances on her, forgetting Stevie for the moment.

The old woman crosses her arms in front of her face to protect herself against his fury. He bangs at her with his free fist. The other one is weighted down by the Oscar. Suddenly, he lifts it like a symphony conductor.

Stevie leaps forward and yanks the Oscar from Sheridan before he can club the old woman. Sheridan assails her with a brief look over his shoulder. He pulls Claire Cavanaugh's hands apart and begins to throttle her.

Stevie sees the old woman is helpless to resist.

Her complexion is turning as blue as her hair, her eyes taking on the attitude of final disbelief.

Stevie screams for Sheridan to stop. He ignores her. She recognizes something must be done fast, or Claire Cavanaugh will be dead. Desperately, she slams the Oscar against his head, above his right ear.

Sheridan's hairy back rises. His clutch on the old woman slackens. His arms fall to his sides. His head swivels, looking for something to do. He aims in slow motion for the bedroom but trips over his shoes after a couple misdirected steps and belly flops to the floor.

Stevie said, "DeSantis said how Claire Cavanaugh heard me screaming the next morning, and so that's when she came to the cottage and found me? Not the way it happened, honey."

"The thought occurred to me."

"That may be what she said, but what I just told you is the absolute truth." Stevie reached across the counter and patted my hand appreciatively. "You feel like another Kirin, honey? I can use one, too."

Our waitress, a petite, rouge-cheeked Asian in a black minikimono and matching Reeboks, acknowledged her hand signal from the other side of the small room and quickly traded two cold bottles for the empties. We already had walloped through a pair apiece at If You Knew Sushi, this unobtrusive Gower Gulch restaurant across from the studio, alone at the counter except for a bald man with a lamp tan reading *Daily Variety*.

"Chin chin." We clanked bottles, and Stevie turned to the eager counter man doing knife tricks to the dead fish on the block in front of us. "Two more orders of toro, Craig-san, and another katsuo . . . an ama ebi . . . and my friend and I will share an order of ikura." Craig-san smiled his approval and set to work.

I dropped my voice into my plate again and said, "You struck Sheridan and down he went."

"Yes."

"And he was dead."

"I think so."

"You think so. Can you do better than that?"

"He wasn't moving, except for one of his legs," she said, lowering her voice. "His leg was twitching a little. His foot. He looked dead."

I rested my chin in my palm, pushed out a long breath of air and shook my head. She recognized the confusion setting in.

"I was more worried about Claire Cavanaugh, honey. Sheridan had worked her over pretty good. I dropped the Oscar and grabbed hold of her before she collapsed. I helped her over to the couch. She could barely stand. She said she needed to stretch out and asked for water. I went to get her some—"

"And Sheridan? Still twitching?"

She shook her head. "Not moving at all."

"Head bleeding?"

"I don't remember. There could have been. I know I hit him pretty hard. The Oscar, it felt like it weighed a ton. My mind was racing, honey. I was coming apart at the seams, but I knew I couldn't let go. I had to help this old woman, and—"

I asked, "Why didn't you call 911?"

"After I got the water, I tried. I couldn't get a dial tone. The cop told you that. Somebody cut the wire."

"Before you got there?"

"Give. Me. A. Break. Neil," she said, exasperated, making each word a sentence. "How would I know if I wasn't there?" She shook her head. Took a deep breath. "Pass the soy sauce, please."

She poured it into the dainty porcelain bowl and added a clump of wasabi, the green horseradish that can bring on a nosebleed, then stirred the combination with a chopstick. I cleaned my palate with gari, the sliced pickled ginger I ate like coleslaw, as the counter man delivered the ikura along with more gari and accepted Stevie's compliments with a bow.

I said, "Let's try out the other version. The next morning, Claire Cavanaugh reacts to your screams and gets the executive director, Mickey Spoon, who finds Sheridan in the bedroom, dead, decorating the pillows with his blood."

"Yes."

"How did he get there?"

"I took him there."

"Sheridan's dead. Why did you move him from the living room to the bedroom? Didn't I once teach you better than to disturb a crime scene, especially the victim?"

"I mean that Mickey Spoon person. I grabbed onto him and I took him into the bedroom, where Sheridan was when I woke up."

"Where Sheridan was?"

She understood my real question.

"I woke up on the couch, Neil."

"Where you said Claire Cavanaugh had stretched—"

"Yeah, only she wasn't around and I was the one stretched out. The first time I knew Sheridan was there was when I went looking, after I saw he wasn't still on the floor. And Claire Cavanaugh wasn't around. Daylight woke me up. The blinds were pulled back. I felt the daylight on my face. I heard the birds outside. I was telling myself, Take ten or fifteen minutes more of shut-eye, Stevie, and then I remembered where I was and what had happened."

"When did Claire Cavanaugh leave?"

"I don't know." A dissecting look. "You. Are. Starting. To. Sound. Like. That. Cop!"

The words drifted out between her clenched teeth. The tiny waitress thought she needed something else and padded over, her Reeboks making scraping noises on the linoleum. Stevie apologized and sent her away.

"It's the truth, honey. Everything."

"Of course it is . . . I know." I pushed the stray hairs off her face and tucked them behind her ear. She pressed her hand against mine to keep it there. "Tell me what you remember from when you dialed 911 and found the line dead to the time you woke up."

"I don't remember; I must have passed out."

"Anything?"

"Not really. I remember wondering why there was no dial tone and then I was waking up on the couch. I went looking and—" A spasm ran through her body. And then, almost as if it had jolted her memory, "Neil, did you say the detective told you they didn't have the murder weapon?" I nodded. "It's a lie, honey. I remember seeing the Oscar on the floor where I dropped it, when I went to help Claire Cavanaugh. Later, I must have said something to that Spoon person. I can picture him afterward. He took the detective over and pointed to it, and then the detective called over one of his people, and—"

Tears welled in her eyes. It wasn't because of the wasabi. She put her hands on the counter to steady herself, but her arms shook anyway. She had gotten too close to the memory that ended with Sheridan's murder.

"It's going to be all right," I said gently, and placed a hand on hers.

"You are my friend, aren't you, Neil?" she asked, without looking at me, her voice a shadow of despair.

"No matter what," I said.

"Excuse us . . . Miss Stephanie Marriner, yes?"

A family of tourists had arrived right behind us and slipped into one of the booths across the aisle. They had not been hard to make. The father was wearing a Hawaiian shirt, the mother a muumuu, and their ten- or eleven-year-old daughter had pigtails and a Disneyland propeller cap. Armed with Leicas.

"We are on holiday from Germany, Berlin, where we see you all the time on the television, on the *Bedrooms and Board Rooms*. We are such big fans and I was thinking . . ." His strident voice trailed off. I started to make an excuse for her. She stopped me with a gesture, smiled sweetly, and said there was always time for her fans. Meant it. Took the menu the man offered and asked to borrow my pen. She wrote a long, warm greeting to the Muller family. Muller wondered about taking a photo, in that polite but pushy German manner, and Stevie expressed appreciation, like no one had ever asked her before. She led him by the hand back to the booth and slid in alongside the girl, who said her name was Anna.

Stevie asked her, "Do you want to be an actress someday, Anna, like me?" The girl nodded shyly. "You are certainly pretty enough, so work very hard and I know that one day your wish will come true." Anna's smile was the biggest as the flash went off and light particles bounced from her braces. Stevie kissed her cheek. "You'll remember to send me a copy, won't you? And, be sure to autograph it for me? 'To Stevie, from her friend, Anna.' "

Impulsively, little Anna lurched forward, engaged Stevie in a hug, and romped off clutching her prize to her chest. Anna's parents gushed more thanks and marched off after her sporting Disneyland-sized smiles. Stevie was smiling, too, with the look she always has when she locks onto some rare, unspoken memory from her childhood. I waited a minute before easing her back to the real world.

I said, "What prompted you to drive out to the MPRE to confront Sheridan last night? Wouldn't it have been easier to quit like you had been threatening to do and make him come crawling to you with an apology. No Stevie Marriner, no *Marilyn Remembers*, remember?"

"Quit?" Stevie spit out the word like rancid milk, then dropped her voice to a whisper and waited for the sushi chefs to move to the other end of the counter. "I never had a chance. The Monster Man, that creep, fired me."

In Stevie's version of events leading up to last night, Sheridan's lavish praise of the early weeks had grown into a blizzard of criticism as an opening date was set and production elements fell into place behind their nightly rehearsals, after she'd finished taping *Bedrooms and Board Rooms* at the studio.

His notes frequently were longer than his script.

Sarcasm and cruelty worthy of an Otto Preminger entered his manner. He routinely assailed her at the top of his lungs, doing a Zubin Mehta with his phallic cane, shrieking uncontrollably, as if trying to wring a performance out of a limp doll, certainly not an actress he supposedly had written the play for and ardently solicited for the part, Stevie of the "incendiary sex appeal."

A stage move or an inflection Sheridan loved and lauded for weeks—applauding madly, pointing to tears she had brought to his callous eyes—somehow turned into "garbage."

"You know what I do with garbage?" he screamed at her. "I throw it outside in the garbage pail. If I was back on the family farm, I would feed it to the pigs."

He seemed to lurk about the stage, waiting until there were others present to launch the worst of his diatribes.

Stevie controlled herself at first, mindful of her deserved reputation for terrorizing the writers of her soap and refusing to say any line she believed was inconsistent with her character. But she understood it was not done that way on Broadway, where the playwright is God, and she gave Sheridan total respect.

That made their eroding relationship all the more baffling, and finally, as her self-confidence and self-esteem evaporated, she started answering back, at first softly, then in kind, and finally in tantrums that turned Black Jack Sheridan into "Monster Man."

I asked, "What made him fire you?"

Stevie shrugged. "He was sweet as honey cake the first hour and I thought, Geez-o, maybe whatever gerbil was chewing up his butt has finished the trip. You know? Like a serious case of male menopause? I was deep into character, the scene where I'm on the phone telling Arthur it's over between us?"

She shut her eyes, pressed her fingers against her temples. Another moment and her eyes flicked open, wet, focused on some distant planet, breaking the bad news to her third husband, the playwright Arthur Miller, in a seductive baby whisper. She was divorcing him. Sorry, Arthur. Time to move on. Rise from the ashes of a union that was never meant to last. Finished, she locked onto my stare, daring me not to like her work.

She must have known I'd found myself substituting my name for Miller's, but she didn't betray the confidence. "I got talent to burn, honey," she said, surveying the room like a matador in the bullring.

"That's when Sheridan fired you?"

She shook her head, picked up the Kirin bottle, and verified it was empty.

"He'd been strutting back and forth, and now he said to keep going without him and vanished into the back of the house. When he returned, he clapped me to stop." She slapped her hands together. "I'm at the part where I'm talking to DiMaggio on the phone, telling him how my life has turned to doo-doo, and here's the Monster Man back mean as ever. He's dressed to split—coat, cap and cockadoodle cane—and announces for the world to hear—" She cleared her throat and spoke in a phony continental accent, "You stink, Miss Marriner, to high heaven. It is over for you. I leave now. I do not expect you to be here when I return."

The sushi chefs looked up from their preparations, exchanged curious expressions. Stevie waited for them to lose interest and shared a disheartened look with me.

"Here, I'd been ready to quit, honey, and Monster Man beat me to the punch. I was shattered, totally, but I was not about to let anyone see me break up, so I put on a great front, letting them know what I thought of Mr. John 'Black Jack' Sheridan. In the back of my mind, I hoped and prayed he would limp back in so we could have it out."

"But he didn't," I said.

"But he didn't."

"So you decided to make the drive to the MPRE."

"I couldn't hang around like a street corner hustler, so I did a Bette Davis and split. I'm halfway home, already suffering a first-stage migraine alert, when I decide, Screw Sheridan if he thinks I am going to spend the night chewing on the bedsheets. You know me well enough to know I wasn't anxious to do a drop dead on Sheridan if we could work out our problems.

"The truth is, the Monster Man was one helluva director and I was learning from him. I headed out to the MPRE figuring he had no place else to go but back home. We'd have it out. Either agree to start tomorrow with a clean slate or—"

I stopped her with my open palm.

Stevie understood. "It was an accident, Neil."

"The DA will call it premeditation and that's murder one. He'll show you had the motive, you had the opportunity, you had the means. The three elements it takes for a conviction. And, for frosting, people in the theater can testify how angry you were at Sheridan. Claire Cavanaugh can place you at the murder scene."

"If you're trying to make me cry, Neil, you're doing a fine job of it."

I gentled a hand on her cheek and felt it trembling to my touch. I was about to say something supportive when I remembered a contradiction about the means—

The Oscar Stevie said she had used to club Sheridan.

That wasn't what DeSantis had said. He'd told me they hadn't identified the weapon. *Identified.* Did that mean there was some question about the Oscar being the murder weapon? Or, only that DeSantis was reserving the call until he had the lab's report?

Did it really make a difference?

I had a great urge to hear DeSantis's unfriendly voice.

An hour later, the cab dropped me at the Heathcliffe Arms, my condo in Westwood. The Heathcliffe, constructed on half a city block in 1972, is a collection of five six-story buildings around a central courtyard, the most attractive condo among the couple dozen that stretch down Veteran Avenue, south of Wilshire and within hiking distance of UCLA.

I moved into my third floor, one-bedroom unit seven years ago, after Stevie organized my departure from the cozy home we had shared as spouse and spice near Santa Anita, where I once spent most of my time and all of our money.

I bought the condo the next year, with a twenty-thousand-dollar down payment I'd borrowed from my ex, who in the interim had blossomed into the highly prized, richly rewarded "Sex Queen of the Soaps." Stevie insists to this day the loan was really a gift, her way of saying thanks; for what, she never says.

Someday I'll decorate the condo, or so I keep promising myself. Meanwhile, its Divorced Male motif functions just fine: thrift shop and late-model Ikea for a cozy dropped-in look, set off by cheaply framed art museum posters and old movie posters like *Casablanca* that provide me more pleasure than anything on TV, except for the old movies themselves.

I found the portable phone on my computer hutch and punched in DeSantis's number en route to the john.

The detective who answered sounded like he had fifty better ways to spend the next minute and reluctantly took down my name and number, promising to leave my message where DeSantis would find it when he came in tomorrow. A pimp's promise, worth about as much.

I finished eliminating fifty gallons of Kirin from my system and headed back to the hutch. The red dot on my answering machine was blinking. A rumble in my stomach told me I'd regret pressing the message playback button, but an overpowering need to know is what makes a reporter in the first place. The need is as vital as his pulse.

I pressed the playback button.

Two calls from Augie.

That's A. K. Fowler, August Kalman Fowler, the brilliant, one-eyed crime reporter, my original mentor at the *Daily*, who resigned years ago to found a spiritual order over by Griffith Park, the Order of the Spiritual Brothers of the Rhyming Heart. He now calls himself Brother Kalman, where I continue to call him Augie, (and most of our old cronies call him nuts).

Augie and I talked at least twice a day, more regularly than a bowel movement. I had become his most reliable conduit to the world, or so Augie had often suggested since becoming Brother Kalman, victim of a desperate passion to put criminal reality behind him.

Also among the jungle of voices—

The *Daily*'s Spider Woman herself, Veronica Langtry, the poisonous deputy editor who had put new life and circulation back into a slew of moribund major city dailies for Lord Dennis Goodwin and since last year was performing the miracle in L.A.

"Return this call, Neil, at once, no matter what time you hear this message," Langtry demanded, leaving her home number.

Not a good sign. I understood the rumble in my stomach and took my nightly tub before calling her back, to be clean for the dirt I expected her to pour on me.

The Spider Woman didn't disappoint.

Langtry said, "Clancy McPhillip tells me he saw you at the Black Jack Sheridan murder scene, Neil."

He had.

A car sweeping past me when I entered the MPRE earlier today had honked for attention. I'd snatched a glance of Al Cavalieri of the *Daily*'s photo department behind the wheel, and the flash of wheat-straw wig next to him sat on McPhillip's high dome like a misshapen roof. Clancy was the Irish dandy Langtry had imported from New York to tackle the front page yarns that once carried my bylines.

"A demon for detail, that Clancy," I said. "By the way, boss, Hello. How most people start a conversation. Hello. Up there with please and thank you in the circles I travel."

"Point well taken . . . Neil, let's make a deal, all right? Let us leave the smart-ass conversation behind from here on in and maybe surprise ourselves at how civil we can be to one another."

"Does that mean now, here on the phone, or as one of life's new rules, boss?" The Spider Woman's heavy sigh sank into my ear. I said, "I'm willing to try again if you are. Hello, Ronnie. This is Gulliver returning your call. Something I can do for you this evening, Ronnie?"

"You know, Gulliver, back home in Texas there are piles of cow dung I'd sooner step in than ever have to work with you."

Obviously, she hadn't been keen for my sarcasm. There was nothing about her I was keen for. She had almost succeeded in getting me fired after McPhillip arrived. The armistice her boss and mine, Lord Goodwin, ultimately stitched for us said I didn't have to go along to get along.

"Thank you for sharing, Ronnie. Does it mean we can go back to being ourselves?"

"Why do you even bother, Neil? Where there are a lot of people who would like to be me, I can't hardly believe even you are happy about being you."

"Then your answer is yes?" No answer. "Your modesty is whelming, Ronnie. Simply whelming."

Drop dead breathing in my ear.

Then, "Let's just cut to the chase, Neil." Her. Every. Word. Measured. Slipping back into her natural prairie accent without a sign of the warmth she turned on and off as easily as flushing a toilet. "You have something I want."

"You're a handsome woman, Ronnie, but I don't mix business and pleasure. I—" I caught myself. Langtry is an easy target. I was being unfair. I was taking out on her the steam building up in me because of Stevie. As usual, using humor to flee the real world. "For what it's worth, I apologize, boss. I have a lot on my mind. What's up?"

Weighing the moment. "Better, Neil. There may be hope for us yet." Her voice back to patronizing me and tipping me there'd be another day when her bloodhound sense told her it was time again to try disassembling my scalp.

I said, "What's your bottom line?"

"Nobody, not even Clancy, could wrestle a statement out of Marriner. She looks smashing in a two-column vertical we're going with on page one, the irrigated eyes look, but that's the best we have for our blue collars. I know how close you and your former wife remain, and I surmise that's what sent you racing off to the Motion Picture Retirement Estates—"

"And you think Stevie may have told me something you can use to help Clancy pep up his copy."

"Precisely."

"Either Stevie doesn't know anything or she wasn't sharing it with me," I lied. "Stevie needed protection from the usual cop bullying, and she knew I could help." To prove my sincerity, I repeated the version of events delivered by DeSantis.

She mulled it over. "All of it is consistent with Clancy's story," she decided. "The old star, Claire Cavanaugh, seems to be the one who can give us a beat on this, but he had no luck running her down. How about you?"

"I didn't even try, boss."

"I'm supposed to believe that, too, Neil?"

"I pulled Stephanie Marriner out and split. Period. Thirty. Over and out. I'm only interested in protecting my ex from the kind of junk justice that gets the wrong people a large dose of lethal coursing through their veins."

"I sense that in your tone, Neil, and that makes it my turn to apologize. Stephanie Marriner is extremely fortunate to have someone like you to call when there is an emergency and to know you are there for her. After all, it's not like the two of you are still married, or—"

"We're kindred spirits. Doesn't come as part of the wedding ceremony and a lot of people who are married till death do them part stumble through life not knowing or ever finding out, with only hollow vows and a certificate to hold them together. If the need ever arose, Stevie would do the same for me." I could have added she already has, but that was none of Langtry's business.

"Yes," she said, "you make me believe she would." I thought I heard something new in her voice, an edge of regret for some closed chapter in her past. "You may want to think about it as a column subject. Food for thought for our hungry readers."

"Great idea," I said, not meaning it. My personal take on life and love is never going to be cooked for mass consumption, like mess hall stew. *On the Go* is a column for and about others. It's written in the first person, but the guy is never me, just some stranger who wanders on and off stage asking questions and fretting over the answers.

"A favor, though? If you do hear anything we can use, call? I'm not asking you to break a confidence or anything like that, just—oh, you know what I mean?"

"If I happen to stumble across anything printable, you will be the first to hear the second I hear."

"You do have a way with words, Neil. Why don't we just leave it there for the time being?"

Something nagged at me as she laid on more compliments. She heralded my newfound spirit of cooperation and hoped time would heal our unnecessary acrimony and let us become friends, and hung up after a floral good-bye. Not the Langtry I knew. My Langtry had something else in mind when she called.

I was certain of it, but I didn't learn what until after a night of tossing in bed, counting shadows cast through the window blinds by a wandering moon, kept awake thinking about Stevie and DeSantis.

If DeSantis had held back on me about the murder weapon, had he also held back something about Claire Cavanaugh? Information he wasn't about to share with someone once related to the prime suspect, someone who also happens to be working press?

I worried for Stevie. Her toughness was an act. Her swearing a defense mechanism when she felt threatened, a relief valve for pressure and anxiety and tension brought on, in this case, by the prospect of being tried for murder one or, if the cops flubbed on evidence, an involuntary manslaughter rap.

By her own admission. She whacked a pervert, Black Jack Sheridan, while defending an old lady, Claire Cavanaugh. Under other circumstances they'd have her up for a medal.

I managed to drift into a brief sleep and roused again at four-thirty, my head throbbing. Body soaking. Muscles aching. Worrying the worst. It wasn't going to get any better than this.

I threw on a robe, fixed myself a cup of microwave instant, and settled in front of the TV. I flipped from one news channel to the next, hunting for early reports about Sheridan's murder. Finally, with the first full light of morning, I went downstairs to pick up the two *Daily* copies delivered to me every morning at the security desk, the Home and the First Street editions.

Both had a row of type as tall as soup cans across all six columns:

SOAP STAR MURDER SUSPECT

The mission behind Langtry's phone call revealed itself in a four-column sidebar under a grab shot of Sheridan sprawled out in bed and another of Stevie silently pleading her case to the media, below a chunky headline revealing:

EX-HUSBAND PROCLAIMS
STEVIE'S INNOCENCE

This story also carried Clancy McPhillip's byline, but not his uncanny ability to turn phrases that wring every ounce of emotion from a situation, the gift that made him New York's king of trash journalists before he was induced west by his friendly Spider Woman.

Langtry must have banged out this tripe after we spoke, with no style and less class, drawing on words and phrases from our conversation, which she probably had taped, letting the copy flow on her own dog-bone thoughts where I had not given her a direct quote to go with.

> "I'm only interested in protecting my former wife from the kind of junk justice that sends the wrong people off to prison," Neil Gulliver revealed to the *Daily* exclusively, his voice breaking at the thought of his beloved TV soap star

> wife being judged guilty of the brutal murder she and she alone allegedly witnessed.
>
> "Stevie would do the same for me," said the prize-winning journalist, whose *On the Go* column is a daily feature of this newspaper. He vowed to protect her from "the usual cop bullying" on his quest to help prove her innocence, even though the two of them were divorced.

Gutter journalism in quest of circulation, thy name is Veronica Langtry.

Augie Fowler's fire-engine-red Rolls was double-parked outside the Heathcliffe. I charged into the street, waving the *Daily* at him and settled onto the soft leather cushions of the passenger seat screaming about Langtry's treachery, repeating a lot of what he had already heard over the phone.

He listened with a bemused expression, nodding at times to show he was paying attention, this curious, cassock-clad senior citizen with one good eye, whose full, deeply lined and leathery face showed the bumps and blue veins of the chronic drinker he no longer was, although he was bound to be carrying a hip flask of some exotic brandy somewhere, for that occasional nip he would never admit to having.

I paused to catch my breath and recharge my indignation, and he reminded me, "Amigo, Langtry ain't the first news hack to work the gutter, just the newest."

"Best of breed," I muttered.

He lowered his window long enough to spit out a few tobacco shreds glued to his tongue by a dead Cuban cigarillo and told me with certainty, "She'll never be like any of the real news hens from my time. Dames like Adela Rogers St. Johns. The one and only Aggie Underwood."

A few minutes later we were on the 405 sailing north, his conversation moving at a faster clip than the Rolls, pursued by a cloudless blue-gray sky.

Augie momentarily slipped out of automatic cruise to slow for a charcoal Honda making a diagonal dash across the lanes to the 101 wraparound, then locked the car back to 65 mph.

He had insisted on chauffeuring me out to the Motion Picture Retirement Estates to retrieve my Jag. I had left it behind when Stevie and I returned to the city in her Cherokee.

It was uncharacteristic of him.

In the years since he had founded the Order of the Spiritual Brothers of the Rhyming Heart and become Brother Kalman, Augie had turned increasingly reclusive.

We'd meet once a week for a leisurely lunch at the Press Club, but Augie rarely strayed otherwise from his growing flock of curious and devoted brothers, who were first drawn to him by small advertisements he placed in the *Daily* classifieds under "Salvation."

The Order was housed in a convent the Catholic church had been looking to unload above Los Feliz Boulevard in the Griffith Park area. Augie picked it up cheap from what always seemed to me to be his inexhaustible supply of ready cash. He had fully restored the double-decker Spanish hacienda built of traditional hand-fired brick and stucco and perfectly measured rows of redwood beams, balconies, and verandas that begged after the presence of fiery señoritas with dark, flashing eyes responding to mariachi bands and flamenco dancers.

Augie could not have bought the hacienda and the two acres it sat on with any money saved from his reporter's salary or the pension he got after abandoning the *Daily*, a stroke of madness in the aftermath of a bomb explosion at the courthouse downtown.

The bomb was supposed to kill him, he insisted, and instead dismembered a cub reporter named Wimpy Angleman, Augie's protégé, as I had once been his protégé, in the abortive attempt to spring a mass murderer who gets dramatized every few years on A&E.

I've always believed that Augie's retreat into a retreat was his way of paying permanent penance, but it's nothing we discuss. Ever. Except for an occasional mellow reflection about Wimpy and the great journalist Wimpy would have become. He prefers it that way.

When I raised the question, challenged his insistence on getting me back to my Jag, he barked into the phone, "It's been a while since I had the blood bucket on the open road and it needs the workout. I'll be out front waiting for you. Take an hour to get your act together? See you at ten."

"Augie, you'd have to drive back alone."

"What friends are for. Ten o'clock. Sharp."

It's impossible to push Augie where he doesn't want to go or, in this case, where I didn't need him to be. I sensed he had another reason and said so.

He charged it off to my imagination. "Don't apply reporter's logic to a simple favor offered out of goodness by a friend."

"The real reason, Augie, or I'm taking a cab now."

"That's extortion, you know?"

"Stop holding back."

"*Real* reason? What's the *real* reason you're going out there? You think I don't hear it in your voice? Why so quick to leave me behind, kid?

"Nice reverse, Augie, but it won't work this time."

In fact, Augie was right.

I had tried DeSantis again and learned he was out there. If he wasn't going to return my call, I'd track him up against the wall. I didn't need Augie around, second-guessing me as he often liked to do for a cheap-thrill reminder of the days when he was the absolute best. These were new times. We had become different people, but our competitiveness had never entirely abated.

Augie pumped air into the phone. Heavy-throated grumbling beyond comprehension. The wheels of his mind turning, evaluating the situation. "Claire Cavanaugh," he said, defiantly.

"What about her?"

"What I also want to know, amigo. She and I are old friends. I haven't seen her in twenty-five or more years, but you've heard me say many times there are no limitations on true friendship."

"You've never mentioned her name to me."

"A gentleman doesn't tell *everything.*"

"From your years in show business?"

"Manner of speaking. When we met, I was long off the boards

and already running the crime beat for the *Daily*. I don't like the idea Claire's missing any more than you enjoy the spot she may have put Stevie in."

"Maybe they've found her by now."

"Negative. I phoned out to the MPRE and asked after I read the page one spread."

"So did I," I admitted.

He grunted a laugh. "I thought you said you were going there strictly for the Jaguar." He pronounced it "Jag-you-are."

"I lied. You taught me that, too, remember?"

"Why?"

I told him about DeSantis.

"My star pupil, definitely," Augie said.

We reached the Retirement Estates and I directed him to my car. He navigated the Rolls into the empty space next to the Jag, checked the locks, and was lighting up when he reacted audibly to an elderly woman walking onto the administration building veranda a short step ahead of Ned DeSantis.

Augie's jaw sagged. He almost lost the Cuban stogie. His good eye squinted, trying to get her in better focus, and began to glisten in the sunlight while the woman cast her head about. She found what she was looking for and raised her arms like she was about to conduct the sky.

"Claire," Augie said, pushing out a deep breath. He hurried forward calling her name.

She didn't know who he was, but it was impossible to imagine Claire Cavanaugh as anyone else. A big part of the gasp-inducing surprise when she put the brush to Shirley Temple's tiny bottom in *Steamboat Sally*, "The Spanking Heard 'round the World," had to do with her image.

Claire was a radiant young Englishwoman, a girl really, who usually played somebody's sister or the grandniece of C. Aubrey Smith, always the innocence of angels to go with a fragile beauty and fragrant voice.

According to legend, it was Darryl F. Zanuck's idea to cast her against type, a mogul's whim that transformed her into the star she became at eighteen, the age Claire already was playing when her parents sailed here from England and began making the studio rounds with their raven-haired, coal-eyed beauty.

She was a tiny thing, except on the screen, where she could steal any scene by virtue of being in camera range. None of the other contract women at Fox wanted to appear with her and only giants like Tracy, Cooper, Tyrone Power, and Fredric March were gallant enough to risk a two-shot.

The passage of time seemed to have diminished her, but not the electric aura she cast, shutting out DeSantis and the stylish young woman who had stepped through the door and stood behind her on the veranda.

Augie took the narrow wooden steps two at a clip in his sandals, hands raising the hem of his cassock to avoid tripping.

Claire couldn't be more than an inch over five feet in a floral-patterned tea dress with full sleeves. A matching scarf cloaked her neck and traveled down her back. "Reasonable" flat-heeled pumps worn by people her age, which I put in the mid- to late-seventies.

Her fragile skin was a kind of camera-ready white that gave her an almost ghostly appearance in person, but on the screen would hide the indignant cracks and crevices of time. Her eyes luminous as ever, sat larger on her arched cheeks. Her royal mouth had been painted a color as dignified as the whitewashed blue of her thinning, tightly cut hair, much the way Jessica Tandy had worn hers in *Driving Miss Daisy*.

Augie was having trouble finding his voice. His stare was intense. When her eyes had drifted from the sky onto him, he said, "Dear Claire," as if a code were passing between them.

She looked Augie in the eye and thought about it before clasping her hands against her modest bosom. "Is Olivia working today, Alan?" she inquired, her voice like an autumn sunset. "I have been promising her I'll make time to get over there to give her a hug and say hello to Errol."

Augie shot me a nervous glance.

DeSantis was bouncing on the balls of his feet, patting his thighs, trying to figure out why I had arrived with someone who had left the set of *Robin Hood* in his Friar Tuck costume.

Augie was of medium height and build but he managed to be physically imposing under any circumstances, more so in the cassocks he had taken to wearing since moving into his Griffith Park sanctuary.

He had the cassocks custom-tailored in a variety of patterns and materials, and his missing eye was either disguised under the same cloth or a cosmetic pair of contacts. Today, he wore a patch, an earth brown to blend with the cassock.

Claire appeared to have confused him with Alan Hale, Sr., the great Warners character actor whose son would one day skipper seven shipwrecked passengers around a television island. She stared at me with no recognition. She seemed light as a feather, about to drift away on a cautious breeze. I wanted to clasp her shoulder and hold her in place. Augie got there first.

He said, "It's me, dear Claire. August."

She smiled back without recognition. "August already? My goodness, before we know it will be Christmas."

He moved his face closer to hers, made a useless noise. He gentled two fingers against her cheek. She winced. Imprudently, he removed Claire's scarf, revealing black-and-blue marks it was meant to hide. Claire had not resisted him, and she continued to address his interest with the whim of a close-mouthed smile.

Augie turned back to me. I didn't like the menu on his face. It was the same need to kill I saw the day the bomb got Wimpy. The look was intended for whomever had hurt Claire.

"I really should get Miss Cavanaugh back to her cottage, unless you need her for something else, Lieutenant DeSantis," said the woman standing behind Claire.

"No problem, Miss Jahnsen. Think we've gone as far as we're gonna get today." He glanced at me. "Besides, I need to have some private words with Mr. Gulliver."

Ms. Jahnsen smiled at us and, gripping Claire by an elbow, started leading her down the veranda stairs.

"I'll go along with you," Augie decided, his voice informing the younger woman she had no choice, and fell in behind them.

Claire said, "Come along then, Alan. Oh, it will be so much fun to surprise Olivia and Errol this way."

I watched them go, wondering how important a role her faltering memory would play in the rescue of Stevie Marriner.

Or, Stevie's conviction.

DeSantis chewed on his temper until the receptionist, Toby Latch, pointed us to the conference room we had used yesterday. She turned her nose away from him as he passed, as if DeSantis had misplaced his deodorant. A copy of the *Daily* was face up on the coffee table.

DeSantis snatched it up and quoted from it without looking, on his way to a leaning spot against the brick facing of a wall dominated by a massive, gas-operated fireplace that looked rarely used. The pile of logs on the hearth was decorative and brittle to the eyes, as if a touch might snap them.

"So, Gulliver the Great is gonna protect his TV star from 'the usual cop bullying,' huh?" DeSantis let the phrase sail across the room. He pressed his back to the wall and found a paragraph to quote. He looked up every few words to check my expression. I searched for a comfortable position on the couch and gave him nothing in return.

"Tell me about the 'junk justice' that sends the wrong people off to prison." His Adam's apple did a little jig.

"The story was a mistake. Not meant to happen, and besides, I was quoted out of context, DeSantis."

He laughed heartily. "Damn, but you surely do sound like brother officers I know who claimed the same after their words were reported in this snot rag you call a newspaper."

"Shit happens," I said quietly, not interested in a debate I couldn't win. "It may have happened to your friends and it did happen to me."

DeSantis mocked my words.

Tossed the paper into the fireplace.

Ran his fingers back through his hair.

I tried changing the subject. "Is it that you didn't return my call or did my answering machine have that pleasure while I was traveling here?"

He exaggerated a shrug. "I figured, Why bother? From the noise Mr. Gulliver is making on page one, I'm bound to run into the knight in shining armor when he tracks out again to tilt at windmills."

"Wouldn't you have been disappointed if I failed to show?"

"Your Jag's out on the lot, and I figured that would be your excuse. What did surprise me was Sancho Panza. Your buddy as crazy as he looks?"

"Brother Kalman? Crazier."

"Then he is the perfect one to talk to the old dame." He drilled an index finger next to his temple. "She's been a lost cause like you seen since showing up this morning. About as much use as tits on a tiger."

"Where was she?"

DeSantis lit up a smoke to buy time. "Wandered off, wandered back," he said after another minute. "The exec, Spoon. He says it's SOP with a lot of people here. The reason why he wasn't more annoyed about it than we saw him yesterday."

"Alzheimer's?"

"A kindergarten version, he said. Sometimes the people are lucid and working on all cylinders. Other times . . ." He rolled his eyes. For whatever his reasons, he was trying to communicate. Or, maybe he thought I knew something he needed and was setting me up for a trade.

I said, "You held out yesterday, didn't you, DeSantis?" The question I had for him when I phoned. I was trying it before his mood changed.

"Meaning?"

"You told me you hadn't found the weapon. I know it was brought to your attention by Mickey Spoon, who heard it from Stevie—after Claire sent him racing to the cottage."

"Spoon told you that?" The corners of his mouth curled upward into a smile. "I didn't think so."

He moved from the fireplace and settled onto the other end of the couch. I prayed he didn't intend to shift closer. He was wearing yesterday's suit and his sad tie had picked up a new grease stain. "What else did your ex tell you that she didn't feel like telling us, the *official* good guys?"

"Were her prints on the Oscar, DeSantis?"

"What I actually said, Gulliver, was we hadn't identified the murder weapon. I did not say anything about not finding the murder weapon."

"Were they?"

"I said I would love to tell you we had Miss Marriner's prints on the murder weapon, only I couldn't." He smirked in stereo.

"Still the best you're gonna do?"

"To do better, what's in it for me?" DeSantis wondered.

"Stevie's version of events."

He smiled. His teeth were vintage smoker's yellow. "You sure you can spare it?"

"Let's say I'm not afraid of it."

We haggled on terms, mainly because DeSantis was out to show me what a steel dick he could be. Before we even started, I knew I would tell him everything I'd heard from Stevie. No percentage in holding back anything. He would learn it all eventually, and I wanted to be in a position to go back to the well.

When I finished, DeSantis aimed a pipeline of spent smoke into the room. "So, the way I make it, you and her are talking self-defense?"

"That, and how she saved Claire Cavanaugh's life. Sheridan was close to choking Claire Cavanaugh to death. The next best thing to self-defense."

"Open and shut if you had the old dame to corroborate, only you don't. Not yet, and maybe never." He leaned forward, poking around the table for an ashtray. Gave up. Squashed the butt on a heel and dropped it into a pocket. "Spoon didn't have to take us to no Oscar, Gulliver. It was there in the bedroom, full of blood and loaded with your ex's prints." He fished out his pack and lit a fresh smoke, studying my reaction. Enjoying himself.

"We got nothing closer talking to Spoon, and of course we still don't have a statement from your former spouse."

I couldn't believe Stevie had made up the story. She was too clever to invent a dead-end lie. "If I hear you right, you took her prints? Before or after you Mirandized her?"

"C'mon, Gulliver, get with the program. I told you it's too early for rights." He tapped the side of his head. "Since I saw you, we pulled a comparison set of her prints from the Feebies. Miss Marriner was on record for a passport from a few years back, when she did a Thanksgiving tour of Korea for the USO. It's no contest, take my word."

I reminded him of the bruises on Claire's face and neck and challenged him to explain them.

"I don't have to, do I?" he said, exhaling a heavy drag. "Believe me, I saw 'em before your friend Sancho Panza. We're gonna take pictures, too, but pending the old dame telling us different, they could of resulted from anything."

"Are you going to charge Stevie?"

"Thinking about it." His gaze drifted around the room and settled on an old *Photoplay* on the table. He briefly pondered the cover illustration of a scamp-eyed Mary Pickford, then snapped his hard stare back into my eyes. "I hear on the grapevine you ain't like all them other newspaper fucks."

"I'm more like one of your basic blow jobs."

DeSantis's grunt, taken with a grin that flared briefly, passed for appreciation. "Also a smart-ass, like I heard."

"I'm the poster boy."

DeSantis shook his head and turned away, but not before I saw another trace of appreciation. He stood, tugged at his pants and jacket like it would make a difference, and walked over to the baby grand piano, hands clasped behind his back. He settled on the bench, exercised his fingers, and began running distantly familiar jazz riffs with a delicate touch that carried the cracks with the notes.

I called over to him, "You listen to a lot of Garner?" The comparison pleased him. "I'm a Bill Evans man myself." He shifted into a pretty fair Evans, and I told him so.

"You got high marks from Jimmy Steiger," he said, putting words to his music. "You put him up to calling me?"

"First I know of it."

It was true. Jimmy, a detective lieutenant friend assigned to a station on my side of the hill, must have decided on his own to say something.

He stopped cold in the middle of something sexy and rejoined me on the couch. "Steiger did a wake-up call on me this morning and gave up some of your history together. You saved his life?"

"I've been paid back."

"I got myself in trouble downtown two, three years ago. The brass was ready to come down on me real heavy until Steiger stood up for me where he didn't have to."

"Internal affairs?"

"Manner of speaking." His gesture said I didn't have to know the details. "Steiger says you're not like them newspaper fucks, no matter how you come off at first. He didn't ask for no favors, just wanted me to know. That's why we're having this talk." His voice hardened. "I also got a call from the DA, wanting to know status, making it sound like he's getting ready to push a murder one on Miss Marriner in time for the eleven o'clock news."

"That's how the twerp plays the game," I said knowingly.

"You don't have to tell me . . . Look, I don't yet know enough to know if your ex is guilty of anything except bad manners, but I ain't giving the DA diddly-squat, so you get a break there. Maybe it lasts a day, a week, before Police Central says we take her in and feed the media. I get hold of more hard evidence than I got now, it's a given anyway. Until then, you got room to play, but I expect you to share anything you turn up, okay?"

"You're sharing with me, too?"

He considered the question. "Where I can."

It was the best I was going to get. "Anything I should know for starters?"

More thought, then, "Before the old dame fell into her trance this morning? She told me how she walked in on your Miss Marriner in bed with Sheridan. Both of 'em were starkers and doin' the nasty."

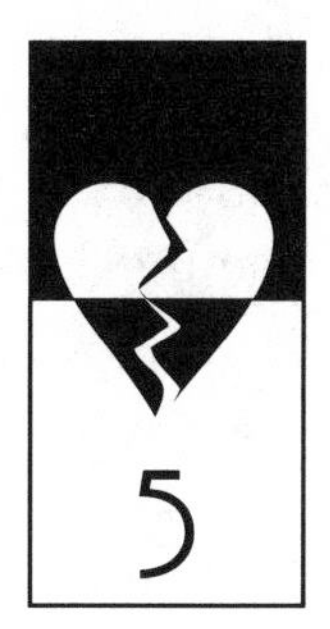

Rapping on the door.

In swept the young woman who had gone off with Augie and Claire Cavanaugh, halfway into a sentence that quit when she recognized she had interrupted our conversation at an awkward moment.

The giveaway had to be my face, the color draining while I drew vivid mind pictures to go with DeSantis's declaration.

DeSantis said, "It's okay, Miss Jahnsen."

"I can come back."

"Nothing that can't wait, ain't that so, Mr. Gulliver?"

I nodded agreement, afraid to test my voice. My throat had been sucked dry by DeSantis's revelation and the confusion of not knowing what bothered me more, the idea that Stevie went to bed with the son of a bitch or that the odds on her beating a murder one rap had just shifted from moderately favorable to bulimic. Or worse if Claire Cavanaugh's memory shifted out of neutral.

DeSantis turned to me. "Miss Jahnsen is Mr. Spoon's assistant and, Miss Jahnsen, this is—"

"*The* Neil Gulliver. I recognize you from your picture on all the bus card ads. Mind if I say you're better looking in person?" I defeated a blush. "I'm a fan of your column, sir."

I rose as she pressed forward, her hand outstretched. Her grip was firm and professional, her galvanic smile part of the tailored working woman's uniform, a gray gabardine pantsuit accented with red and fuchsia pinstripes. Jet black pumps on a stacked midheel that brought the top of her head to my chin. Miss Jahnsen was five four, tops.

Her raven-colored tresses framed her face in a frivolous Clara Bow cut that quit below ears decorated with small diamond chips. Laugh lines playing outside closely set cat's eyes added maturity to a face raging with youth. I had guessed twenty or twenty-one on first glance. She was older, but not by much.

I said, "Neil, please. 'Sir' is what I call my boss."

"Neil, then," she answered agreeably, looking up at me and pumping my hand some more. "I'm Paige. How did you ever manage?"

"Manage what?"

"Getting this far in life with no nickname? I cannot think of anything 'Neil' might be a nickname for, the same way 'Paige' isn't short for anything, except the short person you see here."

Her feisty manner and her bullet-proof voice contradicted her size. She didn't wait for me to tell her I was "Gully" to some people and barely tolerated the idea. Her mind already had jumped to a new subject.

"I've already told the lieutenant, Mr. Spoon had a prior engagement or he would be here himself this morning. It's okay, though. After two years, he trusts me with the important stuff."

DeSantis said, "I hope you're not here to tell me the old dame is lost again."

Paige didn't see he was kidding. "I will remind you, Lieutenant DeSantis. Her name is Claire Cavanaugh, Miss Cavanaugh."

DeSantis showed his so-what? face.

Paige appealed to me. "Residents at the MPRE may not be what they once were, Neil, but they remain entitled to their dignity and our continuing respect. I sincerely hope Lieutenant DeSantis is not one of those unfortunate people who won't be able to understand this until their own golden maturity."

DeSantis gave her a curious once-over before dismissing her with a gesture. "Let me ask it another way. You got the old dame parked back at her place?"

Paige aimed a manicured finger at his heart. "I have her parked, to use your word, Detective, in the auditorium, in the safe and caring company of Brother Kalman. Neil, Brother Kalman wishes you to join him when you're done here."

DeSantis wondered at me, "Brother Kalman?"

"Sancho Panza," I said.

He nodded confirmation. Checked his watch. "Done all the damage I can do around here. You go on ahead, Gulliver. I'll touch base later."

Paige said, "You might think about finding time to call your mother, Lieutenant."

DeSantis pressed a thumb and middle finger against the inner edges of his eyes. Gave Paige an indifferent smile. "My mother, she died a long time ago. She didn't get a chance to leave me the new number."

Paige flushed. "I am terribly sorry. Terribly, terribly sorry. Saying that was terribly foolish and stupid of me."

"Only if you say so," he said, and gave me a wink.

The Motion Picture Retirement Estates was founded about twenty years ago by a show business A-list, many sincere about helping the needy or retired members of the industry, some only looking for new walls to put their names on bronze plaques or in letters ten feet tall, maybe because all the good locations were taken at the older, well-endowed Motion Picture Country Home in nearby Woodland Hills.

Paige explained the rules as she steered our green and gold electric golf wagon at ten miles an hour along the shaded lanes to Warner Brothers Auditorium. Other wagons on the pathway were being used by residents, accompanied by staff members in white outfits or volunteers in gold-colored blazers who were known as Golden Bees. Queen Bees wore matching nursing bonnets, and male Honey Bees sported matching four-corner trucker caps. The foot traffic was energetic, almost as if these residents were out to prove something.

Anyone who'd worked a certain number of verifiable years in Hollywood was eligible for cottages as they became available or as new complexes were added on virgin acreage beyond a spa and the shuffleboard courts. The lucky ones were chosen twice a year by secret ballot of a blue ribbon steering committee. On average, there were three candidates for every cottage available.

"Reasonably good health is a key factor in the selection process," Paige said with a cheerleader's enthusiasm. "We don't yet have the hospital resources of the Country Home. Maybe next year, when our building fund is crackling again."

She had wondrous bee-stung lips and a slight overbite.

When she talked her mouth seemed animated by Disney.

She said, "Whether they were below-the-line—even someone like the best boy—or somebody whose name was always above the title, they all are equal once they take up residence. They sign over all their assets to the MPRE Foundation, which becomes the executor of their estate, as a condition of lifetime residency."

"Sort of like Cults 'R' Us?"

"Oh, poo," Paige said. She slapped me playfully on the shoulder. "You've been spending too much time with Lieutenant DeSantis."

"I like the way you stood up to him."

"Away from him, you mean. The secret is never get downwind."

I laughed loudly at her dagger-edged sense of humor, and so did she, an infectious noise like a playing card rippling against bicycle spokes. She caught my stare with her own, one that seemed to suggest I see her beyond our age difference. Or was that only my ego acting up?

Warner Brothers Auditorium loomed ahead like a multiplex without a marquee, except for the Warner Brothers name stretching above a bank of glass doors.

"Wonderful of them to donate the auditorium," I said. "Must have set the studio back a bundle."

"Not those Warner Brothers, Neil. The funding came from a Beverly Hills attorney named Warner Brothers, like in Dr. Joyce? He had a thing for show business, liked going to cocktail parties and screenings, like that? Mickey stumbled onto him and wheedled the check after he learned how upset Mr. Brothers was when they gave the County Art Museum gallery he had his heart set on to Steve Martin, for goodness sake. Well, excuuuse me! The sad part? Mr. Brothers passed on the week before we dedicated the building. A massive heart attack in the middle of a putt on the fourteenth hole at Hillcrest Country Club. Poor man didn't live long enough to see his name in letters, and not even forty years old."

"Life is supposed to begin at forty."

"I hear that from lots of forty-year-olds. How old are you?" I could have told her, thirty-eight, but I pretended not to have heard the question. She nudged my arm with her elbow and flashed her toothsome smile. "I like you, Neil," she said brightly. "You strike me like a man I can trust. Like my darling pop."

Darling pop.

Darling pop, meet Neil Gulliver's shattered ego.

The house lights were up, revealing an elegantly appointed auditorium designed for five hundred. The area between the stage and ten rows of plush seats—thirty across broken by two wide center aisles, in addition to the wall aisles—was large enough for a symphony orchestra and empty except for six people in wheelchairs. Two were asleep, the others enjoying the action on stage.

A demure gray carpet speckled with colors grew onto the bare walls, absorbing some of the reverb from a sound system pounding out a melody from the original cast album of *Pajama Game*, loud enough to accommodate every hearing aid in Southern California.

This is my once a year day
Once a year day
Felt the morning sun and knew that . . .

It was as if I had stumbled into the Rip Van Winkle road company. Nobody sashaying into view from upstage or the wings—forming an irregular row of sad-shaped sweats and leotards—was under the age of two hundred. They shared a secret energy source that permitted them to move to the beat or, at least, come close, on funny, fragile legs, hippo hips or sheer grit.

These were residents rehearsing for the annual Break-a-Leg Show that gave them the opportunity to strut their stuff for family, friends, and neighbors, Paige explained. Lip-synching lyrics and memories from another time in a world they no longer fit. Taking direction and encouragement from a man who patrolled the apron dressed like he'd just returned from a polo match at Will Rogers Ranch, who slapped his scarred boot with a riding crop to the hypnotic beat, and shouted to be heard over the music.

. . . This was my once a year day
Once a year day . . .

I wondered how many pacemakers were in overdrive.

A piercing whistle told me to look down front to my left. Claire sat in a center-aisle seat three rows back, and Augie, a thumb and finger spreading his mouth, was beside her. He signaled with a wave.

Paige kneeled in the aisle alongside Claire, who smiled and nodded as if she recognized me.

I took the cushioned seat on the other side of Augie, who said, "Miss Cavanaugh, this is my friend, Neil Gulliver."

Claire responded with another sweet nod and went back to watching the dancers trying to keep count. I wondered to myself if she saw Errol and Olivia up there.

The music stopped abruptly.

The director announced in an accented voice, "Wonderful, kids. Perfectly wonderful. We'll take five. Ten for all of you over the age of consent, and don't forget to come back."

The dancers applauded and the director waved his beret in response, skipped down the access steps and over to Paige while the cast dispersed. Some of them worked their way down onto the bare wood floor and sat gasping for breath. Others stumbled in slow motion to folding chairs that lined the fly curtain fronting the bare back wall.

The director squatted alongside Paige, adjusted his camel-colored beret back onto his head. He had a rough-hewn face with Mediterranean features that stuck together like unfired clay and an overgrown, attention-demanding mustache.

"Tell me if you ever saw anything so dreadful in your life? I swear, two of them will be dropping dead in the middle of the show and me not so long after."

Paige said, "Mr. Polyzoides, you silly!"

"I mean it. We were lucky last year. One stroke only. This year—" He threw away his hands. "I think this year, when Chip Ahoy forgets for the first time he ain't doing this for Hermes Pan no more, it will be the last time." He snapped his fingers. "Then, Terry, only because she got her girdle cinched so tight, no blood can get past her Sierra Madres."

"They'll be fine. They'll be wonderful, because you're so wonderful. Because of you, Mr. Polyzoides."

"Okay, so maybe there is something in what you say." He reached up and pinched Claire on the cheek. "Who we should have this year is this great artist, what brings down the house last time with her spanking scene on the little girl we borrowed from the TV. No Shirley Temple, but not bad, either." Claire touched the pinch spot with her fingers, brought the fingers around to her lips. "I mean it, beautiful. Every word. From here." He thumped his jacket above his heart. "You ever hear he was sorry after? Fred Astaire? Regretful, because I said to him, 'Freddie, not Ginger this time. I want you to be great for me with Claire Cavanaugh, what can do it all.' Oh, maybe Freddie give me a mumble before, but never after. After, only praise from his lips to my ears. I mean it, sweetheart. I really mean it."

Paige said, "Miss Cavanaugh should be home resting after all she's been through." The director nodded his head vigorously. "I knew she wouldn't want to miss watching your rehearsal. And, next year, I expect we'll have her up on stage again."

"Dear child, from your sweet heart . . ." He patted Claire's forearm. "You hear what she says about next year, kid? Next year for you, anyway. I should only live so long."

All this time, he had been treating Augie and me like we were invisible. Except for one or two stolen glances. This is a sight deficiency I've observed with stars and other famous faces who seem to feel a danger in being too forward with people they don't know. The Curse of Status? The Celebrity Stalker Syndrome?

Augie said, "Mimi, you old gossip. Have you got so big for your phony faggy riding britches you ignore an old friend?"

The director looked at Augie like he was seeing Alan Hale, Sr., then bolted upright and slapped his cheeks with his palms.

"Oh, God save me! It can't not be, can it?"

Augie unrolled from his seat, excused himself to Claire and stepped past her into the aisle, to give the director a better look. The director shrieked and threw himself into Augie's arms. They did a revolving dance down the aisle to a boisterous tune of their joint imagination.

Paige examined my expression, to see if I might know more than she about Brother Kalman and Mimithos Polyzoides. I shook my head and turned my hands to the ceiling.

Augie swept a golden brown leaf off the asphalt walk and held it up to study. The leaf was translucent in the sunlight, unlike the inner workings of Augie's mind. We were sitting on a stone bench in a small patio area outside the auditorium by a statue of Hal Roach, who balanced Spanky and Farina in his arms while Pete the Pup playfully sniffed at his shoes. We had excused ourselves a few minutes ago, when Augie leaned into my ear to say we needed private conversation.

"Mimi and I were kids together," he said. "Back in the days of vaudeville. Both our families came out of burlesque. 'Stathos and Family,' that was him. Stathos and Melina, immigrant parents with hardly two words of English between them, and the four kids, doing some of the damnedest acrobatics you never saw. Little Mimi was the youngest. It didn't matter how hard or high they tossed him or knocked him about, he always bounced back up no worse for wear. Like Keaton, his idol."

"What were you doing?"

Augie turned the leaf around in his hand, played like he had not heard the question. Finally, "Plotting a way to escape. The war and the movies gave me that and took me out here with a letter of introduction to Colonel Sam Bixel at the *Daily*. The colonel saw something, I guess, because he gave me a chance, but it was up to me to put myself over. The crime beat and the rest, as they say—history."

I sensed this wasn't the private conversation Augie had in mind, but he seemed to need the reverie to dim whatever private emotions Claire Cavanaugh had stirred.

"Saw Mimi years later. By then he was a famous director over at Fox. He had switched from acrobatics to dancing and went on to score on Broadway and after with Earl Carroll, when the Ziegfeld clone moved his *Vanities* out west. You remember any of the stuff Mimi did with Faye or Ameche? Ty Power?"

"*Rancho Pampas Romance. Palm Beach Rhythm. Kootchy Koo,* with John Payne, Carmen Miranda, the Ritz Brothers, and—"

Augie blocked more credits with his hands.

"I'd been meaning to get over there and see him. Never did until that suicide business with Monroe in sixty-two took me onto the lot. I thought there might be more to the story than Noguchi's report let on, so I called on Mimi, who was full of everybody's business; visited other friends; went nosing around in general." He gently replaced the leaf where he found it. "I came up sixes, like everybody else. Probable suicide. In any event, dead."

We sat quietly for a few minutes.

Augie said, "It's not what I wanted to talk to you about." I nodded. He finished a tune he was patting on his thighs. "Amigo, Claire Cavanaugh is play-acting."

My spine went rigid. My eyes caromed onto Augie's face, somber with certainty, as my own drew tight with incomprehension.

"*Verdad.* Claire might have been spaced out when Blackie Sheridan was murdered, or in the aftermath, but she is out and out faking now. She slipped up with me."

"Something she said."

"Nothing she said. Something she did."

"Jesus, Augie, do I have to ask?"

He looked past me. Whatever it was, it was going to stay between them.

I reminded him, "What Claire Cavanaugh saw, what she knows, may be all that's standing between Stevie and a murder one," and briefed him on my conversation with DeSantis. "You don't think I'm going to sit back and do nothing?"

"Exactly what I think, Neil. Why we're talking. You let me worry about Claire while you're worrying about Stevie, and maybe we'll finish up at the same time where we both want to be."

"What are my options?"

"When did I ever give you an option?"

I wanted to say, Don't let me down, Augie, but he'd never done that, either.

He said, "Now that that's out of the way, there's someone I want you to talk to. An old friend from my days prowling movie lots. Maybe you noticed him in the auditorium. Sunset Beaudry?"

"The cowboy star?"

A withering glance. "The used taco salesman."

"Where was he?" I looked around, as if he might have trailed us outside.

"Sunset dragged off home, saying what he had to tell me he didn't want overheard. I told Sunset I wanted to stick by Claire and to expect you instead, *comprendé?*"

"What are we going to discuss?"

Augie dropped his voice another decibel. "Sunset says Stevie didn't kill Blackie Sheridan." His words registered like a kick in the groin. I sucked all the smog from the sky. "Sunset swears he has a handle on who did."

I got lost following Augie's directions. I took the wrong turn on the right lane or the right turn on the wrong lane and wound up a half mile later at a dead end, looking down past a chain-link fence into an undeveloped parcel of land full of crab grass, tall, dry weeds, yellow wildflowers growing lush and lean in scattered clumps, rocky craters, and a clutter of rusted cans, rubbish, and abandoned junk.

I retraced my steps and hitched a ride with a three-hundred-pound Honey Bee wearing a cap full of Olympics pins, impressed I was heading to see Beaudry, whose place was in a wagon train of cottages about a hundred yards west of the compound where Blackie Sheridan, Claire Cavanaugh, and Mimi Polyzoides resided. A cookie-cutter duplicate.

I could have guessed which one belonged to the old cowboy star by the stuffed and mounted pinto strapped to the hitching post in front. It was Buck, a movie horse once as familiar to Saturday matinee kids as the hero who charged him into battle, guns blazing and forever fearless.

"You want I should wait?" the Honey Bee inquired. "I s'pect the old Range Roper ain't there."

"How can you tell?"

The Honey Bee guffawed. "If Buck Junior ain't there, parked alongside Original Buck, then the old Range Roper he ain't there. What he calls that golf wagon a his, 'Buck Junior,' painted up to look like a horse, tail and all."

He was right. After waiting fifteen minutes I had him take me back to the Warner Brothers Auditorium. Paige and Claire were sitting where I'd last seen them. Augie's seat was empty.

Mimithos Polyzoides was leaning against the proscenium arch, stage right, wrapped in himself, playing with his thoughts, head bobbing. He stretched his arm and snapped his fingers.

Music exploded, as deafening as before.

Come and meet those dancing feet
On the avenue I'm taking you to—

A denotation of recorded taps. I recognized the finale from *42nd Street,* Gower Champions's good-bye to Broadway. A Super Chief whistle drew attention to the cardboard replica of a train stage left. At once, the fragile dancers I'd seen earlier came tapping out like a Chinese dragon, breathing fire into the number.

Hear the beat of dancing feet
It's the song I love, the melody of
42nd Street.

My eyes amazed me.

Augie was bringing up the rear.

His cassock hitched above his bare ankles. His sandals supplanted by a pair of gleaming Florsheims. Hefting his bulk to the music. Good eye charging the line to be sure he was matching gestures as well as steps.

The train whistle again.

A slender black man erect in a porter's uniform seemed to rise from inside the cab. He began dancing on the roof, and his moves were unmistakable.

It was the great Taps Vernon, the legendary Taps Vernon, who had won those appellations with every magical step he took, from headlining at the Palace to co-starring in a memorable slew of movie musicals from the late thirties to the mid-fifties.

The slip, the slide. Taps had to be eighty or eighty-five. Closer to ninety. Slide, slip, lift, bounce. A modest pirouette into a split, and—

Taps Vernon stumbled and took a swan dive off the train.

He used his shoulder to break the fall. The crack of a bone echoed. For a fraction of a second, the crack was louder than the music. Louder than his howl.

Jerry Orbach's voice was singing about "*Little nifties from the fifties; Sexy ladies from the eighties,*" but the dancing feet live on stage froze as Taps rolled onto his back and raised a hand, like he was asking permission to go to the toilet.

His hand plopped pathetically onto the stage.

Augie swallowed a stare at the prostrate figure. He rushed forward to the lip and ordered, "Somebody! Call a doctor!"

Mimi Polyzoides turned to the arch and pounded it with both fists. Paige vaulted from her seat and raced to the stage. Claire Cavanaugh seemed not to budge.

A message from Paige was on the machine when I got back to the Heathcliffe. She had nothing to tell me about Taps Vernon I didn't already know, but a search posse of Golden Bees had found Sunset Beaudry in the MPRE cemetery.

He was napping at the grave of a former co-star and outraged over being disturbed. Beaudry was now sleeping off one snoot-full too many. Given his usual recovery time, Paige expected him to be available for a visit by midday tomorrow.

Stevie also had called, anxious to know if I'd spoken with DeSantis and urging me to join her at eight o'clock to meet with Jeremy Brighton, the producer of *Marilyn Remembers*, who was moving ahead with the show as a tribute to the late Black Jack Sheridan.

Great. We had face-to-face stuff to talk to her about. All day, DeSantis's words had echoed in my ears: "Miss Marriner in bed with Sheridan, both of 'em starkers and doin' the nasty." I did not believe it, but I needed to have Stevie tell me herself.

No message from Augie, leaving me to wonder what if any progress he was making with Claire Cavanaugh. Cracking her act. Getting closer to the truth about the murder of Blackie Sheridan.

Lowy from BookSearchers called to say he had found *Shoeless Joe* for less than forty dollars over my top price. He had put a seventy-two-hour reserve on it so get back to him soon, please. This was mortgage week and I was still paying off work on the Jag from three months ago, but I'd figure a way.

The Spider Woman called twice. She could wait.

Jimmy Steiger, returning my call. He came on the line, and I thanked him for his report card on me to DeSantis. He sloughed it off with a noise and asked for an update on Stevie, his voice as smooth as an infant's love. I told him what I knew.

"I've heard worse," Jimmy decided. "Still circumstantial as hell. Simpson walked on more. You keep on playing straight with DeSantis and he'll do the same. Any other problems, let me know, and I'll roll the ball of string as far as I can. How's our girl Stevie?"

"Scared, but putting up a good front."

"That was never a problem with her, pard."

"I'll tell Stevie you said so."

"Why not? She hears it from me often enough."

"Sure, and how's my little Margie, tiger?"

"Ready to pop with number five any minute. Keeps harping something fierce about getting you home for a meal."

"She always loved me best . . . Five times."

The other calls were salesmen hoping to trap someone home.

I grabbed a brew and settled at the computer to finish a column about how subway system construction was turning Sunset and Hollywood boulevards into roller coasters with more dips than a Baskin-Robbins franchise. Two streets that once ran as flat as a postman's arches now qualified as Magic Mountain South.

I uploaded my eight hundred words downtown and stayed in the *Daily*'s system long enough to check for E-mail. The Spider Woman was looking for me here, too, an urgent demand for a call, same as on the machine—or else. I took a shower instead.

Just before eight o'clock, I pulled the Jag into the narrow, rutted parking lot of the Paradox Playhouse on Santa Monica, on the eastern edge of Boys Town, and maneuvered into a narrow space between a late-model black BMW and a blue Cad with rental tags.

The front of the theater, a ninety-nine-seat house rigged for Equity-waiver productions, was dimly lit, except for display boxes on both sides of the shuttered box-office window.

Stevie stared back at me from poster photos in which she assumed familiar Monroe poses. The shots dominated the posters, and except for her name and the play's title, the information was barely large enough to read.

STEPHANIE MARRINER
starring in
Jeremy Brighton's
production of
her one-woman show
Marilyn Remembers
written and directed by
John Sheridan

A spray can artist had applied a red swipe across Sheridan's name and the annotation R.I.P.

Light spilled onto the street from the diner and there was a heavy garlic smell in the air. A panhandler in layers of cast-off clothing and shredding tennis shoes too large for his size nines tugged at the brim of his Giants cap heading over from his handout franchise by the doorway.

"They's inside there, but the door be locked," he said, and showed me a toothless, black-gummed mouth. "Door back where you comin' from, 'round the side there."

He held out an upright palm expectantly, his scrawny fingers protruding from cheap green woolen gloves. I fished some loose change, told him to wait while I sprang a five from my billfold. The panhandler was shocked with gratitude and full of God bless yous. He snapped the bill, tugged at his cap again, then wheeled around and hurried up the street toward La Cienega in a curious, bow-legged gait.

I retraced my steps to the side door, almost to the rear of the parking lot, and entered to find myself backstage. Following an undercurrent of voices, I nosed around a dusty, red velvet curtain and saw the ground-level stage, fifteen feet deep and twelve feet across, bare except for some furniture suggesting a bedroom and a card table being used as a rehearsal table.

Stevie sat at the table facing the front of the house, five escalating rows of school writing desks screwed into the hardwood risers.

Across from her, facing the rear stucco wall in desperate need of painting, was an older woman who looked vaguely familiar.

The man to Stevie's right was good-looking in a scrub-faced twenties sort of way. He reached for her hand, squeezed it, and smiled solicitously. I took an instant dislike to him.

I knew the man sitting opposite from file photos I'd seen.

Jeremy Brighton.

I already didn't like him.

I had checked him out when Stevie first mentioned his name. He came up high in the minus column, an Englishman who had made a career of the courtroom, defending suits brought by ex-partners. Most involved millions and all included allegations of fraud. All were settled out of court, followed by bankruptcies and a suicide or two, while Brighton allegedly deposited his profits in secret bank accounts in the Cayman Islands.

I had seen at once where someone like Black Jack Sheridan, with dreams brighter than his finances—why else did he wind up in an MPRE cottage?—could fall for a praying mantis legging after attractive low-risk, high-yield show business deals.

Stevie blew off my advisory and concerns as none of her business. Brighton was financing Sheridan. Sheridan wanted her. She had an opportunity to prove her worth to all the critics who had congealed into a conspiracy that kept her from starring with Hanks, Cruise, and Gibson.

I knew better than to argue with Stevie.

Gritting my teeth would have to do.

Bottom line, Stevie was a good actress; better than good; maybe not in the Streep category, but better than a lot of movie queens who reached the top because the camera loved their faces, and never developed afterward. The soap was her basic training, seven years of blitzing through three hundred pages of script a week, the equal of two-and-a-half full-length feature movies. Completed and in the can on a deadline tighter than a virgin's knees.

Stevie had become one of the best.

She deserved her pair of daytime Emmys.

And, her dreams.

I had to believe Sheridan recognized that before he reached Stevie with his script and his pitch for *Marilyn Remembers*, the poetry of persuasion directors must have if they're any good at all, and he was world acclaimed in his time.

Conversation at the rehearsal table was stilted, like nobody wanted to say the wrong thing. Pauses long enough to give it the feel of a John Osborne play. I signaled my presence with a cough.

"Neil, honey!" Stevie put a sparkle on her face, rose to greet me with a hug, and hastily whispered, "I really want to do the play, but only if you say so."

Looking great. Face scrubbed clean. Trying to disguise her remarkable body in tight black leather leggings topped by a black silk big shirt brimming with a circus of bright colors and shapes lifted from a Miró painting. Her ponytail sitting like a pretzel pinned on top of her head. Only eighteen-karat gold, diamond-studded Paloma Picasso kissy-X earrings as her passport to the rich and famous.

She felt supremely confident in my embrace, no evidence of the frightened woman I'd left yesterday on a soap opera soundstage, as if she had awakened from some bad dream. A troubled inner voice told me not to ask why, for fear she might tell me.

I announced, "Excuse us for a minute," took her by the same hand the twenty-year-old had been patronizing a moment ago, led her outside to the Jag, and held open the passenger door for her.

She found a comfortable position and asked for a cigarette.

"You don't smoke, remember? We quit together."

"I'm thinking of starting again."

"Who was that massaging your fingers?"

"I didn't invite you over to monitor my friends, honey, but since you ask, Monte Sanberg." My hands did a nervous dance on the dashboard. "You mind letting down the windows? It's stuffy in here." I fired the engine long enough to oblige. "Monte directs *Bedrooms and Board Rooms*. And he is doing one exceptional job, I hasten to add. I thought he could take over for Sheridan and—"

My irritation spun out of control. "You are in trouble up to your plucked eyebrows, Stevie, a candidate for arrest any minute on murder one, and you can sit here calmly and tell me you are going ahead with the damn play? No matter what I think, right?"

"I really feel like a cigarette."

"Stevie!"

"Yes, if you want to know. We both know I'm not guilty, so that's that once the cops get off of their collective butts and find the real murderer. Meanwhile, you can't buy the publicity I'm getting. Jesus, I had to sneak off the lot under a beach blanket in the backseat of Monte's Beemer to duck all the TV reporters. Brighton's been having multiple orgasms about the millions and millions of dollars in free publicity."

"How many multiple orgasms is Monte having?"

She sucked the air out of the Jag.

"It's all right for you to go after the teenage chickie of your choice, but she can't grow up and be interested in younger men? Is that how the song goes? You still a stone freak on the subject of women's lib?"

"Was there an answer to my question in any of that?" Her face contorted angrily. She bit into her lower lip. "The teenage chickie was you, remember? And that was then and this is here and now, Stevie."

"The last time I looked, we were still divorced and free to come and go as we please."

"I love you, Stevie."

"I love you, too, honey. It's only when we were married that I stopped loving you. Why would anyone want to go back to that?"

"Serious question?"

"Course not. Because I'll tell you something else you don't know. This thing you think you still have for me is about as real as the crap dialogue they write for me every day. You're hanging on because everybody needs somebody, and I'm it, in the role you cast me, even though it never was going to fit for long. Jeezo! I swear we had this argument a long time ago and not just once."

"When did you get so wise?" I sneered. Cut her off. Spit out the words.

"Only when you let me," she said, and leaned over to poke my cheek. Her old tactic. Touch and diffuse. She knew where these arguments ended and was determined to stop before we got there.

She said, "Want to know how wise I really am?" She saw I

wasn't going to answer. "This is not about me and Monte Sanberg, honey, so don't try and make it so. You've given me the Gulliver Seal of Approval on other one-note jokes like Monte—"

"Because you ask."

"This jealousy, this old possessiveness . . ." Stevie focused on some invisible star past the windshield. "Neil, Neil, Neil. If I wanted for us to try again, I'd come right out and say so, but I do not need you to help me repeat my errors anymore. I do not. I have proven more than adequate in doing the job by myself."

"You threw me out of our life without asking."

"Some things you don't have to ask, honey." She put a hand on my shoulder. "Meanwhile, bottom line? We are soul mates, me and you. Pals forever. Neither one of us can ever change that."

Stevie's voice faded to a sigh. We locked eyes, and finally I shook my head. I took her by the wrist and kissed the back of her hand.

She whispered, "Let it go, Neil. Let it go." Before I could bring myself to ask if she knew how, she put a hand on my knee and said, "Now, tell me how the cops are still screwing around with my life."

I told her about the bloody Oscar being found in Sheridan's bedroom, full of her fingerprints. She nodded acceptance. About Claire Cavanaugh saying she had discovered Sheridan and Stevie in bed, naked, making love.

She sat up posture perfect and pressed hard against the seat cushion. She hugged her arms to her chest and looked away to keep me from reading her eyes. Her face was a mask of indifference.

She shook and I could feel the vibrations.

"Are you okay?" I touched her thigh, like it was a museum sculpture, and moved my hand to the back of her graceful neck, a harp of taut muscle and nerves.

"Why would she lie, honey? It is a lie, you know?"

"I know. I'm dealing with it. Augie is also on the case. He won't say how, but he knows Claire Cavanaugh from years ago. He thinks she's putting on an act with her revolving-door memory."

"What's he going to do, pray the truth from her?"

I smiled. "You still have a sense of humor."

"I'm a two-time Emmy winner, remember?"

I touched her nose with a fingertip and told her about Sunset Beaudry.

Stevie repeated what the old Range Roper had said to Augie, to be sure she'd heard correctly. "He said I didn't kill Blackie Sheridan?" I nodded. "He says he knows who did?" Another nod. Her eyes darted left and right, absorbing the significance. "Did he say who?"

"Not yet. He was hiding in a graveyard when I went looking today, drunk as a skunk, but tomorrow's another day, Scarlett. I'll be at the Retirement Estates bright and early."

"You think he's telling the truth?"

"He wouldn't be the Range Roper otherwise."

Stevie threw her arms around me.

Swallowed my lips in hers.

Just as Monte Sanberg rapped on the glass.

Sanberg peered a Roy Rogers squint through the passenger window and called in an incongruous honey drawl, like the sound you get cracking walnuts, "How goes it, Rainbow? Mr. Brighton is getting anxious . . ." As if he'd missed her pulling away from me, an inch ahead of her tongue.

She waved a greeting and explained to me, "Monte calls me Rainbow because of the many hues he finds in my acting."

"Not because he recognizes a pot of gold?"

"You be nice, Neil."

I raised my hand to take the oath.

Sanberg opened the door and helped her onto the broken asphalt. She let him wrap his arms around her. She came to his shoulders, which put Sanberg around my size. He looked Malibu coordinated, like he had just been fluff-dried at the laundry, sparkling bright and sunny disposition, tousled rusty-brown hair, and fashionable two-day growth of beard. He wore pleated white chinos that quit a notch short of his ankles, a pea coat with anchor buttons over a grotto blue crewneck sweater, and black deck shoes without socks.

He had the kind of body tone three days a week at the gym can get you and a tan that might be real.

I wondered to myself if Sanberg had ever sailed on anything except the Queen Mary as he looked across his shoulder to me and said, "Rainbow thinks the world of you, sir." Like a college kid come to whisk away his date, but first making nice-nice to daddy. I felt like telling him to have her home by eleven-thirty and no pit stops on Mulholland.

"So do I." Sanberg forced laughter as he tried to decipher the nonsense of my response. I took his hand like I meant it. It was clammy, part of the sea-faring outfit, I supposed.

"Monte Sanberg." He pumped enthusiastically. "I'm her director on *Bedrooms and Board Rooms,* but I suppose she told you?" I said she had. He seemed disappointed not to hear more about himself. He took back his hand. Ran it through his windswept hair. Looked at Stevie for confidence.

"I've told Neil you're encouraging me to go ahead with the play," Stevie said. "I've told him you never let me get away with faking it, but always force me to stretch as an actress."

Sanberg showed his painted teeth. "She's perfect for Monroe. This play is the kind of acting opportunity that comes along once in a blue moon. Besides, it can be tremendous therapy given the shitsky our fair lady is going through right now."

If I didn't want to believe otherwise, I might have believed his concern was genuine.

"Honey, Monte understands it's absolutely a no-go if you don't like what Jeremy Brighton has to say. And, I did mean it when I said it, too."

"Absolutely," Sanberg repeated, draping an arm across her back. She nestled closer, and I was the loneliest son of a bitch the world has ever known.

"Mr. Gulliver, I bow to your presence," Jeremy Brighton said, bowing, then charged at me like I was Breed's Hill. He dwarfed my hand inside both of his, pumped it like it would yield gold coins any minute. "Your reputation precedes you."

His tone was seductive, like a massage and a manicure. I heard the sound of Bow Bells in his voice, a London birthmark that comes without an economic birthright, although he hid it skillfully under an upper crust of his own invention.

In his classic, hand-tailored suit of expensive worsted wool, he reminded me of Charles Laughton in *Witness for the Prosecution*. He was about Laughton's height and weight and had the same exaggerated features, too large for his face, the same way his head was not quite sized right for his body. A paisley handkerchief that matched his power tie hung like a pull chain from his pocket. The white carnation was a trick he may have borrowed from Jackie Gleason.

Brighton turned with a dancer's grace to the woman whom he had just left seated at the card table, "What was I just saying to you, Laura?"

His hair, worn long, was dyed an original shade of subdued orange, and he covered a spreading bald spot by combing it over the top of his skull, right to left.

"You were complimenting me again on the way I got you off last night, is that what you mean, Jerry?" Her laugh started as a stomach rumble and filled the room.

Ten or fifteen minutes ago, I thought she looked familiar. Now, I knew why. There was no mistaking the sandpaper voice stunted by years of nonfiltered chain-smoking or that Mount Vesuvius of throaty laughter, both *Tonight Show* staples when Johnny Carson ruled.

Laura Dane.

Sweeping out from behind the high-rise curtains while Doc and the band pummeled the familiar Rodgers melody to corrupted Hammerstein lyrics: "There is nothing like a Dane, nothing like a Dane," assaulted Sophie Tucker-style by Laura herself.

Brighton responded to her remark with a naughty-naughty index finger and pretended shock at news of their liaison being shared, as if it were a delicious joke. I wondered. That's not the way I heard it, and Laura had told enough stories on herself to Carson and in *Dane, Down & Dirty*, her scandalous autobiography, to make me a believer. If it wore pants, Laura Dane wanted in.

She took the Sherman from the corner of her mouth, held it two inches from her lips like a candle, and blew. The gray ash flew off and the tip glowed a bright red.

Laura Dane said, "Practice, practice, practice. And how about you, handsome? Even in this treacherous light, I'm able to see I am ready to play 'Happy Birthday' on your flute any time you like."

"I'm flattered, Ms. Dane."

"Hear that, Jerry? What I been telling you. He knows me. We aren't all Gloria Swansons. What was it that Gloria said in that Wilder picture? 'We had feces then'? What kinda shit is that to say in a picture, anyway?" She gave it wide eyes and a beat. Laughed uproariously. "Just like Billy. Then or now, I can fill a house fast as your little Miss Ivory Soap star, faster than just about anybody except, maybe, Greta Gargle."

She cocked her head at me, waiting to see if I knew she meant Hollywood's most notorious madam, who ministered to a list of movie stars, studio execs, and other powerhouses in the decade following World War II from a mansion above the Strip on Sunset Plaza Drive. In fact, I had interviewed Greta Gargle, whose real name was Vivien Lehman, about a year before she died an ordinary death in a West Covina nursing home.

She was withering away from several ailments, proud of the eight grandkids whose photos were framed or taped to the wall alongside her bed, but she slid into her notorious persona as easily as a pair of seamless silk stockings.

"They want it, you make them pay for it," she murmured confidentially. "They pay for it, make sure you leave them wanting it again."

I repeated this to Laura.

"Part of Greta's induction ceremony," she said, nodding appreciatively. "The first time I ever did a turn for her. A class act if ever there was."

"I don't remember that from your autobiography."

"Saving it for the sequel," she said, clearly pleased I had read the book. "I kicked around this town plenty, me and Marilyn, Shirley, lotta others, before catching the brass ring. Some girls got by as waitresses. Me, I took up hooking. Hung around Schwab's three, four days a week, waiting to be discovered, but not the same as Lana. Lana, they put in a sweater. Me, they couldn't wait to get out of the sweater. Weekends, if she was expecting a lot of traffic, like after the Oscars, Greta buzzed me and I'd always go out of my way to be available. The pay was first-rate and the hooch sensash, Dom Perignon always on call, and there were other benefits. I got autographs I could send home to show my folks how well I was doing. I got a seven-year contract starting at three-five-oh a week by doing a gag with a studio big shot who Greta's other girls could never get through without upchucking."

I mentioned the big shot's name. "In your book, you said it happened when his Rolls broke down on the freeway and you pulled onto the shoulder to help."

"Translates, I give him a lube job like he'd never forget." She laughed uncontrollably, jarring the table with her girth.

Laura no longer was constructed like the sexpot who tramped her way through dozens of movies in skin-tight outfits showing off her key ring waist and the obligatory conical breasts so popular in her time.

Even next to Brighton, who slopped into obesity, she seemed mammoth, but in a proportionately pleasing way, hardly bothering to hide her weight inside a black silk tent that reached to her ankles and clung to the contours of her ripe body. Her pedicured feet slipped in and out of open-backed flats.

There was an inherent beauty to her face that no amount of Hollandaise and creamery butter could obscure completely. Laura had beguiling gray eyes and a buttercup mouth. A button nose and a small, pointed chin begging to be touched.

She had let her hair go naturally white and wore it cut and styled like a tight snow bonnet, as if she were daring chronology to stand in the way of her desires. It didn't, apparently. *Star* and *Enquirer* photographs always showed her armed with some Adonis sporting an exhausted glaze, her own look smugly singing victory for every woman over the age of sixty.

When she mentioned Marilyn, I remembered they had been

best friends. I told her so. She applauded and urged me to join her at the table. Brighton tagged behind me, and Stevie elected to sit on the bed. Sanberg was ready to take his old seat, but backed off on a subtle hand gesture from Brighton and joined Stevie. The bedsprings complained under their weight.

"Yeah, me and Marilyn. We was quite a pair in our day. I was always Dubinsky to her and she was Norma Jean to me, like she always called Shelley Shirley. Got on like twins at the Studio Club, and after I caught on first, I went for a ritzy apartment with maid service three times a week, over near Gower Gulch, and invited her to park there until she could do better by herself. Should come as no surprise we also shared lovers. You know your movie history, you know that from *Confidential* magazine. No names, please. Names to put flames between your ears, you know?"

Brighton interrupted. "You can understand why I elected to ask Laura to be our technical advisor once I embarked upon this project, Mr. Gulliver."

Laura slapped the table. "Technical advisor! Now, that's a good one!"

Brighton ignored her. "If we were going to do this play, I insisted on accuracy. I insisted on far more than Mr. Sheridan's assurances his script told it like it was."

"Close enough, anyway, Jerry. For Blackie to tell it like it was, he would of had to write it on sheets of asbestos." Laura turned back to me. "Me and Norma Jean had a contest going on between us for years, even after she moved to her own place in Brentwood, over on Helena Drive. We both kept a list, a kind of *Screws Who*. Two or three times a month we got together to—compare notes?" A wink. "Where we had the same names on our scorecards, we graded them as lovers. Where one of us was the first to beach a new candidate for the Humping Hall of Fame, we held off on scoring until the other one had a whack. Let me tell you, neither one of us missed many whacks, you know?"

Laura laughed uproariously, and even her laugh seemed part of a performance she'd given hundreds of times before.

I grazed Brighton. His eyes and a jutting lower lip betrayed the show of interest he was putting on. The eyes were dark, hard and distant from his forced smile. The lip was kept in constant motion by a tic he controlled only by pressing a finger to it. It danced again as he made a show of getting the pair of heavy black frames with thick lenses he stored in his handkerchief pocket.

He fumbled them and they dropped noisily onto the scarred wooden floor. The sound of his grunting swoop to retrieve them served the purpose he doubtless intended. Laura was surprised into silence. She waited for him to sit upright again. He did that after a few more seconds, inquiring, "Well, then, shall we get down to brass tacks?" as if she had finished and there could be no rudeness presumed.

Laura knew she had been snookered but closed her eyes and waved him on. He reached inside his jacket for a stapled set of pages, his bio on Brighton Enterprises letterhead. Worked out the vertical crease. Pushed it across the table with a suggestion I take the time to get acquainted with his credentials.

A column of shows and celebrities Brighton claimed to have done business with ran down the left side of the cover page. The list was impressive. Names designed to bring anyone to the deal line expeditiously.

His personal and professional background was full of rags-to-riches, up-from-the-streets touches that inspire inspiration and appreciation. If it were to be believed, he was a certain candidate for knighthood, especially absent the litigation and allegations I'd uncovered.

"Keep it, should you need to refer to it later," he urged pleasantly, when I seemed to give the bio a tighter inspection than he'd like. I quartered and filed it, patting the pocket to show him how safe the bio was with me.

He volunteered other copies were available if I lost that one, especially if I chose to write a column about him. He said it as a joke, but no one was fooled.

Laura blew smoke at Brighton and told him to cut the crap and get on with it. He answered with a salesman's smile. She answered with more smoke. He mentally wished her away.

"Mr. Gulliver, I suggested this meeting, allowing as Stevie explained how important you are in her life and how she values your excellent judgment."

I turned in her direction. She nodded and gave a thumbs-up, then leaned over and whispered something to Sanberg, who agreed with her, and angled a grin into his fuzzy cheek.

"May I outline the chain of events that has brought us to this point?" Brighton said. It wasn't a question and there was hardly a pause before he dug into the story.

Earlier this year, Brighton had come to Hollywood to explore business opportunities. While lunching at the Friars Club with comedy legend Chick Rainbow, whom he wants to sign for a tour of the U.K., a BBC-TV special, and a home video, he is introduced to Michael Spoon. Spoon explains he is on a fund-raising mission for the Motion Picture Retirement Estates and offers Brighton a tour of the MPRE, hoping to entice a contribution. Brighton accepts the invitation, having gleaned from Spoon's pitch that there might be the potential for an MPRE TV special.

At some point during the tour, he meets Sheridan, who argues persuasively that he has something to Brighton's taste. Never one to reject any proposal without some examination, he visits with Sheridan in Sheridan's cottage and is presented the manuscript of *Marilyn Remembers*. It is written in longhand on composition paper and held together in a three-ring school binder.

At once, the manuscript has Brighton's attention. He asks permission to take it with him, for a second read and further evaluation. Sheridan refuses. It is his only copy. He fears its loss, the way original, one-of-a-kind manuscripts were misplaced and irretrievably lost by T. E. Lawrence and Ernest Hemingway.

Brighton cancels meetings scheduled for the rest of the day. He is excited by the commercial potential of *Marilyn Remembers*. By the time he leaves, he has worked out the terms of a handshake deal with Sheridan.

His greatest concern is agreeing to Sheridan as the play's director.

Sheridan is apoplectic on the subject.

It is the deal breaker.

Brighton reluctantly agrees.

Before he returns to England, he has their partnership committed to an air-tight contract and various elements of the production set in motion.

Brighton's recounting took about twenty minutes. By the time he'd finished, Laura's head was on the table, resting on her arms napstyle.

Stevie seemed to have follow every point intently, less so Sanberg, whom I spotted a couple times stifling a yawn. She had flashed anger when he confessed to having offered the role first to Goldie Hawn and then Morgan Fairchild, but Brighton redeemed her smile immediately.

"Due entirely to an omission in my knowledge of your daytime telly," Brighton explained, not altogether convincingly. "I went to Goldie because of her stature as a movie star and her great popularity in London, but never seriously thought she was right for the part of Marilyn . . . much less the right age." Stevie liked that. "Morgan Fairchild was eager and intelligent and Robin Leach kept ringing me up with words of praise for her, but Laura and Blackie wouldn't quit telling me I must see this beautiful and gifted actress on a daytime soap program called *Bedrooms and Board Rooms*."

Brighton bounced an index finger off his temple, saluting Stevie. She answered with a stagy gesture.

"They were right, of course, and I remain grateful to this moment that we are poised to realize Blackie's vision for his final work of creation—with his first and only choice for the role of Marilyn."

Brighton's glasses were on the table, at his elbow. He put them on and studied Stevie, as if he had found the secret of the universe. She let him. Laura made a snoring sound.

I set my elbows on the table and made a finger pyramid, aimed a pleasant expression and my chin at him, waiting for the con man's hook.

Wherever Brighton's bait and switch was going, it was now in place. He didn't disappoint me, easing into it after a few more laudatory sentences that put Stevie on a pedestal with Hepburn, Davis, Bergman, and, with the calculated cunning and panache of a consummate showman, Laura Dane.

Sanberg nodded enthusiastically. Laura snored louder and made a one-handed lah-dih-dah.

Brighton said, "I wanted you to know everything before I answered questions about the remarkable investment opportunity I am able to offer our star."

Investment opportunity.

Wasn't that my original guess?

Brighton directed a generous face and gratuitous gesture at Stevie, who wouldn't look at me.

"Mr. Gulliver, I need not explain to you the value of the publicity we are getting at present because of Blackie Sheridan's unfortunate murder," he said. "I have no doubt the truth will out in short order and Stevie will be exonerated, of course. I fancy people more than ever will be ready to queue up at the box office to see her, the curious and the sensation seekers as well as her loyal fans. We will outgrow this sorry theater long before I had originally expected, and you should know I have begun inquiries into suitable venues in the West End and on Broadway. The idea of staying in Los Angeles, at a venue like the Doolittle, is not out of the question. We shall go where we're able to secure the best and largest house while the momentum is working for us."

"If you are confident of such an enormous hit, why do you need Stevie's money?" I said. "The play stays your investment and you reap the reward all by yourself for yourself."

"Or so it would appear," he agreed.

"Instead of you talking about her investing, I would expect Stevie's agents to be after you for a richer deal, a larger chunk of the gross."

"You do know the game, don't you?" His glasses had slid down his nose. He pushed them back up the bridge, brought the finger down to his pulsating lip. "To their credit, they tried. Call upon urgent call after the first news bulletins, but I know how the game is played, too. I asked them, 'Boys, if your client is made to stand charges and is found guilty, shall you insist on getting your ten per cent of the poisonous injection?' I have made a career of never negotiating with agents. If I reach a certain point and cannot deal directly with the artist, I move on.'' He smiled emptily. ''If you were her agent instead of a loyal friend, I would have rejected out of hand Stevie's insistence we speak.''

Brighton was spending a lot of words, but I wasn't satisfied with what I was hearing. He didn't wait for me to tell him.

''I see the question on your face, Mr. Gulliver. And me, in your shoes. Why I'm trying to be frank. Our certainty of Stevie's innocence does not extend to the insurance carriers. They have visions of my investment turned to dust if Stevie is unable to continue. All I seek is the difference in the premium, and for that I'm willing to share what I perceive as greater reward than were I to move ahead with another actress as Marilyn. The play has developed an allure of its own off all the publicity. My phone has been ringing off the hook. Ashley Judd's people. Jennifer Jason Leigh. Demi Moore will go blonde for the opportunity if—''

He gestured for understanding from Stevie.

''I am Marilyn!'' She implored me with her eyes. ''Honey, my business managers say I can handle it.''

''How much?''

''A hundred thousand dollars?'' Stevie said, falling back on her helpless little girl voice. She found it easier to look at Monte Sanberg than me. He pushed a strand of hair off her face, the way I still did from habit.

Brighton nodded agreement. ''You probably expected to hear a higher number, but that is all I am asking, exactly what the insurance companies are demanding as an additional premium. I'm prepared to pay Stevie back once I recoup my investment and the general production costs and before either of us dip into the profits.''

''Certainly a man of your stature, who has enjoyed all the successes your bio indicates''—I spanked the jacket pocket where it was stored—''can handle an extra hundred thou.''

''Of course. Let's just say this way purchases another form of insurance. It allows me to be entirely confident that Stevie won't lose interest or leave the show too early for us to enjoy the full fruits of our labors."

"I wouldn't do that to you, Jerry!"

"Of course. No offense intended. But, circumstance can cause that to happen, the same way Mr. Gulliver may decide to convince you my proposal isn't proper and I'm reluctantly obliged to ring up Demi Moore or—"

"Please, honey, what do you say?"

"What else, Mr. Brighton?"

Laura Dane pushed herself up from the table and said with sly invective, "She gets the boyfriend as her director, remember not to forget mentioning that's part of the deal."

Brighton brushed an imaginary speck off his cheek. "My, my, Laura, you do like to stir the pot, don't you?"

"It's for the good of the play," Stevie said, meaning it, and reached for Sanberg's hand. Sanberg avoided my gaze, like there was more to Laura's news than even she knew.

I had a more pressing question. "Mr. Brighton, why don't I believe you?"

His face went blank, as if he had heard a familiar cue, where an honest man would show his agitation. "Can you be more specific than that, Mr. Gulliver?"

Stevie leaped from the bed, hung on one hip, and embraced herself. "Neil!"

I waved her off. "I have a problem with the line you handed out about the insurance companies. I'd be willing to bet nobody is holding you up for another hundred thou."

He trained his dark marble eyes on me and ran a pudgy tongue over his lips. "How much, Mr. Gulliver?"

"I beg your pardon?"

"How much are you prepared to wager? One dollar? Five? Five hundred? Five thousand? Give me a number, and I will gladly cover the wager, Mr. Gulliver. Gladly. I do not take so lightly any effort to impugn my honesty."

He reached for the tired Gucci attaché case next to his leg and hefted it onto the table. The lid was buried under travel stickers advertising countries. He snapped open the combination locks, lifted the lid, and found a Gucci-covered checkbook and a Mont Blanc pen.

"You decide how much. Stevie can hold the stakes until you get your answers right and proper."

It was more con man macho.

It was a dramatic gesture designed to intimidate.

It was going to work, because I currently had fifty bucks to my name, including savings account interest.

I told Stevie, "Do what you want," and left.

I heard her calling for me to come back.

If she had run after me, it might have made a difference. Instead, the breeze on my neck was Monte Sanberg. He caught up with me as I unlocked the Jag. Came down hard on my shoulder, jerked me around. He wanted to do more. He wore the need like some cheap aftershave. I wanted to deck him and I could, if I brought one up now, before Sanberg adjusted to the possibility. And prove what?

I said, "Break yourself of that habit around me, okay?" like a gentle challenge.

Sanberg took back his hand and weighed a fist before shoving both hands inside his chinos. He angled back a step. Caught my stare. Wouldn't let go. "Stevie really wanted your approval, man. It means a lot to her and you know it. You damn well know it. You don't have to hear it from me."

"What's your complaint, specifically, kiddo? I spoke out, instead of playing numb-nuts and letting Brighton sweet-talk her out of a hundred thou?"

"He may be creeping crud, but she needs to do the role and prove something to a lot of people, including you. She can afford the buy-in. You heard her. So, maybe what you should be doing is telling her to go for it, like you believe in Stephanie Marriner. The same way Stephanie Marriner believes in you."

"And, so Monte Sanberg can direct her in the play and prove something to—who? Isn't that part of what I'm hearing from you now, Sanberg? A big, big part of it?"

"You know something, man? You're pathetic."

Pathetic.

The word stung all the way home.

I've been called worse over the years, but never anything as hurtful. It might not have mattered, except that Stevie mattered. Should I have recognized her signals?

I am Marilyn!

Honey, my business managers say I can handle it.

I did the right thing with Brighton.

For Stevie.

Should I have said, "Hey, puss, you want it, take it. You'll knock 'em on their keesters as Marilyn and that money will be back in the old savings kitty before it's missed?"

Said it like I meant it?

Why not?

Just another jazz riff.

Not the first time I would have lied for her.

Thinking about the lies I'd told, often to Stevie to protect her from herself, kept me up long into the night.

Morning brought a distraction, news about another death at the Retirement Estates.

The story and photograph ran as a sidebar to the major front page piece about Stevie, in which Clancy McPhillip reported the DA getting ready to recommend to the grand jury she be indicted for the first degree murder of Sheridan.

McPhillip referred to his unnamed source as "highly placed" and "unimpeachable."

The rest of his copy also was ambiguous. Suspect. It was the half-baked fudge that substitutes for hard news on a major story, absent hard news.

The sidebar headline over two columns reported:

CORONER SAYS NEW MPRE DEATH IS
PROBABLY DUE TO NATURAL CAUSES

There was a three-column photo of Stevie hiding behind a floppy brimmed sunbonnet and giant sunglasses while ducking into the black BMW I had seen parked at the Paradox Playhouse. Monte Sanberg, his face askew, was in the foreground, exhibiting the universal finger for a phalanx of TV and still cameras that must have gotten there after I left.

The shot that riveted me was a two-column vertical publicity still of the "New MPRE Death."

The cutline identified Clarence (Taps) Vernon.

Taps was younger in the still, the genial bootblack getting ready to slide, slip, lift, and bounce little Shirley Temple in *Little Baby Broadway*, in the memorable dance they performed all over Times Square with the statue of Father Duffy. (I shut my eyes and saw Shoeshine and Little Baby Broadway leading the Fighting 69th marching band up Broadway to Central Park and into an iris dissolve.)

The sidebar attributed Taps's death to injuries sustained as a result of a fall while rehearsing for the Retirement Estate's annual Break-a-Leg Show.

I was there. I saw it happen. The drop from the roof of the Super Chief was enough to cause serious damage to someone half his age. I had no cause for doubting. Until I called Augie, who also had been there.

Augie talked murder.

I said, "Read the paper. The ME disagrees."

"Our friend Cuevas was only talking probable. Taps was supple as Silly Putty, amigo. A fractured shoulder, that's all it was."

"Taps was an old man—"

"I knew Taps. He was an elf, a gnome. A gremlin. A kid by fairy kingdom standards. Forever young. Taps was all ready to go again once the doctor set his shoulder and dosed him with a painkiller. Taps had no business waking up dead."

"If I understand you, you're saying an autopsy might show—what? Doctor's error? Taps Vernon was fed something toxic that kicked out his system for keeps? Some anti-inflammatory that turned killer against his ulcers or a bum ticker? Or chronic asthma, or—?"

"The doctor asked him if he was allergic to anything. Taps said no. He was in pain, but he was coherent and knew what was happening."

I reread Augie the paragraphs that quoted Cuevas. Even allowing for perfect health all a person's life, he reaches a certain age and anything is likely to give out, the way an automobile loses the generator and the regulator after the battery dies.

A sigh of exasperation, then his voice took on a harder edge over his speaker phone, and the hollow echo of his tiled bathroom gave it a heavenly quality, like he was coming to me direct from the pearly gates.

"You remember when the doctor asked you to help round up a wheelchair so he could move Taps back home, and off you trotted like a good little Boy Scout?"

"Yeah?"

"I was still goal-tending Taps, crouched down on both knees, letting him use my arm for a pillow. Taps motions for me to lean in closer. There's something he wants me to know. I get down so close he could French-kiss my ear, if he was into that sort of thing. Taps tells me, 'They want me dead, Augie. They also want her dead. Watch over me, you listening? Don't let them kill me.' "

"You suppose Taps was beginning to float? Didn't know what he was saying because of the drugs the doctor had administered?"

"He knew, amigo." Augie blew out the exasperation and added brusquely, "I wouldn't be repeating this if I felt Taps's mind was wandering." Augie took a few seconds to control his irritability. "I asked Taps who *they* were and who *her* was," he said. "The *she they* wanted dead. He got as far as telling me it was Claire. Taps said Claire's name. Then and only then, amigo, did he close his eyes and dance off to slumberland."

"That's it? That's what you base it on, your assumption that Taps Vernon was murdered?"

"He's dead, isn't he?"

"Natural causes, Augie. You're letting whatever it is you're feeling for Claire cloud your judgment."

His voice grew tougher.

"What will you say to me if Claire is next? If she wakes up dead, too? Tell me . . ." I had nothing to say. "Claire witnesses a killing and ever since has been going around with a face, a neck, and Lord knows where else full of ugly bruises, making like she's an amnesiac or worse. Then, I hear that somebody wants her dead from someone who gets there first, and you are inclined to write off his death as 'natural causes'?"

Augie's voice became weary, resigned.

He changed the subject without waiting for my answer.

"You ever talk to Sunset Beaudry?"

"Maybe today. Sunset was still missing when I left the MPRE. Later, Paige Jahnsen left a message saying he had been sleeping one off in their cemetery. I called to tell you, but you weren't there."

"Kid, I know where I wasn't," he said, abruptly. "I got Claire home and was about to head over for Taps's place when Mimi Polyzoides showed up. My going up on the stage and joining the tap routine, it was only a gag—going for a few laughs—and here was Mimi using it against me. He asked me to sub for Taps in the Break-a-Leg Show. I thought he was kidding. He played to my ego and, when that didn't work, called on old times' sake; dredged up family honor. I don't know if it was Mimi's family honor or mine. I figured Taps would need a week to figure how to do the routine without aggravating his shoulder, so I caved in. Besides, it gave me the perfect excuse to hang around the Estates."

"How did Claire react when you said you'd do it?"

"Claire didn't," he said, uncomfortably.

"And you think she's putting on an act."

"I'm certain she's putting on an act."

"Because of something she did, you said."

"Because of something she did."

He still wanted me to leave that subject alone. I heard it in his voice. "What do you think I'm going to learn from Sunset?"

"I told you already. He thinks he knows who killed Sheridan and he says it wasn't Stevie."

"Sunset say who and why?"

An awkward pause. "Not in so many words."

"Maybe just one? Like a name, maybe?"

"Colonel Mustard in the conservatory with a knife." Augie never liked being pressed. "I explained that once before, kiddo; should have been enough for you. He was afraid of being overheard."

"Sunset give you any clue why, any clue at all?"

"Yeah. One. Sunset said somebody wanted him dead. He said somebody wanted him dead with more conviction than I heard later on from Taps Vernon."

I moved the phone from my ear and looked at it with sarcasm, clamped it back. "Augie, you suppose if you had mentioned that minor detail before this I might not have given you such a hard time about Taps or—"

"I didn't want your judgment clouded by what you feel for Stevie," he said, flinging my words back at me, and exploded into laughter. "If you're suing for forgiveness, I forgive you."

Augie, never one to settle for a draw.

I exchanged my sweats for mocha brown slacks and matched them with a navy and tan striped button-down and an Expressionist tie that, along with my Nikes, gave me a touch of individuality. I decided on the camel's hair blazer and found a loud, geometric handkerchief to tuck into the breast pocket.

I liked what I saw in the mirror, except for ten years and fifteen pounds that refused to disappear and hair that was too amenable to the concept of male pattern baldness. I could see myself a few years from now, never venturing outside without a snap-brimmed driving cap like Gene Kelly had worn in public. I went back to the closet and found my Lakers cap on the overhead shelf. Tried it on. Brim backwards. I looked trendy and stupid, I told my father's face in the mirror.

The phone rang. I snapped it up after hearing Doc Cuevas on the machine, apologizing for the lateness in returning my call. He'd been working since five on a drive-by shooting in front of the Lugo post office at Eighth near Olympic, he said. Two dead and two others critically injured.

"Somebody making a statement," the doc considered. "The victims were all garden-variety street. Two with carts, the woman with her life in a shopping bag, and the kid—'' His sigh weighed the world. ''Ten or twelve, Gully, and sad part is he looked happy to be going. You know the expression I mean? That blissful look you rarely see on anybody alive.''

Of course I knew. I started to respond, but he cut me off. Death was what he did for a living, and he had given himself as much of a sentimental fix as the job allowed. Too much and even the best of them start slinking away from competency, into an alcoholic haze or worse, the same way it happens with cops. And with newspaper muggs who've spent too much time hashing over the ugliness of an average day.

I repeated my conversation with Augie.

Doc Cuevas listened attentively, mumbling a few times to let me know he was there. When I finished, he said, ''What your unholy holy man said is a possibility, but we're never going to know.'' His voice had the sheen of ripe berry wine. ''The doc out there certified death by virtue of heart failure and the vicissitudes of old age, compounded by injuries sustained in an accidental fall. It would take more than Augie's conjecture for an autopsy, and frankly, based on what I found when I got there, I go along with their doctor.''

''I'll tell him, but you remember Augie once he's made up his mind.''

''That doesn't make Augie right, Gully, only stubborn.''

When I got to his cottage at the MPRE, the Range Roper was standing on his front porch, supported by aluminum crutches, his ample upper torso pitched forward, toothpick thin legs locked in metal braces.

Except for thickly cushioned running shoes, Sunset Beaudry wore the outfit that never varied from movie to movie, the cattle drover's faded, baggy blue denims, fringed buckskin jacket later borrowed by Shane, and a white bandana knotted at the throat. The tall, white, broad-brimmed Stetson with a single eagle feather in its sweat-stained hatband that was the trademark of his screen persona, as instantly recognizable as Buck, whose gallant, loyal stuffed remains he watched me explore before I skirted Buck Junior, Sunset's pinto golf wagon, and moved on him.

"Gulliver!"

His voice still had the unflinching gargle of resolve that put villains on notice to come out with guns blazing. The notched gun belt and twin holsters were missing, except in my mind, where I could see Sunset's pistols resting butt forward, ready for the astonishing cross-draw that yanked the old neighborhood gang to its feet, cheering madly, and, later, home, to see if we could do it better than the man who was law and order north of the border.

What it always said under Sunset's name on the marquee cards: The Law and Order North of the Border.

"That's right, Mr. Beaudry," I called back.

"Sunset will do fine. Mr. Beaudry, he was my pa."

His grip was firm, stronger than I'd have supposed for a man his age. The movie reference books showed him somewhere between seventy-five and eighty. The strength may have come from pulling himself on the crutches. Beneath a pale mask of sagging flesh, there was still enough chiseled face to distinguish the hero of my Saturday matinees. The nose remained a steep mountain slope that had outlasted a thousand punches, only now it had trails of blue veins and raised freckles that might be skin cancers, like the freckles on his wide forehead.

The honest mouth.

The cleft in his faltered chin.

The half-inch ridge of scarred, discolored flesh below the curve of his left cheek was not as white or obvious on his milk white complexion as it once had been against a dark tan burned on by years of Montana cattle drives, before he became a movie star, or so the stories claimed.

I was afraid my expression might betray to him my sadness at confronting reality, unsentimental destroyer of childhood memory.

"My ma, married to the man going on fifty-three years and I never heard her call him anything but Mr. Beaudry. A different time then, same as my day ain't like now. My day was better, when a man could be a real man and stand up for what he believed."

I said I agreed. His piercing blue eyes washed over my face, looking for the lie. I could see my wet reflection in them and wondered if he already had had too much to drink, although it was hardly past noon. He caught me and made a discarding motion with the back of a hand, like he recognized the thought.

"I'm sorry I missed you yesterday, sir."

"Sunset." He repeated the motion and pointed me to the front door. I stepped aside for him. He insisted I go first.

The living room was furnished simply, decorated like a room at Gene Autry's Western Heritage Museum. Photographs, plaques, citations, trophies, all of it dedicated to the fearless cowboy star who had turned into this crippled, elderly gentleman.

Sunset wondered what I'd like to drink. Wet my whistle. A command more than a question. He sounded disappointed when I asked if he had a diet Coke. We compromised on a beer. He was back in a minute aiming two uncapped bottles of Bud at me.

I took the bottles from him and set them down on the table between us while Sunset leaned his crutches against the arm of the straight-back wooden chair and worked into a sitting position. He winced adjusting his body in the cushioned seat.

I pretended not to have heard and turned back to him when he proposed we toast to absent friends and swallowed generously to my prudent sip. He wiped away a foam mustache with his fingers and rubbed them dry on his denims. He replaced the bottle, leaned back with his arms resting on his paunch, and seemed anxious for me to start the conversation.

In the Saturday matinee movies and serials, Sunset never was one for small talk or reticence.

Now, either.

I must have let a few too many moments pass to suit him.

"Augie says you're trustworthy." He aimed an ear at his shoulder and squinted at me, as if searching for confirmation. Something seemed to satisfy him. "I had important news to share, but Augie didn't want to leave Claire sitting alone by herself."

"I know."

"Of course you know, or you wouldn't be sitting here now." He muttered something indiscernible. "How much did he tell you?"

"Only what you told him, sir."

Sunset ran his tongue around and made a game of rubbing his lips. "Augie says you're married to this actress they think done it. This Stevie?"

"My ex-wife. Stevie divorced me seven years ago."

"You still got this thing for her, Augie says."

"I suppose," I said reluctantly, and thought about Augie's big mouth and what else he might have revealed to the old cowboy.

"I know what it's like. Kinda went through it myself. Me and the wife, Dulcy. We put in shy of fifty years together. We didn't need nobody else. No children. No one. We had each other."

My gaze trailed his to the wall to my left and settled on a large oil portrait in a gilded frame, at least four by six feet, dividing neat rows of framed photographs.

Dulcy Brown had been Sunset's leading lady in his earliest movies for Monogram. Dressed for a gypsy ball, she stared back at us through wise and caring eyes, soft, parted lips about to share a special secret.

Sunset said, "It ain't been a million laughs since the good Lord took her. At least He was kind enough to leave her precious memory and love for me behind. That gets me through most days." He withdrew the index finger he'd been aiming at the portrait and turned back to face me. "Maybe she'll come 'round to her senses."

"I wouldn't count on it, sir. She's very set in her ways."

"Sunset. The only thing you ever really got to count on is yourself. You get that part right and the rest follows. Try and remember."

"I'll try." His head bobbed approvingly. I got us back on topic. "You told Augie you don't think Stevie killed Blackie Sheridan. You think you know who did."

His head swiveled left and right. "I told Augie flat out she weren't the one what done him in. I know who did and I know why, too. Dangerous knowledge to have, but I got it, son." He paused for another swallow of beer and drained the bottle.

Checked over both shoulders for privacy.

Lowered his voice to a soggy whisper.

"It's Elvis who's the responsible party," he confided.

Wiped his mouth dry.

Wondered if I was ready for another beer.

I said, "Elvis?"

"You deaf? Lotsa people around here deaf."

"Elvis Presley?"

"Maybe it got to do with the atmosphere, ever since the smog started squatting the San Fernando Valley."

"Elvis Presley killed Blackie Sheridan?"

I couldn't hide my incredulity.

Where Claire Cavanaugh supposedly lost her memory, Sunset appeared to be going her one better. And, no Augie around to tell me he was faking it, too.

"Is that it, sir? Elvis Presley?"

I rose and was about to say enough polite words to cover my move across the room and out the door. Sunset looked at me like I had just invented *stupid*, then made a mischievous, snorting grin.

"Son, I hate to be the one breaking the news to you, but Elvis, he's deader'n the mules in my uncle Ezra's glue factory." He angled a thumb behind his shoulder. "The kitchen's through there. Bring back whatever's left of the six-pack. We might be here a spell."

I returned with three bottles.

They were empty by the time Sunset had finished explaining how it came to pass that Elvis Presley killed Blackie Sheridan.

His story went back forty years, to early 1956, when Elvis reported to Twentieth Century–Fox to begin work on his first movie, *Love Me Tender*. Monroe was filming *Bus Stop* on a nearby soundstage. It was inevitable the sex goddess would meet the singer whose hips shook up the world and made rock and roll a battle cry of the next generation.

Sunset said, "They fancied the idea, a-course, Marilyn maybe more than him at first. She knew how a photograph would make all the newspapers world over, where Elvis needed Colonel Parker to tell him to go on ahead. It got arranged pronto by Reg Mowry, who was running press and then some for Mr. Darryl F. Zanuck. The fellas in the still department had a field day."

I had a vivid image of the photos he meant. They've appeared in dozens of books and magazines since, the only graphic evidence that Elvis and Marilyn ever met.

I told this to Sunset.

He winked. "They kept on meeting, too," he said. "Sparks went flying the first minute they laid eyes on each other. It wasn't long before that's not all was getting laid."

"Elvis and Marilyn?"

"Reg Mowry managed to keep the lid on, don't know how, but if you know Reg you know his reputation for turning a sow's ear into a silk purse. He wasn't called Dr. Fix-it for nothing."

"Why would Mowry want to keep the lid on? Elvis and Marilyn. It sounds like a press agent's dream."

"Them was different times from today, when a little gossip could do terrible damage to a person's career. Think back on that lady from *Casablanca*."

"Ingrid Bergman."

"Tall, that one," he said, nodding. "Marilyn, she was between husbands or thereabouts. Elvis was young, wild as the wind, and free to dip his spoon into any honey pot, but it would notta set well back home, where folks take their Bibles real serious. A big secret until Mr. Darryl F. Zanuck got wind and called on Colonel Tom Parker, saying the way Elvis was carrying on with her could shut down El's career faster'n a runaway freight. So, the colonel and Reg Mowry got together and took care of things."

"How is it you happen to know?"

"Good question. You ever think about becoming a reporter?" He enjoyed his joke for a moment. "People forget I was in *Love Me Tender*, billed just behind Dick Egan, rest his soul. I was making a transition from all of them programmers to what my agent called *important* films. It worked for a while, long as I did. Elvis, he growed up on my movies, so I was something like a hero to him, and I didn't mind the status it give me. He confided in me a lot, and sometimes, as a favor, I covered for him when he took off to spread happiness, especially whenever it were gonna be with her, Marilyn, and wasn't she some piece of work? You'd think a secret like that had to explode, but it never did. Worked out just fine. Not long after, she up and married her boyfriend, the writer—"

"Arthur Miller."

"That's the one, although I was always kind of partial to Joe DiMaggio myself. And Elvis, after a while he went off to the army and he found himself a bride in Germany." Sunset shrugged and started another brew. "What I'm telling you now, you can't find in any book or magazine, like those pictures, so you know how damned surprised I was to learn it was going to be in that play Blackie Sheridan was writing."

"I beg your pardon?"

"Exactly. He says one day, *'Alfred'*—he was always callin' me Alfred—*'Alfred, I got this here play I'm doin' 'bout Marilyn Monroe, and I'm giving some serious thinkin' 'bout writing up a new scene where she and your old friend, Elvis, get down to some pretty fancy fucking.'* I look at him like he's got one leg on the floor and one out the door. He ain't never heard that from me. He says, *'Don't pretend with me, Alfred. I know you know 'bout that.'* I drift away sayin' nuthin'. A week, two weeks later he joins me at dinner, slaps down his tray across from mine, and says, *'Alfred, you remember what I told you about Marilyn and Elvis?'* Sort of, I tell him, not wantin' to give away nuthin', and he says, *'Well, I been writing up those scenes, and I think I got myself in a mess. I'm scared 'bout things and don't know what to do 'bout it.'* "

Sunset stopped and studied his empty beer bottle, wishing it full again. "Soon after, Blackie, he comes on over again and this time he's white as Aunt Polly's fence. He says, *'You can't believe what is goin' on.'* I agree with him, sayin', *'I might be able you tell me, Blackie,'* only he clams up, like he just seen somebody in the dining hall what is part of the problem. Off. Like that. Not even hanging 'round for dessert."

"And the next time Blackie saw you?"

Sunset shook his head. "Never was no next time. Next time, Blackie was deader'n Kelsey's nuts. So, he was right 'bout bein' in trouble. Now you understand why I can say it weren't your lady what killed him?''

I didn't know what to make of his story and asked, ''Help me out, please.''

He did a trick with his eyes, made a sputtering noise. ''Son, Blackie got himself killed by somebody who knew what he was doing and was inclined to keep it from happenin' in the most certain of ways. Somebody protecting the memory of Elvis.''

''And that's why you blame Elvis.''

''The why and the who of it.''

''You told Augie somebody wants you dead.''

''Little knowledge is a dangerous thing. It killed Blackie. It can kill me, too. Now that you know, maybe I ain't done you no favor either, not that I was ever intendin' to put you behind the same dung heap as me.''

''What were you intending, sir?''

''Augie helped me out plenty in the olden days. I figgered he might have ideas. One was to tell you, so maybe you got ideas?''

I didn't want to hurt his feelings. ''I have to give it some thought.''

''Well, don't take too long.''

''Why is that?''

''Ask Taps Vernon.''

''Taps Vernon is dead.''

''My point, hoss. Taps knew what Blackie had in mind for that damned play of his and how a-scared Blackie was getting to be, and see what it got him?''

''Sheridan also told Taps about the play?''

''Allus was one to share his ulcers, Blackie.''

''The doctors say Taps died of natural causes after—''

He held out his hand like a traffic cop. ''That damned fall he took from the stage?''

''That's what they're saying.''

Sunset's head swung violently. ''Taps could fall off of a tall roof and still come up dancing. He was murdered, son, and not the only one I could tell you about.'' He nodded and gave me the defiant look I remembered from his solitary ride to Desperado Bluff, for a showdown with the notorious Prairie Jack Bigelow.

"Who else, sir?"

I leaned back expectantly, waiting to hear who else was in on the secret about Elvis and Marilyn that didn't seem to be much of a secret after all, except in his rampant imagination.

Sunset investigated my eyes and nodded again.

Before he could reply, there was a rapping sound, knuckles on wood, and we both turned in the direction of the porch, Sunset so startled he had started shaking, like Prairie Jack Bigelow had won the draw this time.

Mickey Spoon, the MPRE executive director, peered back at us, a hand bridging his forehead and the screen door. Sunset had left the door open to catch any breeze before it was burned away by the afternoon sun.

He called in his lilting tenor, "I thought I might find you fellows here. Paige thought she'd suggested you meet us at the office and we'd come on over together?"

I apologized, like I had forgotten.

Spoon joined us without waiting for an invitation. He moved a delicate incidental chair from the wall to the cowboy. Managed to adjust his remarkable bulk onto the seat. Pushed out a cloud of mint and asked amiably, "Having a pleasant chat, are you?"

The mints did nothing for his fogbound eyes or the pool of

heavy air that seemed to fill the space between us. Sunset jumped in anxiously before I could speak. "The pup, he ain't been here more'n enough time to settle down and get comfortable," he said.

Spoon accepted the information with a smile, but his gaze took in the empty beer bottles. Sunset noticed, too, and quickly wondered if Spoon wanted to help himself to one. He put on a slur that wasn't there before Spoon arrived, giving the impression he was responsible for all the empties except the one in my hand. He signaled me with a glance he didn't want Spoon to know what we'd talked about.

Spoon picked up an empty and weighed it. "You kids go right on ahead, unless you mind my eavesdropping."

"Of course not," I said. Sunset inched in his seat. Rubbed the scar on his left cheek. "You'll just be getting an earful of an old Junior Range Roper sharing some memories with his favorite cowboy."

Sunset nodded approvingly.

Spoon beamed. "For a column?"

I smiled noncommittally.

"Wonderful, just wonderful," Spoon said. "It's like a prayer answered. We need all the positive publicity we can get now, Mr. Gulliver. You can imagine how all the ghastly news stories about Mr. Sheridan's death have not helped our fund-raising one iota. We've lost some substantial pledges from people wondering what the hell is really going on out here."

"I was just asking him if he knew the old radio theme song," Sunset said, running his words together. He picked up a bottle and held it to an eye, periscope-fashion, and sang:

Roasted Toasties in the morning,
just like Sunset loves to eat.
With an extra golden spoonful
as an extra-special treat.

I joined in, sounding terrific compared to Sunset, until we both were drowned out a moment later by Spoon:

It's so great for all Range Ropers,
and sometimes even Buck.
But don't horse aroun', when Mom
goes to town—
Tell her Roasted Toasties bring
good luck.

We finished out of tune and were still applauding ourselves when Sunset confessed, "Damned if I ever could figure out what that last line was supposed to mean."

Mickey Spoon said, "I'll tell you what I know, Mr. Beaudry. It was eating all that Roasted Toasties to get my Junior Range Ropers secret decoder rings made me what I am today."

He patted his bass drum of a stomach. Laughed outrageously. The sound grew from a gurgle and filled the room like confetti. His eyes squeezed invisible and evoked tears at the outside corners.

Sunset dismissed the compliment, but Spoon and I looked at one another with the respect of strangers who discover a great secret in common.

I figured his job obliged him to be a gracious glad-hander and wear his cordiality like those notes for teacher that mothers are always pinning to their kindergartners, but he had a generous amount of genuine likeableness. Had I misjudged Spoon, as I seemed to have misjudged DeSantis?

This realization only made Sunset's shift in character more curious. Spoon, meanwhile, had risen to attention and was giving me the hidden thumb Junior Range Roper salute. I returned it, and we both turned to Sunset.

He blew us off with a crusty face that said grown men were supposed to behave like grown men. After a few more minutes of conversation, he asked the time and pretended surprise at the answer. He was late for rehearsal, he said, and began struggling up from his seat.

Once we had helped Sunset into Warner Brothers Auditorium and onto the stage, Spoon pressed closer and murmured into my ear, his voice sparkling with good cheer, his ingratiating grin irresistible, "I need to show you something."

Outside, he pointed me to the golf wagon. He looked like a giant eggplant in his purple slacks and a matching cardigan worn over a rich crimson cashmere turtleneck that reflected the color of his Ferragamo slip-ons.

He stuffed himself behind the wheel. I squeezed into what was left of the seat and we glided out of the space and headed west while he advised into his two-way, "Home, Mr. Micawber here. Come in, please."

The two-way crackled. I recognized the voice of Toby Latch, his receptionist.

He told her, "I'm on my way to Shangri-la, Miss Desmond, but holler if anything urgent breaks loose."

Spoon signed off, watched my expression, and gave me more teeth when he saw what he was after. "I spotted you for a movie buff the minute I saw you, Mr. Gulliver. "*Lost Horizon* is an all-time favorite. I'd give my right arm to see the missing opening sequence; wouldn't you?"

"I'd give your right arm, too," I said. He caught the joke and laughed. There would be a bruise tonight where he had nudged me hard with his elbow. "I thought your receptionist's name is Latch."

"Yes. Toby Latch. But her handle is—"

"Miss Desmond. From *Sunset Boulevard*."

"You got it! Damn, you're good. Miss Latch's favorite."

Spoon made a sharp right turn onto a narrow road heading away from the administration and residential complexes. The sky was clouding over and the breeze was invigorating against my face.

I said, "Why did you choose Mr. Micawber as your handle? Are you a Dickens fan?"

"Much worse than that," Spoon said, and in a halfway decent impression of W. C. Fields added some lines of dialogue from *David Copperfield*.

I said, "Fields can do no wrong in my book, either, but I'm more partial to Keaton and Laurel and Hardy."

We laughed at the names and the instant images they conjured up. The wagon rumbled under his weight.

"What got you hooked, Neil, if you don't mind my being so familiar?"

"Sometimes, I wonder myself, Mickey. The magic of it all, I suppose. The day comes when you realize the actors aren't behind the screen shouting out their dialogue. You need to know where they are and then who they are. Curiosity can be a mischievous companion."

Spoon worked his head up and down, and after a moment, he volunteered somberly, "I'm AA, Neil." The smile slipped from my face as quickly as his credibility.

He gave me a moment to see if his nose was growing, then cracked a grin. "Not what you think. In my life, AA stands for Alcohol Anytime.

"Be damned if I haven't tried to shake the curse a million times, but it sticks onto me like my own shadow. You recall an actor named Martin Sundance, from the eighties? Martin picked up great reviews in Garry Marshall and Martin Scorsese movies, back to back, and then—zip!"

He cheated a three-quarter profile and gulped for air while I scouted for Martin Sundance underneath the molten fat. He had changed so much in barely ten years that, even knowing, he was hard to recognize.

"You don't have to say it, Neil," he said, waving off any acknowledgment. "Hurts me to hear it, most of the time . . . all the time. No Betty Ford for this chump, even if I could of afforded it. I like the sauce too much. It lets me forget how I flopped onto low-budget crap, then a TV series that didn't last out the second episode. An occasional commercial. A few pops on a couple of soaps. Three days on *Bedrooms and Board Rooms*, but not so many lines for Stephanie Marriner to ever remember me."

Spoon's green eyes grew glossy before he squeezed his face and made them slip out of sight behind his cheeks. I felt sorry for him.

He was another of those lost show business souls who come too close to stardom to ever again cope with failure. So they run from it, into a bottle or a needle or a quick fling in front of anything lethal. Spoon's story wasn't new. He was just another name on a long list.

"I tried the other AA between my benders, sometimes three or four meetings a day, looking for the one that brings out the most industry people, especially somebody who might give me a gig. It turned out to be above a bowling alley in Studio City." He pushed aside his nose and pulled in air, first one side, then the other. "It's not hard for me to make friends. One day one of them tells me about this place—that was four years ago, coming up—and how the MPRE needs a new assistant executive director. Why the hell not me? All the good restaurant jobs are taken. I hide my habit and I settle in. Little more than a year later, Mr. Draigo dies. Heart gives out." He snapped his fingers. "Like that. Mr. Draigo did a thorough job of training me to run this place, so the MPRE board of directors didn't waste any time promoting me.

"It's mainly a fund-raising gig that's come a long way since I took over. When I brought Paige Jahnsen on board two years ago, it gave me more time to go among them and lure some of the juicier fat-cat donations that might otherwise go to the Motion Picture Country Home. There's been more pressure on me in the last year, because of a building program to get more cottages and a hospital. Ah, here we are."

We had reached a stretch of lush, beautifully kept weed-free lawn on the other side of a glistening black wrought-iron fence. It was Shangri-la, according to the sign hanging from the tall entrance arch, each letter of the name meticulously carved into a single piece of polished oak.

In the movie, the inhabitants of Shangri-la stayed young forever. Here in the MPRE cemetery they were destined to remain dead forever.

The gates were open. Spoon passed through and a minute later was parking in an asphalted alcove.

The neat rows of chiseled tablets reminded me of the newer sections of the VA cemetery on Wilshire in Westwood, near the Heathcliffe Arms, and made me wonder if any stone carvers were left who could make the monumental tombstones that once haunted the graveyards as well as any ghosts. There was a column in it.

Spoon rattled off a couple handfuls of names of the famous and forgotten buried in Shangri-la, leading me to a section about fifty yards away, and directed my attention to a tablet just off the brick walkway, brighter than any of the others. The tablet was a glistening white, like someone had taken a scrub brush to it. Dressed with a fresh bouquet of wildflowers picked from the patches of yellow and white daisies and golden poppies growing free on the grounds.

DULCINA BROWN BEAUDRY
Beloved Wife of Alfred Edward Beaudry
Rescued from Life, But Never
Far From Those Who Love Her.

She was seventy-one when she died this year. I thought back to Paige Jahnsen's phone call, to say they found Sunset sleeping off too much drink by the grave of a co-star. Here, of course. It didn't take a Spade or Marlowe to figure out that one.

"You knew Mr. Beaudry's wife was Dulcy Brown?" Spoon asked routinely and, not waiting for my reply, said, "They were quite close. When Mrs. Beaudry passed away, he took to drinking harder than ever. Shouldn't be drinking at all in his condition, but Mr. Beaudry finds it faster than we can keep it from him. Somehow, he manages to sneak it past us. Must have hiding places all over. He spends a great deal of time here with Dulcy, bringing her fresh flowers and maintaining the marker like that. The empty plot next to Mrs. Beaudry is reserved for him, of course."

For a fleeting moment, Spoon seemed to recognize some of himself in his description of Sunset Beaudry. He let his eyes study the ground rather than look at me.

"Is there a reason you wanted me to see this, Mickey?"

Spoon looked up again and faced me squarely. "Yes, Neil, there is. It's to emphasize what I want you to understand, in light of what I'll wager you were hearing from Mr. Beaudry."

He angled back expectantly and waited for a response.

I waited Spoon out.

The reporter's trick to getting information from anybody is to offer as little of your own as possible, keep the other guy talking. It obliges him to answer questions he can only surmise might be passing through your mind.

Spoon said, finally, "I walked in and could tell right off Mr. Beaudry was at it again. He has a little too much to drink and tells anyone within grabbing distance we killed his wife. He blames us for other deaths besides Dulcy Brown, too. His death list started growing after Dulcy passed away. I suppose with you he added Mr. Vernon."

"Something like that."

Spoon's head nodded vigorously. His array of chins wobbled like Jell-O. "A wonder he's not also blaming us for Mr. Sheridan's murder." He made it a question that doesn't take a question mark; rolled his eyes.

I nodded.

"It's a dangerous imagination, Neil. I'm usually not this concerned. I've kept the board informed and anyone else, even a potential benefactor, I can take aside and explain. They understand how an aging alcoholic still grieving over the loss of his wife can turn anxiety and depression into accusation. There's a special problem with you, because you write for a newspaper. I dread your leaving here convinced by something Mr. Beaudry said and rushing a column into print."

"Not my style, Mickey."

He shook his fingers at my face. "I didn't mean to imply. I read you regularly. It's just that your newspaper has changed so radically, I . . . One can't be too careful, you understand?"

I did, but life with the Spider Woman was nothing I cared to discuss with Spoon. Before either of us could speak, his two-way interrupted. Toby Latch was calling to advise him that Augie was waiting for me at Claire Cavanaugh's cottage.

Spoon did a zigzag, aiming the green and gold wagon in the direction we had just come from after we traded Junior Range Roper salutes, and as I started up the painted cement path to Claire's cottage, Augie stepped out onto the front porch, wearing sweats right off *A Chorus Line*.

He put a vertical finger to his lips, signaling me to be quiet. "Claire's napping," he whispered. "Why I waited long as I did to find you."

Augie pointed me inside and to a quilted couch covered in a floral pattern as colorful as a spring afternoon. The room could have been decorated by the same people who worked for Judge Hardy and the Andersons. It was drowning in the scent of freshly picked roses. I noticed one huge bouquet in a carved crystal vase on the mantle and wondered if it was a gift to Claire from Augie, but I knew better than to ask.

I pretended not to see the cot along the short wall by the dining room entrance, the corners of the brown woolen blanket neatly made. A small reinforced metal trunk at the foot of the cot had Augie's name stenciled in black capital letters. He had taken up residence here.

"What did you learn from Sunset, amigo?"

I told him.

"How much of this does Spoon know?"

"If he knows anything, he didn't get it from me," I said, repeating what Spoon had to say about Sunset's imagination and the problems it was creating for the Retirement Estates.

"That's all?"

"We disagreed on the top ten movies of all time."

Augie rewarded me with a grunt. If I'd been his pet pooch, he would have stroked my neck. "From what you know about Blackie Sheridan's play, was Sunset's imagination working there?"

"Could be. No Elvis scenes, not from anything I saw or heard and, besides, Stevie would have said something. She knows the time I put in working Elvis's death in seventy-seven, when I was still a kid in high school and writing on spec for *Rolling Stone*."

For a fraction of a second I saw myself at sixteen, the fearless loner stealing off from home and grabbing a bus to Memphis, to soak up atmosphere for a first-person take on the funeral.

"I remember that series," Augie said, like he had spotted a dead bug. "Predictable *Police Gazette* stuff. Excuse me. *Rolling Stone*. Not much difference, though."

"Not much, but it got me an 8-Ball Award from the Press Club for distinguished investigative reporting," I said. "Youngest winner ever." Augie had cut a little too close. I owed him and honored him, but after all he was the one who routinely drilled into me that honesty to oneself was the first consideration in anyone's lifetime. "Wasn't that the same year you were nominated in that category for your series on serial killers?" I said, at once regretting it.

All the while he had been doing knee bends and other warm-up exercises. He stopped abruptly and made a show of adjusting his glass eye. His neck expanded with tension.

Finally, Augie said, "You don't find every fixed jury in a courtroom." I kept quiet. After a moment, he said, "You realize, if Sunset is right about Blackie Sheridan and Taps, it's not only his life in danger. Yours, too, maybe. Also, Claire."

"Major leap of faith, especially on someone who drinks as much as Sunset Beaudry."

Augie didn't like that at all.

"And what's Spoon? The spokesman for Perrier? Even when I was doing the big-league boozing, I recognized the truth, told it, and wrote it. My drinking, being king of the lushes, didn't make it any less true."

I drew a chalk mark in the space between us.

Augie grunted again and gave me his best Popeye squint and eased the pockets of indignation off his face. He said, "Let's just take everything we learn and do the best we can for Stevie and for Claire, okay?"

"Sounds like a plan."

"What are the chances we can wring an autopsy on Taps out of Doc Cuevas?"

"Too late. Spoon told me Taps is toast."

Augie frowned. "Who ordered his cremation?"

"Spoon did, as executor of Taps's estate for the MPRE Foundation. He says he goes that route anytime there are no survivors. It helps keep his budget in line."

"Convenient," Augie said. He put his hands on his hips and slid into what passed for leg stretches. I watched the wheels of his mind turning. "Let's get back to Blackie Sheridan's play. Who might know if he planned to add scenes about Monroe and Elvis?"

I counted off names on my fingers: Stevie, Jeremy Brighton, Monte Sanberg, Laura Dane.

"Sunset said Sheridan was a talker, so there could be other residents he told, besides Sunset and Taps."

"I know one," Augie said. He finished working a kink out of his back and pointed to the bedroom.

"Because of what Taps told you?"

"And something else." He crossed the room to an elegant antique writing desk under an arrangement of framed souvenir photos of Claire with other famous faces of her era or their handsome Bruno of Hollywood portraits, all suitably inscribed.

He pulled down the bowed cover of glistening inlaid woods and riffled a small stack of envelopes and found the one he was looking for.

"This came in the mail yesterday," he said. "Notice, still sealed." He showed me the flap side on his way over. "No cause to give it any thought until now. Check the return address."

It was one of those little stick-ons that come in the mail with an appeal for a donation. Alongside the American flag was the name Reg Mowry and a Kings Road address in West Hollywood.

"Tell me it's coincidence," Augie said. "Sunset mentions Reg Mowry's name, and look-a here."

"Coincidence," I said, viewing the envelope from several angles. "You did a nice job of resealing it."

"I'll be the judge of that."

He took the envelope and worked the flap loose. "Not that nice. Reg was a little stingy on the spit." He puffed inside to make a pouch, turned the envelope upside down and gave it a hard shake.

"Oops."

A piece of folded green paper about the size of a Post-it note fell onto the intricately designed Persian rug.

Augie's knees cracked as he stooped to retrieve the paper.

He opened it and his eyebrows arched.

He shot a look at the bedroom before handing it over.

It was a certified cashier's check for seven hundred fifty dollars.

The check was made out to cash and signed by Reg Mowry.

Augie appeared only slightly more puzzled than I felt. He took back the check. Returned it to the envelope. Put it in a hip pocket. "While I'm looking after business here, maybe you should pay a visit on Reg Mowry," he said.

"Not the worst idea you've ever had."

"Something to ask him." He settled onto the couch alongside me, so there was no chance of his voice traveling. "I worked the Monroe suicide in sixty-two. I remember how Reg was so helpful he was no help at all. All any of us could do was respect him for taking care of business. A real pro.

"Late in the game, when everyone else was working the murder theories, I followed a lead from sources who had told me letters had passed between Marilyn and a secret lover. I figured it was a Kennedy brother.

"I figured, find those love letters and it would be another Pulitzer, for sure. Zilch. It was one blind alley after another. Reg pleaded ignorance with me, but it won't hurt for you to raise the question. This time, instead of saying Jack or Bobby, put the name Elvis with it."

I nodded approvingly. "If Sheridan's information didn't come from some*body*, he might have gotten it from some*thing*. Like—"

"Love letters."

"Love letters. Track the love letters—"

"Track Blackie Sheridan's killer."

"One other thing, amigo."

"Tell me."

"My series on the Monroe suicide? I pumped it out while I was three sheets to the wind and still managed to cop an 8-Ball Award from the L.A. Press Club for distinguished investigative journalism."

"Must you always have the last word, Augie?"

"Not necessarily."

We continued waiting for Claire to wake from her nap. It was long past the lunch hour. I was starving. Augie excused himself and returned from the kitchen five minutes later with a tray of hot meatless stew full of spiced potatoes and carrots, the way he always made it, and thick slices of walnut-rich pumpkin bread.

After another half hour trading notions and theories and no sense, he suggested I head back to the city to see if I could pin down Reg Mowry. Claire would rouse any time soon.

"Weren't we just talking about doing the old double-team routine on Sunset? I can track Mowry after—"

"What is it, kiddo? You don't trust Brother Kalman to ask the right questions?" Augie snapped.

I've seen him edgy, but not for years and never quite like this. Was it about Claire? About a past they shared?

I said, "Not just the right questions. I trust you to come away with the right answers."

He turned abruptly, ignoring my grin, and put in a call to Spoon's office. Toby Latch arrived within minutes to drive me back to my Jag at Sunset's cottage.

She sat behind the wheel of the golf wagon grim-faced and guarded the entire trip, ignoring my attempts at conversation, nervously pampering loose strands of hair, eyes never straying from the road.

She had on a casual sunflower dress that sheltered her large unharnessed breasts, but the hem of the dress had inched over her knees, exposing legs like baseball bats and a flash of red silk panties she made no effort to correct.

Somehow, the contradictions made me wonder how much of her was a professional wallflower and how much was a woman who had never quite figured her way into a relationship with a man. It was still a question when I stepped from the wagon and thanked her for the lift.

"I'll lead you far as the auditorium. You should be able to follow the signs the rest of the way from there," she responded.

When we reached the auditorium, she aimed for an empty space about three slots away from Buck Junior.

I thought about ignoring Augie's admonition and one-stopping to drill Sunset about Elvis and the love letters.

I rolled to a stop, but before I could turn around and act on the notion, I saw Sunset in my rearview. He was on crutches, tracking toward Buck Jr., one cautious step at a time.

Paige was a half step behind him, a hand hanging tentatively between them, like she was ready to grab Sunset if he happened to stumble. She waited until he was secure behind the wheel, then hurried around and climbed in alongside him. He honked a warning. Backed out of the space. Hummed off in the opposite direction.

Miss Latch immediately finished talking into her two-way. Put it below my sight line. Pulled out and trailed after them.

What the hell is this all about? I wondered.

What did I know that I didn't know I knew?

Sunset tells me Blackie Sheridan planned on adding scenes to *Marilyn Remembers* about an affair between Marilyn and Elvis. That knowledge killed Sheridan, he says. He says Taps Vernon also was killed because of what he knew about Marilyn and Elvis. He fears for his own life, he says.

Mickey Spoon tells me Sunset blames the MPRE for the death of his wife, Dulcy Brown, and others, too stewed most of the time to believe otherwise.

So, discount Sunset Beaudry?

But—

Augie also wonders if Sheridan was killed because of love letters that passed between Elvis and Marilyn.

Find the love letters, find the killer? If the love letters do exist, where are they? Did the crime scene people come across them and consign them to an evidence locker?

A question worth raising with DeSantis.

Other questions for Sunset.

More for Claire, whose faded memory—if Augie knows what he's talking about—is an act and who knows more than she's telling.

And Reg Mowry?

What does he know?

I followed the directional signs through the gates onto the boulevard. At the first stop light after the turn, I pulled down the visor to block the afternoon sun.

A sheet of paper spilled onto my lap.

A child, or someone trying to give that impression, had printed in a sprawling red crayon:

> Butt out from other peoples business before it too late.

Not the best grammar, but I got the message.

And instant sweats to go with a heartbeat outrunning the traffic flow.

And the feeling I was being trailed by a rain-crusted white Mazda that had churned out of the MPRE about thirty seconds after me, its license plate too mud-caked to read.

I patted myself all over, then checked the glove for a pack of Luckies, and then tried to remember how many years it had been since I'd had a smoke.

The Mazda followed me onto the freeway and never seemed to be more than six or eight car lengths behind, even after I left the freeway and took Laurel Canyon over the hill.

It had disappeared by the time I found Reg Mowry's street.

Or was it simply that the driver had become more cautious?

Kings Road between Melrose and Santa Monica is a jungle of apartment buildings that replaced middle-income residences during the real estate boom of the midseventies. Little differentiates them besides a name, the tone of their faded paint jobs, and the size and shape of the central courtyard pool.

Reg Mowry lived in the Golden Palms south of Fountain, a mint green and cream-colored, three-story stucco affair with small balconies and wrought-iron railings. A buzz-through front door required visitors to identify themselves over an intercom, and for added security, there were no apartment numbers next to the residents' names in the alphabetical directory.

I punched in the building manager's code when Mowry didn't answer after my third try. A few moments later, a man's nasal voice crackled a question at me.

"You interested in the bachelor?"

The manager sounded disappointed when I told him why I was there. "Reggie's gone," he said.

"Any idea when he'll return?"

"Not for a long time. You a bill collector? He owe money? That it?" His tone mixed curiosity with suspicion.

I thought fast. "An old friend, down visiting for the day from San Francisco. Thought I'd surprise him."

"You're his friend, friends are supposed to know something like that. You go looking in the garage, you won't find Reggie's car either, if you're some collector."

This close to Boys Town, I chanced it. I put an ache in my voice and explained, "On his last visit, Reggie and I had—words. I flew down today with a peace offering."

A murmur of recognition bubbled in my ear.

"Been through that myself," the manager said. "You brought a gift, huh? Small and thoughtful always seems to work."

"Yes." I heard him suck a couple breaths, anxious to know. "Promise you won't tell what?"

"Promise."

"A ring. His birthstone set in eighteen-karat gold. Reggie spotted it and nearly died the last time we did the Castro."

"You romantic, you. If you like, leave the ring with me."

"You don't know where he went?"

"Swear. He packs a couple bags and pays up on his rent a month or two and splits with his hound. Never less than two weeks. If you're worried about the ring, I'll sign a receipt."

"I don't suppose someone else could—"

"No cause to be jealous. Best I can tell, Reggie never has visitors. Keeps to himself most of the time, except for walking Rocky and lunches. Every day, like clockwork. He leaves at noon for the Friars Club and is back by three. Set your watch by him."

"The Friars Club?"

"Wait a minute. You didn't know? Tell me again you're not a bill collector."

I told him, but he was beyond believing now and hung up.

I felt him watching me from a window as I hoofed back to my car, found a gas station with a telephone, and called the Friars Club.

The switchboard operator said Mowry had not been seen in the dining room or card room all week, like it was her fault. Giving out phone numbers was against the rules, she apologized, but she took mine and promised to give them to Mowry first chance.

Climbing back into the Jag, I spotted a white Mazda purring two bays away, the driver trying not to look conspicuous behind the wheel.

It was the same white Mazda with the same undecipherable license plate.

I inched out of the station and onto the street.

A minute later, so did the Mazda.

The driver once again kept a reasonable distance behind me, speeding up only to catch yellows, cheating across a few traffic signals that turned red whenever I tried a slow-and-go to lose him. Even the unnecessary turns, some other tricks I knew, failed to shake him.

The driver might need a red crayon to write with, but he was a class act behind the wheel.

I thought about catching him in a cul-de-sac, confronting him, hearing his definition of the other people's business I was supposed to butt out from before it was too late.

I also thought about maybe getting killed for playing it like I was some Bruce Willis.

About a half mile from the Heathcliffe, the driver made the decision for me.

As I moved into the turn lane to pull a south onto Veteran Avenue, he stayed on Wilshire and sailed past the intersection with what may have passed for a wave good-bye, leading me to two conclusions.

The driver had wanted me to recognize he'd been on my tail since the MPRE. He was too good to be seen if he didn't want to be seen. And, waiting until we were so close to the Heathcliffe before splitting, he wanted me to know he knew where I lived.

I tried to figure out what any of it might mean and how it might link to the murders while I parked and took the elevator up to the lobby, where a surprise was waiting for me.

The Spider Woman said, "You don't return phone calls, Neil, or your E-mail."

"I've been busy."

"That suggests you've been working."

"I have."

"For the *Daily*? For me? Or is there news on the employment front you've neglected to share?"

"You sound pissed."

"Come a little closer and you'll see how pissed I am."

I moved from the double-glass entrance doors to a wall by the armchair Langtry occupied like a throne in the well of the reception area across from the duty guard's station. The guard, who normally can sleep through a Richter 8.5, had left, ostensibly on a safety check, the instant my glare told him he'd welcomed a Trojan horse.

"Right! I see it as well as hear it. That's why you're the boss, boss. You know how things like that work."

The light sneaking in from the entrance blanketed her in a late afternoon glow that strengthened the hard good looks of a carefully made up forty-year-old face. As usual, she carried the New York fashion world on her shoulders.

She was wearing a red and black Chanel power suit, matching pumps, Chanel earrings that also said she was a woman to think twice about. Her long, sleek legs were crossed to be stared at, sheathed in black and finished in a pair of red pumps with black patent toe caps, three-inch heels adding to a height just shy of six feet.

I've never met a tall woman who doesn't confuse her size with an obligation to dominate, and certainly never one quite so deceptively tough as Veronica Langtry.

Langtry's crystal blue eyes worked the room while her words turned conciliatory. "I am here because I've been feeling damn guilty about the trick I played on you," she said. "I extended the olive branch, Neil, and then I fucked you over."

" 'Ex Proclaims Stevie's Innocence,' " I quoted the headline back to her.

"Exactly," she said, her voice stretching the word to gain credibility. "It was ethically questionable, underhanded, mean-spirited, and—"

"What I've come to expect from you, Ronnie."

A look flashed across her eyes and ended with a stretch of her tight, ambiguous mouth. "You never did file a piece on Claire Cavanaugh."

"And you saved me the trouble with Stevie."

Her look impugned my pious expression. She styled her close-cropped raven tresses with her fingers. "You should give better consideration to what I ask of you."

"Or what?" She shrugged, cocked her head, and eased off a nasty expression. "You tried waltzing that waltz with me once before, Ronnie. I'm still here."

"So am I, or haven't you noticed?"

I waited Langtry out.

"I have something for you, Neil." She uncrossed her legs and leaned over to fetch her red leather drawstring bag, placed it on her lap, dug out a beeper and a pocket-sized cellular phone, and held them out to me. "They're ready to go."

I shook my head like a neck coil had sprung. Over the years, I had been successful in resisting both items. I don't like the concept of being on constant call or losing privacy for thought in places like my Jag or the crapper in a multiplex. Beepers and cellular phones are the logical extension of doctors in the best seats at *Phantom of the Opera*.

"Where's the rest of it?" She tried not to show she wasn't following my logic. "You know, boss, the electronic ankle cuff, the slum lord model, in case I should stray from my hovel without authorization?"

She said, "You brought it on yourself, Neil," and set down the beeper and the cellular on the side table. "I want you when I want you, not when you elect to be available."

"This brought you here? Don't you normally leave the muscle flexing to one of the *Daily*'s high-priced, button-down lawyers?"

"Your bullshit attitude brought me here, Neil. I wanted to watch your face when I told you what you would have learned if you had the simple courtesy to return one of my phone calls."

I took two steps forward, to give her a better look at my face, and didn't like what I was getting back.

She leaned forward and aimed an index finger at my chest. "You know I'm wired like Western Union to the DA's office. I got word they've pulled a sealed murder one indictment against Stevie Mariner from the grand jury. I wanted you to know that before it came down, so you could prepare your sexpot ex for the boys who will be knocking on her door with the warrant and cuffs."

A shudder ran through my body and my heart pumped iron as dismay flushed my face.

I had visions of the ugly hysterics Stevie would go through if the visitors came as a surprise, and no doubt the DA would be there, too, accompanied by a few hundred of his best pals from the media.

Langtry leaned back and studied me. For a moment, I imagined her concern was real. She said, "I figured I owe you. You still have some time—the way it now looks, we run with the story day after tomorrow—so in my little black book all accounts between us are square."

I coughed my throat clear. "Thanks."

"You almost say it like you mean it," she said, easing back into Spider Woman territory.

"Temporary insanity."

"Work on it some more. It becomes you."

We were smiling, but there was too much history between us for the humor to be permanent. She got up to leave. I wished her gone, so I could call Stevie.

"One more thing, Neil. Clancy will do the main story. I expect the sidebar from you. Complete details on how Marriner responded to the news. The exclusive gush and mush that boosts circulation. No excuses." Then, like an ace up her sleeve, "If you know what's good for you."

The instant Langtry was out of sight, I used the cell phone to call the production office at *Bedrooms and Board Rooms*. Stevie had left a half hour ago. She wasn't home or not picking up and had not checked with her service for an hour.

I left urgent word.

Called the Paradox Playhouse.

A guy with a Jersey accent answered on the twelfth ring. I identified myself and told him why I was calling. "Stevie is not expected, sir. Our producer, Mr. Brighton, has canceled tonight's rehearsals. They're recalendared for tomorrow."

Maybe they were together, I considered, Brighton and Stevie, Brighton coddling his star and cash cow over a pretentious meal somewhere. Maybe—

Maybe there was a message waiting for me upstairs.

There was; not from Stevie.

Augie, to say he was spending another night with Claire at the

MPRE, leave word with either Brother Ian or Brother Gerard if I learned anything worth sharing from Reg Mowry.

I left a callback for DeSantis.

He'd be able to tell me if anything that smacked of love letters had been found in Sheridan's cottage and, possibly, add to Langtry's news about the grand jury's indictment.

I felt good about having information to trade with him. Most of what I had heard from Sunset, Mickey Spoon, and even Augie was incidental and irrelevant, but it would show DeSantis I was honoring our agreement.

I tried Stevie's home number and hung up on the service.

I thought about logging onto the *Daily* celebrity database for Monte Sanberg's numbers but abandoned the idea for the same reason I hadn't asked for him at *Bedrooms and Board Rooms*.

If Stevie and her director were together, I didn't want to know.

"Progress, Neil," I congratulated myself, while my memory raced back to the first year following our divorce, when I would spend hours parked across the street from the house we'd shared in Arcadia, usually as full of booze as despair.

I had my drinking under control now, and it had been a long time since I felt the need to host myself to a slumber party in the backseat of the Jag, outside the Beverly Hills mansion she had picked up on foreclosure after the soap opera bucks started paying off like a winning lottery ticket. An investment, Stevie said, against the day somebody came along with better bleach and bigger titties.

Her words.

And the phone rang.

I snapped it up.

Jeremy Brighton. Returning my call. Doing his impression of my best friend, as if last night's disagreement never occurred. I let him carry on until the pause that said he'd run out of small talk.

"There's something we need to discuss, Brighton. I'd rather not do it over the phone."

"If it's about my investment proposal—"

"What we have to talk about could be worth more than a hundred thousand dollars to you."

Now I had the con man's full attention. "You make it sound so mysterious, Mr. Gulliver. I don't suppose you could give me more of a clue?"

In fact, I didn't want to give too much away. At the same time, I wanted a gauge on how much Brighton might know. I said, "It's about Elvis Presley."

"Elvis Presley?"

"Elvis Presley and Blackie Sheridan's play."

The sucking noise he made sounded like a whale swallowing its tongue. "I don't quite follow you." His change in manner betrayed him. He followed all right, so I kept the lead.

"A matter of some letters?"

He weighed the question. "Yes. Yes, I do see, Mr. Gulliver. I've been away most of the day and presently am not where I can talk freely. Your first suggestion works best."

We agreed on breakfast tomorrow morning at the Beverly Hills Hotel's Polo Lounge.

After a couple hours, I tried Stevie's numbers again. A sweet soprano at the service assured me the computer wouldn't lose my earlier messages or any of the dozen others waiting for her.

A dozen others?

That distressed me.

Stevie was a phone-aholic who might let two or three calls back up, but a dozen? I invented reasons and applied all forms of logic to a concern that drove me to what I had so far managed to avoid, deal with the son of a bitch who had called me pathetic.

The *Daily* database showed two numbers for Monte Sanberg, one unlisted, as well as a service number and an agency contact. Some burden he was carrying seemed to ease, almost with relief, when he heard it was me calling. Before I could put the question to him, he wondered, "Have you talked to Rainbow?"

"No, why?"

"She's uptight, I don't know about what. She said she was going to call you."

"I have calls in to her. I thought she might be with you."

"Not since we wrapped. We were going to grab a fast bite and do notes after I gave the rest of the cast theirs, but Stevie had split by the time I finished with them. No messages. Not a word.'' Sanberg gave it some thought. ''You're worried after her, too.''

''Yeah.''

''It's not like her not to return calls. What's going on?''

''I hoped you'd be able to tell me,'' I said, and knew I was in for another nightmare sleep.

Interrupted by a middle of the night call from Stevie, so abrupt I thought I was dreaming.

''Where the hell are you?''

''Honey, I'm scared. Somebody has been following me since yesterday and tried to kill me and—'' I heard a crashing noise. ''Oh, shit! The bastard broke through the door . . . Oh, shit, shit, shit!''

''Stevie, where are you!''

The connection went dead.

I had to call the cops and—

What?

Do what? Say what?

I woke Jimmy Steiger, who cleared the sleep from his throat and let me know what he thought, but only until I told him why. His concern was immediate, for me as well as for Stevie.

''I'll get on it now,'' he promised. ''Get an unmarked over to her place, check it out. Get back to you ASAP. Figure on an hour max.''

''Nothing official, Jimmy. This is us. Personal. I'd have gone myself, not bothered you, except I want to be by the phone if Stevie calls again.''

''Of course. I understand. Strictly personal. I'll make it clear and no questions asked. And what's with this 'bother' crap, Gulliver? You wouldn't do the same thing for me if Margie was in trouble?''

''I get warnings left in the Jag and someone sticking to me like a bedsore, I can handle that. But if anything bad happens to Stevie . . . I want Stevie okay, Jimmy.''

''So do I, Neil. Don't go hysterical on me, okay? Don't fall off the mountain. Stevie can take care of herself. She's pulled out of worse with no help from either of us, and more than once. Now hang up so I can make some calls and get someone over to her place.''

I roamed the bedroom like a nervous groom, trying to make myself believe Jimmy was right. I wanted to try her number again, but it was more important I keep the line open, and when it rang about forty-five minutes later I leaped for it awkwardly, twisted a searing pain into my left side.

It was Jimmy, reporting that Stevie's place was clean. No broken doors. Nothing out of place, except for her Cherokee. It was missing from the garage, so he had ordered an advisory APB, with instructions to approach with discretion.

''This was supposed to be between us, Jimmy.''

''It still is. Stevie won't be brought in, nothing like that, trust me. Instructions are to have her call you at once regarding a family emergency.''

''You also log the Mazda?''

''Yeah, and the 'white and filthy' description is certain to turn it up.''

His sarcasm was intended to get a laugh and it worked on me, enough to momentarily ease the tension charging through my system like a massive attack of gastritis.

He refused to hang up until I promised I would try to get some sleep. I did when my worrying turned into anxiety overload and my system shut down involuntarily.

Only for a few restless, tossing hours, but at least, in my dreams, Stevie came back to me unharmed.

I woke up ragged, red-eyed, drowning in sweat. No desire to keep the breakfast date I'd made with Jeremy Brighton, but it was too important to Stevie for me to cancel.

Blackie Sheridan's murder.

The Presley and Monroe letters.

I was certain Brighton knew something he wasn't telling. His voice had given him away.

I drove to the Beverly Hills Hotel and found a parking spot on Crescent Drive, by the freestanding bungalows. Brighton had negotiated a seven o'clock date in the Polo Lounge to be certain we scored what he called a "proper booth" in the pink and green majesty of the main dining room.

The white-haired hostess in a garden-variety dress from the fifties brightened at the mention of his name and led me to the only empty booth against the far wall to the left of the patio entrance.

It was set for two. I thought I had arrived first. As I settled in, a crumpled linen napkin and a half-full coffee cup informed me otherwise. I surveyed the room.

A Ray-Ban convention. Show business types bonding over the scrambled smells of power breakfasts—

And recognized Brighton's arched back.

He was hunched over a circular booth across the way and talking animatedly to its three occupants, one of whom looked like Shirley MacLaine, all of whom were making an uncomfortable show of appearing interested.

He swept some new arrivals with a glance, noticed me, and signaled. Retreated backwards from the MacLaine table on shared insincere laughter. Arrived after a stop at a center table to trade greetings with a pair of executives in splashy California Casual uniforms, who traded thankful eyebrows once he'd moved on. Brighton was dressed for a bankers' convention. A custom-tailored suit with stylized lapels. A fresh white carnation in the lapel. High-gloss pumps.

He waited until he was settled before engineering a double-handed handshake. Moved into a review of the elaborate tour of English cabarets he had just proposed to MacLaine.

"She's mine," he confided, the words slipping out the side of his mouth, "if I can also deliver a week at the Palladium and her own BBC special."

"Can you?" I asked, not really caring.

His lower lip danced while he removed his black frames and swallowed me in one of those foolish-boy expressions the English are so fond of.

He popped the glasses behind his jacket handkerchief and

leaned over, an elbow on the table, a hand shading the side of his mouth from the world. "Jerry Brighton has his special ways," he boasted. "Another case where you should not bet against me, Mr. Gulliver, as you were ready to do over the investment I was seeking for *Marilyn Remembers*."

It was as close as Brighton came to mentioning the reason for our meeting until we were halfway through our meal, orange juice and oatmeal for him, for me a toasted bagel, black coffee, and trying not to show my concerns about Stevie.

He stuck to small talk, all designed to escalate him in my opinion, and his eyes routinely prowled the room like a wild boar hunting for fresh meat until he perceived I intended for him to raise the subject.

I could have, but I wanted him off balance.

A reporter's trick that works as well as a lie detector.

Brighton protected his coffee cup with his palm when I offered to pour from the large metal serving pot. "Yesterday evening, after I rang you back, you said something about dear Blackie's play and—Elvis?"

I refilled my own before repeating Sunset's story without mentioning who I got it from. Brighton listened impassively. His cold eyes stopped roaming and betrayed his keen interest when I got to the part where Sheridan had revealed he was adding scenes about Marilyn's secret affair with Elvis.

I used the coffee for intermission. When Brighton finished repositioning stray strands of his orange hair, he stopped his ticking lip with a finger, swallowed his breath, and said, "I don't assume Blackie told you this?"

"It came from a reliable source."

"Journalists and their reliable sources, plentiful as those secret sauces one learns about in restaurants. Back home London, I've been assailed by those reliable sources more than once."

I let it pass.

"You also mentioned letters last night."

"I did?"

"Come, Mr. Gulliver, too late to play coy with me. In for a penny, in for a pound. Allow me to save time. Did the reliable source say the scenes were to be based on, shall we say, certain letters involving Elvis and Marilyn?''

I made a Sergei Eisenstein face, his to interpret.

Brighton took it affirmatively.

"Did the reliable source show you the letters, perhaps, or say where they might be found?''

I shook my head.

Brighton made a little noise of despair.

He said, "I intend to be straightforward with you, if you give me your word what passes between us keeps between us.'' A vague teetering had encroached on his bedside voice and snapped his air of confidence.

I sipped my coffee and watched Brighton survey the room. He used it like a stage wait while he marshaled his thoughts. "Are we agreed?'' he asked, his voice restored to full strength.

I wanted everything on the table. "What makes you think you can trust me? We barely know each other, and I'm hard pressed to say I trust you, Brighton.''

"Stephanie Marriner,'' Brighton said, disguising a smile.

Had he seen the flinch her name had caused?

Brighton continued, "She trusts you and that's fair enough proof for me. For someone like Stevie, to bestow trust does not come swiftly or irrationally or without merit, but you have it. I understood this instantly night we met. Whatever you may think of Jeremy Brighton, he knows women. That you can depend on. So! Do I have your word?''

People are always asking newspapermen for their word, like words are sold by the pound. Whenever it happens to me, I recall Augie's admonition over the years that resulted in more than one exclusive: You *give* your word. You *keep* a promise.

I nodded assent.

Brighton's shoulders sagged and he gave the appearance of relaxing, but the sweat pebbles irrigating his forehead and forming a mustache below his putty nose showed something else.

As he had done last night, he went back in time to reach the present. I heard how he had visited the MPRE at Spoon's urging. Read *Marilyn Remembers* under Sheridan's supervision. Grasped the play's potential. Drove a hard bargain to tie up the rights.

Now that I'd given my word, there was more to the story.

"Marilyn, a magical name, Mr. Gulliver. A love goddess for memory, for myth, forever," Brighton explained unnecessarily. "I entertained no doubt a production would do quite well. To strike a better bargain, I hid my enthusiasm and maneuvered Blackie into the sweaty position of selling me hard. When it appeared failure was knocking at his door, he revealed his secret about Elvis and Marilyn. I have seen enough zircon my time to spot real diamonds when they come along. This one was larger anything Dickie Burton ever purchased for Liz. All I could do to keep my trousers dry before asking Blackie he was ready to include those scenes in the play, in order for us to have a deal. He made out like he was agonizing over the thought, but I knew how badly he wanted to direct and waited him out. Finally, he offered to trade off, the scenes for the right to direct."

Brighton's expression begged appreciation for his negotiating skills. I slapped cream cheese on the other half of my bagel and reached for the jam jars. Offered him a look that encouraged him to tell me something I did not already know. He played with his face and continued.

"At once, I had a horrid thought. What if Blackie invented the story about Elvis and Marilyn to win me over? I told him I needed proof. He grew quite angry and we traded back and forth. When he saw how firmly I held my ground, he revealed there were love letters to back up his claim.

"Dear God! Love letters! This was a whole cache of diamonds, Mr. Gulliver. There were tremendous sums to be made mining those letters. I don't have to remind you there are newspapers ready to pay a small fortune for love letters exchanged by Marilyn Monroe and Elvis Presley. A small fortune? Barely a tidy sum compared to what the letters can bring at auction.

"Think of Jacqueline Kennedy Onassis. An old cigar box sold for more than half a million? A set of golf clubs sold for almost three quarters of a million? Who would have thought? Marilyn and Elvis, that same league, greater for the pair, Mr. Gulliver. And all Blackie Sheridan cared about was directing his little play."

"And you encouraged him."

"Sincerely and gladly and knowing it put me within reach of the letters."

"But you never got them."

An exasperated sigh. "I proceeded to rehearsals on Blackie's assurance they would be forthcoming. They were not where he could put his hands on them immediately, he said, and it was always one thing after another. He would quote from his new scenes to prove good faith, but the scenes were never satisfactorily finished for him to deliver something on paper.

"At the risk of embarrassing myself, I'll tell you it began to seem I may have been taken in. He denied it, of course, so I gave him an ultimatum: forty-eight hours to deliver the letters and the scenes or I was calling off our deal. I had an iron-clad contract give me rights in perpetuity. I guaranteed Blackie his play would not see light of day—ever—he failed come through." He acknowledged himself with a look and poked a thick finger at his temple.

"How did he respond?"

"As you might suppose. More excuses, but he understood I meant to stand by my threat. Later that same evening, during rehearsal, he exchanged words with Stevie and stormed from the theater. Stevie left, too, more upset than I'd ever seen her. I waited about, supposing it was one of Blackie's usual tantrums. And hers. And, they'd return due course.

"Instead, after about an hour, he rang me up to say he had the letters and I was welcome to come fetch them in the morning. I was understandably delirious with joy and had my best night's sleep in weeks.

"The next morning, I turned on the telly to learn Blackie had been murdered and Stevie the prime suspect." I started to speak, but Brighton put me off with a motion. "Although my first thought was Stevie may have killed Blackie from anger, I did not believe it for a moment, actually, and a phone call later in the day set me straight—a strange voice saying he had the Elvis and Marilyn love letters and they were mine for a price."

"He." My pulse was sending anxious messages.

"It could easily have been a she. The voice was muffled and distorted, but exact in its demands. I was welcome to the letters for one hundred thousand dollars, arrangements for delivery to be made immediately I agreed. That's it, you see? Blackie was killed for those letters."

"Only a hundred thousand, when the letters could be worth millions?"

Brighton made a go-figure face. "One does not stare down a bargain, Mr. Gulliver."

"The hundred grand investment you wanted from Stevie."

"Yes, precisely. Are you wondering why I didn't simply withdraw that amount from my accounts?" He surveyed the room for eavesdroppers. "I'm a tad short funds right now, you must know, given recent reversals I shan't belabor. It would take me time organizing that amount, where I was certain Stevie had it with the flick of her signature. I was too anxious to risk delaying the deal and see the letters fall into other hands." His voice lowered two notches. "Not at all unusual for me, Mr. Gulliver. I have managed to build an extraordinarily successful career by my own wits and other people's money."

Brighton's look invited applause. I wondered to myself if people like this knew how easy they are to dislike, or if they care. I needed Brighton, so I forced a smile, and he smiled back like he'd bought it, both of us knowing better.

I said, "When I mentioned Elvis and the letters, you thought I had them or I knew who had them or—"

"Stevie had them or knew who had them," Brighton finished the thought. "She was at Blackie's that night. It's reasonable to assume that if she didn't kill him, she saw who did."

"The way you assume his killer was after the love letters?"

"Precisely."

"What if your caller doesn't have the love letters but was bluffing? What if he couldn't find them after he killed Blackie and they're still in Sheridan's cottage?"

"Are they?"

I shrugged.

Brighton pushed back against the booth and weighed me for sincerity. Sent a noise from his throat. "Your reliable source wouldn't know?" We exchanged stares while the waiter poured me another coffee. "It's worth your while for us to approach this situation together," he said, eventually.

"What does that mean?"

"Come, Mr. Gulliver." Brighton puffed out his cheeks and sucked in the room. Brooded over a sigh. "Putting it out to you straight. I want those letters for my reasons, you need them for yours. Help me to acquire them. They'll get Stevie off the hook by revealing Blackie Sheridan's killer and I'll cut you in for a proper share of the proceeds, auction and all." He looked at me questioningly.

"You mean cut Stevie in."

"Whatever you choose to do with your share is your business, Mr. Gulliver. The play and the career opportunities it represents is all Stevie's purchasing from me. I suppose her gratitude might satisfy some of your own dreams for the future."

I wanted to decorate Brighton's peep-show grin with a fist. My knuckles went white in my lap. I forced myself to keep them there.

"Did your caller say when you'd hear from him again?"

"Only to expect a call in due course."

"When he calls, agree to whatever the terms are and let me know immediately."

"We have a deal, then, I take it?"

He leaned forward and extended a hand. It was wet to the touch. "Good. Delighted. What's our next step, partner?"

Partner.

The thought was chalk scraping across a blackboard, but the alternative to his game was cutting off a source of information.

I grinned back and said, "How much of this does Laura Dane know?"

Brighton pondered the question and finally decided, "I wonder myself. More than Laura lets on?"

"Why?"

"Straightaway I learned what I did from Blackie, I looked her up. I remembered her often carrying on about Marilyn on the telly, Carson, and thought she could be helpful. Always room for a technical advisor." He gave the term a salacious twist. "Laura has been helpful at that. Knows her stuff and had been correcting details Blackie got wrong."

"And you mentioned the letters to her?"

"Indirectly at first."

"Pillow talk."

"I am a cautious man, Mr. Gulliver. I trust only myself. It becomes laborious after that. Laura didn't bring them up, or anything about Elvis, so neither did I. I kept hoping her need to tell stories would spill over onto those subjects . . . something to brag on, but so far—"

"When did you say something to her?"

"When it appeared Blackie could not or would not deliver as promised."

"What did she say?"

"She said Blackie was lying. There were no letters because there never was any romance between Marilyn and Elvis."

"She was certain."

"She was persuasive, but there's an element of doubt back here." He patted the orange fluff at the base of his neck. "Her response came too anxious and too easy. After Blackie's murder and the phone call, I put the question to her again. Somebody having a poke at my backside Laura claims, only that."

"Were she and Sheridan friends?"

"From the old days. He didn't want Laura coming around at first but learned to tolerate her after I insisted, and because Laura didn't mind acting as his driver, I suppose."

"His driver?"

"Gimpy leg, you know? War injury, he claimed. Dragged it after him like it weighed a ton, and an odd prick-handled cane for support. Somebody from the MPRE dropped him off and Laura delivered him back."

"Did she take him back the night of the murder?"

"Yes, chased after him following his outburst, but if you are thinking what I suppose, it leads to a dead end. I drove to Laura's flat after I gave up waiting and she was back in normal fashion. Only time to drop Blackie off and come home, as usual."

"You often drove to her flat?"

"Often." His expression played with the obvious, daring me not to understand the relationship. "Her technical advice. Unlike any I have ever received. Like a woman half her age."

"When she returned, what did she have to say?"

"Only how Blackie had complained the whole trip."

"About what?"

"What is it any director complains about? Everything and everyone, so Laura turned up the radio and drowned him out. She dropped him by the doorstep and that was that."

"She said."

"Yes. She said."

"You think she knows something she hasn't shared."

"You ask her. Comes to that, you are the professional, Mr. Gulliver. Anything she's keeping from me, you might be able to pry from her." He arched an eyebrow, in case I didn't get both his meanings.

"You have her phone number?"

"Better."

He got our waiter's attention and made a phone of his thumb and pinkie. The waiter returned with a plug-in. Brighton shortly was spewing pleasantries into the mouthpiece, cupped for privacy.

"She'll expect you anytime after eight o'clock," he said, replacing the receiver. He retrieved a leather-covered memo pad and his Mont Blanc pen from an inside jacket pocket, wrote out her address and phone number, and pushed it at me.

"Laura may offer you more than cocktails and conversation, Mr. Gulliver. As my lady friend is one to kiss and tell, like that Monica Lewinsky girl, I'll take no offense whatsoever if you, what's that expression?, get it on?" Laughing like he meant it. "We are, after all, partners?" Ha-ha-ha. "I'd have suggested meeting at the theater, but we'll not be back there until after the weekend. Stevie's flu, you know?"

"Stevie's what flu?" I challenged spontaneously. If she had the flu, the *Bedrooms and Board Rooms* office or certainly Sanberg would have said something to me.

"The flu her doctor rang me up about yesterday, obliging me to cancel rehearsal. Another message earlier this morning, saying she still was much too ill to consider rehearsals, at least until Monday, when he'll know better." He eyed me curiously. "She does have the flu?"

I said I'd forgotten and changed the subject.

Brighton made a show of accepting my explanation and, while his vacant gaze shared nothing, his manner made clear I wasn't fooling him, or that he believed for a minute trust would be a hallmark of our "partnership."

I left him about ten minutes later.

He gave me another wet handshake and angled off to invade a booth across the room, where Whitney Houston and a lamp-tanned agent-type looked up from their conversation and smiled gamely at him, knowing they were trapped.

I rushed for one of the lobby phones.

A call to Brighton from Stevie's doctor this morning, *this morning!* had to mean she was alright wherever she was, safe and well, and maybe the doctor knew where.

First, I dialed my own number, hoping to hear her voice on the machine. Other callers, mostly sales pitches, but not Stevie. I found the doctor's number in the phone book. A nurse told me it was his golf day, she didn't know which club this time, and, no, she knew nothing about Stevie's flu.

I called Jimmy Steiger to brief him.

He interrupted me.

"I took a run by *Bedrooms and Board Rooms*," he said. "They told me about Stevie's flu, and something else. Stevie's dressing room door. Somebody cracked it during the night. Other signs she was snatched from there."

"But the doctor."

"I'll see if I can run him down," Jimmy promised. "A doctor on a golf course. Only slightly better than a dirty white Mazda on the road."

This time his sarcasm evaded me.

"If she's been harmed in any way—"

"Stop it, Neil! Stay on the mountain. Anything wrong, I'll be there to go off the mountain with you," Jimmy said, too calmly to be kidding.

Two minutes later, I saw the Mazda.

I had followed the winding garden path past the bungalows back to my car. Sunshine was eating through the remains of the early morning dew as I climbed behind the wheel.

I turned the key and, in the same moment, saw the Mazda parked across Crescent Drive. White. Dirty. Obscured license plate. Definitely the Mazda.

Empty—

Because the man I assumed was the driver was now rapping at my passenger window. His smile said one thing. The .45 he was pointing at me said something else. He was using it to signal me to unlock the door.

He was probably half a head taller than me, disproportionate like a body builder. His neck was the size of a couch and refused the top button of his dress shirt. His tie was hanging loose and dragged down his appearance as much as the blue blazer pulling at the seams and too tight to button at the midriff.

Otherwise, Blue Blazer's appearance was ordinary. He had a bland, midthirties face that made no impression, except for teeth too white to be natural and a barely noticeable scar that may have resulted from childhood surgery to correct a harelip. Marine-cut dark hair. Whirlpool eyes. I knew I could take him in a fair fight, because that's what wishful thinking is all about.

Something distracted him. A dog on a long leash, a pampered French poodle with dozens of pink ribbons in her hair trying to climb his leg, her matronly owner, equally pampered and mouthing commands for the poodle to stop. She saw the automatic before he hid it inside his jacket. Froze. Threw up her hands. Dropped her Vuitton bag and the leash. Stared mutely as the poodle raced down Crescent Drive toward Sunset, and—

Blue Blazer fled for his car.

I gunned the Jag and played bumper cars in clearing the space, intent on tracking him and, this time, trapping him.

He was gone by the time I hit the lane.

I drove aimlessly for about fifteen minutes, bringing my heart back below the speed limit and making sure I wasn't being followed before I once again tried to store Stevie in the back of my mind and headed for Venice Beach and a drop-in on someone I hadn't seen in years.

Sunset Beaudry said Elvis and Marilyn had had a love affair.

Laura Dane had told Brighton they didn't.

If Hank Twitchell was home, he could be the tie-breaker.

And a key to the love letters?

Hank Twitchell lived behind Ocean Front Walk on Hurricane Avenue in a planked wood shanty smelling of dry rot and ocean, like so many other places in the neighborhood that were worthless today, except as real estate.

At least, I expected he was still there, twenty-one years after the death of his pal, Elvis.

It had been Hank's home for a dozen years when we sat down to talk after "The King" died. We got along well enough for Hank to help grease my way inside Graceland when I expressed interest in going to Memphis for the funeral. Country music was our common denominator. I knew enough about Western swing, Hank Williams and the Opry, Sun Records, and country's debt to race music to make him comfortable, but Hank's taciturn nature got in the way of his adding to what I'd already learned about Elvis.

He always spoke slowly, polishing a thought in sentences that began in the middle and worked out in both directions, not always making sense to anyone but himself, or so his intelligent eyes signaled. We wound up spending social hours together, too, and I always left him wondering if it was his nature or an act.

Hank was in his late fifties then. Half his life and most of his career had been spent with Elvis. They'd met when Elvis went to New York to sign his first music publishing deal. Hank worked for the publishing company and there was some instant chemistry between them, because he was sitting behind Elvis and the colonel when their jet took off for LA.

Hank had worked from a small office on the sixth floor of the old RCA Building on Sunset near Vine, two doors down from Colonel Parker, until a year after Elvis's death, when both of them were invited to leave on short notice.

So far as I knew he was still the only confidant who had not cashed in with a tell-all book. One evening he dug out from the back of a kitchen drawer a book contract that would have paid him an advance of two million dollars.

I wondered, "Why not? If the money's that good, you can bet everybody else will be writing about Elvis."

He barely mulled the point. "Then there's no need for mine, is there?"

It took fifteen minutes to find a parking spot and another ten to locate Hank's place in the middle of the block. It was squeezed out of sight between two narrow, dilapidated apartment buildings that weren't there in seventy-seven, sitting at an angle and half off its foundation.

What remained of the faded brown paint was peeling. Cardboard squares filled busted windowpanes. The angled roof had lost most of its wooden shingles. A mud garden laced with cans and bottles had replaced the lovingly tended lawn and orderly stretches of colorful flowers I remembered. A single-car garage barely stood at the rear of the property line at the end of a slender driveway protected by a fat, rusted metal bar locked into place between two steel poles. One of the doors hung by a hinge. Both had been spray-painted with gang names in primary colors.

The bell didn't work.

Rapping on the door, I wondered if Hank ever had regretted passing on the book offer. After another minute, the door creaked open half the length of the chain latch.

"Neil Gulliver," Hank said, his banana-ripe voice swelling with delight, as sprightly and familiar as yesterday. "Wondered when you'd think to come over."

"You sound like you've been expecting me, Hank."

"Just so happens I have, son."

There was half a pot of coffee in one of those old-fashioned metal percolators simmering on a gas six-burner that must have been built before Sears met Roebuck. By the time I'd filled two ceramic mugs and returned to the living room, Hank had changed from his pajamas and robe into work jeans and a lumberjack shirt that hung loose over the sway belly that disrupted his otherwise rail thin frame.

He wore his age elegantly for someone in his late seventies, except for earlobe flaps and the discreet gold band dangling from the left one. His strong blue eyes were vigilant behind half-moon glasses perched on a finely etched nose. A trim, modified gray and white goatee hid all but the fierce cheekbones on fissured, liver-spotted parchment skin showing the effects of too many tans over the years.

Hank's shoulder-length, silver-gray hair was pasted back from a widow's peak that had retreated an inch or two from his crevassed forehead, the same way he may have shrunk an inch in height in the intervening years.

He raised his mug for a toast to go with eyes glistening with good intentions and a Santa Claus smile that exposed two uneven rows of nicotine-stained teeth. "A sight for sore eyes," he decided, padding across the faded carpet of the claustrophobic room to a cracked and chipped, carmine-colored leather easy chair that hissed under his weight.

He sipped the coffee for taste, signaled a thumbs-up, and assumed a whimsical expression that informed me it was my place to begin the conversation. Time had not made him less cautious.

The coffee was strong and had the instant caffeine kick of freshly roasted beans. I answered his raised thumb with mine and refitted myself into a corner of the couch so we shared a sight line. I pondered how much he knew and might share with me about Elvis and Marilyn, given he was yet to explain how or why he knew I'd be dropping by.

The room was neat, well tended. Simply furnished. The only visible clues to Hank's past were erratic rows of framed gold records filling the half wall along a corridor leading to the bedroom and two framed photographs on the wall strip between curtained picture windows.

In the faded photo, a moonfaced girl about five or six years old sat astride a sassy pony with bows in its tail in front of a tenement stoop showing melting signs of a recent snow. Her hands held onto the brim of a cowboy hat too big for her. Her eyes were cautious, her smile too nervous to be real.

I could only suppose who she was and how she fit into Hank's life, whereas I recognized the crafty face of the man in the other photo, Colonel Parker, bobbing in a swimming pool with only his head above the water, teeth bared and locked onto a cigar, mock fierce visage daring the world to dispute his presence.

"Pretty much like I remember the place," I said, breaking the silence. "Warm and hospitable."

"You had to think the worst after you saw the outside," he said, and smiled impishly. "Confuses the burglars. They take one look at the mess I designed for outside and figure there's gotta be better pickin's down the road. The streets were safe once upon a time, but, lately, they're as much a part of the undeclared war as anywhere else." The floor lamp cast Hank's face in a curious orange glow.

I nodded agreement.

The side table was piled with used paperbacks, the corners curling back from constant thumbing. A large green glass ashtray was full of the brown and broken stumps of cigarillos, like the Sherman he lit now. He took a healthy drag, puffed out his cheeks, and pushed out a jet stream. The odor dissipated quickly into the intoxicating ocean smell that was as much a part of the wallpaper as the English manor countryside it portrayed.

"I finally made good on my promise to quit, Hank." Making small talk. Creeping toward the reason for my visit.

He said, "I remember you with a butt always dangling from the side of your mouth. The cancer scare?"

I nodded.

"I also thought about quitting," he said, taking a fresh drag. "Especially after the doctors took one of my lungs. How's that for a warning signal?" He raised an eyebrow and an amused look crowded his sharply angled face. "Ease up, Neil. I'm fine, really. You know how long John Wayne lasted with one lung?"

"Nine years," I answered, too quickly, like a quiz show contestant. I regretted it at once. I had no idea when Hank had undergone surgery. My cheeks heated with dismay, but he didn't give me a chance to apologize.

Instead, he glanced away and made a show of doing his own math. After a few moments, he turned back and said somberly, "On that basis I've been dead for a year and a half."

He exploded into hearty laughter that seemed ready to go on forever before it turned into a coughing jag that told a sadder truth about his health, not visible in his appearance. Another moment and we were staring at each other again. Hank had never been one for small talk, and appeal registered in his eyes. All the while, a kitchen radio had been playing in the background, tuned to KZLA, the country music station. The new Garth Brooks hit faded out and we caught ourselves listening to Randy Travis, who had dominated the charts until Brooks came along.

I remarked about the fickleness of the record-buying public. Hank was comfortable with a subject he knew well. We talked that way for a while. A Vince Gill record faded into a commercial, the commercial into Billy Ray Cyrus.

"You ever see him on television, Hank?"

"The Nashville Network."

"Billy Ray moves like you-know-who."

"No," he said, gently, his eyes letting me know he was offended by the comparison.

"I hear a lot of people say that."

"People say lots of things anymore."

"I heard a new one the other day." Hank smiled. He put down his coffee mug and waited for me to finish the thought. "Never mind. It's too stupid to even repeat." He crossed his legs and body-wrapped his arms in a way that let him scratch imaginary itches. "About Elvis and Marilyn Monroe? A love affair?"

Hank took it calmly. He considered the two names, playing them against one wall and then the other with his eyes. Rejecting them with a slight shake of the head, he gridlocked his fingers and decided, "Yes, too stupid to repeat."

"Too stupid to be true, Hank?"

He pretended to think about it. Maybe he was deciding what to tell me. His look gave away nothing. He said, "You ever wonder why people can't leave the past alone?"

"All the time. I usually decide it's because the present gets so painful, we need to escape to where we think we can't be hurt anymore."

He rewarded the thought with a smile. "Sometimes the past is where the real pain is, the hurts that keep on giving. In the present there's a chance to stop the pain before it starts."

"Becoming a philosopher so late in life, Hank?"

He shook his head. "Learning to share is all."

"The past or the pain?"

"A little of both, maybe." He sat erect, as if snapping out of a nap, and exercised a crick from his neck. "Why do you want to talk about this so many years down the road? I'd hate thinking you're into that kind of journalism now."

"You know better."

"Even if I didn't, I would. The Blackie Sheridan murder and your former wife suspected of killing him. You'd have to live on another planet not to know what's going on, so I get the Marilyn part, but Elvis?"

"Too stupid to be true, Hank?"

A flip of the wrist. "You were around after El passed on. You stumbled onto a shitload of women, movie stars and otherwise, in the course of business, so I ask you, Don't you think you would of found out about Marilyn Monroe, if she was one?"

"You were awfully good at hiding what you didn't want me to find, Hank, even after we agreed on ground rules that let us be a hundred per cent honest with each other. If it makes a difference now, the same ground rules apply."

A smile tilted the corners of his mouth upward. "Hell, son, with or without our rules, I only ever cribbed on what there was no cause for the world to learn is all, remember?"

"Like Elvis and Marilyn?"

"I see you still got a stubborn streak."

"When it comes to family and friends." His body stiffened, as if he sensed where I was going with the thought. "Reminds me, Hank. How's that boy of yours?"

His smile turned forlorn. He knew all right. I was about to collect on a debt. It's nothing I do as a rule. I like to believe you get as good as you give without forcing the issue. Sometimes, circumstance obliges otherwise.

A year or so after Elvis died, Hank's fourteen-year-old son, Roy, had come back from Italy, where he had been living with his mother and her second husband, a director of spaghetti westerns. Roy had developed a smack habit. His mother, unable or unwilling to cope any longer, bought him a one-way ticket and scooped him into an Alitalia jet to LAX.

When the vice squad arrested Roy for lubing West Hollywood johns to support his hundred-dollar-a-day craving, Hank phoned me. He knew I'd made some great contacts through *Rolling Stone*. I made a few strategic calls and helped get the kid out on his own recognizance and into a Riverside rehab hospital. Last I'd heard from Hank, Roy was clean and doing fine in school.

"He's dead," Hank said with an edge of wonderment. He turned to stare at the photos by the door, as if he were making certain they knew, too. Colonel Parker and the girl on the pony.

"Christ! I didn't . . . I—"

He held me off with a hand.

"It didn't make much of a splash," he said. "Roy come out of that place you arranged for and both of us worked at keeping him straight. It took because he wanted it bad as me.

"He went off to a movie with friends one night, and after they went for burgers and fries. Heading back to the parking lot, a car rolled on by and slowed long enough for the bastard in the passenger seat to take my son Roy's life with a shotgun."

"I don't know how I missed the—"

"What would you of said or done? Anything you could of said or done to bring Roy back to life? They never caught the one who did it, so I suppose I will never find out why he chose my boy." Hank took off his glasses, rubbed at his eyes. "You were asking about Elvis and Marilyn Monroe," he said, and turned back to me.

"It's not necessary, Hank. We don't—"

"We do," he said, forcing a smile. "I still owe you one."

"Not now, this way. I can come back—"

"It don't never get any better'n this for me, son."

Hank refilled our mugs, then sank into the easy chair and stretched and overlapped his stringbean legs. He rolled the mug between his palms occasionally, rinsed out his mouth and finger-dried his whiskers while I told him what I had heard from Sunset Beaudry:

Elvis filming *Love Me Tender,* Marilyn *Bus Stop*. They meet. The affair takes off, helped by Sunset, Elvis's boyhood hero and setside confidant, who covers for him whenever he sneaks away to meet Marilyn. Zanuck finds out. He summarily orders the Colonel and Reg Mowry to put an end to the romance before the two careers are destroyed. The affair ends.

Hank listened with closed eyes to forty-year-old memories.

Every so often, I saw the flicker of a smile or some harsher judgment, or heard a heavy breath pushed out in response to one of the old Range Roper's allegations, the heaviest reserved for the notion that Elvis was responsible for Sheridan's death.

"How'd he come to figure that?" Hank said, trying to sound bemused, but I felt he knew where the question would take us.

"Sheridan told Sunset he was adding scenes to his play that would expose the affair. At dinner a week or two later, he tells Sunset the scenes have caused problems. He says he's scared."

"Like what problems?"

"Sheridan wouldn't spell them out, and a short time later he's murdered."

"By Elvis." This time he let me see the smile.

"Your reaction is about the same as mine was when Sunset told me, Hank. He's absolutely convinced it's *because* of Elvis. Somebody protecting Elvis's memory."

"It appears Sunset don't do much reading. If he did, he'd know there isn't much left of El's memory to protect. Marilyn, neither. Just stirring the waters, ol' Sunset."

"You haven't said yet if it's true, Hank. Were they having an affair?"

"Would it make a difference?"

"Yes."

"Anything left to tell me?" he said.

"Not yet."

"I ever tell you how they were going to call that picture *The Reno Brothers,* almost to the day production got going? El was one of the Renos, of course, and Dick Egan was another. Sunset, I think he played one of the soldiers who winds up killing Elvis with Neville Brand. El looked good in his Confederate uniform, acted good, too. Worked damn hard at it, trying to impress the producer. The producer was the same one who did *Rebel without a Cause* with James Dean, and El always went out of his way to prove he should be the one to play Dean if the producer ever decided to do a movie of his life. El idolized Dean, more than he did Sunset Beaudry, and that's saying a mouthful." He raised the coffee mug above his head to emphasize the point.

"You're ducking my question, Hank."

He took exaggerated offense, left palm over his heart and the other hand outstretched, then wondered slyly, "Do I recall you saying there's something you haven't yet told me?"

"The same way you haven't said how you knew to expect me."

"You go first."

"I've already gone first," I said.

He closed his eyes and thought for a moment or two. "You remember what 'Love Me Tender' replaced on the charts as number one? Two songs, actually, back-to-back hits. 'Don't Be Cruel' and 'Hound Dog.' They were in the top spot eleven weeks. Eleven weeks was a record, son. Maybe, still is. Haven't checked in years."

Hank cocked his head and picked under his fingernails, arched his eyebrows and gave me an analytical stare, knowing he had me. "Your turn to go first again."

I answered with a finger salute and my best Steve McQueen grin, then repeated Augie's ideas about love letters and how his suspicions had been confirmed by Jeremy Brighton.

Even before I finished, Hank was searching the room for guidance. He pushed himself from the easy chair and came around the coffee table to join me on the couch.

"It's the truth about El and Marilyn," he said. He sat with an arm using his belly as a table, a hand guarding his mouth. His voice conspiratorial. "But not all of it, Neil."

He fished out a fresh Sherman, found a match, watched the smoke trail dissolve before confiding the details.

"I wouldn't call it a real romance, and maybe affair would be too strong. A fling. It lasted a couple of months and then it was history. She came after him like a hurricane in a hurry. I don't have to explain what kind of an impression it made on a youngster like El, although he already could have his pick of the girls, to have this ripe sex goddess ready to park her body beneath his.

"He counted on Sunset to find safe places for them to meet. Sunset's trailer usually, although Sunset had to be more creative whenever Colonel Parker was nosing around the set.

"The Colonel was my responsibility. My job was to steer him away or send out a warning signal to El if he got too close. I wasn't too good at it, but I knew the Colonel would discover the truth sooner or later, anyway. Man had a sixth sense. For a time, he thought about picking up a phone and calling the news wires, but after he weighed the publicity against the damage it could do to El's career, he sat down with Reg Mowry and they did what had to be done to kill the story. Forty some-odd years, and it takes a murder to get people talking again . . ."

I caught his inquiring stare as his voice trailed off.

"How do you explain Laura Dane?" I asked. "To hear her tell it, she was Marilyn's best friend and they whored around together. Yet, she says there was nothing between Marilyn and Elvis."

"Goes to show you how well the secret was kept. Best I can do for you with that one, Neil."

"Tell me about the love letters."

"Son, aren't any letters to talk about."

I must have bolted when Hank said that. I became aware of his hand pushing down on my shoulder. An instant later, he was patting out *all right* on my thigh, the way my grandpa used to do.

I said, "Brighton?"

He shook his head again. "Somebody playing games with him, same as Blackie Sheridan did. I know that whacks holy hell out of your hopes for finding such love letters and getting your ex off the hook, but what is is, son."

I searched Hank's eyes for another answer. They were clear and unflinching. He shook his head. I rose and stalked the room, with one hand in my pocket, the other gesturing to thoughts I had not figured out how to express. Hank's smile was supportive.

I tried an idea on him. "You and I were talking secrets. If there were letters, why would you or anyone have to know? They could have stayed a secret between Elvis and Marilyn—"

"And the United States Post Office?" I had to strain to hear him. "I told you it never got so serious, at least, not with El. From what I saw, he got tired of her after the mystery was gone. The same with her, probably. Elvis was no great lover, Neil, but on that fact you will just have to take my word. A couple months and then—"

Hank gestured, made a noise like he was popping a balloon. He moved from the couch to my side. He ran an arm across my back and squeezed me closer, dropped his voice lower.

"I'm going to share something only a few people knew outside of El's immediate family. The Colonel knew, and I found out in a roundabout way. The public record shows that Elvis Aaron Presley graduated from L. C. Humes High School in Memphis, and that he was a so-so student. He could read and write, but not either as well as he could sing, if you get my drift. Also, humble as he truly was, El had an ego.

"If I show you a man who had trouble with a postcard saying he was having a wonderful time and wished you were there, are you prepared to tell me he'd risk making himself out a laughingstock by writing love letters, love letters, dear Lord, to anyone, much less a world famous star?

"On my dear son's grave, Neil, I swear there are no Elvis or Marilyn love letters to talk about, that's how certain I am."

I said abruptly, "How did you know to expect me here, Hank?" He thought about it for a moment, grinned, and surrendered his hands. "Does the name Paige Jahnsen mean anything to you?"

Two hours later, back home, I snapped on the lights to the immediate sense somebody was there. Any cop or newspaperman or badge can tell you how presence changes the weight and volume of any enclosed area and propels waves of normally static air against your face.

I felt it now.

Backing out fast and banging on neighbors' doors until someone let me in to roust security would have been the wise thing to do.

Instead, I reached for the Maltese Falcon replica on the mail table in the entry hall and hefted it like a brick. The statuette weighed about six pounds, enough to bust a cheekbone.

I inched forward.

Even before taking a cautious peek into the front room, I caught the fragrance of recognition. I knew I wouldn't be needing the black bird and replaced it on the table.

Stevie.

A two-ton gorilla fled my back.

She was asleep on the couch, contorting fitfully, wrestling for a comfortable position, snoring the way she did whenever she was troubled. I pushed out a sigh of relief and melted into the easy chair.

I leaned forward, arms resting on my thighs, hands clasped, and studied her inside the blanket of daylight racing through the unguarded window.

She was wearing black stirrup pants that hugged the curve of her long legs and a matching lambswool turtleneck top that punctuated the rhythm of her breathing.

Her blond hair was unharnessed, veiling much of the exposed side of her face, unlined in repose, and making her more than a memory of the kid I had once romanced. The smell of her favorite perfume, Obsession, lingered in the air.

I leaned closer and the chair creaked. She stirred and her eyes sputtered open. They were more a sparkling yellow than green in the light and captivating in their intensity as she maneuvered to get her bearings.

"Hi, honey," she said, her throat still full of sleep. She finger-brushed silken strands of hair off her face and held me with a wistful smile. I felt we had retreated to a scene played out a million times years ago, before the divorce. "What time?" she asked, working the sand from her eyes.

I smiled and blew her a kiss. She tossed it back, as if she also were lost in time. Until she remembered something. And her smile evaporated. And the nostalgia lesson was over.

Stevie pushed herself off the couch, stepped over, settled onto my lap with one arm across my back, brushed her lips against my face, and begged, "Help me, please?" Her tears spilled onto my cheek while she told me what had happened.

I got this feeling we were being followed home from the playhouse. Not that I saw anything, honey, just a feeling. It could have been some paparazzi, it could have been nothing. He wanted to come up, Monte, but—the truth? I thought it could be you following us, so I didn't want to stir the pot any more than it was already."

I shook my head.

"I know. Next day, going to the set, the same feeling, only this time I spot a car. It's parked about a half block down from the house and it pulls out after me."

"A Mazda. Dirty. White."

She looked at me curiously. I motioned for her to continue.

"The Mazda goes through a couple of reds in order to keep up and that's what tips me for sure. I do some lane changing and braking that lets me get a good look at him. When the light changes, the bastard lizard-tongues me, fires a finger gun, and splits."

I described the gunman in the blue blazer.

Stevie said, "Maybe you should be doing the explaining?"

"Not yet. Tell me the rest."

"I tell myself it's just another one of those obsessed fans who maybe belongs in deep analysis, only he had a cold look that absolutely terrified me, honey. I barely got through blocking and the run-through, is how scared I had made myself."

"Why didn't you call me then? Right then?"

"So you could laugh at me? Besides, he can't get past studio security, and I could have Monte follow me home after we did notes and sushi. After taping, I'm in my dressing room and I figure the knock on the door is Monte. I call him in, only it's the guy from the Mazda. The bastard pushes me back inside the room and locks the door. He's bigger than a fortress and I'm grade A scared.

"He wants to know where the letters are. I ask him, *'What the crap you talking about?'* He says, *'You know what, bitch,'* and aims a gun in my face. I say, *'Oh, you mean those letters. Why didn't you say so?'* I point him to the walk-in closet. *'Top shelf, behind the scripts,'* I tell him, like I know what the hell he's after. I make like I'll go and get them. He waves me down with the gun and goes over himself.

"Now's my chance, right? I'm out of there faster than you can say Jack Shit. He's right behind me, chasing me through the empty hallways. I'm screaming, and there's nobody around to hear me. I'm looking for an exit that will get me to the parking lot, only I don't have my car keys. They're in my purse which is back in the dressing room.

"I make it inside a supply closet, turn the dead bolt, and pee in a bucket, shaking harder than the official Brazilian maraca team, and fall asleep standing like a broom because I'm too scared to do anything else.

"I don't know how many hours go by, but I open the door a crack and suck up the rug dust and go back to my dressing room for my keys. I call you, and that's when the Incredible Hulk breaks in. Right away, he's on me like cheap cologne.

"I struggle a hand free. Yank off his earring. He starts to howl and rain blood and I somehow get loose and kick him in the balls. You always told me that would work, and it always does."

"Do I know from balls or what?"

"When it comes to a ball, nobody better."

Stevie had been clinging to me like tinsel on a Christmas tree. She managed her first smile since starting the story and released another avalanche of tears.

"I grabbed my bag and got the hell out of there," she said. "I jumped into the Cherokee and split, thinking about heading for the nearest police station, when the radio tells me the district attorney is about to issue an arrest warrant, thanks to a damn grand jury indictment. Not exactly *Entertainment Tonight*, honey. I drove around. For hours. I got onto the Hollywood Freeway and, zip . . . Go with the flow. Next I know I'm in San Diego. *San Diego!* Can you believe?

"I stopped at a gas station and called my doctor to have him call Brighton and cancel me out of rehearsals and call the studio and tell them. It's the pro thing to do. You don't just not show up, not if you're a pro, right? After, I crossed over the bridge to the island and parked. Stared at the sailboats for hours. I freaked, worried the next cruiser in my rearview would be a cop flashing red, asking me one question too many, so I headed back."

"To me."

"To you."

"Monte Sanberg?"

"To you, honey. Don't ask me why, please? Monte, he's okay, but you, you're—family. *Family!*" My heart skipped a beat. "My mom and her current are doing Europe again and I could of holed up at their place, but I didn't want to be alone, you know?" She ran her hand over my head, squeezed gently at the tension knotting my neck. "Besides, I knew the cops were more likely to check there than here, us being divorced and all."

"Where'd you stash the Jeep?"

"Behind your Jag. I slid through the parking gate behind a Honda. You weren't here, but I never gave you back the spare key. I went berserk, sat down to think about everything, what to do next, and then you were here. You were here, honey."

Stevie kissed my cheek and steered my face around so she could reach my lips. Familiar touch, dry and electric. I was hungry for more. Wondered if she was, too. I was certain I saw the question burning inside her half-closed eyes, but I pulled away. It wasn't a thank you I wanted or needed. She understood, smiled back wistful understanding.

While Stevie showered and freshened up, I made her a light meal of vegetable soup, cheeses, and what was left of the French bread. She swept through everything without her usual cautions about diet and figure. I sat by her at the counter, sipping a Heineken and wondering if the law could hold me as an accessory to murder, as well as harboring a fugitive.

She sensed my thoughts.

"I could turn myself in, hon. I could call my lawyer and—" I reached over and shielded her mouth. "Don't mean for you to get into trouble be—" I replaced my hand and underneath felt the grateful smile.

I got up and led the way to the couch with her coffee and my beer. I angled into a corner. She settled into the opposite side, one leg tucked under the other, while I told her about my meeting with Brighton and what Hank Twitchell had to say, and our mutual assailant.

Stevie had scrubbed her face clean but couldn't wash off the worry lines or rinse away the bloodshot eyes. The lines had deepened and spread by the time I finished.

"He came after us for love letters written by Marilyn and Elvis? He thinks we have them?"

"It looks that way. One or both of us. Probably you, since his note told me not to get in the way."

She shivered. "Somebody put him up to it?"

"He didn't get our names out of a raffle bin."

"Who?"

"Whoever murdered Blackie Sheridan. The killer was after the love letters. When he didn't find them, he came after you because you were also there that night and a logical candidate. I was the afterthought."

"Jesus, honey! I didn't ever mean for you to get into any—" I touched my hand to her mouth. She warmed me with her look and ran an anxious hand around my thigh. She said, "What about the Twitchell person saying Elvis and Marilyn made love, but there were no love letters?"

"Augie thinks there might be and Sheridan told Brighton there were. Sunset Beaudry told me Marilyn and Elvis were tighter than Siamese twins. Laura Dane said the opposite . . . You get the feeling I may not be the only one flunking some quiz?"

"I know that tone, Neil. What are you cooking in your mind?"

"How does it stand about Brighton getting his hands on your hundred thousand?"

"My business manager is drawing up the deal memo to go with the check. It's supposed to be ready today."

"Call him. Tell him not to turn over the check to Brighton without phoning here first for my okay. When Brighton hears from the mystery caller, I don't want him able to move ahead without me knowing it."

"Honey, I don't want you sticking your neck out."

I waved off her concern, secretly pleased. "By then I'll have something worked out with Ned DeSantis."

"DeSantis?" she said, and made a bad medicine face. "He was ready to take me to death row the minute he laid eyes on me."

"We have an understanding. DeSantis is an acquired taste."

"You mean an acquired smell," she said, crinkling her nose.

Stevie lifted herself from the couch, readjusted her outfit, and crossed to the phone. A minute later, she was talking to her business manager. She gasped and wheeled around, eyes as wide as a Missouri horizon. "Buddy says Brighton came by an hour ago and picked up the cashier's check for the hundred thou."

I couldn't locate Augie at the MPRE.

DeSantis was at the precinct, griping about paperwork.

"If you're calling to surrender your wife, I accept."

"What are you talking about, DeSantis?"

"Like you don't know from the grand jury indictment?"

"Why I called. Did you have a hand in that?"

"Is Miss Marriner with you? I figure she is, the way she counts on you, like a moron uses his fingers."

"Is that your specialty, DeSantis? Morons? The department have you working at your top speed?"

"My, my, Gulliver, touchy, aren't we? She is with you, huh?"

"Of course not."

"Thought so," he said. "I'll forget we had the conversation, okay? For now."

"Are you saying you don't think there's a case?"

"It's inconclusive as shit," he said. "The DA doing his usual grandstanding. Anyone ask me first, I would of said hold off, but that doesn't mean I vote Miss Marriner any clean bill of health, unless you got something more better than us?"

No amount of police veneer could disguise the sincerity I heard in his tobacco-starched voice. I was liking DeSantis more and more. I told him about the love letters.

"Elvis and Marilyn, huh?" The silence built as he considered what he'd heard. "Gotta figure the clue crew did a thorough sweep at Sheridan's place. I'll spec it out."

"If you don't turn up the letters, what are my chances of poking around the cottage?"

"You thinking of bringing Miss Marriner with you?"

"You got that answer already, DeSantis."

"Do you say things like that with a straight face?"

"How about tomorrow?"

"The yellow tape is still up, but so what? I was going out there anyway. Some details I need to check with Miss Jahnsen."

"Paige Jahnsen?"

He tried to suppress a childish giggle. "Some looker, you agree?" Giggling again.

"DeSantis, none of my business, but is something going on between you and Paige Jahnsen?"

"Right," he agreed. "None of your business."

And he giggled.

I was relieved I hadn't mentioned how her name had come up in conversation with Hank Twitchell. Learning how Paige fit in all of this was part of my business now, and I feared the answer might not be good for a giggle from DeSantis or anyone.

Stevie had heard my end of the conversation.

"Why didn't you tell him about Godzilla? Because of me?"

"And because there's nothing he can do about it."

"About some guy trying to turn my ass and yours into cream of fertilizer? A little protection might be in order, even if you only mentioned you, not me."

"A memory refresher from your days as Mrs. Crime Reporter. Cops aren't in the prevention business. They don't stop murders. They investigate them. If we were dead, they could do something."

"I'm encouraged. Thank you. You still keep your gun around?"

Stacked in the back of my bedroom closet are maybe a dozen Nike shoe boxes, containing the treasures of a lifetime, including the Beretta 92f semiautomatic Stevie meant. It was a thank-you gift from somebody whose life I saved years ago, when I was young and stupid. Tucked snugly in its own box, inside a watch cap, loaded with sixteen rounds of 147-grain hollow point misery, including the round in the chamber.

I told her where it was and said, "Look, when I leave for my rendezvous with Laura Dane, you don't answer the intercom. Don't answer the door. Don't stroll the building. Don't take a dip in the pool or the sauna. You know the drill. Fill your time doing something you enjoy, like looking at yourself in the mirror, and you won't need a gun."

Stevie put her fingers in her ears and shot a thunderbolt at me. "I plan to use it on you if you don't shut up," she said.

Laura Dane lived on the third floor of a designer-scarred apartment high-rise in Hollywood, on a steep hillside north of the boulevard, west of where the boulevard turns residential.

The building address was painted in numerals six feet high on a tarp that was lit by spots and stretched across the entire side visible from as far away as Sunset.

The Royal Hollywood offered short-term leases and discounts to prospective tenants who acted quickly; no credit check, down payment, or security deposit required. Nothing distinguished it from any of the other apartments that had replaced the rows of quaint single-family residences that dominated the area before the talkies, when Charlie Chaplin's studio at Sunset and La Brea was a safe ten-minute stroll away.

I parked on the street, about six minutes closer.

It was a lovely night to be outside, the temperature at a comfortable sixty degrees while a high-watt, three-quarter moon sailed effortlessly in a seamless gray sky.

Only a few people were chancing the sidewalks. A jogger puffed by me in mismatched sweats, pretending I wasn't there, mind tuned to his headphones. A bent old woman, her chicken neck extruding at an awkward angle, strained to keep up with a frisky pair of black-and-white toy Scotties. Two women in bib overalls, lumberjack boots, and outdated Beatles cuts strolled hand in hand, whispering and giggling.

Knee-high lawn lamps illuminated an eccentric brick walkway to the outer entrance, lined with wind-dazed hula palms. I found Laura's name on the wall directory and tapped in her number. I was buzzed through without verification. Laura obviously was a believer in the goodness of man.

I rode the elevator with a midfortyish biker, all black leather and beer belly, black helmet cradled under his arm, who must have entered from the underground garage. He tried not to show how hard he was studying me, appeared to have lost interest by the time we both exited on three.

He ushered me ahead of him with a gesture that showed off the grinning skull decorating his left wrist and hesitated when I inquired after the apartment number. There were no directional signs on the wall, only a cheap print, a painted desert sunrise.

The biker pointed a direction and headed the other way. Two left turns and a dead end later, I realized he had been guessing and backtracked past the elevator in the direction he had taken. The door numbers started making sense after a second right turn.

The cream-complexioned, barefoot blonde who opened Laura's door looked to be in her midtwenties and wore her frosted hair piled frivolously on top of her head. Her almond-shaped blue eyes had the tired, moist allure of a starlet not quite ready to trade in her dreams for a bus ride back home.

She studied me carefully. I thought I might have the wrong apartment and identified myself. Her reply escaped through lips frozen in a pucker that exhibited just enough of an overbite to be tantalizing.

"I know. Come in, Mr. Gulliver," she said, in a natural, sexually charged voice. "I'm Marnie."

Marnie extended her hand, pulled it away after a tentative handshake, and led the way inside. She wore a white ribbed scoop-neck top that showed off tantalizing breasts that seemed larger than they were on her petite frame. Her behind was squeezed into white jeans a size too small and swayed to a metronomic rhythm I couldn't hear but was appreciating as much as a Gershwin melody by the time she had settled on the living room couch, legs tucked yoga-style.

She invited me to choose a seat. I settled for a thrift shop straight back by the wall, moving it closer to her. There was a large bowl of dried fruits and nuts on the table between us, a pitcher of orange juice, and some jelly glasses. She refilled her glass and told me to help myself.

I played at sipping my juice and forced myself to study the room instead of Marnie—who appeared to study me—anticipating Laura's grand entrance, sweeping in like the movie star she once had been and commandeering the conversation, the way she always did with Johnny Carson.

My head was full of questions tougher than any Carson had ever asked her, including Hank's: If Laura and Marilyn were so tight, why didn't she know about the romance with Elvis? If she did know, why had she lied to Brighton? If Laura had lied about the love affair, had she also lied when she told him there were no love letters?

If Laura changed her stories tonight, especially about the love letters, did that also mean Hank didn't know Elvis as well as he thought he did? If both were right and there were no love letters, who gave Sheridan the notion that may have killed him? Who was offering to turn over love letters that don't exist to Brighton for a hundred grand?

The living room was crammed with unmatched furniture. Some of it was expensive-looking. Other pieces looked like lawn sale bargains. An oak cabinet with etched glass doors dominated one wall, shelves packed with leather-bound books and scripts with gilt-embossed titles on their spines. Walls and surfaces held various framed photos, movie posters, and career artifacts, like those I had seen in the cottages of Claire Cavanaugh and Sunset Beaudry. The dust of this lifetime's baggage was hidden under the sweet lemon scent of room freshener.

Marnie said, "She sure was some beauty in her day, wasn't she?" I continued studying the elegantly framed photos of Laura in various moods, costumes, and theatrical poses. "Beauty can be a curse, you know?"

"Not as well as you would."

She considered my response. "That's a compliment."

"I meant it that way."

"Thank you. Aunt Laura says you're a newspaper writer, a columnist, but the way you said it made me wonder if you ever were a movie or a TV producer."

"I'm sorry. I didn't mean—"

"It's okay, Mr. Gulliver. You're just catching me on a bad day. They screw with your mind trying to screw with your body. Aunt Laura says it has always been like that and nothing will ever make it change, not even for a damned good actress, which I am. You wouldn't believe some of her stories, about people like Darryl F.

Zanuck. I never would have believed before what the *F* in Darryl F. Zanuck really stood for."

I gave her a who'd-ever-think gesture and asked, "Laura is your aunt?"

"My great-aunt, on my grandmother's side—her sister. More than that since I arrived here from Columbus. More like a saint. Saint Laura." She said it with reverence. "She's a wonderful aunt and a wonderful teacher. To me and to all the actors she coaches. How she makes her living. Or did you suppose it was from those talk shows and, once or twice a year, *Diagnosis Murder*?"

"I hadn't given it much thought. I—"

"They could be out on the street pushing a cart or begging for quarters outside the post office, the old-timers, while we think of them like they'll always be in the movies. Aunt Laura, too. She is too generous, giving away more than she takes in and she won't listen to anybody who says otherwise. This place? Aunt Laura will be out when the lease is up. How she helps make ends meet. Moving from place to place, wherever they don't demand a first and last month or where they're so hard up they give you the first three or six months free, just to fill up the empties. Aunt Laura stays the three or six and then it's on to the next. The students help her move. They're devoted to her. Loyal. The way she deserves."

"I didn't—"

Marnie brushed at her eyes, shook the finely sculpted tip of her nose and sniffed it clear. Forced a smile into place.

"I'm sorry, it's just that it gets very depressing sometimes, especially when I find her reading that darn old book of hers or going through an old script or scrapbook, her eyes washed out by tears, hardly able to speak a word. Am I? Speaking too much, I mean? Telling tales out of school, I suppose, but I love her so very dearly."

"She's fortunate to have someone like you."

Marnie shook her head and tapped her chest with an index finger. "If I ever do make it in this business, it will only be because of her. Molded me from wet clay. I thought I was hot crap when I got here, ready to go for my first Academy Award, but she made me see better. I am a damned good actress because she made me one."

She reached for the script on the seat cushion beside her. It was bound in mocha leather. "I can prove it to you. This movie is *All about Eve*. I've been working on it as a scene study exercise."

"I'll take your word for it."

Marnie suppressed a pout, then lit the room with her smile and said, "You should see the title page." She held the script open and displayed a handwritten inscription, which she recited from memory: "For Laurie, the best friend I have, the very best actress I know and a fellow escapee from the Copacabana School. With all my love forever, your partner in crime, Norma Jean."

Norma Jean.

I angled in for a better look.

There were flashes of flamboyance in her capitals. Otherwise, her handwriting was schoolgirl neat, legible, reaching out to be understood, yet small enough to hide behind. A message of contradiction presaging the Marilyn Norma Jean Daugherty became.

Marnie said, " 'The Copacabana School,' that's a line from the script."

"George Sanders."

"He won an Oscar for it. Really something, huh?"

"Really something."

"He played a newspaper columnist, like you, only you do it for real. Why you came over? To interview my aunt?"

"We have some business to talk about."

"About Marilyn, she told me. Why, I thought it could be for a column. I confess why I said some of the things I did, so maybe you'd write her up in a way that tells everyone how wonderful she is and how Aunt Laura deserves a role to fit her great talent."

"I'll think about it."

Marnie peeled off another winning smile. "Thank you, Mr. Gulliver. Really. It makes me extra sorry that tonight isn't working out."

"What does that mean?"

"Aunt Laura had to go. She got a call. We were in the middle of scene study, so she asked me if I'd mind waiting here for you and tell you, so you wouldn't think she stood you up or anything bad like that."

"Did she say how long she'd be gone?"

"Only she was sorry and to call her tomorrow, if you want, so the two of you can choose another time."

"I don't suppose you know who phoned?"

"Of course I do. Her producer boyfriend. Jerry Brighton?" She made a face. "Whatever it was, he said it couldn't wait, so Aunt Laura threw herself together and was all pretty for him when he picked her up."

"How long ago was that, Marnie?"

"You're not mad at her, are you? You'll still think about doing a column?"

"I promise. How long ago?"

She checked her Pocahontas watch. "About an hour? I helped Aunt Laura get her lips on straight and she went to wait for him out in front, all giddy and smiling one of those precious sweetheart smiles of hers."

My mind flashed on Jeremy Brighton, sitting anxiously behind the wheel as Laura forged her large frame into his car. Brighton must have called Laura after being contacted, after picking up the cashier's check from Stevie's business guy.

Why not me?

Maybe Laura had never said there was no affair or no love letters? Maybe Brighton had lied to me about that? Maybe they were in on it together?

Anything she's keeping from me, you might be able to pry from her. Isn't that what he said over Shirley MacLaine and a toasted bagel at the Polo Lounge? When he encouraged me to meet with her, did Brighton already know about tonight? Was he making certain I'd be preoccupied, grounded here, when he and Laura sped off to trade a check for the love letters?

The cemetery is on the way home, five minutes from the Heathcliffe. Maybe that's why I had the thought as Westwood Boulevard loomed ahead. A sudden, irresistible urge to visit Marilyn Monroe.

In the fraction of a second it took me to decide, I swung a left off Wilshire at Glendon, the side street feeding an Avco Cinema parking structure and the Pierce Brothers Westwood Village Mortuary.

The street was empty. Crimson-jacketed parking attendants milled around smoking and gossiping, waiting for the movies to break. A Bel Air Patrol wagon blocked the mortuary entrance. A pair of uniformed guards in tan pressed pants and tight neckties were pulling shut and padlocking a wrought-iron gate that, like the brick wall it rolled from, was a good twelve feet high.

I checked my watch. Quarter to nine. The guards were closing the cemetery fifteen minutes early. They probably didn't want to be late for a coffee break.

I accepted the lockout as a personal challenge.

Easing my Jag around the patrol wagon, I zigzagged south to an open parking lot adjacent to the cemetery. It was closed for the night. A lit sign said leave four dollars under a windshield wiper blade in the provided envelope. There were around two dozen parked cars, and eight or nine motorists had obeyed.

I pulled in, ignoring the envelope dispensers, and parked parallel to the west brick wall of the cemetery. It was about six feet high.

The moon was glowing inside a porphyritic umbrella cloud and protection overheads were turned on all over the lot, but I was relatively obscured from view by the lush shadows of trees that overhung the wall. I stepped from the hood of the Jag onto the brick shelf and used a branch for balance while I chose an open spot to land in the garden below.

It's not a large cemetery.

It took only a few minutes to move on past the executive offices and chapel, across a central island of discreet grave markers, to the banks of crypts along the north wall, beyond an imposing mausoleum reserved for the Armand Hammer family.

Marilyn's crypt wasn't difficult to find.

I'd been there once before, researching a column on burial places of our greatest celebrity icons. It was in one of the last sections facing the courtyard, by the Sanctuary of Tranquility, whose most notable guest is Buddy Rich, the great jazz drummer.

I had followed one of the groups of camera-toting tourists anxious to have their photos taken alongside Marilyn, to show the folks back home in Kyoto.

They had stood in an informal line, a respectful few feet away, and patiently waited their turn, then popped a smile and pointed to a fresh red rose nestled in the wall container before the shutter was snapped.

If one believed the story newspapermen like me had helped mythologize, it was the red rose replaced daily, on permanent order from Joltin' Joe himself.

Tonight it would just be Marilyn and me. The moon reappeared and seemed to throw a spot of light onto her plaque as I stepped up to the wall.

The light brown marble was edged in gilt, and the name blossomed in inlaid eighteen-carat gold:

MONROE

There were twelve individual vaults across each of four tiers. Most were occupied.

Marilyn's vault was on the third level from the top, second row in from the left. The vault to her left was empty. That it was being held in reserve for DiMaggio was also part of the myth grown up around their love story.

I had to wonder, though. The flower vial on her vault held wilting red and yellow marigolds instead of a red rose. Had Joe given up the ghost or had he never read up on the legend? That's the best thing about all the truths we create for ourselves. They can be anything or nothing at all.

"Like love letters, Marilyn?"

I allowed her a few minutes to answer me.

She didn't.

I started back for the car, my retreat less anxious than my arrival. I paused to survey the flowers flourishing in the beds fronting the cemetery's administration bungalow. There were red, pink, and white rosebushes among them.

What was it Stevie used to call me?

An incurable romantic.

I listened for foreign sounds, checked for problem shadows, then snatched the largest, most appealing red rose and retraced my path to Marilyn's crypt. Tomorrow, the tourists would pose and point and not be disappointed by the reality of wilted marigolds.

And what would Stevie call me now?

She was doing Goldilocks in my bed when I got home and was still asleep when I left the next morning for the Retirement Estates, after spending a restive night on the couch doing more worrying for her.

Saturday morning traffic was light and I made good time.

Shortly before eleven-thirty, I pulled into the parking lot by Sheridan's cottage. DeSantis was waiting on the porch, pacing back and forth, his hands clasped behind his back as if he were tracking a thought.

We exchanged perfunctory greetings and he sent an umpire's thumb flying over his shoulder. "Notice anything funny about the doors?"

Sheridan's screen door was standing open against the stucco wall.

Broken strips of crime scene yellow danced aimlessly in the breeze that often drifts leisurely along the valley floor.

The arched front door was open an inch or two. Its official seals also had been cracked.

"I spotted it right off," DeSantis said. "Called it in and the lab's crime busters are on their way, so now I'm gonna play peekaboo." He stepped up to the door and used his shoulder to open a passageway. His service revolver was out of the holster and parked against his chest. "I smell empty," he said. "You stay here until I say so."

I gave it a moment, then followed DeSantis inside.

Curtained gray light heightened the musk of time and the smell of recent death. He flipped the light switch. My eyes adjusted quickly. Stevie's description made me feel like I had been inside before.

DeSantis moved forward a few feet.

Stopped like he'd banged into a clear glass wall.

"Holy shit!"

I moved in for a look and was startled by a sight that had been invisible from the doorway.

Laura Dane was stretched on her back on the brown leather couch, her arms crossed at the wrists and resting gently on her chest, like an oversized corpse without a coffin.

My eyes swept from her to the nearby recliner and the still figure of Jeremy Brighton, one cheek cushioned against a shoulder and laced fingers capping his belly, also asleep or dead.

DeSantis saw me and ordered, "Just freeze a minute."

He checked them for pulse, first Laura and then Brighton, noising something indiscernible, rose quickly, and searched for the phone. It was halfway to his ear when he remembered, "Fucking line's dead."

I slapped my pockets for my cell phone.

I'd left it in the glove compartment.

DeSantis barked, "Outside, call from my car. Tell Dispatch we need paramedics and the meat wagon, too. One finished and the other one still breathing. Can't say for how long."

I started to ask him who was which, but he shot his finger at the door, picked a direction, and headed off in double-time.

I was back in a few minutes.

DeSantis was coming out of the bedroom. He saw me and threw a thumb over his shoulder. "You got a friend in there," he said.

He stepped away so I could get inside and see who he meant.

He meant Augie.

Augie was on his back, spread across the unmade bed like a restless sleeper, arms askew, a leg dangling over the side, his face turned away from the door. I urgently crossed the room to the far side of the bed, to verify what DeSantis called out to me: "Friar Tuck, he's breathing."

Augie's pulse was soft, erratic.

I pushed open the lids of his good eye; it could have been his blind side. I put my mouth against his ear and whispered his name. No response. I got back onto my feet and stepped backward, my mind swimming in questions he couldn't answer.

His color was a murky white, contrasting sharply with the finite drinker's veins dressing his prominent nose and cheeks like monuments to a forsaken past.

He had been cold to the touch. A clammy sweat clung like raindrops on glass to his broad forehead and the wide scarred ridge above his mouth. I brushed my palms down my jacket lapels, as if I were warding off infection.

There were no visible wounds, no sign of what pushed Augie into this condition, but clearly he was not dressed for a nap. He had on blue sweats and a pair of scuffed running shoes. The sweats were adorned with silk-screen versions of Picasso's peace dove admiring interlocking crimson hearts, the emblem of Augie's order. I feared for him; slightly less for myself and the concept of surviving in a world without an Augie Fowler.

In the distance, I heard the wail of a siren and willed it to grow louder faster. Maybe it's because MPRE residents share a working relationship with death, but the arrival of the screaming ambulance and, shortly, the meat wagon did not attract the crowd of curiosity seekers that might have gathered on a public street.

Fewer than a half-dozen people had bothered to check out the scene by the time the paramedics were ready to move Augie and Laura outside to the ambulance. They knew Sheridan was dead and could not fathom what might be happening now. DeSantis delivered a guarded explanation like a favorable weather report, and they nodded appreciatively, said thank you, sauntered off.

I wanted to climb inside the ambulance and make the ride to the emergency hospital with Augie. The paramedics wouldn't allow it. They smiled benignly through my outrage and made calm, quiet sense while gentling me away from the rear door, as if they, not me, knew what was best for him.

DeSantis clamped an arm across my shoulder and told me we could make the trip together, only later. I pulled myself free, in anticipation of his stale odor, and realized it was absent. The detective smelled like he had been born again, in a vat of Bijan. I noticed how expensively he was dressed this morning. A buff gray pinstriped suit. A clashing power tie. A pair of dress Ferragamos that on his salary would have him devouring processed cheese spread on soda crackers for a year.

DeSantis had upgraded his appearance to Lieutenant Kojak for Paige Jahnsen, I was certain, by the way his body language kicked in when she came rushing to us, like some kid bluffing around the fact he was too shy to ask for a date. He tried not to stare at her, chose his words carefully, and ran his fingers nervously through his hair, smoothing strands into place. His complexion glistened. I couldn't decide whether he'd used makeup or Dutch Boy to disguise his acne scars.

Paige had to have noticed DeSantis's transformation, but she didn't let on. Her questions and her catalog of expressions were afloat in genuine concern for the victims. She nodded animatedly. Occasionally, her eyes widened in fascination as he added to the description of events.

I left them that way. Raced to Claire Cavanaugh's cottage. If I couldn't be with Augie, for his sake I needed to check on Claire, make certain she was safe.

No answer to the bell or my knocking. The door was locked.

I strolled around, searching for a window that would permit me to check inside, but all the curtains were tightly drawn. A kitchen shade was raised about five inches. I stooped awkwardly. Strained my neck looking for any signs of activity. None.

I tested the back doorknob. It depressed all the way and the latch clicked back. I entered a narrow service porch off the small kitchen. Open-faced cabinets were stocked with canned and packaged goods, home supplies, and scrapbooks and keepsake boxes piled irregularly to the full height of the upper shelves.

A work counter running the full length of the area was lost underneath more scrapbooks and boxes, orderly stacks of old movie magazines slick with thick top layers of dust. I finger-dusted a copy of *Photoplay* to check the date—1958—on a hunch, brushed the cover with a circular, sweeping motion to get a cleaner look at the face straining to be recognized: Claire. Captured for all eternity by the magic lens of the great George Hurrell.

The kitchen was tidy except for a pair of breakfast dishes on the sink counter, oatmeal judging by the residue in the bowls. An opened carton of fresh orange juice and emptied juice glasses. A last slice of whole wheat toast in a sterling silver server. An old-fashioned kettle on the gas range.

I tapped the kettle gingerly with an index finger; cold.

The antique mahogany table, almost too large for the dining room, had not been cleared. One fine bone-china teacup was empty and the other one barely touched. Hardly any brownies remained on the dessert platter. I recognized them by their size and shape as Augie's secret recipe. The man loved his chocolate chip brownies as much as he once reveled in his whiskey.

I stepped into the pale light of Claire's living room and at once became aware that something was not right. Was it only my imagination working overtime, jolted by what DeSantis and I had discovered next door?

"Miss Cavanaugh?"

I called her name a few more times. My gaze settled on the bedroom door, anticipating it might open and Claire would sail through with the enchanting grace Loretta Young had displayed every week on TV.

I crossed the room cautiously, observing the neat military corners to the brown blanket on Augie's cot. Reference books were stacked on his trunk and their titles suggested he was boning up on gardening. Not surprising. The strolling gardens at the Order of the Spiritual Brothers of the Rhyming Heart were one of his personal treasures; he always made a point of showing them off.

I brought my ear to within an inch of the door and called for Claire again, disturbed by the picture of tragedy forming in my mind. I swallowed all the air in the room, turned the knob, and inched the door open, ready to be shocked by what I would find.

The bedroom was empty.

Her canopied bed was neatly made, smothered under hand-embroidered scatter cushions. The folded comforter's floral pattern matched the fitted sheet and the valance and seemed perfect for the scent of roses and daffodils hanging in the air.

I relaxed, pushing out my breaths like a learner, stepped over to the bergère armchair angled to face the bed, and sank onto the golden velvet plush. I heard myself saying to Augie, "Claire is okay, old man. You better be, too, or somebody out there will answer to me."

A vague noise outside set the birds chattering. I moved to the window and stood in a way that let me peek unobserved through the ruffled curtain.

A Honey Bee was purring away in his golf cart, and Claire was heading up the cobblestone path as if it were carpeted in royal red, cherishing a bundle of long-stemmed, yellow flowers like those I'd seen growing wild the day Augie sent me looking for Sunset.

I had the front door open and was pushing aside the screen door by the time she reached the top of the veranda, holding the handrail and measuring her steps.

She had on a basic trapeze dress over a classic blouse and a flowing scarf wrapped around her neck, a simple outfit in earth tones devised to cover up the wrinkles and gravity of aging. The facial bruises she suffered the night of Sheridan's murder were barely visible under a careful layer of makeup.

Claire hesitated, as if she were about to wonder what I was doing inside her home. I also saw a glimmer of recognition before she averted her wondrous coal black eyes and sailed past me as if I were the usual footman.

I called after her, "Are you all right, Miss Cavanaugh?"

"Fine, and how are you today?" she responded, her voice like fine champagne. "You're Mr. Hale's young friend, aren't you?" She invented a question mark and searched the living room for a clue.

"Alan," she called. "I've returned, Alan. Shall I fix a pot of tea for you and your young friend?"

"You mean Augie Fowler, Miss Cavanaugh, not Alan Hale."

She stared back at me the way Lillian Gish stared at Robert Mitchum in *Night of the Hunter* and for a moment had me believing I was the one acting crazy.

She searched the cottage for Augie and, satisfied he wasn't present, urged me to make myself comfortable while she prepared tea for us. "I suppose Alan is off doing his exercises," Claire suggested en route to the kitchen. "Jogging is so good for the heart, the doctors tell you. The way Alan goes about it, he will live to be a hundred." Her famous dancing laugh was ingratiating.

"Augie will be lucky to live out the day," I said, settling onto the couch, preparing to tell her what had happened.

She answered with another laugh. "Not luck at all, young man, but always God's decision for all his creatures," she said. She paused under the archway to cross herself.

Was Claire acting? I wondered.

If so, she was impeccable.

It wouldn't even be a consideration, except—

Augie had said Claire was faking it, and if she was faking it with him she was faking it with me.

I wondered what secrets they shared.

What was the strong bond that, after so many years, caused his moving in here to protect her from death threats now not as vague as they once seemed, except she was still alive and Augie was barely clinging to life.

Could she tell me why Augie was in Sheridan's cottage? What did she know about Laura Dane and Jeremy Brighton? Would she have any answers to any of the puzzles of the past week?

I had to find out.

She returned, assuring me our tea would be ready shortly, wondering if she might tempt me with a slice of fresh, homemade pound cake.

She glided to the mantle on her leather sandals, carrying some of the yellow flowers she had brought inside from the golf wagon and replaced the fading roses in the carved crystal vase, adjusting and readjusting the new flowers.

"Maybe you didn't hear me before, Miss Cavanaugh?" She made a pleasant noise. Returned to humming a tune I didn't recognize. "I said our friend, Augie, could be dying while you pretend not to know who he is, pretend he's somebody else."

"Alan, you mean? Do you mean Alan isn't his real name? How amusing. *Augie*. Alan never mentioned changing his name to me, but I would not be surprised. Many of us did it one time or another, Mr. . . ." Her laugh again. "Did you say *your* name? I know Alan told me once. He told me what a pleasant young man you are and quite a treasure as a friend, but I fear I've forgotten your name."

"Mickey Mouse," I said, out of frustration. She turned and gave me the kind of reproving look I'd get from teachers before they ordered me to the vice-principal's office. "It's Gulliver. Neil Gulliver."

"Do you travel, Neil Gulliver?" And laughter, as if she were inventing a joke I had never heard. "Oh, wait, I remember now . . ." Claire paused and tilted her head back, as if the memory were an elusive butterfly sailing above her, then returned to puttering with the flowers.

"I'm a newspaper columnist, Miss Cavanaugh. Years ago, Augie Fowler and I worked together. He was my teacher and more, and now he may be dying, something I know neither of us wants to happen."

"Yes, newspaperman. That sounds right," she decided, adding a smile of undefiled innocence that made you want to sweep her into your arms and protect her. Is this what attracted Augie to her, his insatiable need to rescue innocent damsels in distress?

I eased up from the couch and walked over to her, felt her shiver as I gentled my hand on her shoulder, and said softly, "He must have told you you can trust me."

Claire didn't answer, pretending the flowers had her full attention.

I said, "My ex-wife, Stevie, Stephanie Marriner, has been charged with Blackie Sheridan's murder . . . You were there when it happened and you know better. Before he died, Taps Vernon told Augie your life was also in danger. He said someone wanted you dead. Augie got the impression you were not the only one whose life was being threatened." I checked my watch. "About two hours ago, in Sheridan's cottage, we found a man named Jeremy Brighton dead. Someone else you know, Laura Dane, was close to dying. So was Augie. I think it's time now to stop your deception and speak to me, before you or anyone else winds up dead."

Claire stopped puttering with the flowers, and I studied her reflection in the mantle mirror as she tracked her eyes after old memories.

She looked past her shoulder at me and said, "Laura Dane, such a fine actress. Laura and I made several movies together, you know? Of course, I was always billed higher than she, above the title, but billing is not an accurate measure of talent . . . Is there any truth to what I hear, Mickey Mouse? Laura put on quite a few extra pounds in recent years?''

Was she toying with me?

I took a deep breath and pushed it out through my nose to keep from losing my temper. And said softly, ''All of this has something to do with Marilyn Monroe and Elvis Presley, doesn't it? About Marilyn and Elvis and what you know about their love affair? Their love letters?''

Claire smiled enigmatically, touched my cheek with her fingertip. ''You say you're a newspaperman, but the way you invent stories maybe you should consider becoming a screenwriter?''

''My interest is the truth.''

''Documentaries then?''

I flashed on the antique desk and the envelope Augie had shown me the last time I was here, decided to try some shock therapy on her.

Properly applied, surprise is a meaningful weapon of war.

I learned that lesson the hard way, on the crime beat, where more than once I almost became a statistic in a sack before I taught myself to make surprise work for me. It kept me alive. Here, it might—

What?

Save a few lives, maybe?

I said, ''What if Reg Mowry is the next one to go, Claire? Will the seven-hundred-and-fifty-dollar checks he sends you also disappear?''

She looked blankly at me.

''Those love letters? What if I told you I had them?''

She almost tripped on the question. She stepped to the wall and pushed it with a hand, for balance. Recomposing herself, she declared in a voice less certain than before, ''Perhaps this is a good time for us to share our secrets, Mickey Mouse.''

''Secrets?'' Paige Jahnsen said. ''Aren't they fun?''

She was standing just inside the front door and I wished I had thought to lock it. How much had she heard?

She was dressed for a cocktail party. A long-sleeved, two-piece dress in a rainbow of horizontal stripes, the drawstring cinched tight and showing off a tiny waist that slid onto the kind of luscious hips and long, limber legs featured in health-club ads. Open-toe red pumps added three inches. Diamond ear studs and gold-plated mesh cuffs added to her dazzle.

"Hello, hello, hello," she called, and ticked off a two-fingered salute to the brow. Her grin accentuated her overbite. "Ned—Lieutenant DeSantis—sent me looking for you, Neil. He thought I might find you over here. He says he needs to go over some stuff before he splits?"

Claire disappeared into the kitchen.

Paige surveyed the room and shut off a gurgle of surprise with her hand over her mouth when she saw the cot. I was struck by the realization that Augie's stay had not been authorized by anyone. She shook her head and closed her sloe eyes to whatever kinky pictures she had invented.

"Miss Cavanaugh and I are about to have tea."

"That's all you're planning, I hope." She winked broadly, gestured away any need for an answer.

"And some pound cake."

"Strictly yummy, her pound cake." She smacked her lips with her fingers. "I think it has something to do with the chemicals in the water. Not all chemicals are bad, just the bad ones. Well, you know what I mean."

"Join us? I'm sure Miss Cavanaugh wouldn't mind."

"Thank you, but I got the impression from the lieutenant that seeing you is urgent."

"I wouldn't want to disappoint her."

"You're such a sweetheart! I'm sure I told you that before!" Paige marched across the room and pounded a fist into my arm. "People rarely make time for even relatives who end up in lonely, isolated circumstances. Usually, we hear a fancy excuse and get some guilt money. The guilt money is very important, but the excuses make you want to puke."

I hid my impure motives inside a blush. "Miss Cavanaugh's movies have given me a lot of pleasure."

"It's something else, too, isn't it?" Paige said, eyeing me with mock suspicion. She lowered her voice a decibel. "Maybe Miss Cavanaugh knows something about Mr. Sheridan's death—to help get Miss Marriner off the hook? One of the secrets you meant?"

Paige was no fool. "Caught," I said, and raised my hands in mock surrender.

"Pretty smart of me to figure out that one, huh?" She tapped her temple. "Not! Ned—Lieutenant DeSantis—told me that. He said the two of you, you and Ned, the lieutenant, are trying to find out what really happened."

"Sort of," I said, wondering how much DeSantis would trust Paige if he knew about her phone calls to Hank Twitchell. "I'm also working with another friend of yours," I said, testing the waters. "Hank Twitchell."

"Hank Twitchell?"

I almost believed she didn't recognize the name and played along, describing him.

She squeezed her eyes and, after a moment, shook her head. "I don't think so. He says he knows me? What else?"

"He says you called him, asking about Blackie Sheridan, Taps Vernon, and Sunset Beaudry."

"Hank Twitchell?" She sounded genuinely perplexed. Her head swiveled left and right. "I don't ask questions and I don't say word one to anyone. Not people I don't know, and especially not to all those calls from those stupid tabloids and TV shows that pry into people's lives without a care for who they hurt, like people are just so many garbage cans."

She cocked her head and fixed her mouth determinedly. Struck a defiant pose, feet apart and arms akimbo like Peter Pan, as if challenging me to disagree.

I let it go for now.

Later, I'd run it by Hank.

One of them wasn't reciting the whole alphabet. Knowing what I knew about him, the smart money had to be on Paige. Except, she came off so naive and engaging, trusting, caring and sweet, I had to wonder.

"Look who's here!" Claire had returned carrying a sterling silver tray with tea service for two, the china pattern I'd seen on the dining table, and a ceramic plate full of delicate pound cake wedges. "How good to see you, Gene. A delightful surprise. Ty, you know Gene, of course."

She was into her act.

Gene Tierney and Tyrone Power.

Whatever secrets Claire intended to share, she wasn't about to include Paige, who sneaked me an arched eyebrow.

"So lucky, this beautiful creature," Claire said, and set down the tray on the glossy black lacquered TV table by the armchair. "If I hadn't been shooting *Down Two Dangerous Streets* for Blackie Sheridan, the delicious title role in *Laura* opposite Dana Andrews was mine for the taking. It will do absolute wonders for your career, dear."

Paige said, "Thank you, Miss Cavanaugh."

"Claire, please. Remember? How many times must I tell you? We were about to settle down to a pot. Join us?"

Before Paige could answer, I said, "Gene was just telling me how Mr. Zanuck sent her over to bring me to the set, Claire."

Claire smiled appreciatively. "Well, then, we'll just have to postpone our tea, won't we? It's never wise to keep Mr. Zanuck waiting."

The outside of Sheridan's cottage was a TV scene again. Residents creaked by—heads drifting knowingly, acknowledging police cars and fresh yellow tape, the coroner's meat wagon parked where the ambulance had been—but never pausing to ask questions or confirm an answer they knew by heart.

A fuzz-mustached uniform lifted his sunglasses and made a show of remembering Paige. Gave a brief, nodding approval to my credentials. Lifted the tape to let us through.

Doc Cuevas was leaning against a living room wall, cooling a cheek with a can of Miller while his people went through the usual motions in rhythm with a crime lab team sniffing around the yellow strip outline where Jeremy Brighton had been. A burst of light startled us—the photographer's strobe lamp.

"I hear I missed Brother Crazy trying to check out of this place," Cuevas called to me. Reading my face, he lost the grin. "S'okay, Gully; chill. I been getting status relays from Valley General. That old bastard was still pulling his bips on the blue screen five minutes ago. The lady, too." I told Paige to wait and joined him. He held out the beer. I waved it off. "Laura Dane, I hear. The old actress?"

"Yeah. What's the honest read on Augie?"

"She was some looker, that one. I remember getting hard-ons every time she was in a scene. I couldn't of been more'n twelve or thirteen, sitting in the Saturday matinee and playing pocket pool while eating Laura Dane's face off the picture screen." He repeated her name and made it sound like a wet dream.

"Augie, Doc. The prognosis."

I bit down hard on my back teeth. No reason to explode at Doc. We've had lots of conversations like this over the years, but the jokes you tell to protect against the horrors don't work when someone close to you is toe-dancing on the high wire.

He knew the difference, too, and shrugged.

"Emergency says nothing visible on either of 'em, Augie or Laura Dane. They haven't scored the problem yet, so all bets are on ice. Too early to quote odds."

"Do it anyway."

He thought about it. "Seventy-thirty, the best. No, not even that, they don't isolate the cause pretty soon, Gully."

"Laura Dane?"

"Fifty-fifty. She's also in Dreamland, but she didn't fall as far down into the rabbit hole as Augie."

"Why?"

"Dunno."

"Something they ingested?"

"If you mean like a bad tuna fish sandwich—"

"Doc, you know what I mean."

"They're running tests, okay? Remove your fangs from my neck, Gully. Christ!" He searched the room for relief. "No signs of any needles, so they have the lab running blood. I fudged some urine specimens, to see what they might turn up. Modern medicine versus the clock, and ya know what?"

"I know what."

"We crawl before we walk, but the clock is always running."

"I'd swear I said I know what."

Doc dropped a hand on my shoulder, meaning to comfort me. I swept it off. He moved in close enough for me to smell the beer on his breath and seethed through his teeth, "It's not my fault, Gully." Making certain the words sank in.

I signaled a field goal with my hands and apologized. Cuevas faked a punch to my chin. "I ever need a friend, Gully, I hope to hell you're available."

"Up yours, too, Doc."

He laughed through his nose. "Only if you're Laura Dane and I'm ten years old."

"The corpus, Jeremy Brighton?"

"No interest in fucking him, any age."

"Cause?"

" 'Cause he's not my type."

"Doc—"

Hands out defensively. "Okay, okay . . . All I can give you is best guess." I made a gathering motion. "Same as the other two, Gully. Internal."

"Poison?"

"Why not? If you bother to notice, you'll see we're already running what we can here, and I've put a code one on him. Maybe we can help 'em out at Valley General, 'specially if they haven't come up with any answers of their own on Augie and Laura Dane by the time the stiff's downtown and racked."

I remembered I hadn't heard anything yet about the post on Blackie Sheridan.

"Small world," Cuevas responded. "We had Sheridan under the lamps this morning. We were about to sign off on fatal trauma to the head induced by heavy blows, blunt instrument, when this call come in."

"Did you run the basics?"

He made a dumb-question face. "Should I remind you someone drummed on the victim's head like they was breaking open a ripe coconut?"

"To obscure the real cause of death? Especially if an overworked coroner trying to get through the backlog on ice decides to fudge on basics because the visible, obvious evidence—"

"Jesus! You're as subtle as a street whore. You ever know us to do that?"

"Yeah."

"Then, I'll rephrase the question: Check back with me later on the hot line number. Good plan?"

"What's a good plan?" DeSantis's question sailed past my ear. He had stepped up behind me. "Something I should know?"

"Gulliver here asked if it would be okay for him to go on over to the hospital. Hang out until they know one way or other about his friend, Fowler."

The doc's lie was guesswork, but on the money.

"Swell, no problem," DeSantis said, "but after him and I talk." Turning, I saw on his mobile face the anxiety I'd just heard in his voice. "Let's find somewhere private, Gulliver."

He took hold of my jacket sleeve and, with a nod for the doc, led me away.

I caught a glimpse of Paige standing alone in a corner of the living room, flaunting a hip, hands tightly woven, unsettled eyes stalking our progress. Something was bothering her, almost as much as I felt DeSantis's bother.

Valley Emergency was a fifteen-minute cruise east on the 101 freeway, inside an oak tree–lined industrial park on South Custer Avenue, an efficient, two-story, medicinal white structure with two matching wings extending like stereo speakers from the main building. The hospital was never going to win any design awards.

I parked the Jag near the emergency entrance behind the west wing and got directions to ICU from an indifferent receptionist with a bad nose job who barely looked up from buffing her nails over the new issue of *People* magazine to advise my backside as an afterthought, "No visitors except for immediate family."

Augie and I are close enough to qualify. The nurse on the wall phone disagreed. She said his condition was still "extremely critical" and refused to buzz me through. Check back in an hour, she said, suggesting I camp out in the public cafeteria, and disconnected my tantrum.

I followed the directional signs and a painted green stripe running down the middle of the scarred linoleum past double doors connecting to the main building, then up a stairway to the second floor, trailed by a pungent disinfectant smell.

What passed for a cafeteria was a small assembly room lined with vending machines. A chalkboard hanging from a view window of the food tray railroad said it would reopen at five. The moonfaced wall clock said almost three o'clock. I was starving.

I invested in an egg salad sandwich on whole wheat, a bag of Cheeze Wows, and a can of Diet Coke. The egg salad had too much pepper, but I finished it anyway, and tried escaping my thoughts by studying the six or eight people spread around the rectangle at Formica-surfaced tables arranged study hall fashion. Over food baggies and plastic coffee cups, they contemplated the realities of their own problems.

The Cheeze Wows were too salty. I ate them anyway. I absentmindedly patted myself for the pack of smokes that wouldn't be there and thought about canvassing the room for a smoker who would empathize with my frame of mind. Applaud my determination to resume the habit at this moment in history. Trade me grief stories between deep-throated drags and sumptuous smoke rings. And sympathize with my concern for Augie and his damn, dumb, dying act.

"Mind if I join you, Neil?"

Mickey Spoon interrupted the memory. He hovered across the table, holding a white Styrofoam coffee cup and a package of bear claw miniatures. I responded with a motion.

Spoon pumped out a generous smile and slid onto the bench opposite me. It groaned under his weight. He found a place for the cup beyond his right elbow and tore into the package. He had on an untucked, parachute-sized, cranberry-colored madras buttondown over a tailored pair of rhubarb-colored chino cutoffs and matching tube socks that underscored his toothpick legs.

"Bear claw?"

I gestured, pointing to what was left of my own meal. Spoon popped one. He made a yummy sound and got in several chews before swallowing. He dipped in for another. It disappeared as quickly; so did the third.

He adjusted the angle of his Dodgers cap, wiped a layer of sweat from his brow. "I rushed over soon as I heard about Miss Dane," Spoon said, not waiting the question. "Paige had Miss Latch track me to Hillcrest. I was on the ninth green, schlepping around with three old-time comedians who were betting on whose jokes would get the biggest laughs out of me." He rolled his eyes. "Had to swallow my tongue several times, because I couldn't risk offending Danny Powell. Mr. Powell is the one most likely to make the largest donation to the MPRE, and he kept forgetting punch lines, so I just laughed on the beat every time and kept laughing until Mr. Powell took a victory bow."

"How's Laura?"

"The doctor downgraded her condition to critical, and she was showing enough improvement to get moved out of ICU, but Miss Dane didn't look so terrific to me." He made a face and sneered, "Modern medicine can kill you faster than it cures you nowadays."

"Did Laura say what happened?"

He shook his head and his chins jelly-wobbled. "Miss Dane lays there out of it, Neil, looking slightly this side of Glenn Close in *Reversal of Fortune*. The nurse said she's not likely to wake up for hours yet." His hand slid over his mouth. "Unless she takes a turn for the worse."

"Augie is still listed as extremely critical."

"I know. I went first to intensive care, and they told me. Poor Brother Kalman, and such a good dancer. Mr. Polyzoides is beyond hysteria with concern. First Taps Vernon. Now, Brother Kalman. Mr. Polyzoides believes the Break-a-Leg Show is jinxed this year and screaming about quitting. Miss Latch reminded him the show must go on and that quieted him. Bound to get bad again when Mr. Polyzoides realizes how we don't have another hoofer on the campus. Chorus boy material is all."

A question crowded my mind.

How did Mickey Spoon know Laura Dane well enough to come charging over here? She chauffeured Sheridan and so would be driving to and from the Retirement Estates, but was there more?

I asked him.

Spoon cocked his head and gave me a strange look.

"Some deep, dark significance to this, Neil?"

"Should there be?"

"It's the way you asked. Like I should tell you something you don't know based on something you do know and haven't told me. Why do I suddenly feel like I'm in the last reel of a Lone Wolf B-movie?"

"Curiosity, Mickey. I apologize. I'm reacting badly because of Augie."

Spoon nailed me with a squint while he thought about it. He shook his head. "It's *The Lone Wolf in the Hospital* and I don't mind. I have nothing to hide." He leaned back from the table and unlaced his fingers. Held up a hand. Pushed himself up and said, "First, let me get a fresh cup of coffee. You? My treat."

A few moments later, dropping sugar cubes into his cup, he said, "I spotted Miss Dane at an AA meeting over in the valley, above the Palooka Bowl? Lots of celebrities there, and after, I asked for her autograph. An autograph, sure, she said, but I had to buy her a drink at this little bar on Cahuenga she favored. A lot of drinks, it so happens. Turns out Miss Dane was only acting about quitting on the stuff.

"She said she wasn't about to give up a habit it took her most of her life to develop correctly. Those AA meetings served another purpose when she was between acting jobs, which was most of the time. She said they made it possible for her to practice her craft in front of an appreciative audience. She said there was nothing better than the rush that comes from the immediate response of live applause, not even the booze. She grilled me about her career and it turns out I knew as much as she did. I knew stuff she had forgot years ago, so we hit it off solid as Plymouth Rock and we've hung together ever since.

"Miss Dane and I are buddies. A wonderfully old-fashioned

word that, *buddies*. But it applies. Nothing racier, in case you got thoughts. I have too much respect for Miss Dane. Sometimes, she visits at the MPRE. Other times, I go over to her home. She even allows me to sit in on her classes. It's how she makes most of her living—acting classes. Miss Dane is an inspiring teacher and coach, on top of being a tremendous actress and human being, no matter what she might pretend."

"You knew about her involvement with Blackie Sheridan?"

"Sure. Mr. Brighton remembered her from the *Tonight Show*, carrying on about her friendship with Marilyn Monroe. He tracked her down after making his deal with Mr. Sheridan, and it was Miss Dane who urged Mr. Brighton to get Stephanie Marriner for the part, you know that?"

"I heard."

"Mr. Sheridan also put in a good word."

"You introduced Brighton to Sheridan, didn't you?"

Spoon studied me before answering with a modest shiver of appreciation. "My goodness. We are playing *The Lone Wolf in the Hospital*."

"Brighton told me."

"If it was me, I would have remembered," he said, pulling himself up. "It's so. I met him over at the Friars on one of my hat-in-hand visits, and one thing led to another. Mr. Brighton . . ." He reflected on the name. "Leveling, Neil. This may sound harsh, but I don't care that Mr. Brighton's dead, even if I'd believed him when he dropped hints about coughing up a sizable donation. Not a nice man in any sense of the word. Usually I spot it the first time, like I spotted you being a nice man, but he fooled me. He was awfully good at deceiving, like he was born to it."

"Exactly how did Brighton deceive you, Mickey?"

He analyzed the question and, for a moment, didn't look like he planned to answer.

"Like I said, the dangling carrot. Always talking about the check he was going to write out to the MPRE, always just before he needed something, even if it was a simple request, like using the phone. Or he would ask my permission to have Miss Latch do work for him, like call to confirm some appointment or take his dictation, type out a few memos. The dangling carrot.

"He had this neat little trick. He would show up next time with some cheap perfume or junk jewelry in a gift box and say to me—" He introduced a passable version of Brighton's accent. " *'Guv, you mind if I give your Miss Latch a token of my thanks, to show her how much I appreciate the work she does for me?'* I got to say sure, don't I? He lays on the gift to her and makes himself out to be the great hero . . . Never without an ulterior motive. You ever meet people like that?"

"All the time. Laura seemed to like Brighton."

A dismissive frown. "Business is business and we all do what we must in the name of survival. When he offered Miss Dane the job, he swamped all over her and took the credit for remembering her on the Carson shows. The honest to God truth is I nudged him that direction, same as when I encouraged Mr. Sheridan and Miss Dane to think about Miss Marriner for Marilyn Monroe."

"It sounds like you're wasting your real talent at the MPRE, Mickey. You should be a producer."

"Thanks, but no thanks, Neil. I don't have the personality or the temperament for the job. If people are going to accuse me of being an asshole, I'd rather it's for what I really am than for what comes as part of a producer's job description. A seat on the thirty-yard line is good enough for me."

"What do you know about Elvis Presley?"

Spoon didn't seem to know what to make of the question. "All the lyrics to 'You Ain't Nothin' but a Hound Dog,' but I won't sing them, no matter how hard you beg." He let his smile lapse when he saw I wasn't sharing it and inquired, "Am I going to like what I hear next?"

"You'll tell me," I said.

He listened with increasing wonderment as I spelled out the story of Elvis and Marilyn and the love letters. When I signaled I was through, his hands rattled the air and his mouth cast about for words that translated as unintelligible sounds.

Then he draped one hand over his chest and the other on his

gluttonous belly and started laughing so uproariously the bench sounded like it was about to give under him. His eyes disappeared inside the folds of his red-soaked face.

He acknowledged the fish-eyed attention he had drawn from others in the cafeteria who could hardly pretend they had not heard him, and, turning back to me, said, "That is the damnedest story I have heard in some time, Neil." Deliberately. Adding a space between every word. "Comes as news."

"Did Laura ever talk to you about Marilyn and Elvis in any context?"

"Sure. All the time. You know how she is when it comes to adding to Monroe legend and, not so incidentally, polishing her own a bit. There are Elvis stories, also, from when she worked with him, not so many and only when somebody thinks to ask, but all of it strictly press agent stuff. Elvis was a nice guy. He showed promise as an actor. He loved singing. Blah, blah, blah. Then she's talking about Marilyn again."

"Maybe there's something Sunset said to you that—"

Spoon shook his head and finger-toweled the sweat off his face. "Doesn't confide much in me at all, less since he got the notion I'm somehow responsible for the death of Dulcy Brown, Mrs. Beaudry."

"Didn't Dulcy make a movie with Elvis?"

"Same as Mr. Beaudry did. Not much of a part, but enough to be noticed. Almost like a favor, or just to keep busy. This was before she became a regular member of John Ford's stock company. Mrs. Beaudry and I chatted about those times whenever we strolled around the Estates; she always appreciated me tagging along after her, given Mr. Beaudry's condition and all.

"She loved to putter in that mutt of a garden we have, and she had quite the green thumb. The plants and flowers flourished under her touch. Once Mrs. Beaudry was gone, everything withered and died, missing her as much as we did. Nobody's ever been able to do as well."

"And she—"

"Unh-unh. Her Elvis stories were just as innocent as Miss Dane's stories. Not so much as a whisper about Marilyn."

Spoon seemed to have grown uncomfortable and was having a hard time looking at me. His eyes seemed to prefer focusing on a dirt stain on the table.

I thought I knew why. "Tell me what Laura Dane told you about Marilyn and Elvis."

"I already said," Spoon said. He used the butter knife handle to scrape at the stain, which appeared to be chili.

"Range Roper salute?" I gave him the hidden-thumb salute.

The salute is one of life's lessons a true-blue Range Roper never forgets. He started to return it but stopped halfway and slapped the table with his hand.

"Darn it, Neil. I gave Miss Dane my word I'd never tell."

"Code of the Range Ropers, Mickey."

"You invoking it?"

"It could help my ex get off the hook, Mickey."

For a moment, I thought he was going to burst into tears, and then he related the story:

Marilyn and Laura. Joking about Elvis the week he checked onto the Fox lot. Exchanging one outrageous guess after another about how good Elvis the Pelvis worked his gyrating nothing-but-a-hound-dog hips horizontally on a mattress. Beset by the madness of their starlet days, they bet on who can score first with him.

Laura wins the coin flip. She begins visiting the *Love Me Tender* set and proves an inspiration to members of Elvis's young, horny Memphis Mafia. However, nothing she does gets more than a sultry-eyed, side-of-the-mouth grin from Elvis.

When it's Marilyn's turn, knowing the direct approach won't work because it's already failed Laura, she chooses a simple ruse that worked years before with John Huston. She sends Elvis a mash note. The note bluntly describes what lies ahead for Elvis if he has any curiosity at all about Marilyn.

Laura delivers the note. Within the hour, Elvis's answer is dropped off by Sunset Beaudry. It also is specific and inventive, and by nightfall Marilyn and Elvis are locked inside Sunset's trailer. Curtains drawn. Lights off. Flesh yielding to flesh and fantasy.

Spoon raised his shoulders, frozen inside a forlorn stare, obviously disturbed at having violated one moral commitment to keep another. I didn't care. My priority was Stevie. I pressed him to tell me more.

"Marilyn sent Elvis a note and Elvis sent Marilyn a note," I said. "Did Laura say more notes were exchanged?"

"Uh-huh. A lot of them got delivered back and forth, right until the affair got broken up."

"Got broken up? It didn't just end?"

"Unh-unh. When Mr. Darryl F. Zanuck heard what was going on, he told his PR guy to do whatever he had to do to put an end to it. Reg Mowry? In the olden days at Fox, everyone called him Dr. Fix-it."

"I know. I've been looking for Reg Mowry."

"So, it might interest you to know—"

Spoon aimed a poking index finger downward.

"Meaning?"

"Reason I left Miss Dane. He's with her now. They allow one visitor at a time, so when Mr. Mowry showed up, I come up here for coffee and claws. I need to bring him a black coffee and a—Hey, Neil! Hold your horses and we can go back down together."

I paused in the doorway to Laura Dane's room to let my eyes adjust. The curtains were drawn. The only light was the blue one flickering from the TV set mounted on the wall to my right.

I recognized Crosby and Hope. One of their road movies, *Road to Morocco*, the sound lost below the steady, snorting breaths of the patient lumped underneath a single sheet in the tilted bed by the window. Laura was asleep under a tangle of lifelines.

I stepped inside cautiously, careful to keep my Nikes from making squeaking sounds off contact with the linoleum. The other bed was empty. So was the rest of the room, unless Mowry was in the john. I cocked an ear toward my left, heard nothing at all until an instant later:

The squeeze of a heel against the floor.

I angled in place and glanced over my shoulder expecting to see

Mickey Spoon. The motionless figure sketched in shadows, his back lit by the corridor fluorescents, was too trim and erect to be him.

"Neil Gulliver?" he said, like the answer was attached to the question.

"Reg Mowry?"

Reg Mowry's voice was quiet and calming when he said my name, while I had to push out his through snatches of anxious breath.

"Seen your handsome face on a million billboards and buses," he said. "Reading you, too, since our mutual friend Augie Fowler turned me on to you. Lots of times I find myself quoting you to friends."

I wheezed out a thank-you and eased into an upright position while he tossed out a few more compliments. Press agents do that as easily as firing up a gas stove burner. Reg Mowry was always considered the best.

"You've been looking around for me." His smile was too easy for the truth.

"Yes."

He raised his arms in surrender. "About Blackie Sheridan's murder."

"Yes."

"Elvis and Marilyn?"

"Yes."

"Something about love letters?"

"Yes. How do you know so much?"

"Used to be my business to know *everything,*" Mowry said. He retreated a few steps. "I found a quiet place looking for a phone a few minutes ago," he said and, as if he were following up on a suggestion I had made, led me to an empty room across the way and two doors down.

I perched on the edge of the bed nearer the window, legs crossed at the ankles, facing Mowry, who stood an uneasy parade rest alongside the door.

"The Friars message said something about a column, and that

made me curious as a Century City lawyer,'' he said. ''What kind of column could Neil Gulliver need me for? I wanted to know what I could be getting myself into. Or not. I thought Augie could tell me, so I went and tracked him down, some religious compound over by Griffith Park.''

''It's not just Hollywood that's changed.''

''Brother Kalman, what the old devil wants to be called now.'' Mowry smiled, adding cracks and fissures to sun-bleached leathery skin that traveled in all directions, like busy streets on a page in the *Thomas Guide.*

Mowry was in his late seventies or early eighties, and his Wedgwood blue eyes widened and brightened behind his oval-shaped bifocals. The lenses were mounted in thin, cherry red frames that stood out like a personal trademark against the quiet reserve of a perfectly creased gray herringbone suit, its age exposed by the broad lapels, and polished, burnished brown Oxford wing tips that played games with the reflected light whenever he tapped a foot.

Dressed like this, Mowry could walk with kings, but still retreat into the background, the way PR people are supposed to do, despite a six-foot height that gave him a commanding presence he resisted by assuming a butler's stoop.

I said, ''Augie told you about Marilyn and Elvis, the love letters. What else?''

''Not as much as he learned from me, Neil.''

''Are you going to tell me, too?''

Mowry made a show of considering the question, trying to make up his mind between me and the walls, shifting his weight from one foot to the other.

Finally: ''Are we off the record on this?''

His eyes pinned me to the question. He saw me weighing the question. Anyone who has been around as long as Mowry knows the way to keep something off the record is to keep your mouth shut. I reminded him.

Mowry nodded agreement and moved his fingers closer to his chin, then tossed them away. ''Augie said you can be trusted, but indulge this old press agent, anyway. Off the record?''

I coughed my throat clear and agreed, "Off the record." It was the truth, too, unless I heard something that had to go back on the record in order to clear Stevie.

Augie would know that, whether or not he had mentioned it to Mowry. It was one of the first lessons I learned from him on the crime beat: "You do whatever it takes to get the story, kiddo, and then you're free to make the rules fit the headline."

Mowry's memory was almost letter-perfect as he told me about the Twentieth Century–Fox lot in the glamorous fifties, when Marilyn and Elvis were working there and the streets and soundstages throbbed daily with people who could turn reality into make-believe for a screen credit.

He frequently Mr. Malaproped his metaphors and was prone to wander from the main road whenever a name or incident caught his imagination.

When that happened, I let him drift until he was satisfied, trusting myself to piece together a coherent story later. It got harder the closer Mowry came to the present, and his yesterdays took on the coloration of a rumor. Trying to remember a name or a date, some other elusive detail, he squeezed his eyes, did tricks with his nose, scratched thoughtfully at his cheeks, begged the ceiling, and, ultimately clueless, he laughed in frustration and moved on.

The way he told it, he first learned Marilyn and Elvis were having an affair the day he went searching for her with contacts from a gallery shoot with Andy Varington. Varington was the only photographer on the lot Marilyn trusted, but she refused to waive her kill approval for anyone, and Mowry was under the gun to get sets printed and planted with the fan magazines.

Marilyn hated making decisions and had put him off for two weeks. More delay could cost Fox advance exposure for *Bus Stop*, including layouts in *Movie Mirror*, *Silver Screen*, and the book that mattered most when it came to selling a picture, *Photoplay*.

Zanuck was on the case personally, even calling once during a morning lube job from some aspiring starlet, cataloging demands at a feverish pitch, leaving Mowry to wonder if they were for him or the girl whose face was buried between Zanuck's thighs.

He reached the soundstage shortly after eleven. No Marilyn. She had disappeared after the driver dropped her off three hours late for a six-thirty makeup call.

They were still waiting for her in makeup and Josh Logan, the director of *Bus Stop*, was wandering all around the set with Milton Krasner, the cinematographer, making rude insinuations about her while he anxiously looked for another cover angle to shoot using Don Murray and Claire Cavanaugh.

"Marilyn always had this acting guru with her, and she was on the set," Mowry said. "That meant Marilyn was close by. The guru wasn't talking—never to me—so over to Laura Dane I went."

"Her best friend."

Mowry nodded. "Her best friend. She was visiting, sitting out a suspension at Warner Bros. over some piece of crappola she wouldn't make with Lancaster. I spotted Laura flexing her curves by Marilyn's set trailer, kibitzing a grip, stroking his ego and his overalls, her way of passing time. I put the question to her and recognized immediately by her lame answer that she knew where Marilyn was. I reminded Laura she still owed me for favors I had once negotiated on her behalf with DFZ:

'You're putting me on the spot, Reggie.'

'Marilyn's put us both there, baby.'

'Can't I just suck your dick and call us even?'

'I think you have me confused with my boss.'

'Not the first time.'

'Maybe not the last, either, but not this time.'

'Okay, but promise me not to spill the beans to Marilyn about who told.' "

And she stuck a tongue and a whisper in his ear: Elvis. He should have known by the signs that weren't there, the way they had avoided each other after he'd posed them together for Andy Varington in what became "The Snapshot Heard 'round the World."

Mowry waited out the flashing red light at the door of the *Love Me Tender* soundstage, then went hunting for her.

Elvis was on the set, every inch the gun-slinging cowboy immortalized in Warhol's paintings. He was getting his makeup freshened while the crew relit and moved the camera for a two-shot with Sunset Beaudry and responding good-naturedly to some sideline kidding from Dick Egan and Neville Brand.

"Bobby Webb was the director. I got his permission to borrow Sunset for a few minutes, outside where we couldn't be overheard. Sunset gave me a desperate look, like he knew what was coming. I felt Elvis's eyes tracking us all the way. Even before I finished asking, Sunset was denying any knowledge of Marilyn and Elvis.

"I put it to him straight. I told Sunset none of his Range Roper crappola. He could answer my question or he could answer direct to Mr. Zanuck, and that might take care of any thought he had about escaping out from under the Curse of Monogram Studios here at Fox. Sunset looked liked Chicken Little must have looked, only his sky really was about to fall on him. Without so much as a word, he dug out of his pocket a key to his trailer and handed it over. 'I didn't tell you a word, not one single word,' Sunset said, like it made a difference. Maybe it did, the way Sunset's mind worked."

"Marilyn was in Beaudry's trailer?"

Mowry shook his head definitively. He said, "I knocked good and loud a few times but did not risk calling her name. I heard sounds, so I unlocked the door and climbed inside, and what I saw next, you could bowl me over with a feather."

"It wasn't Marilyn," I guessed. He pushed a hand between us. Paused. Debating whether to share the rest of the story. I said, "We're still off the record."

Mowry took a deep breath and pushed it back out.

"The two of them were naked in the aisle, sweaty and smelly like filthy bedsheets in a quickie motel. Blackie Sheridan was grinning at me under a tall, black Stetson, like he welcomed an audience. And Dulcy Brown, her eyes were screaming loud at me to go away and keep her shame secret."

My memory flashed on Dulcy's grave marker in the Retirement Estates cemetery, Shangri-la, and the empty plot next to hers, waiting for Sunset, who brought her flowers every day.

Mowry said, "You would have to know Dulcy as well as me to understand how unbelievable that was. Except for Loretta Young, I never my whole career have dealt with anyone else so true to her beliefs, so there had to be something drastic that put Dulcy with a cock hound like Blackie Sheridan. He was a damn fine director, the reason DFZ tolerated him so long, and a first-rate charmer. But, Blackie also was a cock hound and a rat. Whoever once said 'Time wounds all heels' had Blackie in mind."

Mowry dug his hands into his pockets and surveyed the room for contradiction.

"What made Sheridan a rat?"

Mowry thought about it and shrugged. "The law of averages, I suppose."

"Dulcy?"

"The tit of the iceberg." A corner of the ceiling caught his interest. "Taking it all into consideration, it's a miracle that Blackie lived as long as he did before someone separated him from his next breath."

"Like Sunset? After he learned Sheridan and his wife—"

"Absolutely not! Never!" Mowry shook his head violently and withered me with a four-alarm, pop-eyed stare. He excused himself and crossed to the bathroom on urgent legs. I heard water running and, a moment later, he emerged sipping from a small waxed cup. The brown prescription vial in his other hand disappeared into a jacket pocket.

"My ticker," he explained sheepishly. "I'm not supposed to get excited. I should never of come here for this except for the telephone call from—"

He flung aside the rest of the thought and got comfortable on the other bed, facing me.

Had Mowry forgotten the name or didn't he want me to know?

He closed his eyes until he remembered where he'd left off.

"Sunset never found out about the trailer. I made Dulcy pull herself together, and right in front of her I told Blackie in no uncertified terms he was through in this town if he ever breathed a word or dared come on to Dulcy again. I could destroy him with a whisker in DFZ's ear, and he knew it. I was not the power, but I was close enough to make things happen."

His eyes became as narrow as his voice. His face warped into a mask of conceit, like the ones worn by people operating in the shadow of command.

"Blackie's word meant crappola," Mowry said, "so I steered a few pictures his way by planting the notion with Mr. Zanuck, and I made certain Blackie knew. One picture DFZ had in mind for Jean Negulesco even got him another Oscar nomination. Once he checked off the lot for the last time, I saw to it the right people heard what I wanted. Not all at once, so it was obvious, but over the years. When I finished with the rat, he never knew what hit him.

"Last year, when he was so pushed and desperate he needed a place like the MPRE to stay, Blackie drove on out to my chicken ranch and begged for help. I got some perverse satisfaction from writing a letter of recommendation. I called over there and even had certain friends with money for clout call and put in a word."

"Why did you bother?"

Mowry trained his eyes on the water cup, finally nodded agreement with himself. "It's easier to live with guilt when you're young, Neil; nobody tell you that yet?"

"Augie says, Forgive and remember."

He shot me a harsh glance. "If Augie pulls through, he will be well advised to remember to forgive, especially if he plans to keep on acting the holy man."

"I don't pretend to understand what it's about, Mr. Mowry, but I've never felt being Brother Kalman is an act with Augie."

Mowry excused my defense with another look. "People make a habit of finding God after they lose themselves. They'd be better off by starting the search earlier."

I wasn't about to argue theology. "When you helped Sheridan, weren't you concerned that the Beaudrys were living at the MPRE?"

His expression absorbed the question and evaporated into a somber smile. "I checked first, before lifting a finger. Made a breakfast visit one morning. When we had a minute, I asked her. Dulcy assured me Sunset had no knowledge what happened that day, and, as for herself, she said—

"I can live with it, Reggie."

"You sure, sweetheart?"

Dulcy's fingers wandered to the petite crucifix around her neck, fondled the encrusted-pearl surface. She closed her eyes to the past, nodded gently, reached for the teapot. "This is our Claire's favorite blend, her version of Earl Grey. It's scented with bergamot, Reggie. What gives it its lavender-like bouquet."

"Don't change the subject on me, Dulcy." She moved her hand onto his and patted it gently, like a mother reassuring a child. "Make me believe you, sweetheart."

"It will be all right, Reggie. Believe me. I was never that good an actress."

"Says who?" Sunset challenged her from across the room, posturing on uncertain, metal-bound legs, using his umbrella-handled, gnarled wood canes to sustain a delicate balance. "In all my years, ain't never come across one who's better."

"Oh, piffle, Alfred."

"Don't you go piffling with me, Mrs. Beaudry." He faked a scowl. Inched ahead, the canes one after the other carrying the forward thrust of his upper torso while he urged his legs across the room. He clamped a firm hand on the back of her chair, leaned in to kiss her earlobe.

Dulcy swept around a hand to embrace his cheek. He took it in his own, squeezed it gently. "She's gone and done it to me again, Reggie. This old girl is piffling with me . . ."

Mowry seemed mesmerized by the memory.

I said, "Now tell me about Claire Cavanaugh."

He arched back. Eyed me suspiciously.

"Claire's supposed memory losses?"

I repeated what I heard from Augie.

Mowry lifted the red frames for better access to a mottled liver spot below his right eye and sandpapered it with his fingers. Gave the spot a final swipe and replaced the frames. "Augie told me the same thing, Neil. I'll tell you how I answered.

"In her time Claire was as fine an actress as they come, but what we're seeing is not playacting. Her mind glides. Here today and gone tomorrow. I have visited enough to know."

He flew a circling finger from his temple to the sky.

I said, "How did Augie respond?"

"He did not believe me. You would know that just by knowing him. Augie is one of those people who must stumble onto the truth himself, before it becomes the truth. I can see it is a trait he managed to install in you."

I said, "Augie and I believe each other. That's saved us a lot of stumbling over the years."

Mowry lifted his bushy eyebrows, swept them down, and pushed threads of henna-rinsed hair off his temple. He held off a smile.

I said, "You have a problem with that?"

"Let's say I respect your sincerity."

"How about my problem now: believing you?"

"I respect your honesty."

An annoying edge had filtered into Mowry's tone. Discreet. Enough to remind me who controlled the situation.

I pushed up from the bed and strolled the room, stretching, working out the kinks in my legs and between my shoulder blades, keeping my back to him, not wanting Mowry to see how well he was manipulating me.

I said, "Earlier today, Claire magically regained her senses when I told her I knew about the seven hundred and fifty dollars you sent her."

Mowry shrugged. "You caught her in a lucite moment. There's no mystery to the seven five oh. I told Augie when he asked, like I can tell you. I've been sending checks to Claire for years. Not only Claire. A lot of old-timers. You want a list? I can give you a list. You want to know why? I can tell you that, too."

Turning, I held Mowry off with a gesture and said casually, "I also told Claire I have Elvis and Marilyn's love letters."

Astonishment tanked over Mowry's face.

Except for the hum of the fluorescents, the room got quieter than a graveyard chorus.

Mowry removed his glasses and inspected the lenses. Used his jacket handkerchief to rub them clean. Played out a laugh in his chest. Poked the red frames back up his schoolyard nose. Stared at me defiantly.

I was in control again.

When Reg Mowry finished studying me, as if I were some bug under a microscope, he said, "It's my turn not to believe you, Neil. If you had Elvis and Marilyn's love letters, your ex-wife would not be getting ready to star on post office walls all over America. The cops would know who killed Blackie Sheridan and, I suppose, the others, also, and she could flee like a bird."

A hint of smile briefly fractured his noncommittal gaze. He pointed me back to the bed and waited until I was settled before continuing.

So much for me being in control.

"I was giving you too much credit," he said. "I expect the youngsters to look at people my age and say, 'Relics, dinosaurs, off with their hats!' but you should know better. If you're not able to give me your respect, show me enough courtesy not to try a cheap theatrical trick. I was on to stunts like that before you were in knee pads.''

I apologized. He dismissed it with a gesture.

''Do you know what honor is?'' he said. ''I do. To this day I honor the wishes of my boss, Mr. Darryl F. Zanuck. With honor comes obligation.''

Mowry's eyes glistened with memory. His devotion to Zanuck was obvious. He propped an elbow against the hand wrapped over his stomach and stared into space, played finger games over his lips, cleared his throat.

''I was going to tell you about Claire's seven five oh,'' he said. ''For years I've been in charge of what DFZ and I called the Fund. It wasn't a lot, maybe a few hundred thousand collecting a high interest in an account DFZ kept at a small commercial bank in Riverside where nobody would ever think to check, especially not DFZ's wife, Virginia.'' He balked at the thought. ''I used the Fund to pay off debts and obligations that fell to a high roller like DFZ. The gamblers and those girls he groomed for stardom, if you get my draft?''

I said I did.

''Over the years, he had me putting hundreds of people on the list. Most were one-shots, fast payoffs. Others made DFZ's secret payroll for the long haul. He was generous to a flirt. We talked in shorthand, never on paper. DFZ was too smart for paper.''

His voice took on a melancholy edge.

''In 1979, shortly before DFZ passed on in Palm Springs just three days shy of Christmas, in his seventy-seventh year, I went over for a visit. There wasn't much left to him by then, except in the Hollywood history books.

''I drove over to the Springs to pay my respects and drop off some eggs from my ranch, sort of a Christmas present, and it hurt to see him failing so fast. When we had time to ourselves on the patio, DFZ gave me the high sign and I moved over to his chaise. Leaned in real close to hear him. He said he was glad to see me, because he had been meaning to invite me over. He wondered about the Fund, but not like any test, because he knew I could account for every penny if he ever bothered asking. I told him his Fund was earning a higher interest rate. He seemed to enjoy that, but he shut me up when I tried to tell him the balance. It wasn't the reason for his question, DFZ assured me.

"He said I was to go on paying out like always and to feel free to take what I needed personally. He said, 'You'll always be my man, Reg.' Isn't that something?"

Mowry was wearing the quote like a medal.

"Claire got what she made while she was under contract to Fox, and that's why," he said. "Seven five oh a week. Not like today, where the millions flow like wine. Fairies who can't act their way out of a paper hat get more for one movie than a Dana Andrews or Vic Mature made his entire career, know what I mean?"

"Yes." I needed to stop Mowry before his memory started another rollback. Under other circumstances, over tap beer and pretzels, I'd be begging for the E-ticket tour in his castle of gossip. "How much does Laura Dane get?"

He angled his head, glancing across at me with one-eyed curiosity. "When did I say anything about her?"

"You mentioned a list. I assumed she was on it. Sorry if—"

Mowry's hand dismissed me.

"None taken," he said, easing back, pushing his palm at me. "The time comes when living in memory is like walking barefoot. Comfortable, but expect to step on a pebble or rusty nail every once in a blue moon. She gets two grand."

"Two thousand dollars a week?"

"A month. Two thousand a month."

"For forty years."

"Going on forty years. Less than Claire because Laura was never under contract."

Finger math. "That's nearly a million dollars. What could be worth a million dollars?" He waited for me to guess. "You know what I'm thinking, Mr. Mowry?"

"I wasn't born again yesterday, Neil. You're thinking, was Laura Dane's way with DFZ's dong that special?" Mowry's laughter turned into a phlegmy cough. He wiped his hand dry on his jacket handkerchief and rearranged it in the pocket. "Actually, she gets paid for keeping her mouth shut."

"About Marilyn and Elvis."

"No, about Lassie and Rin Tin Tin," he said, making a face of mock exasperation. "That was the deal DFZ ordered after I got to recognizing the gift that keeps on giving, mash notes and all, and got Laura to tell him the whole story and he saw what kind of problem he had. Laura didn't want any reward or anything, but DFZ insisted. He was grateful to Laura. He knew the career-destroying impact for his two stars if word started leaking. Right away, he wasted no time. DFZ summoned Tom Parker, Elvis's manager, and laid down the law. He handled Elvis and I handled Marilyn and—that's all she rode. The romance ended faster than you can spell hump."

He grinned easily, checked his expensive Baume & Mercier, and glanced toward the door. "You suppose Mickey Spoon is still across with Laura, wondering what became of us, while my coffee grows colder'n a witch's tic?"

He made a move to get up from the bed. I held him there with a gesture. Something below the surface of his story was nagging at me. Waiting to hook it, I said, "We still haven't talked about the love letters."

"Destroyed," he said after a moment.

"You're certain?"

"Is tomorrow"—bringing the watch six inches from his face—"Sunday?"

"Who destroyed them, Mr. Mowry?"

"Laura. Marilyn was saving hers all bound up by a pink silk ribbon like a silly schoolgirl bitten by the love bug, hidden away in a dresser drawer. After Elvis kissed her off, she threw one of her tantrums and told Laura she didn't ever want to hear his name again, to go get the letters and burn them. Laura did. Turned on the gas jets in the bungalow fireplace and piled on the logs. One by one, sent them to the dead letter office."

"Marilyn's letters to Elvis. Did she also burn them?"

Mowry gave me a look that wondered how that was possible. He shook his head. "Seems Elvis wasn't as sentimental as Marilyn. He consigned a letter to the circular file soon as he read it."

"You're certain?"

"No reason for doubt. The Colonel was a rascal, but he saw there was too much at stake for tomfoolery. He took Elvis's word, but he also had Hank Twitchell search around, just to be on the safe side."

"Hank Twitchell?"

"He was Elvis's man."

"I know Hank, Mr. Mowry. I visited with him. He told me there were no love letters."

Mowry digested the information like someone waiting for a bus. "Well, there aren't. Besides, Hank was never one to spread anybody else's manure."

Mowry mumbled something else about his coffee and rose. I tried a question while he traveled across the room slowly, as if my questioning had had a tiring effect.

"Mr. Mowry, if what you've told me is true, why was Blackie Sheridan certain the love letters exist? So was my ex's producer, Jeremy Brighton. Somebody phoned Brighton and offered him the love letters for a hundred grand. He went to the MPRE to buy them and was killed for his trouble. My ex has been attacked for the love letters and somebody even came after me . . ."

Mowry did a shuffling about-face and accented his smile with a shrug. "If what I've told you is true, you said? You are a trusted friend of Augie's and we are off the record. I have no cause to lie."

"How do you explain all this, Mr. Mowry?"

"I don't have to." He studied his watch. "At this hour and with the freeways, I got a long trip ahead of me, Neil."

"Time reveals what the truth conceals, Mr. Mowry."

His look challenged the thought. "Come visit me sometime at my ranch. An open invitation. See what a boyhood dream can be all about. Tell Mickey Spoon I've gone? Tell him I said you are welcome to my coffee."

Mowry slipped out the door.

I knew it was useless to chase after him.

He was in control.

I picked up the phone and pressed zero.

The ICU nurse's hollow voice advised that Augie was resting comfortably, no change in his condition.

I paused at Laura's door to look for Mickey.

He wasn't there.

Marnie, her great-niece, was, looking great.

She was in a visitor's chair alongside the bed and stroked Laura's arm gently while conducting a one-sided chat too low for me to understand. Her tone was gentle and full of bright-spirited laughter, like she was ministering to an ailing pet.

The overhead lights had been turned on and I could see her blond hair discharging static electricity in all directions. Exotic eyes owlish behind wire-framed oval lenses that couldn't distort her fresh beauty, even with her memorable body buried inside a baggy jogging suit, work boots, and a fractured bomber jacket.

The dark mass near the window was the beefy biker in black leather I had seen at Laura's apartment last night who had given me the bad directions.

I thought it over and decided to head for the parking lot.

I had more important matters to puzzle over.

The cell phone beckoned about the time the Jag was defying the 405 incline at the Bel Air pass.

I needed a moment to recognize the muffled tinkles emanating from the glove. I gripped the steering wheel and managed to hold a steady course in the center lane while fumbling with the latch.

Yanked open the mouthpiece.

Anchored the gizmo between my shoulder and ear.

Said my name.

"Honey, it's me." She sounded out of breath.

"Stevie. What's up?"

"My blood pressure. I keep hearing noises outside the door, like someone's trying to get inside."

"Did you look through the spy hole?"

"Yeah, and I saw James Bond," she said, annoyed. "I'm scared, not stupid. There was nobody there."

"Call down to security, then get 911 on the line."

"Screw that!" she said. "I got your gun aimed at the door, and if it opens—"

"Stevie, please do what I say."

There was distortion, then the phone died in my ear.

Dead battery.

It's an imperfect world.

I had set a new land speed record by the time I got to the Heathcliffe around six o'clock. I fumbled with the key. Charged into my apartment. Froze two steps into the living room.

In the middle of the room, about five feet in front of me, was Blue Blazer, late of the Beverly Hills Hotel and later an attack on Stevie. He stood militarily correct in tight jeans and a wide-lapeled black leather jacket like the one I had just seen on Marnie's boyfriend. Spit-shined boots.

My Beretta was in his left hand, aimed like he knew how to use it. He looked almost happy to see me here as he swung it in my direction, then adjusted it past his body to the other side of the room, invisible from this position, then back again, like he was having trouble making up his mind.

His eyes danced anxiously behind the yellow-tinted lenses in his aviator frames.

Moments like this, those inclined to end a life, can last a lifetime. I had survived more than my share and every time walked away swearing I would never again get myself in this position.

"Stevie?"

"Shut the fuck up," he said gently, with not quite a lisp.

I answered Blue Blazer's tough expression with a look that said I was mad and capable of getting madder if provoked. He saw it and shook his head enough to tell me better.

"Honey, don't do anything crazy," Stevie said, from a corner of the room I couldn't see.

Blue Blazer tracked her voice with the Beretta.

"Stevie, you okay?"

"No thanks to this moron."

"Shut the fuck up, you, too, cunt," Blue Blazer said.

I said, "I called the cops. They'll be here any minute."

"Whadja do, dial 911?" Blue Blazer snorted. "That stands for the number a minutes it takes for 'em to respond. You'll be dead before that, you and the bitch, unless I get the letters."

"No letters here," I said.

"Then where?"

"The post office?" I suggested.

"Where you looking to get buried? Forest Laugh?"

"Put away the gun. You're killing me with your humor."

"Just give me the letters, okay? I'm outta here and nobody gets hurt." He was becoming the kind of anxious that accidentally pulls triggers.

Stevie charged into sight in a pair of my cotton pajamas, taking long-legged strides to Blue Blazer, shoulders hunched, shaking a fist as if she couldn't decide what to do with it.

"Back, you crazy bitch!" Blue Blazer shouted and straight-armed the Beretta at her.

Stevie was not quite between us as her fists crashed down on his left shoulder.

Blue Blazer made a noise and his hand flew up reflexively.

The Beretta caught her under the jaw.

Her arms flew asunder. She stumbled backward on her heels.

"Crazy bitch!"

I charged forward and reached him in time to feel the butt of the Beretta bang down on top of my head. My hands fell and my body reeled haphazardly on my knees.

"You insane, too?" Blue Blazer said, astounded, looking more pained than I felt, and I was feeling lots of pain. It was bolting down me like a broken elevator. I pirouetted on one foot while Stevie shot past me.

I heard a smack and a heavy-duty scream behind me while I rubber-legged into the hallway. I hit the wall hands first, hard, reminding old healed wounds how to hurt me again. New pains exploded in my shoulders like the bones were trying to crack through my skin.

I willed myself to remain awake, somehow managed to wheel around. Through a biting fog crowding half-shuttered eyes, I made out Stevie battling Blue Blazer for possession of the Beretta. Blue Blazer held it above his head, out of Stevie's reach.

She tried climbing him like a ladder. There were no steps for her feet. Their legs became entangled as he swayed backwards.

He lost his shades. Her nails dug at his face as she struggled to hold on. He yowled another, harsher scream. I imagined what she had done to cause it as they toppled onto the coffee table. The table collapsed under their combined weight.

Stevie shook her head clear and tracked the Beretta.

It was still locked in Blue Blazer's grip.

She rolled onto her knees on top of him and began batting his face with her fists, inventing new curses.

Blue Blazer brought his arms down and across his face to protect himself without letting go of the weapon.

"Dung-swallowing skunk!" Stevie screamed.

She leaned forward and adjusted her body in a way that let her bury her teeth into the fleshy mound below the thumb of Blue Blazer's gun hand. He yowled and his fingers sprang open.

Stevie snapped the Beretta away. Lifted it into the air like the Statue of Liberty's torch.

She freed the safety, pressed the mouth tightly under Blue Blazer's wide, frightened left eye, and hissed in an ice cube whisper, "You got lucky and got it from me last time, garbage face. Try it again, I blow your brains to the Bel Air gates."

Blue Blazer's answer was an unintelligible buzz as I sank into the pitch-black whirlpool washing away my pain.

I hated to leave the dream.

In it, I slew the dragon and rescued the fair maiden and regained the kingdom by dispatching a villain who substantially resembled Blue Blazer. Dreams like that are hard to come by and at the moment it was preferable to the hacksaws cutting through my temple bones and the shredded glass sloshing behind my eyes.

"It's about time," Stevie said. She was sitting on a stool at the counter that divides the living room and kitchen.

I twisted into a position somewhere between sitting and leaning on my elbow and acknowledged the truth. "My hero," I said.

"It was either that or listen to the two of you trade more of your macho bullshit," Stevie said, toasting me with a jelly glass of my cheap Napa Valley red and keeping the Beretta pointed at Blue Blazer, who sat stiffly two or three feet away, across the flattened coffee table. He kept his hands clasped on his lap as if getting ready to pray. "It's been ten minutes. Where are the cops you called?"

"Another nine hundred and one minutes to go," Blue Blazer said, recycling his punchline. Smiling nervously. All his menace lost inside uncertainty.

Stevie faked taking aim. "Who asked you, dick brain?"

Blue Blazer cringed and hid his face behind his palms.

I said, "I lied about the cops. I was buying us time."

Blue Blazer made a smug I-knew-it-all-the-time noise and turned away from Stevie like a mutt who knows he's done wrong.

"Why didn't you phone down to security?" I said. "Didn't I tell you to call 911?"

"I wanted to listen to you we'd still be married," she said. "Besides, when you hung up on me, I thought it was so you could call the cops."

"I didn't hang up. The damn cell phone went dead. Battery."

"Happens to me all the time, so I started using a lighter plug-in," Blue Blazer said, and retreated from our nasty stares.

Stevie said, "I was about to dial when I hear this pile of snot calling something about flowers for Miss Marriner, so I go over and check the peephole again."

My eyes followed her gesture to a bouquet of bright yellow, gold, and white wildflowers wrapped inside green tissue and tied with matching ribbon.

She said, "I figure it's been my imagination acting up and what a sweet surprise from you, forgetting that you never go in for sweet surprises, so I let down my guard. I open the door and next thing I know the ape man has wrestled the gun away from me. I convince him I don't know about any letters, and we settle in to wait for you.''

"The way she had the safety off, she could of killed someone. I don't put the safety back on, I could have really killed someone,'' Blue Blazer said.

Stevie said, "Will you shut up? Can't you tell we are trying to have a serious conversation here?''

"Okay, okay. I'm sorry.'' He appealed to me with a look. "I really had you believing, didn't I?''

I said, "Stevie, couldn't you see it was the same guy?''

She looked at me curiously and after a moment shook her head. "What are you talking about?''

"When you checked at the spy hole. The guy who came after you at *Bedrooms and Board Rooms*.''

"Because that's not him,'' Stevie said. "This is some other degenerate pond scum lowlife.''

Blue Blazer nodded agreement.

"When I described him to you, you said—''

"It was close and cudda been, especially after you got the car right, but that muscle-bound moron is walking around now with a piece of his ear missing.''

Blue Blazer nodded.

I asked him, "Who the hell are you?''

"I'll tell if you promise you won't call the police.''

I made like I was mulling the deal.

"You have my word,'' I lied.

"Where would you like me to start?''

"How about with your name?''

His name was Larry Grenedier.

He was one of Laura Dane's prize students.

She had put him up to playing a bad guy and coming after Stevie and me for the missing love letters.

Laura had told him it was an acting exercise involving his favorite actress, Stephanie Marriner. How could he pass up an opportunity to meet Stevie?

"What else did Laura say about the love letters, Larry?"

Grenedier squeezed his face into a question mark. "She say? They were just a prop, the letters. Like, you know? Secret plans to destroy the universe?"

"How did you know Stevie was here?"

"From the other guy in the exercise. True?"

"Is what true?"

"No, that's his name. True. True Something-or-other . . . We traded off. I started with you and he got Stevie. How long you been studying acting with Laura? You played that blackout scene just great, dude. And you, Miss Marriner, great improv. Simply awesome."

Grenedier flashed his smile at Stevie and me and saw the truth in our expressions.

He said, "This wasn't an exercise, was it?"

There are definite benefits to being an incurable pack rat.

In the box of collectibles I keep under my bed was a Will Rogers lariat I acquired about three years ago at a Butterfield and Butterfield auction of Hollywood artifacts.

I used it to secure Grenedier to the armchair I pushed in front of the TV and for good measure cuffed his hands behind his back with a pair of handcuffs Jimmy Steiger gave me almost a decade ago as a souvenir of a tough case we'd broken together.

I wasn't certain everything Grenedier had told us was true.

I didn't want him free to send warnings to anyone before I followed up on an idea that had flashed like a comic strip lightbulb.

I called DeSantis.

I told him about Grenedier and said I'd leave a spare key with the security guard at the main entrance.

"Breaking and entering, attempted burglary, ADW, and what else, Gulliver?"

"He has bad timing and a lousy sense of humor."

"C'mon. I know you're holding back."

"What he doesn't tell you, I'll fill in when I see you."

"Not good enough. I need to hear more if you expect me to pick up this joker and run him around the precincts for a day."

"This arrest will help make you a hero in Paige Jahnsen's beautiful eyes."

"You don't fight fair, do you?"

"Never where beautiful eyes are concerned," I said and overlayed his retort with a quick goodbye before hanging up.

I tuned the TV to the Comedy Channel at Grenedier's request and reassured him the condo would not catch fire before DeSantis got there.

"What if it does?" he said anxiously. "Will somebody know to come up and get me?"

"No," I said, "but I promise I'll never toast another marshmallow without thinking of you."

He was still appealing as we left the apartment and Stevie remarked, "Did I ever mention you have a very, very sick sense of humor, honey?"

"I married you, didn't I?"

She whacked my shoulder and had a snotty answer, several, in fact, throughout our drive to the Paradox Playhouse. The argument was in good fun, unlike the arguments of our married years, or is it just that time makes a joke of everything?

Or, was our relationship changing again?

Sometimes, when I looked over at Stevie, I thought I could see her asking herself the same question, and I wondered if she was any closer to the answer than I was.

The watchman looked up from his *New Yorker*, over the thick bifocals sliding down a modest nose, and recognized Stevie. He asked for an autograph before unlocking the stage door for her.

I settled against the trunk of the Jag to wait for her.

She emerged about twenty minutes later wearing a cropped blond wig, huge pearl button earrings and a bosomy white outfit straight out of *The Seven Year Itch*. She hip-switched for the Jag, her skirt billowing like a sail caught on the brisk alley breeze, revealing her tight thigh and an intoxicating snatch of white panties.

The watchman's awestruck eyes trailed her all the way.

Stevie leaned forward to suppress the skirt, her green eyes catching moonlight, chin pointing to history, a smile to start a war. I sucked in my breath and had to remember it was Stevie, not Marilyn, and hoped the act was good enough to fool Laura Dane.

15

Valley Emergency was in its overnight mode.

The antiseptic corridor held an eerie quiet, except for the slosh of an old-fashioned mop being pushed by a barefoot janitor intent on revitalizing the scuffed linoleum.

Stevie and I hurried past the floor station, where a nurse as starched as her uniform engaged in somber conversation with a tired-eyed intern, and snaked into Laura's room.

Zombie snoring.

A good sign for what we intended.

I stood motionless in a corner by the corridor wall, eyes acclimating to the darkness. I could hear everything unobserved from here. My heart was pounding with anticipation.

"Dubinsky, it's me, Norma Jean." Stevie gentled Laura's shoulder the way a mother rouses a napping child. She leaned closer and poured another breathy whisper into Laura's ear.

"Dubinsky?"

Laura barely moved her head, as if hearing her real name tickled. Her snoring filled the room louder than the sound in a Bruckheimer movie.

Stevie tried again. "Dubinsky?"

On the fifth try, Laura's eyes fluttered open. She made a gargling sound and turned her face to investigate the presence in the visitor's chair by her bed.

"Hear you almost bought it, Dubinsky."

Laura thought about it. "Norma Jean?"

"You were expecting maybe Jean Harlow?" Trying for a Yiddish accent. Throaty laughter.

"Where am I?"

"It isn't Kansas, Toto."

Stevie laughed again, the way Marilyn might have with her best friend as they prepared to trade stories of another night on the town. Laura squinted into the lukewarm light cast through the open bathroom door. It was the only light into the room, too dull to give away the secret of our deception.

She said, "How did you get into this sorry state, girlie?"

Laura craned her neck for a better look and folds of fat floated with the movement. "Can't tell you." Her voice sounded parched, like she was speaking through a blender.

Stevie walked to the sink. She filled a dispenser cup with water, helped Laura manage several sips, and set down the cup on the utility table. "You gave away your cherry. Hundreds of times. You were always able to tell about that. Whatever could be more important than your cherry?"

"I promised."

"You promised?" Laura made a noise. "Dubinsky, since when is a promise more important than me?" Laura's noises were lost under Stevie's spicy Monroe laugh. "You also promised you wouldn't tell Zanuck about me and Elvis, but you did, didn't you?"

"He made me."

"Zanuck, you mean? That yahoo from Wahoo made every broad who ever got within a foot of his polo mallet."

"Sizzemimman," Laura pushed out from the back of her throat.

My best guess, she was trying to pronounce sixty-minute man.

Stevie said, "I got to thinking, Dubinsky, about how pissed I was at Elvis for throwing me over."

"Sorry, Norma Jean, I—"

"Puh-leeze. Not your fault. You did what you gotta, though I was stuck for a long time on that big lunkhead. More than I ever was with Jack the K. Always ready to climb into the sack with him faster'n you can say Frankie Sinatra. Always grinding better'n the last time, that Elvis, but never better'n me."

"You better," Laura croaked.

"Absa-postively right, me better. Wear 'em out and throw 'em out, that was my motto. Remember? I taught Elvis a few new tricks and ruined him for anyone else. Then, before I could say, *'Thanks, but no more thanks, Baby Hips. Start dipping your wick in somebody else, Norma Jean has other fish to fry,'* he dumped me."

"Other fish," Laura agreed.

"I was sure pissed, wasn't I? Pissed enough to burn all his letters. Didn't need the letters any more'n I needed that hound dog eating from my bowl like it was chock full-a peanuts."

"Bowl."

Stevie glanced at me.

I nodded yes, go for it.

Stevie said, "So, what's this I hear about the letters, Dubinsky?"

"Peanuts."

"A little birdie tells me you kept Elvis's letters instead of burning them?"

"Birdie."

"I told that little birdie to go and shut his beak. My partner in crime Laura wouldn't play games like that on Norma Jean. I wasn't buying into that, no how."

"No . . ."

"You know who the birdie was?"

"Beak."

Stevie leaned in and whispered the name like it was some military secret.

She said, "Same person who's responsible for putting you here?"

Laura tried raising an arm.

It fell limply onto the mattress.

A rattle escaped her lips.

Stevie called her name in a voice filled with alarm, then swung her head around and said, desperately, "Neil! Oh, honey, I think—"

I was at Stevie's side before she could finish the thought, on jellied legs, panicked over a death I may have caused by this deception. I reached over to check Laura's neck for a pulse and started to say something to Stevie about screaming for a doctor.

And Laura said, "Help kill . . ."

Startling my fingers, like I'd touched lightning.

"Brighton . . ."

Stevie's shoulders fell a mile. She pushed out a breath big enough to sail a boat to Catalina. Shook her head clear. Became Marilyn again.

"Helped kill? Dubinsky, you crapping on me?"

I retreated to my corner as Laura made noises she may have believed were words.

"Take your own sweet time, Dubinsky. I got all night with no place to go and no one to go down on. Who's this Brighton? Don't recognize the name, honey . . . You run across him where? Ciro's? The Mo? Not the Band Box! Tell Norma Jean everything."

Stevie said she wanted to make love.

Maybe she was still playing Monroe.

She had stayed in character driving back to the condo and remained stimulated by the sex talk about Elvis and Marilyn and the realization we were close to exposing a killer and, perhaps, finding the love letters they had written one another.

We were both certain they existed now, no matter how often their existence had been denied, or by whom.

The question was, Where?

I expected the answer to come in the morning.

She expected something else.

Inside the apartment, Stevie immediately stepped out of her Monroe costume and stripped free from the rest of her clothing.

She demanded I undress, too.

I was about to explain why it didn't make sense.

But who says it had to make sense?

I needed her, too.

Stevie watched with a growing passion, her tongue playing around her lips and her fingers finding places to stroke, while I fumbled out of my clothes.

She studied me admiringly.

"Lay down on the floor," she demanded, and in a wink she was on top of me.

She pressed hard to push me deeper inside her and rode me faster and faster until we screamed on cue and her back arched and her arms flew back and she twisted off me and onto the bed, exhausted, moaning with delight.

"I do love you, Neil," she said, and fell asleep on those words, before I could say I loved her.

My head was telling me there was too much history for us to ever get back together, but my heart was saying we would never be far apart, Stevie and me.

I was too restless to sleep.

I slipped out of bed and stared out the bedroom window for what seemed like hours, until I gave up waiting for the moon to pass through a fleet of fat, dark clouds that added gray mystery to the somber, silent street below and stumbled into bed seconds ahead of a fitful sleep.

My dreams verged on nightmares and generally made no sense, even though Blue Blazer and Laura had helped turn suspicion into sad truth. Chaotic, confusing images continually reinvented the day and recast principal players, telling me something else, but I didn't know what.

The alarm woke me at six.

I refused to open my eyes and gripped the sheets so tightly my palms began to cramp, not wanting to let go until the dreams told me everything.

I was bone tired, in a cold sweat, and fighting to hold on to remember—

What?

No use.

I kissed Stevie's cheek and shoulder. Stevie showed no signs of rousing. On weekends, noon was an early wakeup call for her. I stroked her shoulder. She flinched it away.

Just as well.

What I had to do now I could do better by myself.

I skipped the morning jog, showered, shaved, consumed two bowls of dry cereal, threw on some Sunday sloppies and my ragged Nikes, and aimed the Jag for Venice on empty streets that, two or three hours from now, once the day guaranteed sunshine, would be bumper-to-bumper with beach-bound traffic. I lowered the windows and enjoyed the clean, carbon monoxide–free air.

A parking spot opened up about three blocks from Hank's place. I'd almost overshot his street assessing the odd mix of early morning risers hurrying to stake claims to the best spots on the beach or view tables at one of the walkway cafes weaving in and out among the souvenir shops along a two-mile stretch of carnival atmosphere that pervades the weekends. Sun-baked surfer girls in invisible string bikinis and outsized shades, tossing around their trim, naked hips and buttocks, were ready to defy the cancer-charged rays another day. Muscle-builders clutching gear bags bounced side to side in that awkward strut that comes with gargantuan lats and pecs. Tight-faced sidewalk hustlers and anxious clowns with animal balloons were warming up in front of shuffling homeless and crafty panhandlers displaying crude signs that begged odd jobs and spare change.

Hank wasn't home.

A note taped to the screen door told someone to meet him at Popeye's on Ocean Front Walk and gave the cross street. I knew the place. I had written about it.

Popeye's was a landmark that started as a pickup joint for sailors during World War II. Sawdust on the floor. Peanut jars on the bar. Cozy rumps in tight-fitting outfits roosting on the high stools. A rumor the Black Dahlia dropped by her final night was still conversation for veteran regulars. Heaping portions at budget prices delivered by surfer boys and bunnies, inside or on the patio for customers who enjoy the drama of the promenade with their toast and jam.

Hank's front door was unlocked. I decided against exploring inside. There was no time on his note and I didn't want to risk being caught inside.

Glancing up the driveway, I considered the steel security bar guarding the worn-out garage doors, decorated with new gang graffiti since my last visit. I wondered what great treasure Hank might have stored there rather than inside his Pisa-like shanty castle to merit the protection.

A classic Harley was parked on the right, a foot or two beyond the kitchen door. Sleek. Heroic. Midnight Black. As well kept as a *Fortune* 500 mistress. The engine was warm to my touch. No personal ID. I jotted down the license number on somebody's business card I found in a zipper pocket of my windbreaker and headed off for Popeye's.

Popeye's was doing brisk business. All the outside walkway tables were occupied by couples, young families with kids in tow, and a few lonely-faced people with their heads praying over the *Daily* and breakfast plates delivering a sweet mix of familiar scents to passersby.

Hank was sitting at a table for four along the tarnished brass railing separating the cafe from the sidewalk. He had one of the view seats.

The biker sat across from him chewing animatedly on a hunk of Danish, the same side of beef in black leather and a Grateful Dead T-shirt I remembered from Laura's elevator—except the light was better here than at the hospital yesterday and I could see a fresh bandage where he used to wear an earring.

The biker's shades disguised his eyes, so I couldn't tell if he was as pleased to see me as Marnie, who waved delightedly. I resisted the urge to give him a complete facelift.

Some other time.

More important considerations had brought me back to Hank.

"Uncle Hank, look, your friend, Mr. Gulliver!" she called out excitedly, pointing.

Marnie occupied the aisle seat alongside Hank and seemed indifferent to shifty-eyed halter inspections by patrons and passersby. She spilled over the top of it like breakfast cream, exposing enough of her cherry blossoms to quick-start a voyeur's tool kit. Her blond hair was as disorganized as bedsheets in the morning, draping her face to emphasize the sensuousness of her features. She wore no makeup except for mascara and a dab of lip gloss.

Hank waved and gestured me to sit next to the biker, who retrieved his helmet and moved it to the cement floor between scuffed black marching boots that needed a shine. He added a finger-shot of recognition to his nod and decided, "The other night at Laura's."

I nodded.

Hank said, "The fella we were just talking about, True, the reporter." The main section of the *Daily* was on the table, folded to page three and my column. "Say howdy to True Mullen, Neil. From the old Memphis Mafia days. True was just a kid then and one of El's favorites, as reliable as they make 'em."

I offered my hand automatically. He ignored it and wondered in a cartoon voice, "What wrote the story about the boy dying in the bathtub?"

Hank assured him I was.

True nodded approval and exploded into serious praise, not for me, but for the fasting kid, whose protest would be forgotten by Monday's early edition.

He said, "Somebody willing to die for a cause, bro, the only way to go, that kid. Put 'er there." He leaned over the table as far as his belly allowed to dwarf my hand in his overripe grip.

I pretended not to feel the knuckle-crunching pain of our instant comradeship as Hank wondered, "Is it serendipity brings us together so soon again, Neil?"

He saw the answer on my face.

"Neil and I have some things to talk over in private," Hank said, and we left them lingering over coffee and fresh hot apple pie to join dozens of other barefoot strollers leaving temporary footprints on the cold, damp shoreline, my Nikes tucked under my arm, Hank's leather sandals stashed in the back pockets of roomy blue denim cutoffs that exposed knobby knees and beanpole legs.

"A curious couple," I remarked out of earshot. I was making conversation to keep my anger from spilling over before I had the answers I had come for.

"Looking, you hafta think they're as mismatched as Ali and Quarry," Hank said, smiling inwardly. "Laura never pictured an old beer gut hanging over the bars of a Harley being right for Marnie. You'd hardly even take him for one of her students."

"Tell me why, Hank? Tell me why you lied to me about there being no love letters and—for Christ's sake!—on Roy's grave. On your son's grave."

The words were out before I knew it.

I don't know which of us was more shaken.

Hank gave the impression the world was shutting down around him. Tears welled in his eyes.

"I didn't lie to you, Neil."

"And Pinocchio will be here any minute to go into his act."

"What I swore on Roy's grave, I said was no love letters to talk about, Neil. Far as I know there's still no love letters to talk about. You seen any? I haven't."

"Dammit, Hank. I know they exist."

"Sunset Beaudry feeding you more pap?"

"Laura Dane," I said.

Hank looked at me like he was transfixed by a speeding train heading straight at him. He swiped at his eyes. Didn't know where to put his hand. Settled on his heart.

"When's that?"

"Last night."

He cocked his head and examined me disbelievingly.

"Laura was in no condition."

"Last night she was. To Stevie."

"Why would she tell Stevie anything?"

I explained it to him, the Marilyn deception.

Hank decided finally, "I can imagine how that happened. You always were too clever by half. What exactly did Laura say?"

I shook my head. This conversation was about revelation, not confirmation, and Hank knew it. He started to say something else. Stopped short. Turned to explore the horizon, his eyes battling a glare bouncing off the ocean's shimmering blue-green surface.

He took a final drag on his Sherman.

Flipped it into the fizz water lapping at our bare feet.

Smoothed his goatee and adjusted the rubber band securing his ponytail.

Tugged at his gold earring like it completed some ritual.

He said, "Dr. Fix-it is what Reg Mowry was called back then, for the way he could always solve Mr. Zanuck's problems. An actor getting brain-dead drunk and taking wild swings at the cops. Some actress who slipped up taking the proper precautions and needed a doctor who could be counted on. Straightening out that song-and-dance man who was always sneaking into women's wardrobe to dress up like Carmen Miranda in—"

"The love letters," I said, too angry for patience. "I need to hear about you and Laura and the love letters. Tell me or tell the police, Hank. At the very least, it's suppression of evidence in a homicide investigation. Your choice."

"Threatening an old friend, Neil?"

"Beats lying to an old friend."

I had wounded him again. He looked for somewhere to bleed, then extended his arms, as if getting ready to embrace the entire ocean, and sent a sigh against the breakers.

"You'd really ring in the cops?"

"They're in it already. You're too smart not to know someone tried to kill Laura because of the letters. You should be trying to keep her safe, same as I'm trying like hell to prove Stevie Marriner didn't kill Sheridan."

He said, "We been seeing each other a long time, seems like

forever, Laura and me,'' as if he owed me some explanation. ''Laura didn't break up my marriage, though. When we decided to do something together with our lives, Julie Anne and I were living under one roof, but it had been a long time for us between the sheets. Laura had already taken up with that damned Frenchie director.

''I had had my fill of marriage anyway, and Laura wasn't into it at all. She may of been the first of the modern women. I went into this relationship with both eyes wide open, knowing we would have each other, but at a distance. There was my life and Laura's life, and only after that, our life.

''Sure, I minded her other men, but you gotta give to get. Even with people like that Brighton. They come and go like bad dreams, same as Laura's problem keeping the cork in her bottle, but it isn't all sex between us. Never was.''

He turned away from me as he said it and let his gaze drift lazily down the beach and found something to laugh over without sharing.

Eventually, he said, ''Laura has always been there for me, through the best and the worst of times. Same as I'll always be there for her. You able to say that about a woman in your life?''

I saw he hoped for some response.

I thought about Stevie and how close she had come back to me once the violent passions of divorce were spent. Even closer now, working to keep her out of jail for a murder she didn't commit.

These were truths I had no urge to share, so I turned my palms to the blue velvet sky and gave him a who-knows look and said, ''Tell me about the letters, Hank.''

He flicked the corners of his mouth and rotated a palm to the sun.

''Reg Mowry paid me off to make sure the letters never got talked about, same as he paid off Laura. All this time we been getting bought off.''

He looked at me like that was it.

We both knew better.

''You know what I think, Hank?''

''What?''

''Talk is cheap. The printed word costs extra. I think you and

Laura were paid for more than keeping your mouths shut. You kept the love letters as insurance."

"Laura said that?"

I scooped up a smooth white pebble the size of a doughnut hole, swallowed gallons of salt air, pitched the pebble into the ocean as far and as hard as I could toss. It landed in a silent splash as fast as a heartbeat.

Hank made a career of finding his own rock and threw it at least as far as mine.

"A retirement plan," Hank said. "An annuity. If the letters meant so much to Mr. Zanuck and Reg, we figured they must mean at least as much to us. And we never went back on our deal with Reg. Why I couldn't say anything to you. To anyone. That was the deal. What would you of done in my shoes, son?"

Who ever knows for sure? I suppose I'd have done the same thing, putting obligation in front of honor, but I didn't tell him. Although I felt better about it, his lie was still in place.

"How did the letters get away from you?"

He cocked an eyebrow. "Says who?"

"If you had the letters, you wouldn't have needed to send anyone after Stevie and me."

"How am I supposed to take that to mean?"

I didn't respond. I wanted his truth about Larry Grenedier on my footprints and True Mullen scaring the crap out of Stevie.

Or, another lie, which would tell me as much.

Hank stared down at the sand.

I said, "Sheridan claimed to have the love letters. Somebody offered to sell them to Brighton. Both of them are dead because of the letters."

"You saying I'm a murderer? Hoss, I'm so old, nowadays I got enough trouble killing a pint of whiskey."

Hank tossed another rock at the ocean. It scattered some gulls. My rock went farther than his.

He nodded appreciatively and said, "One day out of the blue, Reg Mowry calls me up to say what in hell is going on, Hank? He's gotten wind Blackie Sheridan is going around and claiming to have

Marilyn's love letters to El. He wants to know, if that's so, why has he been paying out Mr. Zanuck's good money all these years?

"I'm at a loss, but it comes to me after some hard thinking. Same as Elvis and Monroe, Blackie sometimes used Sunset Beaudry's trailer to practice his cocksmanship. I won't give out the lady's name; besides, it don't matter no more. But it could be anytime Blackie came across a letter there in the trailer, before it got thrown away, he took it for his own, seeing value down the line. Blackie's mind worked like that."

I knew Hank was talking about Dulcy Brown. He'd always been a gentleman, same as he was honoring his deal with Mowry ahead of any obligation to me.

"How did Mowry react?" I asked.

"Then he wanted to know about the Elvis letters that Laura said she had burned. Letters, hell. They were hardly even notes. Boyish scrawls. Marilyn's back to him were exotic, erotic even. She was the original Energizer Bunny, that one . . . I got Laura on the phone with Reg and she just kept up the lie. After, we went and looked where she had been keeping the letters all this time."

"Where was that?"

He must have thought he heard something in my voice. "Where Laura told Stevie they were," he said smugly, and chalked one up for himself in the air.

"And they were missing."

"They were there. They were there after Sheridan died and they were there when I looked yesterday."

"So, the only love letters Sheridan could have had were the ones Marilyn wrote to Elvis."

" 'Pears that way, Neil. When they didn't turn up, I thought Stevie might have taken them the night of the murder. Either she had them, or maybe she gave the letters to you. I guess not."

"Why not Claire Cavanaugh? She was there, too."

"When I said that to Reg, he said Claire was too dotty to even know her own name most of the time."

"So then you phoned Jeremy Brighton and offered the letters to him for a hundred thousand dollars."

"Absolutely not." Hank was adamant. "First we knew was when Brighton told Laura about the call and how he would be getting the money from Stevie. We got right to Reg. Figured it would show our good faith and make him think twice about shutting off our money. Reg was pleased. He said for Laura to stay as tight to Brighton as fleas on Fido. Why she went off with Brighton to the MPRE when he called."

"Even knowing she might be confronting Sheridan's killer."

"We was both scared, son, but mindful of Reg, who said Laura would know for certain when she saw the letters if they were the genuine article. So, you know what it's like when time travels on crutches? I'm rolled up tighter than a twenty-dollar ball of yarn when it gets way past the time my girl says she'll call by.

"After an hour, I'm kicking myself real hard for letting my girl go off that way and thinking I should go to the MPRE myself, when the phone rings, lifting me a good two feet off the couch." His goatee swept the air. "Laura is whispering how she can't talk right now, but not to worry." His voice cracked, his eyes glossed over. "Next thing I hear, Marnie and True call to say they're on the way to the hospital."

I stepped closer and squeezed his arm. He patted my hand, appreciatively.

"When Laura called, did she say who was with them in Blackie Sheridan's cottage?"

He hesitated, the way people do when they're about to share uncertain news. "No, only that they were still waiting, but not at Blackie Sheridan's. She and Brighton were at Claire's, having tea and dessert with Claire and Augie Fowler."

He checked his watch while I computed this newest surprise and muttered something about Marnie and True. We headed back over the sand to Popeye's.

"You gotta tell me one thing," Hank said.

"If I can."

"When Stevie and Laura talked last night, what exactly did Laura say?" When I didn't answer immediately, he said, "It was nothing was it, hoss, what with my sweetie lingering just out of reach of the Lord?"

"Nothing," I said, paying him back for his lie.

Instead of getting angry, he seemed to enjoy having guessed right and he laughed the rest of the way.

Marnie was ready with another bright smile and wave. True's eyes darted anxiously between Hank and me, as if he were looking for clues to our conversation.

He wondered, "Joining us for breakfast, bro?" and gestured me to the empty place.

"Save it for Larry Grenedier," I suggested.

True's expression grew ugly. He pressed his palms against the table, making to rise. Hank settled him back with a subtle head shake. Marnie looked puzzled, but she was a good actress, and I decided she understood what I had meant.

"We got a problem?" True said.

I left him without an answer, but he knew what it was.

We both knew it wasn't over between us.

16

The drive from Venice to Twentieth Century–Fox took a half hour on surface streets. By the time I reached the main gate off Olympic Boulevard, Jack Hummell from the publicity department was waiting for me at the security booth.

He signaled the guards to raise the road barrier and waved me through.

Jack was a little guy, small enough to have qualified as an agent if he'd made a different career choice, but filled with big ideas that had served the studio and its productions well through recent owners. He was notorious for opening-day stunts that added millions to the box office.

Jack blew me a kiss and jumped into the passenger seat, and immediately began pitching me a column about Jodie Foster's next movie, making certain I knew that was the price I had to pay for getting him here on a Sunday, as he directed me to make a left at the first intersection after the administration building.

"Thar she blows," he said, pointing to the third structure on my left, a faux New England–style cottage I thought I knew from *Portrait of Jennie* or *Carousel*, maybe both. "That one was Monroe's."

I aimed the Jag into the vertical-lined space directly in front. The other spaces were empty and there was no foot traffic today, only a light breeze kicked up by the ghostly memories of a million movies I'd seen growing up.

As we trudged up the cobblestone path, bordered by rows of brightly colored flowers that could have been rubber, Jack kept up a lighthearted banter honed over years of dealing with the media.

"When I said thar she blows, I was talking Monroe, not Moby Dick," he assured me in his potato-shredder voice, "although Marilyn also had her share of those. I know guys who were licking Marilyn long before she was on a postage stamp." He made a ba-da-boom rim shot noise.

Jack found the master key he was looking for on a metal ring as big as the Elephant Man's hat size and a moment later ushered me inside. His gap-toothed smile broadened and his eyes, always looking for an angle, twinkled as he rattled off an impressive list of actresses who had resided here before and after Marilyn, but he saved his best lines for her.

"Almost got the studio renamed Twentieth Century Fucks," Jack averred inside a wall of fingers and sounded a rim shot.

"You remember her co-star Yves Montand? She made *All About Yves* over there," he said, pointing to a deep-bedded sofa by the brick fireplace. Rim shot. Indicating the door to the bedroom he said, "Her movie *Don't Bother to Knock*? It was almost filmed in there as *Don't Bother to Knock Her Up*." Rim shot. "Her and her pal Laura Dane used to toss some wicked barbecues here, turning wieners into hot dogs, I was hearing just the other day from Reg Mowry."

"Reg Mowry?"

"You remember Reg, old Dr. Fix-it himself? He stopped by to drop off some eggs from that retirement ranch of his and he was telling how DiMaggio never struck out here. Kennedy neither, although he was a different kind of Yankee for Marilyn. Frank Sinatra—"

"Jack, when was Mowry here?"

He made a gag of counting on his fingers and told me. I could see he was dying to know why, but he didn't ask, maybe because of the way I looked back at him.

"Can you give me about five minutes alone, Jack?"

He continued to study me hard. My face gave away nothing.

"Something that might come back to haunt the studio, Neil? Rupert Murdoch has a lot of stockholders to answer to anymore."

"I should have a sit-down with Murdoch about his production plans for next year," I said, "maybe just in front of your next annual meeting. Is this something you want to personally broach to him?"

Jack beamed extravagantly, a creature of the game. "Take ten minutes; hell, take fifteen," he said, and left.

Less than fifteen minutes later, I had the answer that had brought me to Fox.

DeSantis was nowhere near as gracious as Jack Hummell when I reached him at home on my cellular, but his job was catching the bad guys, not courting publicity.

"What is this, Gulliver, National Wake-up-the-Cop Sunday?"

"Crime waits for no man, Lieutenant."

"Hah fucking hah. First Doc Cuevas and now you." He cleared his throat and grumbled something unintelligible.

"What did Doc want?"

"He wanted you. I told him I'm learning to like you, but not that way."

"Seriously."

"I am being serious. I told Cuevas I'd rather stick my dick in the mattress, and the Mex butcher said he figured that's what I do anyway, the cocksucker."

"Was it about the autopsy on Sheridan?"

"Yeah. When he didn't get you he figured he'd bother me. He said a woman answered when he phoned over to your place. I don't suppose it was our star, the future post office pinup?"

"You know harboring a fugitive is a chargeable offense."

"So do you, right up there with aiding and abetting unlawful flight to avoid prosecution, so why don't I believe you?"

"All cops are cynics. You're a cop. Therefore—"

"Yeah, that must be it. Otherwise, I might have a car on its way over already."

"Do you?"

"I would if I thought she did it, whoever that was."

"Something Doc Cuevas said?"

"It helped."

When DeSantis finished telling me about the coroner, I gave him an abbreviated version of the past twelve hours. He asked a couple questions and thought about it.

"You sure, Gulliver?"

"Not sure at all, but it appears to tie in with everything we know or suspect. I'm on my way to the MPRE. I need you to do some things for me."

I told him and he thought some more. "The easy part, done," he said. "The rest, I'll see what I can do." His voice took on the sound of a lonely Saturday night, like he had been drinking. "You know, I been playing around with it in my head and I can't figure out what Paige sees in you."

"Me, neither."

"I'd make a better father."

"Something else we agree on."

"Already have a couple of my own, you know?"

"You've mentioned them."

"Love kids."

"And, you're experienced at it."

"You sticking it to me?" I could have said something cute, but the pain I was hearing was too intense. DeSantis said, "Well, maybe you can drop the word." And the poor, lovelorn slob clicked off without waiting for an answer.

Another twenty-five minutes of empty freeway and I reached the MPRE. There was a fair amount of street and walkway traffic inside the gates, family and friends on weekend visits.

A squad car with West Valley markings was parked near the Sheridan cottage. I pulled up alongside and waved at the young cop sloped behind the wheel. He answered me with a fingertip to the forehead, removed his Walkman earplugs, and eased onto the asphalt.

"Mr. Gulliver?" I agreed. "I'm Trafficante. Lieutenant DeSantis said to give you the run of the place once. Any idea how long that might be, sir?"

I told him I didn't. He smiled resignedly, talking about today's playoff game as we headed away. He was tall, lean, and black, twenty-one or twenty-two, with a five-inch difference between a cop and a basketball scholarship.

When I emerged from the cottage about an hour later, he was leaning against a porch beam, doing body rhythms to the rap music spilling from his Walkman.

Trafficante motioned at me and walked over. "Message for you from Lieutenant DeSantis, sir. You know a guy name of Grenedier? Larry Grenedier?"

"A bad actor."

"The lieutenant said to tell you Grenedier must of had some friend in high places because he's been on the sidewalk since an hour or so ago."

I must have showed my alarm, because he said, "You okay, Mr. Gulliver?" I told him I was and started away. He halted me with a tight grip on my arm and started to say something else, but I was not hearing him.

I pulled free and raced to the Jag and the cell phone and tapped in my number and got my recording.

"Stevie, if you're there, pick up. Stevie, pick up, please."

I had this picture of Grenedier and a wised-up True Mullen teaming up and making a new try for the letters. They might not be tied in with Hank, but they were working for someone, and if it wasn't Hank, I was pretty certain now of who.

"Stevie? It's me. Pick up, please."

No answer. Was she still asleep? Showering? I would have to count on her to obey the rules if there was another knock on the door. Keep it locked. Call security upstairs on the double. Call 911. Get my Beretta and—

I had the Beretta with me. I'd stuck it in my linen ankle holster and stashed it in the glove. Just in case, I told myself. Just in case what? I wondered now.

I'd try calling Stevie again in a few minutes, I decided, and walked across to Claire Cavanaugh's cottage.

Claire wasn't home.

The front door was unlocked.

Twenty minutes later, I'd seen enough and left the same way I had come, leaving everything as I had found it, including the lock, as a toot-toot sounded at my back. A Queen Bee. Her nursing bonnet atop a gossamer cloud of sunburned orange, her golf wagon parked at the head of the path. Waving yoo-hoo at me, expressive eyes exploding with conviviality.

"You looking for Miss Cavanaugh?"

I answered with my best grin.

"She's gone." She saw by my reaction that I'd misunderstood her and said quickly, "Not gone gone. A friend picked her up and took her off for the weekend, yesterday afternoon."

I described Reg Mowry and explained, "They were supposed to be back by now. We had a picnic planned."

"Sounds like him but I can't be certain," she said. "I sure hope you won't be eating lunch alone."

I thanked her. Wished her away.

Her painted smile made clear she expected me to move first.

"Give you a lift?"

I pointed to the Jag.

She nodded. Waited. Tracked me with her eyes until after I had gunned the motor and backed out of the parking spot.

Whatever happened to trust in the world?

Too many break-ins?

I cruised over to Sunset's cottage.

His golf wagon, Buck Junior, was gone, but eternally loyal Buck stood faithful, stuffed and mounted guard at the hitching post by the gate. I gave the Junior Range Roper salute and headed up the walk. Inside the screen door, the front door was being held open by a brick.

I called Sunset's name several times without a response and thought twice about trespassing on the private life of a boyhood hero. Called myself a bad name for dishonoring the Junior Range Roper code. Went inside.

I was looking for two items.

They could be anywhere.

I scanned the front room and was caught, as I had been once before, by the dominating portrait of Dulcy Brown, as beautiful as I remembered her. Dulcy's gentle eyes followed me as I came closer to pay my respects. I was struck again by how her parted lips seemed ready to tell a secret.

"I'm listening, Dulcy," I said.

She didn't answer me.

Until I got to the bedroom.

There was still a ranch house flavor to the decor, but the feminine influence was visible, especially in an elegant canopied bed that looked like it came off the set of *The Three Musketeers*. Satin balloon window curtains trimmed in lace. A delicate crystal chandelier.

A marble-surfaced wash table occupied the closet wall, full of personal photographs in silver frames. Mounted above it was an intricately handcrafted, sparkling silver and gold altar. The lit prayer candles ate away at the stale dust permeating the room.

I checked out the closet. Shoes and boots neatly arranged. Clothing secure inside plastic zipper bags. Sealed cartons on the overhead shelves identified with Sunset's name or hers, contents indicated in black marking pencil, in a small and precise woman's script. "Keepers," someone once called them, the incidental stuff of a lifetime with no real purpose, but too precious to toss.

What I hoped to find of Dulcy's was much more than that.

I turned first to the antique cedar hope chest at the foot of the four-poster and located what I was looking for, tucked inside her wedding dress, along with an inlaid pearl crucifix.

Dulcy's diary.

Before I left almost two hours later, I found what else I'd come searching after.

And I'd still been unable to connect with Stevie.

My heart started doing an unhappy dance at the sound of my own voice again on the answering machine.

Warner Brothers Auditorium was dark.

I next tracked the road signs and familiar landmarks to the MPRE cemetery. Sunset was picking at the weed grass and arranging bunches of flowers around Dulcy's grave marker.

He'd taken off his metal braces and was as uncertain on all four as a newborn calf. The braces were within reach, along with his walking canes and a canteen lying on his half of the double plot. I didn't suppose the canteen contained water. Water was too sissy for The Law and Order North of the Border.

Buck Junior was parked on the path in front of the old Range Roper. Toby Latch, seated on the passenger side, was reading a magazine. She had a stack of them on her lap and used one hand like a visor against her forehead, warding off a late morning sun advertising today's scorcher.

Sunset paused and settled on an elbow to take a swallow from the canteen. He recapped it, tossed it aside, brushed his mouth with the back of a hand. He looked for the birds twittering back and forth, like he wanted to join in their conversation. After a moment or two, he set his wide-brimmed Stetson down beside him on the grass, rolled over onto his back, and eased his locked fingers under his head, content to stare at the traveling sky.

What we had to talk about didn't need an audience.

Especially Miss Latch. A stern, nervous Miss Desmond to

Mickey Spoon's Micawber, and what else were they to each other? For certain, she fit into what had gone on here like one of those Russian nesting dolls.

Mickey Spoon, also?

And Paige, was she also part of the ill-conceived plan I'd been working over and over in my mind?

Who else?

Names flashed as I shortcut over the grass, attempting to fit the Russian dolls in proper order.

"Miss Desmond."

Toby Latch reared up from her *Premiere* magazine, startled momentarily at hearing her nickname. She saw it was me and her recessed look turned stark staircase cold.

"I need to be alone with Mr. Beaudry," I said.

She started to argue.

I cut her off with a gesture. "I'll get him home. You just toodle over to the set. Mr. DeMille needs you for your close-up."

Her stringbean lips trembled and I braced myself for more debate. Instead, she killed me with a brick-faced glower, keyed on the golf wagon battery, and took off like a schoolgirl on a skateboard.

Sunset was still examining the sky. I settled alongside him campfire style and gave the Junior Range Roper greeting too loud for him not to hear. His eyes blinked recognition. That was all, and for a while I said nothing, then waffled on a way and a place to start.

This went on for ten or fifteen minutes, Sunset lost in the clouds and me to the misfortune of having to say I knew enough of the truth to imagine the rest.

I said, "You killed Blackie Sheridan, Sunset."

The words didn't come any easier than Sunset's slurred reply after a moment or two. "When you say that, smile."

The canteen was out of his reach. I retrieved it for both of us. It was empty. I told him and took a sniff before setting it aside. Straight whiskey. I'd be lucky if he had comprehended half of what I said.

"Allus wore the white hat," Sunset said, maybe to himself.

I craved a smoke. "I also know why it happened and I can't blame you. I would have killed the bastard, too, if I'd learned he was responsible for what happened to my wife."

Her diary had told me a lot.

Adding to what Hank knew from Laura.

More than even Dr. Fix-it knew.

Blackie Sheridan caused Dulcy's death.

All those years ago, in fifty-six, when Reg Mowry had walked in on Sheridan making it with Dulcy in the trailer, he thought Sheridan had forced himself on Dulcy.

In fact, Sheridan and Dulcy, like Elvis and Marilyn, were carrying on their own quiet affair.

Who knows why or how such things happen?

They do.

And end as this one did, with Dulcy Brown another name on a Sheridan list longer than his credits.

Dulcy's diary only covered the last three years, but she had made an allusion to the romance following Mowry's visit to ask if she would mind having Sheridan move into the Estates.

"I can live with it, Reggie," Dulcy wrote, the same response Mowry had reported to me. Only, to herself, Dulcy had gone on to reveal the truth of the affair. How the affair had disturbed her for years, but she thought it finally made her a better wife, one worthy of Sunset's devotion.

It might have ended there, but for Sheridan's cruel streak.

He often taunted Dulcy, passed dark hints that he might one day expose *their* secret to Sunset, and let the truth slip to Mimi Polyzoides and God knows who else, considering his blabbermouth whenever he had too much to drink.

Dulcy, weighted down by grief and guilt, decided to end her life. She set about putting what was left of it in order, knowing suicide would not make worse the afterlife her religion reserved for adulterers.

I said, "I found out about Dulcy's suicide the same way you must have found out after she was gone, Sunset."

"Never gone!" he shouted abruptly, and his eyes went narrow, as they always did before the showdown on Main Street.

"I found her diary. I read it."

I'd spoken gently, not in any accusatory manner, but Sunset reacted as if, by invading her privacy, I had called her a dirty name. Faster than I could dodge, he rolled over and began beating on my thigh with his fists. Blue veins grew at his temples. The pink scar underneath his left cheek deepened to cherry red. Tears washed his face.

He cursed me savagely, screaming his demands. "You watch your mouth, you foul bastard! Don't you ever talk that way in front of my Dulcy!"

I looked away rather than see him crying.

"After Dulcy's death, you found her diary and you learned about her affair with Sheridan while Elvis was filming *Love Me Tender*. Was that when you vowed to revenge her?"

I did not expect an answer and I didn't get one. Sunset was on his back on the rear seat of the Jag, eyes closed and mumbling incoherently, occasionally swatting the air. He'd agreed to come with me after I promised to drop the subject until we were away from Shangri-la and Dulcy's hearing, and immediately became dead weight. Unable to bend him into the front seat, I negotiated him head first into the back, came round to the other door and tugged the rest of him inside.

"You waited for your chance. It came unexpectedly through Claire, when she called you from Sheridan's. Desperate. Barely making sense. You were confidants. Dulcy wrote fondly about your relationship in her last diary entries, didn't she, Sunset? She wrote how she could leave you without notice, because she would not be leaving you alone. You would have Claire to comfort you. I want to believe your only thought in responding to her appeal was to help her. You couldn't do it alone, so you called for your pals, Taps Vernon and Mimi Polyzoides."

As horrible as my conjecture was, I had to battle the smile trying to form at the vision of three antique men banded together for murder. If they were sentenced to life terms by a jury, what would that add up to, eight or nine years total?

I said, "The three of you made certain Claire was all right, moved my ex to the couch, and carried Sheridan to the bedroom. You were disappointed Stevie had not struck him hard enough with his Oscar to kill the son of a bitch. The rage festering inside you got to be too much to bear. He probably twitched, something like that, and you exploded . . . Sunset?"

No response.

"You looked around for something you could use and saw his favorite cane was near the bed. Stevie described it for me last week: shaped like a giant penis, balls for a handle. Dulcy talks about it in her diary, how he was always wagging it at her face. At Claire. At Laura. A surrogate, as if he still had enough to go around."

"Laura! Face in the misty light!" Sunset began humming the old movie theme song.

"You had the motive and the opportunity and now you had the weapon, the method. Blackie's cane. Meant to be? A symbolic way to kill the bad man? You brought the cane down on him again and again before Mimi or Taps could pull you off. Maybe they didn't even try? Maybe they were as happy as you to see him dead?"

"Face in the misty light!"

"In my mind, I picture Mimi directing Claire on what to do and say the next morning, when she supposedly discovered Stevie and Sheridan's body. One of you cut the phone line to create the impression of an intruder, possibly, to turn suspicion away from Claire, in case she blew her lines and became a suspect. All the talk later about Elvis being responsible? More diversion?"

Sunset began humming the Roasted Toasties theme.

I pulled into a parking space by his cottage walk, lowered the windows and turned off the motor, opened the door, swiveled sideways in order to stretch my legs.

My entire being craved a smoke.

I sucked in air, inventing nicotine content.

"When you were finished doing those dumb things, you added to the list by taking the murder weapon. I checked out Sheridan's place, Sunset. I found canes, but not his cock cane. I found the cock cane in your place—after I found the diary. Cleaned up and hidden in plain sight, in the floor rack with your own canes and crutches."

"Nobody suspect, nobody look."

"It would have come out eventually, Sunset. You may even have been on the verge of telling Augie Fowler when you saw him at the Break-a-Leg Show rehearsal or me the day we met . . . Are you listening, Sunset? I want to be certain I have your attention for what I'm about to tell you next."

"You have mine, Neil."

Mickey Spoon.

Peering at me through the passenger window. I had not heard him approaching. He moved quietly for a large man. He was aiming a revolver at me.

"It's the real thing, Neil, and I know how to use it, so no foolish moves, okay? It's a Colt single-action Peacemaker, like Wyatt carried. A gift to me from Mr. Beaudry. You might recognize it from *Daughter of Dodge*, one of the matched pair he wore cross-holstered?"

Behind him on the path, Toby Latch sat tightly at the wheel of Buck Junior. She may have been smiling. I made a one-handed wave. Mickey followed the gesture with the pistol.

"Nothing foolish, please?" He signaled for her to join him. "I am going to hand the Colt to Miss Desmond. She'll be keeping serious aim while we move Mr. Beaudry inside."

"Perfect timing, Mickey. I was saving the best for last."

"Of course you were, Neil."

"I was about to tell Sunset he didn't have to kill Blackie Sheridan, because Sheridan was already dead."

"So I was right all along," Mickey said. "We're in a Lone Wolf movie."

I repeated the story I had pieced together for Sunset once Mickey and I managed our boyhood hero into bed. Sunset hadn't resisted. He let us get him out of his cowboy duds and into a light cotton nightshirt and was snoring before Mickey closed the door behind us.

Mickey and I sat at opposite ends of the couch. Toby Latch sat across the couch table, her chair angled in a way that gave her a clear shot at me. Her finger was firm on the Peacemaker's trigger and her head palsied slightly as she chewed nervously on a floral patterned hanky dangling from a corner of her mouth. She reminded me of a morose Zasu Pitts with bad manners.

"Fascinating," Mickey said when I signaled I was finished, "but what did you mean when you said Sheridan was already dead?"

"Poisoned, Mickey."

"Poisoned?"

I could almost believe he was surprised; he may have given up too soon on his acting career.

"According to the coroner, the heavy trauma to Sheridan's head was enough to kill him under other circumstances. Here it obscured the real cause of death until he worked through poison traces detected in the victim's system. You ever hear of aconitine? A poisonous alkaloid found in plants from the monkshood and larkspur families? Another name is wolfsbane."

Spoon made a puzzle of his face, jowls dancing as he shook his head. He pushed a flop of hair from his forehead.

"Wolfsbane thrives in garden soil, especially in the shade. It's growing all over the Estates."

His eyes disappeared inside a disbelieving smile.

"You're serious about this?"

I showed him the Junior Range Roper salute.

"Once the coroner isolated the poison, he sent the lab boys back. Those pretty yellow flowers you see around? Someone knew to harvest them, grind them into pulp, and stockpile the wolfsbane."

"And poisoned Mr. Sheridan?"

"And poisoned Mr. Sheridan."

His eyes canvassed the room. They settled briefly on Miss Latch, then returned to me. "Now, I know what you must have been thinking, but it was not me, Neil. I had no cause to poison Mr. Sheridan."

"Putting you in a distinct minority, but if you're telling me the truth why the gun?"

I was pretty certain I already knew the answer.

Mickey's jowls activated again and sweat lit up his face. For a moment I thought he might change his mind about answering. He gave a sideways glance to Miss Latch. A puff of resignation. "The Lone Wolf, definitely," he said. "When Miss Desmond—Miss Latch—came back to the office and reported you were in Shangri-la with Mr. Beaudry, I guessed it was about Mr. Sheridan and somehow with your nosing around you'd discovered our part in killing him. I got afraid and grabbed the gun and hurried on after you."

"Don't say one more word, Mr. Micawber!"

"It's foolish for us to continue this way, Miss Desmond; I should have behaved better the first place. Mr. Beaudry did not have to phone anyone when Miss Cavanaugh called him, Neil. I was already with him, the two of us spending another evening together over alcoholic libation. We began doing more and more after Mrs. Beaudry passed over, the least a Junior Range Roper could do, and the tales he shared were so glorious, not like in any movie book on your shelf or mine. I got Miss Latch on the phone. I told her hurry on over to Mr. Sheridan's. You know how lost I'd be without someone like Miss Latch?"

I nodded.

Toby Latch recoiled, as if the compliment hurt.

Mickey continued, "I'm the one moved Mr. Sheridan, and when Mr. Beaudry started to lose his reason and reached for the cane, I stopped him from using it."

"And you bashed Sheridan."

Miss Latch made a despondent noise.

"The absolute least a Junior Range Roper could do for Sunset Beaudry. I didn't even have to think about it. Just took the cane and administered a little vigilante justice."

"What about Sunset?"

"He hung back, like he wasn't used to playing the Walter Brennan role, shaking his head something fierce, like maybe he already thought better of the idea; like, maybe, it should not end this way."

"Bad scene, Mickey."

He opened his eyes and sighed.

"But it was too late for a retake, Neil. I worked out what to do next. Miss Latch got Miss Cavanaugh out of there and away until Miss Cavanaugh knew how to act and what she should say to the police."

"Mr. Micawber, I wish you wouldn't."

"Everything going to be just fine, Miss Desmond. Can't have Mr. Beaudry accused of anything to tarnish his star on Hollywood Boulevard, can we now? Besides, you heard what Mr. Gulliver said about the wolfsbane. I murdered a dead man, so it shouldn't go as bad on me as it might, or you at all."

"Would you have shot me otherwise, Mickey?"

His eyes glossed over and he shook his head.

"Just afraid, Neil. I truly apologize."

I pushed a palm between us.

"Do you care who poisoned Sheridan?"

"You know then?"

"Consider this, Mickey. Aconitine is relatively fast-acting in a sufficient dosage. The victim's pulse gets weaker. His blood pressure begins falling. He gets lethargic and then weak. He gets confused, cold, finally, dead.

"The coroner's report noted a substantial amount of brandy in Sheridan's system the night he died and made it evident the aconitine was in the brandy. Nobody noticed Sheridan drinking or drunk before he stormed out of his play rehearsal, so assuming he didn't set out to kill himself before Stevie got to his cottage, it suggests Sheridan was poisoned sometime in between."

"All that's in between was Miss Dane driving him back here," Mickey said. "You can't mean Miss Dane poisoned Mr. Sheridan?" It was as if the screw holding his neck on had popped. "You couldn't make me believe that in a million years, Neil."

Miss Latch squeezed her troubled face and made a series of left and right head turns in disagreement.

"Not my intent, Mickey. If it were, I'd also have to believe Laura afterward gave herself and Augie Fowler enough aconitine to kill both of them."

Miss Latch's head switched to an up-and-down direction and she suggested, "To throw off suspicion?"

"Miss Desmond!"

"I'm sorry," she said, retreating into herself.

I threw her one of my Steve McQueen grins.

She looked the other way.

"Last night Laura roused from her coma to say Sheridan was stone cold sober on the trip back to the MPRE," I said. Probing for a reaction, I added, "She told us a lot more," and ended the thought with a fly-away gesture.

Miss Latch appeared to be giving birth to an octopus.

I turned back to Mickey. "So, how did Sheridan come by his deadly aconitine cocktail?" His look grew puzzled. He shook his head. I said, "He got it from someone who knew his travel habits and waited until he was dropped off by Laura, then knocked on a pretext, possibly something as simple as delivering an expensive bottle of brandy supposedly left for him earlier by a friend or a fan. The someone was a someone he would expect to be making such a delivery, and—" I mimed a toast and bottoms-up for Miss Latch, who made it clear she didn't appreciate the attention. "How close am I, Miss Desmond?"

"Miss Desmond?" The name flew out of Mickey.

"Did you leave immediately, or did Sheridan invite you in for a nightcap?" I said. I renewed my Steve McQueen grin and winked.

Miss Latch raised the Peacemaker from her lap and aimed it at me with uncertainty. She said finally, "I should shoot you just for having the filthy thought."

"Did Reg Mowry also want you to look for the love letters, or were you just in charge of the killing, as usual?" She looked confused. "Oh, didn't Mowry tell you about that part?"

Mickey said, "Reg Mowry? Neil, what the hell is all this about?"

"Ask her," I said. "Miss Desmond has chalked up quite an enviable record for Mowry. Haven't you, Miss Desmond? How many residents did you poison for him before you poisoned Sheridan? You strike me as a very organized person, so I'd bet you kept a tally."

She gave a nod that went nowhere.

"What number was Dulcy Brown? Taps Vernon? Did you have a nonresident category for Jeremy Brighton and, if they also had died, Laura Dane and Augie Fowler?"

She cocked the Peacemaker and drew a bead.

"I could do it, too, you don't stop your insulting ways," she announced, pleading, "Please, don't listen to him, Mr. Micawber."

Mickey smiled at her. "And, you be careful, Toby, okay? I'd like you to put the gun down."

She didn't seem to hear him.

"Think what you want, but I didn't do it for Mr. Mowry," she seethed at me. "I did it for Mr. Micawber."

"Me?" So much incredulity in a single word.

"Trying to do such wonderful work here and always too busy and never enough money to achieve your dreams or even get done the necessities. Going like a beggar to people who are not good enough to hold your hat. He is a saint, Mr. Gulliver, only he doesn't know it. A saint should not ever have to go begging."

"Neil, I had no idea—"

I put a finger to my lips and turned back to her.

"Well, you are, Mr. Micawber. Well, he just is . . ."

"So, you found a way to help, repay him for his kindness."

"Yes."

"You began poisoning residents."

"Yes."

"Who to choose. The information you needed was in the MPRE files. They told whose deaths would provide a financial windfall through insurance or real property the MPRE was holding a quit-claim on, or—"

"Gawd! You make it sound so coldhearted!" She rolled her eyes and appealed with a glance to Spoon. "Seeing Angela Lansbury in *Sweeney Todd* gave me the idea, but Mr. Mowry helped me, too. I chose people who weren't long to be with us, like Mr. Vernon. Bad heart could go any minute, and him dancing and carrying on like he was still a child anymore."

Spoon was pained. "Toby, Toby, Toby. I wish you'd discussed this with me first."

Their eyes locked momentarily.

"I knew what your answer would be. Besides, if anything ever went wrong, it should not be you has to pay the price."

I said, "Unless someone looks for it, aconitine is almost impossible to detect. Add the deceased's age and any doctor would write 'by natural causes' on the death certificate without giving it another thought. She counted on that. Your policy of cremation always worked out for her, Mickey."

"Dear, dear, dear."

"It could have gone on forever, except for the screwup with Sheridan. Stevie showing up unexpectedly . . . Claire . . . Miss

Latch managed to get rid of the brandy bottle and otherwise clean up, probably after you called her to help you, but there was nothing she could do about the body."

Miss Latch listened like it was all news to her, too.

I asked her, "How did you learn about the wolfsbane growing here? How did you know what it was or what to do—"

"It doesn't matter."

Spoon and I exchanged glances.

He said softly, "I'd like to know, too, Toby."

She turned her head and the Peacemaker toward him in a single synchronized move.

In the same instant, a voice I'd grown up with, sotted out of shape but distinctive as ever, boomed large behind her.

"Time for some law and order 'round here!"

Sunset had the Peacemaker's twin cocked and aimed at Miss Latch. He used his free hand and steadied the elbow of his shooting arm, but his red-flaked feet were about twelve inches apart and he was having trouble keeping his balance.

He had on his tall Stetson. It made him look all the more foolish in his nightshirt.

As a startled Miss Latch turned in his direction, her finger jerked nervously on the Colt's trigger.

Cuh-rack!

The accidental shot caught Spoon in the chest as he lifted himself from the couch, getting ready to say something to Sunset. Whatever he intended to say became a pitiable squeak. He elevated slightly. Plunged forward from the waist. Cracked his head hard on the surface of the table.

Cuh-rack!

Sunset's Peacemaker also had discharged awkwardly.

The shot passed through Miss Latch's eye and broke her face in half before exiting from the other side and smashing into the wall, en route shattering his Lifetime Achievement Award from the Cowboy Hall of Fame.

She dropped the Colt. It bounced to within a couple feet of me. She briefly hung in eternity, then slumped to one side like a rag doll, her cheek nesting on her shoulder and one arm dangling uselessly. Her face turned crimson and blood began to stain her dress, the chair, my memory of a moment not yet ready to end.

Sunset's gaze swung between his revolver and her.

I sensed his confusion, as if this scene were not in the script, until he bit down on his back molars and let his mouth betray the slightest hint of satisfaction. A self-congratulatory nod. He tried slipping his Peacemaker into a holster that wasn't there. More confusion. He looked around dazed, his mind wandering faster than his feet. Grew shakier. Got a grip on top of a chair in time to keep from falling.

As DeSantis and Paige walked through the front door.

DeSantis saw me first. "We thought we heard a—what the hell?" He swung an arm around to push Paige back, moved to one side so that his body protected her.

Paige shrieked. She inched past him and hurried over to Miss Latch. "Oh, my God! Oh, my God!" Slipped onto her knees and stared at the dead woman through startled eyes, her lips lost behind her hands, making nonsensical sounds.

The old Range Roper may not have recognized Paige as he redirected the revolver away from DeSantis and fired off two quick shots. He appeared lost in a Saturday matinee somewhere. His first shot sailed past my head by inches. The second came even closer to Paige, barely missing her shoulder.

Before DeSantis could lunge or get to his belt holster, Sunset's Peacemaker was back on him.

DeSantis angled his hands in surrender.

His eyes went as narrow as Sunset's.

He said, "Sir, if you know what's good for you, you will not do that again. You will not fire again at either Miss Jahnsen or Mr. Gulliver."

Sunset reminded him sharply, "I'm law and order north of the border."

He pulled back the hammer with his thumb and took careful, arm's length aim.

Paige pleaded, "Mr. Beaudry, please don't."

Sunset shot blindly in the direction of her voice.

The bullet thudded harmlessly into the floor.

I jumped from the couch and started toward him.

He fired at me. I felt the heat of the bullet as it passed. It threw me off stride. I tripped over the table leg and came up with Miss Latch's Colt aimed at Sunset's chest.

Sunset's aim was back on DeSantis, who'd managed to get his revolver out of the holster and pointed at Sunset.

The cop couldn't miss at that distance.

Me either.

"Two against one," Sunset announced. "Hardly fair enough odds for fellas like you. Ten against one more like it."

"Drop it!" DeSantis commanded.

I understood the look on the cop's face.

Him or me.

Better him.

"You been counting, you know there's one bullet left," Sunset said, and cocked the revolver defiantly. "Least that gives you a fighting chance."

Paige appealed to him. DeSantis repeated his warning and took careful aim down the length of his arm. Sunset answered with belligerent laughter.

I'd been counting and knew Sunset was right. He had one bullet left, not that it made a difference. He was not going to get off a shot before DeSantis. This was not *Guns of El Domingo*. Sunset had managed the trick in that one. Two against one, with only a single bullet remaining in his Peacemaker. He maneuvers Jack Holt and his henchman, Noah Beery, Sr., in a way that—

Of course!

For Sunset, this was *Guns of El Domingo*.

I shouted, "Cut!" and called, "Best take of the day, Sunset. We'll print that one and move on."

Sunset accepted the compliment with a nod.

He eased down the hammer and held out the Peacemaker for someone to take.

Paige was to him in an instant.

"Lemme know when you're ready with the next setup, boys," he said and, with a wink for DeSantis, turned and headed for the bedroom. Shoulders squared, as erect and steady on his feet as I'd ever seen him. Humming the Roasted Toasties theme under his breath.

DeSantis turned to me for understanding. I didn't even try. He turned to Paige, who now was looking at him with adoring eyes short of a swoon. I saw he wasn't sure how to read her and helped the romance along.

"You're the real hero here, DeSantis, the way you stared down Sunset's gun barrel and were ready to take a bullet if he fired at Paige again."

He froze a blush and finally thought to stammer at me, "Not you?"

"You mean because you probably saved my life, too?" I gave him a gesture that said he had to be kidding.

"To protect and serve, all it's ever about," he said, and now seemed to catch the significance in Paige's eyes. Her smile widened at him and hinted at better to come for the two of them.

Meanwhile, I was too busy working out in my mind a load of unfinished business I wasn't ready to share with him, including the murder of Jeremy Brighton and the identity of Brighton's killer.

And, finally, the truth about Marilyn and Elvis and their love letters.

Of one thing I was certain, however:

Reg Mowry was responsible for everything that had happened.

Dr. Fix-it.

The mastermind.

Everything.

All I lacked was proof.

I thought I knew where I could find it.

"Honey, please. You're doing it all over again, trying to tell me how to behave. Don't. Please don't. Okay?"

"You should have stayed put in the damn apartment, Stevie. How smart was it, going out and walking around Westwood?"

"For the zillionth, trillionth time, I. Did. Not. Walk. Around. Westwood. I jogged. I put on one of your jogging suits and I jogged. My sunglasses. One of your stupid basketball caps."

"Jogged for two hours, three hours, what's it been?"

"Long enough to take in the movie at the Bruin. I was up for the role, and I would of been sensational, but it went to Cameron Diaz." A rumble in her throat.

"Long enough for True Mullen to get to you again. It's not over yet, Stevie. Not as long as people think you might have Elvis and Marilyn's love letters. Can't I drum that into you?"

"You're not banging this drum anymore, can't you remember that? Thank you for caring, but I can take care of myself well and fine. Can we stop now?"

"Promise me you'll stay put until I get back."

"I think what I'm gonna do is go back to my place, maybe over to Monte's."

"Please, Stevie, stay put. Don't be stupid."

The phone clicked off. I counted out ten seconds, but this time she didn't call me back.

I called her.

She let the phone ring.

I had called from Toby Latch's desk in the administration building. DeSantis and Paige were still at Sunset's bungalow, waiting out the arrival of cops and coroners. I had plenty of time before I would be needed for my statement, and I intended to fill it at Miss Latch's computer.

I hung up the phone, began running through Windows Explorer, looking for files with promising names. An actor or someone else who might have known Reg Mowry. Even been supported by the Fund. Even been cremated.

All I found were normal deaths, until it struck me to stop looking for the obvious and put myself inside Miss Latch's mind, the organized mind of a movie fan steeped in movie history.

A Trivia directory contained a hundred or more files of information downloaded from America Online and the Internet. Two of them jumped out at me, Examiner and Starkeeper.

I smiled at her subtlety.

The Examiner was the role played by Dudley Digges in *Outward Bound,* who tends to a group of passengers sailing off to their rendezvous with death. Starkeeper was the heavenly angel played by Gene Lockhart in the 1956 movie version of Rodgers and Hammerstein's *Carousel.*

The two files yielded the name of every MPRE resident marked for premature demise by Miss Latch. The method she had used to dispense the aconitine. Dates of death and cremation. Any special or unusual circumstances she wanted to memorialize. Screen after screen of musings that revealed a troubled woman murdering out of misplaced love for her sainted Mickey Spoon.

And a list that got my stomach doing a Riverdance—containing the names of each and every victim who had been specified by Reg Mowry.

I had him.

And, I shortly would learn, more than I had bargained for.

I went home by way of the hospital.

Augie had been taken off the critical list and moved out of ICU. I watched him sleep for a while. Once he roused long enough to give the impression he knew it was me before falling back into a snoring trance.

My questions would have to wait.

Laura was still under heavy sedation, and the doctors figured she'd be well enough to go home in a few days.

Marnie was visiting and greeted me like an old friend. She was sorry I hadn't stayed for breakfast, she said, as I looked around for True Mullen.

No sign of him.

No sign of Hank, either.

I asked where they were.

"True had some personal errands to run this afternoon," she

said, "and Uncle Hank . . . you know, I think Uncle Hank is afraid of hospitals."

I didn't tell Marnie I was reasonably sure why.

Because his son, Roy, had died in one.

Stevie wasn't there when I got home. No note. Nothing that even smacked of a thank you and goodbye. I threw away my hands and hit the fridge for a Bud.

By eleven the next morning, the empty sky gone from gray to a pastel blue, the weather warm and encouraging, I navigated the I-10 at an illegal seventy-five miles per hour. I was about halfway to Reg Mowry's chicken ranch.

The rush hour and Los Angeles was behind me and the freeway lanes were relatively wide open. I kept the radio tuned to heavy metal at an eardrum-battering level to retard any chance of my falling asleep behind the wheel.

Once again I'd had trouble sleeping. I'd twisted and turned and wandered the night trying to make the pieces of the puzzle fit better, and every time I'd come up with pictures I didn't want to see or believe.

The suburbs dissolved into roadside communities buried under an avalanche of advertising signboards. By the time I reached the Badlands approaching Beaumont the rest of the view had reduced to cactus and rolling sagebrush, boulders, an occasional squirrel or rabbit.

I whizzed by Banning and ten minutes later took the Cabazon exit into an AM/PM, where a fill-up and a tuna sandwich on limp whole wheat bread got me directions to Reg Mowry's place from a toothless counter man in bib overalls who smiled at Reg's name and heaped praise on the quality of the eggs he regularly bought at Mowry's ranch.

Fifteen minutes and five freeway exits later, I maneuvered onto an access road near a deserted truck-weighing station, then made a sharp right turn south onto a smaller dirt road that was barely wider than the Jag.

After about a mile, I passed through an open, rusted iron gate and followed the overlaid patterns of sun-dried tire tracks to a half-dozen weathered mobile homes arranged like wagon trains at angles around a central courtyard. Interior walkways connected by fiber-glass or canvas enclosures. Canvas stretched on tubular poles set into the ground provided protection from the sun for dozens of neat rows of wire mesh chicken coops stretching west and south of Mowry's own roost. Canvas walls were rolled open, but they could be moved quickly in the event of desert storms or any other threat to his noisy broods.

Some of his flower, fruit, and vegetable gardens were inside the courtyard, visible over a knee-high, glistening white picket fence, recently painted. More were beyond the gated area east of the main trailer, seasonal bounties lush in the rich brown soil.

The paint smell lingered in the air from twenty yards away, where I parked the Jag near Mowry's Pontiac wagon. The smell was nothing compared to the roosters and hens, whose troubled sounds signaled the arrival of a stranger.

Mowry stepped forward onto the platform steps of the main trailer, which faced the road. A smile played on his face. He waved as if he had been expecting me, inquired about lunch, and grimaced when I told him about the tuna sandwich.

"A miracle your stomach hasn't exploded," he said, taking my hand. "That's the general reaction to one of Grover's sandwiches. It could of been worse, though. Could of been his egg salad." He threw a thumb over his shoulder. "Inside, I got just the cure. A fresh vegetable stew from the garden, my specialty, steaming hot, with homemade butter biscuits, and a tall glass of tap beer to wash it all down."

"You know why I drove here, Mr. Mowry."

"You think so?"

"I've arrived at the truth."

He smiled pleasantly, parroted my words. "You've arrived at the truth. From your expression, dollars to doughboys you're also here for something else."

"The rest of the story," I said.

Mowry stepped aside so I could pass into the trailer first. He was wearing a tailored turtle-green safari suit with trouser creases permanently hand-stitched into the sturdy cotton fabric and highly polished cordovan chukkas. Multihued ascot, matching silk handkerchief cascading from a breast pocket, enough red bursting from the ascot and the handkerchief to make his eyeglass frames a part of the costume.

"Truth is stronger than fiction," he said. "With truth you know where you're going. With fiction, you sometimes don't even know where you've been. You know who told me that?"

"Mr. Zanuck."

"Mr. Zanuck told me. About the time we began doing all those documentary dramas, like *Boomerang* and *The House on 92nd Street*. You ever catch *Boomerang*? One helluva picture. Made Gadg Kazan's reputation . . . before that dreadful commie business."

"I'll level with you, Mr. Mowry. I know where I've been and have a better idea where I'm going now."

"Whenever we spoke before, it was always the truth, Neil. Certainly so on my part."

"Your version of the truth, you mean. Beautifully delivered and designed for self-serving mass consumption, Dr. Fix-it, the master, still at the top of his form."

His eyes almost twinkled. "As DFZ used to tell the boys, the house does not have to be on 92nd Street, any more than there has to be a house at *13 Rue Madeleine*. We show the audience only the truth we want to show. We invent the rest to suit the story."

"With all due respect to Mr. Zanuck, this time I'd like you to consider the whole truth and nothing but the truth."

The trailer home was neat, like a set dressed for the first day of a shoot. I had noticed the same thing about the MPRE homes I visited, Laura Dane's, too. They gave me a new sense to an old saying: pretty as a picture. The picture stays pretty, no matter how ugly the truth becomes.

"Why should I? Because you talked to people?"

"Because they talked to me."

"That and a dollar will buy you fifty cents," he said. "You got nothing that points to me. Sit down over there, please."

He indicated a milk chocolate leather lounger too large for the conversation corner he had created in what once had been the driver's area. A stuffed chair whose expensive fabric matched the cushions on the breakfast bench angled from the trailer wall.

The driver's window was lost behind an expensive silk shoji screen out of an old Gump's catalog and served as a backdrop for eight or nine framed photographs on the dashboard mantle. Mowry was in all but two, inscribed portraits of Zanuck and Claire Cavanaugh. Zanuck had written a terse thank-you in a bold hand. Claire's appreciation was addressed to Dr. Fix-it.

Mowry said, "Relax, get comfortable while I get those beers, or is there something else you prefer?"

"Diet Coke?"

"Maybe one Diet Pepsi left."

"Good enough."

The fridge was on the other side of the buffet counter. He returned in a minute with the Pepsi and a flute of draft. Eased into the stuffed chair. Tugged at his trousers. Smiled. Toasted me with his glass.

"Salud!"

"Salud!"

He gestured for me to continue.

"You have more deaths painted on your fuselage than any Top Gun, Mr. Mowry, including Blackie Sheridan and Jeremy Brighton. Except for a minor miscalculation, Laura Dane and Augie Fowler?"

Mowry tried reading my face. Swallowed hard when he saw I was giving away nothing else. Examined his nails in the subdued yellow glow of the ceiling tube lights.

He said, "A cast of thousands you might say?"

"MGM used to boast about having More Stars Than There Are in Heaven, little suspecting you would be the one putting so many of them there."

"Metro had Howard Strickling for that. Someday I'll have to tell you what he told me about Paul Bern and his supposed suicide and Jean Harlow and what really killed her and—"

"Why, Mr. Mowry?"

"Something more current? How's James Dean and his supposed car crash? Natalie Wood and her supposed drowning?"

Is there no graveyard for memories? I wondered.

I wondered if more than Reg Mowry's thoughts were drifting.

Where do minds go after they unhinge?

I said, "I may already know most of the truth. I'd like you to fill in the missing parts."

Mowry took off his glasses to massage his eyes and made a ritual of refitting them. He ran his left hand up and down his right arm, squeezing the muscles, pushed out a noisy breath.

"What constipates most of the truth?" he asked.

"The usual. Money. I can't put a date to it, but I'm sure that little commercial bank in Riverside you told me about will after the DA shows up there with a court order."

My announcement hung like a cloud.

"I never stole a penny of Mr. Zanuck's Fund!" Mowry raged suddenly, and I thought for a moment he might rocket out of the chair at me.

"I'm not accusing you. Maybe Mr. Zanuck erred on the side of generosity, or you paid out longer than he ever intended, or lower interest rates and inflation took their toll. Or, over the years, as other

Fox names became needy, you added to the list people you were sure Mr. Zanuck would want to help if he were around."

His chin rose defiantly and his eyes developed a rain gloss.

A tick roamed from the right corner of his mouth onto his richly tanned, fissured cheek.

I said, "The Fund was running low. Almost empty. You decided to fix that by reducing your financial obligations, and Toby Latch became your unsuspecting dupe. When did you first learn about the wolfsbane? Did Claire Cavanaugh tell you? Dulcy Brown? Or was it Mimi Polyzoides? Augie said Mimi is quite a gossip."

He caught his breath and said quietly, "This is your story, Neil. You're the reporter."

"And you're not stupid, Mr. Mowry. You've accomplished too much in your career for anyone to ever think that." He took the compliment flat-faced. "There had been too many deaths by sudden heart attack, almost always followed by cremations, for you not to wonder. Maybe one of the victims was someone you knew or a Fund person, too healthy to die like that. Dulcy's diary makes clear that Toby Latch knew about the presence of wolfsbane. You probably took her aside, and either by charming her or with some sophisticated threats, you got her to confess.

"Next, you amazed Miss Latch by saying you didn't want her to stop. You wanted a hand in the selection process. What choice did she have? You began designating Fund beneficiaries and Miss Latch went about helping you reduce your overhead while the MPRE continued to benefit from insurance or inheritance. Were you as thoughtful as Miss Latch said she was, only picking those with a limited time left? It could not have felt good killing off old friends, but you were committed to respecting Mr. Zanuck's dying wish that the Fund live after him. What choice did you have? You were Zanuck's man, after all."

That impressed him, and he seemed ready to comment. Our eyes held for another moment, then he turned away, gestured helplessly and laughed into the air.

"When Blackie Sheridan showed up on your doorstep, it wasn't generosity that motivated you to help him. Once a snake always a snake. Sheridan blackmailed you into helping by revealing he had the love letters Marilyn wrote Elvis and threatening to go public with them. Until that moment, you thought they had been destroyed years ago. You got on the phone to Hank Twitchell and forced the truth out of him.

"You were honor bound to keep your commitment to Mr. Zanuck to keep a lid on Elvis and Marilyn's love affair, even after all these years, so you made the calls that got Sheridan his cottage at the MPRE. Maybe, you would have let it rest there, except for two things.

"Someone had told Sheridan about the Fund. He cut himself in by again threatening to go public with the letters, adding to the Fund's cash drain.

"Then, you got wind his play about Marilyn was being revised to include scenes about her romance with Elvis.

"You demanded he give you the letters once and for all, and when he refused, you moved him to the top of Miss Latch's list . . . Or, maybe you didn't even bother asking, knowing Sheridan was not one to honor his word. Miss Latch brought him a bottle of brandy laced with wolfsbane and by morning you had the love letters, but at a price. Instead of the usual poisoning, cremation to follow, you wound up with a full-blown murder investigation, the cops and people who could mention your name. Bring you into it." He seemed to be paying more attention to his glass of beer than me. "How am I doing so far, Mr. Mowry?"

Mowry looked up and studied me hard.

"Where was I the faithful night, Neil, lurching in the bedroom or hiding in a closet? Waiting for the moment all was right again with the world and I could collect the letters, is that how your story goes? If I was so bent on suppressing the letters, why did I turn around and offer to sell them to Jeremy Brighton for a poultry hundred thousand dollars, especially if I was pressed for money and knew I could sell them privately or at an auction for a great deal more?" Mowry shook his head and made a loud breathing noise. "Better yet, what reason did I have to murder him?"

"Poisoning Brighton was a resourceful expedient. You knew

from Laura he couldn't resist the thought of a bargain, so you used him as a decoy to get Laura to Claire Cavanaugh's cottage. Laura was your intended victim all along. She knew too much. She had lied to you all these years. You no longer trusted her. She was expendable. She would be another name off the Fund list. You told her to go with Brighton, meet this mysterious seller, make sure the letters were real."

"Why not Claire, if she saw me at Sheridan's?"

"She was your designated killer. It would be made to appear as if she had poisoned Brighton. You anticipated what an autopsy would show, that Sheridan had been poisoned, and that would make her the prime suspect overall. Claire was no real danger to you. Her memory slips in and out, you said so yourself. It would be simple convincing her she had done it. And if the DA took her to trial, the worst she'd get is first-degree funny farm."

"Then why bother moving Brighton and Laura to Sheridan's place? Why not leave them at Claire's?"

"Because of Augie. Because he wouldn't let you. He stumbled into what was going on and forced you to change your plan. Augie was not about to let you put the woman he loved in harm's way, so you poisoned him, too. Doesn't it ever end, Mr. Mowry? Can it? Do they all have to go before you feel entirely safe and the Fund is healthy again, although I'm not sure who'll be left to benefit by then, except for you, of course. Is that when you'll finally be satisfied, when it's only you?"

My questions jarred him. He looked around the way people do to show they're searching for someone else who might have spoken the words.

"Happy endings. That's what Mr. Zanuck always said, to me, to the writers, to his producers and directors. Give me a happy ending. I'm only doing my job."

"Where did you train, Nazi Germany?"

He dismissed my sarcasm with a wave.

I said, "It's time to quit."

"You can't prove a thing, you know. Are you counting on Laura to blab or Hank? Maybe Augie? Well, don't count on it, son. Dr. Fix-it here has always been better at the math than anyone."

I said, "I can prove it, Doctor."

Now he was looking at me like I was the crazy one, until I told him about Toby Latch's detailed records on the MPRE computer system.

He made another loud breathing noise and scoffed, "They do not make typewriters like they used to. Besides, I already saw to it all those records were erased by friends in high places, you might say. Quite the keeper that Toby, a regular squirrel in more ways 'n one."

"Not the records I found," I said firmly. "I also took home a backup copy."

I dipped into a pocket, pulled out a floppy disk, and tossed it at him.

He bobbled the catch and the floppy landed at his feet. He let it stay there. Checked out my eyes. Didn't like what he saw.

"I made that second floppy for you, Mr. Mowry."

"You say so . . . Why didn't you go straight to the police with your evidence?"

"Maybe I did."

"No, or I'd have heard by now."

"I told you, I came for the rest of the story. And I've also come for Claire."

Raising six indignant inches, he fixed me with a hard stare and said, "What's that supposed to mean? Why would she be here?"

"You picked up Claire at the MPRE Saturday and brought her here, maybe because you changed your mind and decided this was no time for someone as unstable as Claire to be running loose while you cleaned up after yourself? You feared Claire might stumble into reality long enough to give away your secrets. Augie wasn't around to protect her, so why not?"

His blue eyes blinked codes of confusion behind his glasses. I couldn't tell what he was thinking until he said, "You are a damn fool if that's what you believe. I brought Claire here to the ranch to protect her."

"Protect her from who?"

"From herself, God damn it."

"I'd like to hear that from her."

"There's not a thing Claire can tell you." He sighed again and, getting up from his seat, said forlornly, "C'mon."

Something about the moment made me wish I had not left my Beretta outside in the glove. I would have felt more comfortable with the holster kissing my ankle.

Reg Mowry asked, "You remember what Claire said on the night she won her Best Actress Oscar?" I said I didn't. "Claire thanked me. Not by my name, only enough to let me know."

His gaze drifted into the sky, to a memory beyond sharing. We were about a half mile behind the compound, on a noisy gravel path. He halted to scoop a handful of the white-and gray-flecked pebbles and tossed them randomly as we headed toward the shadow of the San Jacintos.

I said, "It sounds as if Claire was special to you."

"To the world," Mowry said. He moved his fists to his chest, like he was clutching the handle of a baseball bat. Or, an Oscar. He began to say something else. Changed his mind. Threw away the pose. Resumed walking like he was in no hurry to get to wherever he was taking me.

His silence grew as loud as a jazz band at a funeral.

I considered how safe I was heading nowhere with a man I had accused of mass murder. Mowry could have any number of surprises waiting for me out here. A fire burned inside my stomach.

I asked, "What happened at Sheridan's, Mr. Mowry? What did Claire see that night that made her call out, 'Not again'?"

Mowry stopped in the road and turned in my direction.

"Off the record?"

"You have my word," I said, and immediately felt smarmy, Augie's old lesson banged on my head. You give your word. You keep a promise.

Small valleys materialized between Mowry's hairy brows. His eyes looked for a landing place.

"The real Claire was never her image, Neil, any more than the real Marilyn was the Monroe she presented to the world. Like other actresses of her time, Claire gave to get. She put out for Mr. Zanuck. She put out for Sheridan. From Mr. Zanuck, Claire got stardom. From Sheridan, she just got fucked.

"Mr. Zanuck kept her on his payroll, the Fund, and Sheridan threw her away. She didn't know it until the night she walked in on him humping some Zanuck reject in his bedroom. Their exchange of verbs became physical. Sheridan attacked her and beat her up pretty bad. She never forgot it, but by the time I moved him to the MPRE, her mind didn't know one day from the next and it did not even matter that they were neighbors.

"That night, you ask? That night her mind started wandering backwards and so did Claire. Who the hell knows how these things happen, besides the shrinks? She wound up at Sheridan's place in time to see him attacking your ex-wife.

"In that moment, it was Claire being attacked all over again, and she screamed out at him, 'Not again!' " He shrugged. "Sometimes it's simply not possible to throw away the past, Neil. The future doesn't present that obstacle until it happens."

Mowry pointed in a new direction and we veered off the path, toward a shaded wood. Increased his pace and pulled ahead of me. About ten yards later, he stopped at what I saw was a pioneer's grave. A tall mound of stones artfully arranged on top of freshly turned earth and gnarled branches laced into a rugged cross with rawhide strips. Bouquets of fresh wildflowers.

There was no marker, but no marker was necessary to tell me who Mowry had buried there.

"This does the job for the time being," he said. He saw my question and shook his head. "Claire wanted it this way, not me. If I'd of known she brought wolfsbane with her, I would of tried talking her out of it, even though the stars always get the final word. We spoil them and we have to live with the result, you know.

"She sent me off with a shopping list and a soft kiss on the cheek. When I got back, she was curled up in the big chair, like she had dozed off in front of the TV, as beautiful and as serene as ever, watching Oprah. She liked Oprah. And Rosie. Larry King, also, on nights she couldn't sleep. She was having lots of those lately."

Something had pushed the cross off center. He concentrated on fixing the problem, working the horizontal branch with both hands, easing it around in the rocks.

"I left her like that and headed on out here with a shovel. I finished what had to be done by nightfall. The sky was alive with desert rainbows as far as you could see, like all of heaven was opening wide to greet Claire. I recited a simple prayer over her and sang one of her favorite hymns, the wind and the noises of the wild creatures my choir, and, so—here we are."

He started a song I didn't know.

His voice broke after a few bars.

"It's better this way, too," he said. I couldn't be sure he was talking to me. "Why should Claire be around to have reporters and cameras stalk her, hear the press talk about her the way they would, tarnishing her memory and treating her with disrespect? A laughingstock. Someone to be pitied. Claire was too great a star for that. Better to let her go out a star and be remembered that way, for the star she'll always be." He nodded satisfaction with the cross and looked up to gauge my reaction. His face redefined misery.

I said gently, "This has to be reported."

"I think not. Claire Cavanaugh being missing will make news and headlines briefly, I'll see to it. Then, all will go back to normal. Only, if I play my cards wild, a hundred years from now, they'll still be writing and talking about her disappearance, the way we remember Valentino and Harlow. Carole Lombard. James Dean, and, sure, Marilyn and Elvis. The staff of legends, Neil. That'll be the tombstone that matters for Claire, as it should be."

"This has to be reported."

"I think not. It's off the record, remember? Off the goddamned record!"

His sudden move startled me, but he was only pulling out the Sulka handkerchief. He ran it over his face, removed the frames, and gave his eyes a gentle rubdown. Cracked tired joints one leg at a time, then worked out the stiffness from his knees. Rubbed and massaged his hands. Laced his fingers and made the knuckles crack. Came around the grave to within one foot of me and leaned into my face.

"Let's talk about it," he said, softening again. His smile sweeter than his cologne. "You think Toby's files or your damned fluffy disk matter? I don't." Dr. Fix-it ready to operate. "What happens to me doesn't matter one aorta, Neil. Between you, me, and the gold post, it all boils down to what would happen to someone near and dear to you . . . Augie Fowler?"

Augie is needed at the Order of the Spiritual Brothers of the Rhyming Heart. His old friend, Reg Mowry, offers to spell him for a night at Claire's. Mowry has been looking for an excuse to get Augie away for a few hours.

Immediately, Brighton is called and told where to bring the hundred thousand dollars. They'll trade his cashier's check for the Marilyn love letters after a spot of tea and some of Claire's wonderful cakes.

Augie unexpectedly returns from the sanctuary, too concerned about Claire to stay away the night. Claire is wandering about in a daze. Brighton is already dead weight. Laura is on her way. Toby Latch, cleaning up in the kitchen, panics at the sight of him.

Augie recognizes what has happened and what it can mean for Claire. He rebukes Mowry. He is not about to let Claire become a scapegoat. It is not that easy, Mowry announces. Augie owes him favors, he says. He is collecting on all of them tonight.

Augie helps Mowry and Miss Latch move Brighton and Laura to the Sheridan cottage. They ferry the bodies most of the distance in a golf wagon, but it's still a struggle. Neither Brighton nor Laura are lightweights. Mowry and Augie aren't kids anymore and Miss Latch is too fragile to be much help.

Sweating profusely in the warm night air, out of breath, Augie accepts a glass of water from her, not even thinking it might be flavored with wolfsbane. It turns out, as with Laura, that the amount has been a best guess and a bad guess. Augie is also alive when DeSantis and Neil find them.

Mowry finished the story and said, "Accessory to murder is accessory to murder, even when it involves garbage maggots like Sheridan and Brighton. You inform the authorities and I guarantee you our friend August Kalman Fowler will add a vertically striped cassock to his wardrobe."

"You'd do it, too, wouldn't you?"

"I'll give him up as fast as a crow flies, same as you dare presume exposing me. Your boyhood hero, too; Sunset Beaudry will suffer. Can you see him surviving when the world learns the whole ugly truth about the diary and his beloved Dulcy Brown?"

"Did you always conduct business like this?"

"In the olden days, you mean? Hell, no! In the olden days I was one tough motherfucker. You play the game, you play to win."

"Is this a contest?"

"Life's a contest, boy."

His expression dared me to dispute him.

I said, "I'll let you know," turned and headed to the path.

His voice calling my name cut through my jacket and wheeled me around. He thumped an index finger on his chest.

"Not what it used to be, Neil, this ticker. It's turning to dust faster than movies shot on nitrate. I got my house in order and I got the Fund back in shape to take care of the last people who really meant anything to DFZ after I go. I need you to help me write a happy ending."

"Meaning?"

"Meaning your word simply won't do anymore, Neil. For the happy ending, I need your promise, not your word."

"What makes you think I'll give it to you?"

"Because, if it turns out Augie doesn't matter enough to you, understand I got Stephanie Marriner," he said triumphantly. "I got her and either you give me the deal I want, you tell me where Toby Latch hid that information on her computer, you give me any more fluffy disks you have, anything else that links to me, or I promise you, I *promise* you, you will never see Stephanie Marriner again . . . not alive."

I was crazy for ever thinking Mowry was crazy.

19

An inexpensive voice on the hospital switchboard said Augie had been released earlier in the day. I phoned the sanctuary and was told Brother Kalman was under light sedation, but might be up for visitors tomorrow, Wednesday at the latest. I promised I'd call first. I was lying.

I tossed the cellular into the glove compartment and chased the sinking sun back to LA, navigated the curving hillside above Los Feliz Boulevard, satisfied the disembodied voice inside the security box, and waited for the iron gate to pull back and admit me to the Order of the Spiritual Brothers of the Rhyming Heart.

The last musical chime was still resonating as the DeMillean front door swung open on greased hinges. Brother Ian was reciting one of his rhymed prayers of greeting, losing most of the words inside his bird's nest beard, when Brother Saul loomed over his shoulder, not pleased to see me.

"I really don't know why I didn't have you turned away at the lower gate," Brother Saul said, and looked at Brother Ian as if the flush-faced, liver-freckled older man were to blame. "I said tomorrow or Wednesday, did I not?" Brother Ian closed his eyes to Brother Saul's disciplinary tone. "Did I not say to call first?"

"I was in the neighborhood."

"The neighborhood will be here tomorrow and Wednesday."

"Not if the Big One gets here first."

Brother Saul understood I wasn't leaving until I spoke with Augie. He sent me a noisy sigh and waved me inside. I thought I caught a sly wink from Brother Ian.

Heading down the main hall, I paused at the open den door for a fast glance at a Charlie Russell oil that owned the room: cavalrymen still riding to the rescue against an unseen enemy. A bugler sounding the charge. Flags caught on the breeze of a fresh prairie dawn. Swords drawn. Rifles aimed. Pistols blazing.

Especially now, I identified with the painting.

"Come," Brother Saul insisted, guiding me to an open door at the end of a secondary corridor at the rear of the sanctuary. He signaled me through, urging, "Be brief and try not to tax Brother Kalman's energy."

The door clicked shut.

Augie and I were alone.

He stood barefoot across from the entrance, a few feet inside French windows that opened to a view of Griffith Park, his hands locked behind his back military style. Smoke drifted up from the slender Cuban cigar angled Roosevelt-style from a corner pocket of his mouth.

Using the wall for balance, he engineered a turn. He took the stogie from his mouth and pounded it into an ashtray on the dresser. Drew a bead on me with his real eye. "Good to see you, amigo. Way I feel, it's good to see anyone."

"You're better?"

"Compared to what?" The only light source was a naked bulb

glowing in the floor lamp alongside the desk hutch. It couldn't obscure the fact he looked dreadful.

Augie was colorless, except for the road map of broken booze blossoms on his cheeks and nose, and the ordeal had stripped away ten or fifteen pounds. He was lost inside satin pajamas the same violet shade as his eye patch.

"The good Lord takes care of his own, and here's one more time I qualified," Augie said, stretching out on the bed. I settled on a handcrafted mission-style bench and found a position.

"So, you visited Reg Mowry, did you? Reggie called me two hours ago to tell me. He said you are quite a piece of work. A genuine compliment coming from Reggie, kiddo." The persuasion of his voice sputtered in and out. "I suppose I should have told you everything up front, but you know how I am about secrets."

"Maybe that's the part that hurts most, Augie, having to hear it from a stranger."

"Reggie, also from the old school. Tip of the iceberg you share. What's underneath you treat like an ordinary ice cube."

"He told me a lot."

"Ice cubes, and they melt. What you got left is a sea of chance, the shifting waters of common doubt."

"You must be getting better. You're starting to sound like your old self, which is to say I don't know what the hell you're talking about."

He resisted a smile. "He says he worked you pretty good on the hunch you'd drop the story before you hung me out to dry."

"Or to melt?" I said, for the time being letting it go at that.

Augie drew a vertical line in the air.

I said, "Mowry is counting on our friendship."

"So am I," he said.

"Then tell me the truth, Augie. Mowry didn't tell me the truth, but I expect to hear it from you."

I repeated the story Mowry had told me.

Augie's one-eyed gaze stayed fixed on the redwood-beamed

ceiling, like he expected it to crack open, rarely showing any emotion except for the occasional fleeting grin.

When I finished, he rolled onto one side, with his back to me, and said, "Sounds good to me, amigo."

"Stow it, Augie. I let Reg Mowry rattle on, hoping to learn something new. I won't stand for you also playing me for a fool." I drew a stuttered breath and told him what I saw the last time I had explored Claire's cottage.

It had been cherry-picked clean. Not to the casual glance. On closer inspection, much of her clothing was missing. Also the heavier baggage that stars carry, the scrapbooks and memorabilia that reduce a public life to private storage and are dusted off for review on a lonely whim on lonelier nights. And Augie's cot was gone. Augie's trunk was gone. As if he had cleared out of the cottage with no intention of returning, not temporarily to take care of business at the sanctuary.

When I finished, he asked in an exaggerated voice full of false humor, "To what ominous purpose?"

"You knew what was going to happen after Brighton arrived. You moved your gear out early so you wouldn't have to explain your absence later."

He eased around to face me, saw how the knot in my gut was twisting my face.

I said, "Were you in Claire's cottage all along, waiting to help Mowry and Toby Latch kill Jeremy Brighton and Laura Dane? A bigger part of the plan than he let on to me?"

Momentary silence.

"I was there to make certain Claire was safe. I intended to bring her here afterward, where she would be well taken care of. When I got there doesn't matter, any more than the dose of death I swallowed. I'm still an accessory to murder."

"Not if the cops don't find out."

"Even if they do. The question, amigo, is simply this: Do you tell them or do you become an accessory to murder, too?"

He trapped my eyes and wouldn't let go.

And I imagined a pain that hurt so much I begged for it to go away.

Augie said, "What you don't know starts in the sixties with Marilyn's death. Reggie and I became chummy around that time. My boyhood pal, Mimi, got me on the horn and put us together when it seemed the suicide story was ripe to explode and wipe out lots of the wrong right people. I was boozing pretty heavily and not much into ethics. I yanked a few strings attached to favors and helped Reggie out. He paid me back to where I won the Press Club 8-Ball for investigative reporting on the Monroe yarn. He pulled a few strings of his own later, when my DTs turned into more deep shit than I wanted to handle and was ready to swallow a .45 I borrowed from one of the boys in Homicide.

"Reggie Mowry saved my life and my job. Reggie helped me get back my integrity and self-respect, and—he put me with Claire." His voice sank to a whisper. "You know what it's like to catch a moonbeam, then lose it?" His throat tightened around the thought. "Of course, you do," he said. I was remembering my first sight of Stevie, the precise instant she stole my breath and my life away. "You savor the moment, kiddo, and—when it's gone—the memory." Augie moved to a sitting position, his feet pressed to the floor and fingers locked in his lap. He leaned forward like he was praying. "It wasn't meant to be forever, of course. Anyway, not to Claire, and so it never was. It was over in less than a year, nobody the wiser, except Reggie . . ."

"Who also loved her."

His expression denied the concept.

"Who loved them all. It was Reggie's job to love them and take care of them. He'll still be at it the day after he dies." Augie let the thought sink in. "I didn't want it to end but she did. A gentleman must respect a lady, even one who won't answer the questions that make him cry.

"When you and I went out to the MPRE, it was the first time I had been so close to Claire in three decades, and I immediately understood why Claire had stayed in my mind. I knew about her old affair with Sheridan. I saw I needed to help her, exactly the way you were looking after Stevie. So, we both had our reasons."

"Because she gave you a sign."

"Nothing you have to know. I pulled Mimi into a corner and

later I learned more from Reggie to know to move in with Claire and protect her from herself . . . Your priority was Stevie, amigo. Mine was Claire.'' Augie's head inched left and right. ''I sent you to talk to Sunset when probably I shouldn't have done that. My own personal curse, an inability to let go of a good story, even when it turns into an exclusive for a friend.''

''You thought I couldn't dig out the story myself?''

''This isn't about ego. Give me some credit for loyalty.''

''What you expect from me now.''

''No, I expect you to do the right thing.''

''What is the right thing?''

''Whatever you make of it,'' Augie said, a bittersweet smile playing on his lips. He shifted his body in order to look at me full in the face. ''What are you going to make of it?''

I said, ''Did Mowry get the letters and destroy them?''

''What did Reggie say?''

''Yes, but not where or how.''

''Me, too.''

''Where and how?''

Augie turned on a dumb expression. ''I didn't ask. He didn't volunteer, but why should that matter to you anymore? The good guys got the bad guys.''

''Not the real bad guy, Augie. Not Reg Mowry.''

''Would blowing the whistle on Reggie change anything? Would it really change anything?''

''Only the truth,'' I said.

''Stevie is off the hook. That's the truth that should matter to you.''

''You know who True Mullen and Larry Grenedier are?''

Augie nodded. ''A couple of Reggie's bad eggs,'' Augie said. ''Mullen knew Elvis from the old days. Reggie put him with Laura, to keep an ear open for him, help him track after the Elvis and Marilyn letters. Mullen got Grenedier involved.''

''Reggie also had Mullen and Grenedier snatch Stevie. She was his ace with me, if it turned out you weren't.''

The news caught Augie short.

He pushed out his arms and wagged his hands. "What are you aiming for, kiddo? He'd never pull a stunt like that, not with me around, knowing what you and I are to one another . . ."

"Hurts to be wrong, doesn't it, Augie?"

That night, shortly before ten o'clock, I walked out of the Heathcliffe and strolled the three blocks north on Veteran to the Federal Building. Mowry had instructed me to wait in the middle of the immense parking lot, empty at this hour but brightly lit, as if the government feared someone might somehow sneak off with the asphalt.

We would be making the trade here.

"It is so theatrical," he had agreed with me, "but that's my background, isn't it? It's also safe. I always choose safety to any amount of promises."

Walking over and now squatting for comfort and rubbing my hands against the cold night air, I reflected on elements of the story I'd never be able to tell, for Mowry had bought my silence as well as my copy disk as the price for Stevie's safe return.

It had become clear that between what I had been told and what I had found out for myself since that first frantic message from her after Sheridan's death, I was only certain I would never know the whole story anyway.

From Mowry, once he was armed with my promise, I learned how the murders began with Claire's green thumb. How she came across the wolfsbane and knew it for what it was and, because this was before her memory turned too sour, knew enough to warn someone.

Unfortunately, the someone was Toby Latch, who was inspired to use it as her weapon of choice, and began moving residents to a place where only God is billed above the title.

And, of course, Mowry also learned about the wolfsbane from Claire—

Through Mimi Polyzoides.

Mowry said, "From the old days to this minute, Mimi is the man who knows too much. Everybody told Mimi what went on. He was the gadfly of the Fox lot. Landing on everybody's stools. Always coming to me with the best shit. You think Mimi was added to the Fund because DFZ had something for Greeks? Better directors than him were around, but he was our own special CIA." He studied his beer glass, toyed the foam with a finger. "Sometimes, for a juicy piece of information, I fed the little bugger a special reward, a starry-eyed chorus boy with ambition where his brains should be."

"Is that how you found out about Dulcy's diary? Mimi?"

"Dulcy adored Mimi. She felt safe around him. But I'll tell you something else. No matter how much she longed for it in her diary, Dulcy Brown didn't commit suicide. She was poisoned, just like the others, by Toby Latch and Mickey Spoon."

"And Spoon?"

I almost dropped my Coke can. I placed it on the mantle of the trailer dash under trailing eyes making certain I used a coaster as he let me know he understood my surprise.

Mowry said, "What, you believed that crappola about Spoon not being part of it? Close but no horseshoes. From the git-go, Neil. To convince you, the two of them must have put on quite a show before Sunset whacked them, but think of the irony. Sunset revenged the death of his sweetheart without even knowing it. I can't see you telling that to the police. That information gives Sunset a motive for first degree murder, and even old cowboys are allowed to die by lethal injunction."

He sent me a smile that seemed to take credit for keeping another of his people out of trouble.

"You went with Hank to Fox and picked up the Elvis letters where Laura had stashed them, in Marilyn's bungalow."

"Did I?" His head inclined and he fixed me with one eye. "I heard from young Jackie Hummell you were there dropping my name. Let's say Hank and I have a new understanding now. Hank will say nothing to you or to anyone hereafter and he won't have to worry ever again about Laura's health. In fact, both are due for raises from the Fund."

"A cost of living increase."

"For all parties, you might say," he decided, undercutting the words with a grunt of laughter.

"And you got Marilyn's letters from Sheridan. Where did he have them hidden?"

Mowry took off the glasses, checked them while letting the question register, adjusted their arms behind his lobeless ears, pushed the frame against the bridge of his nose, scratched his head.

"When you get to be my age, you'll discover that memory is no diamond," he said.

"Did you destroy them? Or are you going to cash in the way Brighton intended to cash in?"

"Neil, please," he said, frowning. He worked his collar. Adjusted his buttons. "Consider those letters dead and buried, same as Elvis and Marilyn."

Shuffling footsteps on the Federal Building asphalt.

I looked up to see Larry Grenedier approaching, his toothy smile illuminated by a burning full moon in a cloudless sky, his bulky body gliding along at a gandy dancer's gait.

"Hey, hey, Neil Gulliver," he called, his speech impediment having unintentional fun with my names. He was carrying a laptop and, after sitting down alongside me, positioned it on top of his crossed legs. "Gimme," he said, holding out his hand.

"Where's Stevie?"

"First the floppy."

I wished a fist in his face, but I had no bargaining room. I fished the disk from my pocket, wondering as he slid it into the slot and began playing with the keyboard.

After a few minutes and a few more scrolls, Grenedier said, "Yeah, it's what the old fart said to check for. You keep any other copies?"

"I told Mowry it was the only copy. It's the only copy."

"Hey, don't peel my skin, dude. Only doing the *Mission Possible*. Nothing personal here, dig?"

Grenedier slapped the computer shut, shifted back onto his feet, and made an overhead signal with his right hand.

An engine gunned alive from a dark corner of the lot about two hundred yards away and at once a motorcycle zipped toward us. It was Mullen's Harley, Mullen in the saddle, like a vision from *The Wild One*—and Stevie behind him, her hands gripping his midsection and her head looking anxiously past his shoulder.

Mullen braked to a noisy halt and looked at Grenedier, who nodded.

"No mistakes?" Mullen said.

"Just like the old fart ordered," Grenedier said.

"Okay, bitch, off."

She dismounted and rushed to me, wrapped her arms around my shoulders, and said breathlessly, "I'm okay, okay?" before I could ask the question. My hands locked around her waist and I felt her body trembling. "They didn't have the balls to try. If they did, they wouldn't have had the balls to try again."

She said it loud enough for them to hear, reserving a nasty face for True Mullen, who mirrored it back.

Mullen drawled, "The stupid cunt just waltzed into my arms, in case you been wondering. The guard in your building tells her it's her boyfriend downstairs, and she's through your door faster than you can say ass fuck."

"I was the guard," Grenedier said proudly. "My first voice-over."

Stevie said, "He said he was Monte, honey."

Her eyes appealed to me. I put my fingers to her mouth and told her it was okay, then to Mullen, "Speak to her like a lady or speak to me, True."

"You shudda heard her before. I had a mouth like hers, I'd will it to the National Museum of Filth," Mullen said. I felt violence renewing itself inside me. He knew the look. "Don't try to be a hero, okay? Not what this is about, okay?"

Stevie put her lips to my ear. "Let's just go, please?"

I flicked off a corner smile and a curt nod at Mullen.

He nodded back and told Grenedier, "Climb aboard, camper, and we'll be on our way."

Mullen gunned the motor, and as Grenedier settled onto the passenger seat behind him, I called, "Next time let's keep the women and children home."

He rolled the bike closer and said, almost hissing in my face, "I like your writing, but that's not enough to stop me from making horse pie out of you."

My body tensed and I took a step toward him.

Stevie tugged me back.

Grenedier said, "By the way, you might try and catch *ER* next Thursday. It's only five lines the old fart got me, but I act rings around Anthony Edwards."

Mullen angled the bike around and sped off toward the black hole he'd emerged from, laughing against the night as Grenedier flag waved good-bye.

It should have ended there, but it didn't.

A moment or two later, before Stevie and I could start a kiss, the sound of the bike grew louder. Mullen had dropped off Grenedier and was heading right for us, like some Manoleté on a motorcycle.

I barely managed to push Stevie out of the way.

Mullen circled and made another pass at us, close enough to boot-kick me onto the ground. Grenedier encouraged him with calls of *Olé!* from the darkness.

Mullen made another circle, another pass.

I rolled out of the way.

He never stopped laughing.

Stevie shouted fresh obscenities at him.

It diverted Mullen from me. He aimed at her, instead. Her body angled aside in time. His front wheel shield passed an inch from her denims.

Mullen drove to the end of the lot, circled, paused briefly to monitor our positions. I was half sitting, with the weight of my body supported upright by one arm on the ground. Stevie was on her haunches alongside me.

Mullen charged. He had something raised in his arm. As he drew closer, I saw it was a tire iron.

I flung Stevie sprawling and rolled as he sailed past, the iron swinging hard where my head had been an instant before.

As Mullen prepared for his next charge, I yanked at my Beretta in my ankle holster. I steadied myself and took a careful two-handed aim at his chest.

Mullen recognized the pose. He was too close to do more than brake and adjust the bike's path abruptly. The bike flew out from under him at an angle, flopped onto its side, skidded into one of the cement barricades the government had installed all around the Federal Building perimeter as an antiterrorist measure.

He was about ten feet from me, on his back.

I limped to him and aimed the Beretta at his face.

Stevie hollered, "Honey! Don't!"

"Do it," Mullen said, certain I wouldn't.

"Fuck you," I said.

And blew away one of his kneecaps.

And told Stevie it was time to go home.

At this moment, even if I had known, I could not have cared less that the rest of the truth, the real truth, about Elvis and Marilyn's love letters was yet to come.

20

The Motion Picture Retirement Estates stayed at the center of a news blitz for another couple weeks. Shows like *Hard Copy, Inside Edition,* and the other purveyors of glamour mayhem offered the MPRE residents bundles of instant cash for comments about the serial poisonings, about Toby Latch, about Sunset Beaudry's role in what the Spider Woman memorialized in the *Daily*'s headlines as the "Gunfight at the OK Cottage."

They turned the residents into buffoons, marionettes with faltering voices, palsied gestures, and hopscotch memories. They disregarded the fact these people had been victimized already by an aging process that plunders dignity as well as years.

I said so in a column, then had to sit back and laugh. The few critical letters I received were from these very residents, who were thriving on the attention. Such is the allure of lost stardom found again.

What I didn't write about was Reg Mowry, the Dr. Fix-it of Death, and wouldn't my Spider Woman have sprung multiple orgasms given that appellation to play with in a headline?

Paige, who'd been asked to assume management of the MPRE by the board of directors, called in exterminators to rid the place of the *aconitum napellus*.

They found most of the stately herbaceous perennials growing wild among the weeds in undeveloped acreage, some as high as four feet, and in the pathway borders and shaded gardens maintained by the Golden Bees. DeSantis and I agreed that a small, well-tended garden behind the administration building was the one Toby Latch had given her personal attention, but there was no way of knowing for certain.

Not for DeSantis, whereas I knew it positively from Reg Mowry, Exterminator to the Stars, and wouldn't the Spider Woman also have come and come again over that one?

DeSantis and Paige were officially an item now.

As a favor, I tagged along when he picked out an engagement ring he intended to surprise her with over wine and candlelight at a romantic Malibu restaurant overhanging the ocean, whose name and an impossible reservation I scored for him through our dining editor.

I'd rather have given my love-embalmed cop the name of Reg Mowry, mastermind extraordinaire, but I couldn't do that. For now I couldn't even tell Stevie, who I was certain had sensed I was holding back on her from the moment we left True Mullen screaming epithets in the parking lot.

By the weekend, Stevie and I weren't confident about where we were with each other, if our new emotional drowning pool had been caused by what shrinks call a shared experience or because we had come to our senses about being madly, passionately made for each other forevermore, again.

Stevie's way of finding out was to drop all communication for the time being, while she used a hiatus from *Bedrooms and Board*

Rooms to seek out investors for *Marilyn Remembers* in New York, where she and Monte Sanberg would be sharing an East Side penthouse overlooking the river loaned to her by Aaron Spelling, who was developing a movie-of-the-week based on her ordeal.

I refused to cooperate, even as Spelling's offer became more and more tempting. Not only because of my deal with Reg Mowry. I have an aversion to fiction based on true stories, the specialty of this particular TV commodity.

It's enough hell to deal with in real life.

When DeSantis phoned me with the news, I had no doubt Mimi Polyzoides had staged his death for the Hollywood history books. Mimi, the master showman taking leave. His body found by a Honey Bee. Reclining on a chaise lounge on the auditorium stage. Naked underneath a crimson smoking jacket, one of those funny little Chinese caps with the dangling tassel, and patent leather pumps. His face fully made up. Thick, false lashes a mile long. Exaggerated bee-stung lips, colored a delicate purple. Full red moons on his cheeks. A suicide note running to a dozen pages held in place on the chaise by his cock and balls, which he had painted to match his lips. The cover page decorated in a light sprinkle of semen.

Aconitine, the lab boys said.

Mimi had been hoarding it, his farewell message announced. Against the day he could no longer handle the remorse growing inside him, because of the crimes he had committed at the MPRE.

He confessed to everything hanging open on the books, including Taps Vernon and Jeremy Brighton, and some deaths that were not, like Dulcy Brown. Spelled out reasons that would make sense to people who didn't know better. Took credit where I knew other names belonged, because I had found the real truth hiding in a computer.

Mimi begged forgiveness. Asked to be cremated and his ashes thrown in the face of a certain director residing at the Motion Picture Country Home.

I wanted to believe Mimi knew what he was doing when he

dressed up to play the damnedest corpse since that old movie star Albert Dekker, whose bizarre death in a hanging noose, handcuffed and dressed in a housewife's frock, had established a new zenith for kinkiness back in the late sixties.

I believed otherwise.

Paige organized a simple memorial service for Mimi at Warner Brothers Auditorium, where half-mounted sets and stray props were all that remained of the Break-a-Leg Show, which she had canceled in honor of Mimi's creative contributions to the MPRE.

At the main entrance, security cops checked for ID before guiding vehicles through a maze of reporters and broadcast vans, and paparazzi aimed their lenses at limos that might be hauling a celebrity. Laura Dane was the biggest name they got.

Laura came with Hank Twitchell and her niece, Marnie, and cried louder than anyone during the service, genuine tears, like she was the one who had taught The Method to Stanislavsky, but I could not decipher how much of it was acting.

Marnie also cried, not as convincingly as Laura.

Some day, maybe.

Not today.

Hank passed me a few looks that said he was living with a secret as dark as my own. I wondered to myself if he knew how Mowry had arranged for Mimi to take the fall, but recognized it would do no good to ask—Reg Mowry had seen to that—so we parted on a decent handshake, as firm as a farmer's rainy day thank yous to God.

I had not expected Sunset to show up.

He didn't disappoint me.

Why would he want to pay final respects to the man claiming responsibility for poisoning Dulcy Brown? Unless he had licensed the pissing concession on Mimi's grave.

Sunset was never meant to know the whole truth about his beloved, or so I hoped as I went looking for the old Range Roper after the service.

I found him at her plot, arranging the flowers. He barely took notice when I called his name. The smell of alcohol was on his breath like a permanent stain.

"May I say hello, sir?"

Sunset removed a cloth handkerchief from a pocket of his denims and rubbed at the name tablet, already bright with the afternoon sun.

"Dulcy and me, married going on fifty years and we shared everything every damn day of our lives."

"I've seen many of her movies. She was lovely."

Sunset brushed away a tear on his cheek with the back of a hand. His mouth moved wordlessly until, "Be seeing my Dulcy real soon."

Then, it was as if I didn't exist, only the two of them.

He said, "Real soon, precious. Real soon, darling mine."

Driving home, I began to fear what Sunset meant by *soon* and that he might be planning to put a Peacemaker to his head, until I realized he had died a long time ago.

One way or another, they were all dying, taking the Golden Age of Hollywood with them.

Reg Mowry's death barely got attention a month later.

The *Daily* gave him the fat paragraph on the obit page that signals someone worth mentioning, someone who used to be important. A quarter century ago it would have been page one, with a sidebar on the jump, photos of Mowry attending some of the stars he had helped create.

Television ignored him completely. American Movie Classics tied together old newsreel footage from its library, grainy shots of Mowry looking elegant and antsy in the background of a press conference or news event he had invented—like Zanuck attending a New York premiere with his latest small-breasted discovery; Jane Russell and Marilyn immortalizing their hands and feet in cement at Grauman's Chinese, as if it were their hands and feet that the public paid to see—and dedicated a movie festival to his genius.

The obit said he had suffered a heart attack at his chicken ranch in Riverside County.

Given Mowry's age and a history of chronic heart problems, the county coroner specified "natural causes" and released the deceased's body to a great-niece, Paige Jahnsen, for burial on Mowry's ranch in a peaceful and sheltered grave at the back of the property. At Mowry's request, there would be no funeral or memorial service.

If it wasn't Mowry's heart turning off naturally, but self-administered poison, the way he had hinted when we made our final deal, I didn't want to know.

I didn't want to know about the coincidence of Paige being his great-niece, because then I'd have to consider it was Paige who had erased Toby Latch's files, and later, after he got the names from me, the Examiner and Starkeeper files, and then work out how to share the news with her nervous fiancé.

Anyway, DeSantis was no fool.

Paige would slip somewhere and he'd pick up on it and maybe then there'd be something to connect Mowry to the deadly business at the MPRE.

Hopefully, nothing to connect Augie.

That had mattered.

That was on my end of the deal with Mowry.

I had made it hoping that, in time, I would be able to live with what I knew.

Keep the faith by hiding the truth.

An accessory to friendship.

The day Mowry's death notice appeared, I combed the *Daily*'s birth announcement log looking for newborn infants with names similar to his. It's step one in my ritual whenever anyone I know hits the high road.

Last month, a five-pound eleven-ounce Mame at Valley Pres was as close as I could get to Mimi. Today there was a Reginald Dwight and a Regina Arno. I called my florist and ordered a fresh bouquet of roses sent to the mothers with my usual unsigned card of congratulations.

People die, but life goes on.

It wasn't long after that I located Elvis and Marilyn's love letters.

I hadn't been looking for the love letters.

Or thinking about them.

Except when I got the occasional phone call from DeSantis, bemoaning his loss of Paige, who had dumped him for no reason, wondering if he'd ever find another one like her.

Or the middle-of-the-night panic call from Stevie, telling me about new setbacks with *Marilyn Remembers* or sharing another hysterical explanation about why it might not be working out with Monte Sanberg, but was still not ready to see me.

By now there was nothing left to the MPRE story to merit more than an occasional squib at the back of the Metro section. Usually it was another failed heart, excuse enough to mention the Blackie Sheridan murder. Sunset Beaudry's last shootout. Claire Cavanaugh, who was still missing and presumed a victim of her own failing memory.

About Claire I knew better, because of a letter I received from Augie.

It had been mailed from one of those tropical islands on the outer edge of nowhere that exist by printing and selling souvenir postage stamps. His generic name for them was Lombago or, if they were large, Lombago Lombago, and he would always fancy himself in a sarong, forty pounds lighter and shimmying up a swaybacked tree after coconuts, chasing Dorothy Lamour over the clean white sand, jauntily navigating an outrigger atop tall white-bearded waves, diving for coins tossed from the bridge of a four-masted schooner by Clark Gable or Ray Milland.

Eight miniature stamps on the envelope portrayed Elvis at various ages and stages of his career, and I recognized this as Augie's idea of a joke.

The postmark was nine weeks old. I allowed another week for the handwritten date on the first page of the elegantly embossed stationery Cunard reserves for first-class passengers of the *QE2*.

Augie wrote:

My son,

All's well that bends well, a tennis pro once told the Bard. He must have had my knees in mind. So many stairs on this vessel, they're useless within an hour of my wake-up, as the morning sun starting its speculation at the edge of creation, just about the point where Columbus lost his fourth ship.

I thank you for the sad news about Mimi.

You recall he and I go back a long way, so I would have liked to have been there for one final salute to the little snoot. I agree with you about the act Mimi put on and I know for a fact it was a grand way for him to turn out the light before leaving the room.

I suppose he did it for Reggie because Reggie had taken such good care of him and those others all those years. Here was some way to make it right and keep it going, that Zanuck dough back to the brim for whatever other obligations Reggie had we might not know about. Or, whatever it is he meant to have them doing at the MPRE through that great-niece of his, Paige. He sure did love that kid.

Did I know it was going to happen?

No, but I might have guessed if I had put on my thinking cap, given what I did know.

No, I would not have done anything to prevent it.

Mimi would have gone soon anyway. His pisser was not in the best of shape, whether at rest or leading the charge, which Lord knows he did a lot of in his day. He told me how hurtful it was to pee and how it was past getting better. It was like he could only pee inside his system and spread the poison, so you see why that stage show meant so much to him. It was going to be the last one. Too bad. For me, too. Gene Kelly would have bitten his nails down to the quick if he had been able to see what this hoofer was able to pull off.

The last time Mimi and I spoke, he was in agony and mincing tears the way he usually walked. I reminded Mimi of the old gent who complains to the doctor he can't pee. You can't pee? the doc says. How old are you? The old gent says, I'm ninety years old. The doc says, You've peed enough.

You know how boring a boat can be? Be thankful I didn't ask you to join Claire and me.

Claire travels in her own private world most of the time. She has good days and she has bad days, increasingly more of the latter, when she forgets everything that happened before 1955 or 1965. I become Alan Hale and she wanders the decks reciting lines from her movies, desperately determined to have them right before the director calls for the first take.

No pattern to it, except when somebody recognizes her and wants a picture or an autograph. And, this boat is up to here with people old enough to remember!

She sparkles when that happens. She peels away layer upon layer of depression and becomes the giddy girl I fell in love with once and never lost the knack. But she never goes up in her role as Sister Dolores, never lets on to the most ardent and discerning of her admirers, whether her memory is full or bent with the run of the sea.

Claire is radiant and saintly in her robes. They match mine, and we look more like brother and sister than fugitives on a voyage from reality.

Claire is secure, and I intend to sail on my own fantasy for as long as time and circumstance allows, amigo. What didn't work for us once works for us now. If she thinks I'm Alan Hale, that's okay, too. I know who Claire is. My lucky star.

Did you know she was in the sanctuary the day you faced me off there? Could you smell her perfume in the air? Recognize what her presence meant for the flowers in my garden? See beyond the clouds to the rainbow she had built for me over life itself?

Maybe I should have told you everything then, but I saw you weren't ready for everything. Besides, most of your guesswork was good enough to count as the truth. I hope by now you've quit the idea you're guilty as sin for what you did.

First off, nobody can tell you how guilty sin is. Second, you know the word "compassion"? You got it up the kazoo, amigo, and that gets you bonus mileage on the score sheet they keep at the Pearly Gates.

Reggie did what he had to do. Me, too. And, you. It's doing what other people want that ultimately creates all the problems. How many times do I have to teach you that lesson? At least, this time you got it right and for that I'm eternally grateful. What's that? you're wondering. Did Augie actually mean "thank you"? That was Brother Kalman using the pen, kiddo, and you know better than to ever confuse us. Life does that without any help from you.

When will I be back? No telling yet. A lot of that answer depends on Claire, who just returned to the cabin after a nice nap on the top deck, looking like, well, what do you know? Words escape me. Like a movie star. How's that? Looking like a Movie Star. A MOVIE STAR. I just told her who I'm writing to and she has lit up the whole cabin with her smile. She says to tell you, "Hello, Mickey Mouse." What's that all about?

Better watch it, amigo. You have enough women in your life without hungering after mine. What do I mean by enough women? One. Just one. If she's the right one. The trick is in figuring out which one the right one is.

Bless you.
Augie

The business about the Elvis and Marilyn letters came back into my life with a call from the customer relations department at Westwood Village Mortuary, informing my machine it was time for the annual review of final arrangements and an inspection of property.

A different cheery voice told me she was certain they had the right Neil Gulliver. One moment, please. Clack of computer keys. Confirmation of the address and phone number on file. My address. My phone number.

"Oh, I see why the confusion," she said, sounding like a twenty-year-old trying to sound forty. I was the new *transfer* owner of the subject crypt, a gift passed along in the probated will of the late Keith R. Mowry. "It's only happened in the last two days. I suppose you haven't been officially informed yet?"

"Not even unofficially, unless this counts."

"We pride ourselves on our service," she said, merrily.

Tawny Zimmerman and I arranged to meet at eleven the next morning at the mortuary.

She was waiting for me with the kind of paste-on smile the morticians wear.

She was twenty and looked forty. Mousy brown hair cut short, hanging limply around a plowman's face. A thick body that could stand to lose about fifty pounds inside a three-piece, funeral-black suit topped by a scarf bow accenting the color scheme in shades of gray and grayer. Comfortable Rosa Klebb shoes.

She marched me from the administration bungalow, across the courtyard, to the crypt I had visited one dark night, the Marilyn land of a million tourists, chattering nonstop about the wisdom in early purchase of an appropriate final resting place, trying to draw me out on the subject. Her smile never budged.

"There," she said, pointing to the checkerboard squares of subtle brown marble, "where that fellow is taking his pictures." She drew closer and said something to the spaced-out kid toting a Canon 35, who grunted his reply and grudgingly stepped aside.

Tawny checked the Post-it on the cover of her day organizer, held out a hand like she was presenting the next act, indicated one of the blank-faced vaults adjacent to Monroe.

I said, "I thought that one was reserved by Joe DiMaggio."

"Who?"

"Marilyn's husband."

Tawny thought about it. "The baseball player!" A self-congratulatory expression whizzed across her face. "Husband number two. First was the former policeman and a man who wrote stage plays was after." I congratulated her on her acumen. She deciphered the word and satisfied herself it was not derogatory.

"Here's the one I think you mean," she said, guiding her finger to another vault. "I can't answer with certainty, though. We are discreet about what we tell anyone, especially if they're a newspaper columnist?" She pronounced it "colyumnist," the first indication she knew who I was.

"The other one. Mine. It was previously owned by Mr. Mowry?"

"I suppose."

"Why didn't he use it?"

"Beg pardon?"

"If Mr. Mowry owned the crypt, why didn't he use it? Why did he have himself buried on his chicken ranch, in a grave—"

"Beg pardon?"

This time I heard her and realized I had been thinking aloud. I dismissed my words with a wave and sank into quiet thought.

In a grave he'd meant for himself all along.

Not in a crypt near Marilyn that—

"It was never meant for him," I said.

Tawny replayed her puzzled look of a moment ago. "What was never meant for who?"

"How long ago did Mr. Mowry purchase his crypt?"

She shrugged, turned her palms upward. Before I could ask another question, she pointed and said, "The information you can have is all in there."

In the office, Tawny had handed over a thick, letter-size manila envelope. I'd glanced at the front and saw my name on it, hand-printed, along with the caution, "Only to be opened by him in the event of my death," and signed by Mowry. I had shoved it under my arm and forgotten about it.

I excused myself and retreated to a stone bench away from fans with cameras who had arrived after us. Did a fast run-and-read through the contents. Found a receipt for purchase, signed by Mowry in 1962, one week after services for Marilyn, a gilded certificate of ownership, various maintenance reports.

In a cover letter addressed to me, composed on an old Royal or Corona and full of struck-out words, lines, and entire graphs, Mowry explained how the love affair between Marilyn and Elvis, no matter what anyone presumed, was never casual or concluded.

The affair remained torrid, sustained for years, long after the events I already knew about.

Mowry wrote:

On the day of Marilyn's funeral, imagine my surprise when my secretary said it was Elvis on the line for me. At Elvis's urging, we met for dinner at his favorite steak joint, The Steak Pit, a place over on Melrose that always looked to be closed. Where they locked out everyone else whenever Elvis wanted privacy. His tips more than made up for lost business.

He told me then that he and Marilyn had to go their own way in public, but he still loved her deeply and was certain she died still loving him at least as much. Elvis said, "You're Dr. Fix-it. Dr. Fix-it, there is something I'd like you to fix for me."

He was a nice kid, decent, who never did anybody any dirt that I knew about, and truly grieving. I was happy to go along with him, especially since I might need a favor sometime.

Elvis said he wanted to be as close to Marilyn as possible for all eternity. He wanted me to buy him the crypt next to hers. The one he chose was already sold—I heard later it was bought by Joe DiMaggio—so I got Elvis the next best one.

I'll tell you just how appreciative Elvis was. You know my ranch? Elvis got wind I couldn't afford a parcel that size on my salary. DFZ was a generous man, but the really big dollars never went to people like me. Elvis made it happen, although I did not know that for years and years. Until old Hank Twitchell spilled the beets, I went around believing I had smooth-talked the owner into lowering his price.

Maybe, when he died, Elvis still meant to be laid to rest next to Marilyn. It's something we can't know for sure, given a wife and daughter that came later on, and the sad circumstances surrounding his own death and everything afterward.

Except for catching his show in Vegas once, we lost touch. We shook hands in his penthouse suite at the Hilton, but nothing was spoken and the look Elvis gave me could have meant anything. When he died, there was nobody to ask, nothing I could do about it, you understand that.

Well, Neil, whenever you open up your new crypt, you'll see a stack of powder blue envelopes with Marilyn's name engraved in the corner in a fancy, flowery script.

It's Marilyn's handwriting. I saw it often enough to know the difference from the signatures that came out of my publicity department, answering the zillions of requests Marilyn received day in and day out from her fans.

The bonus is Elvis's letters, in a stack of white envelopes like you could get in a five and dime store. A handwriting expert will tell you they're the genuine article, too.

I felt they belonged with Marilyn, but you can't believe the red tape involved in getting the mortuary to open her crypt. I could have pulled it off, of course, if I gave myself another week or so, but I was too tired and anxious to move on.

You know where the love letters came from. They're the rest of the story you pursued so diligently, my parting gift to you for keeping your word to me and to Augie, or you would not be reading this. I don't know if it's Pulitzer Prize stuff, but it's sure to win you a prize or two if you use it.

All I ask is one last favor. Whatever you write, please don't mention my name or my part in any of this. I want to leave this earth the same way I came, nobody's business but my own.

As if to emphasize the point, no signature.

Close to dizzy with excitement, I stuffed everything back inside the manila envelope and charged over to Tawny.

"Can we open the crypt?"

She gave me an odd look. Her mouth scrunched up one side of her face. She was concentrating. "I suppose it's—I could call my supervisor and he could authorize maintenance to—"

"Call your supervisor. Please."

Within the hour, the area had been cleared and a pair of security guards were stationed where they could hold back the curious while two workmen in bib overalls built a sweat easing the door slab from my vault and onto a mattress cushion.

When Tawny gestured me forward, I could not bring myself to move. I was entrapped by thoughts that had frozen me in place and would not let go. The thoughts were hammer hard and pointed as an ice pick, and they had the voice of my conscience.

"Mr. Gulliver? If you like, this here flashlight will allow you to get a complete picture of the quality of the workmanship that goes into the entire—"

I was asking myself, Do I deserve the story?

Do I deserve a reward for having contributed knowingly to criminal acts?

An award?

The Pulitzer?

By letting the bad guy get away, hadn't I become one? Is there ever a good enough reason to spit in the face of justice?

Friendship?

Loyalty?

Love?

Could I continue to hide the truth and live with it? With myself? With my award?

The Pulitzer?

Augie's letter was right. It's doing what other people want that ultimately causes the problems.

Get real, Neil.

Do what you have to do. You've already collected several lifetimes of lies in this world. So what if you add one more to the mix? Why not?

Do what I have to do.

"Mr. Gulliver? Come, have a look. How strange . . ."

Driving home, I tuned to a jazz station. After a while, a Billie Holiday record from 1937 came on. I sang along, trying not to drown out her voice:

I'd lie for you, I'd cry for you.
I'd lay my body down and die for you.
If that isn't love, it will have to do.
Until the right thing comes along.

And wondered where Stevie was, what she was doing.

Acknowledgments

Thank you.

You know who you are.

Most of you, anyway.

I think so.

I hope so.

You're the people who have the author's enduring thanks for your words of encouragement or some expression of belief during the creative process and the even longer time it took to fall in with the magicians who made the dream come true, beginning with my agent in Los Angeles, Lew Weitzman, whose steadfast support brought me to Susan Crawford, my tenacious literary agent in New York, who, in turn, paired me with the exceptional Natalia Aponte, my editor at Forge, my guiding light, and a stellar example of the people at Tom Doherty's organization, whose love of books keeps publishing an art as well as a business.

Family and friends I cite by name to avoid sleepless nights, at the risk of forgetting a few people and offending a few others:

Deborah Gwyn and David Scott, Therese and Stephanie, Erin and Daniel; Judith Joy; Bertha; Grelun, Alex, Chris and Karen, Jay and Brenda, Harvey, Saul, Macey, Stan, Ron, the other Sandra; my parents, Helen and Al, who in their lifetime always led the cheering squad; and—

—your name goes here:

____

Robert S. Levinson
Los Angeles, California
January 1999